Prologue

Sensing a slight buzz from the alcohol, he knew he shouldn't have had that last Margarita but still felt in control. No one could out-drink a military man with so much experience, he thought to himself. John Davenport, Captain, U.S. Navy, in charge of special operations and rapid reaction forces for the Pentagon, was responsible for covert military operations including extraction or extermination of non-friendly personnel during wartime or peacetime. Having been through Vietnam in some of the worst hellholes, conducting insertion and extraction operations in the Middle East, Russia, Yugoslavia, Panama and Yugoslavia, his exploits were never publicized because no one was supposed to know they happened. That never concerned him. He wasn't in it for the glory, he just wanted to stretch the limit and do things no one else could. In most cases that was true, since no one was better at it, at least no one to date.

Davenport had spent a lifetime getting his body in the best physical condition throughout high school and collegiate sports, as well as competing in major Karate competitions when it was still considered a new event. With broad shoulders, strong arms and tight stomach, each muscle was finely tuned. Although thinning slightly, his hair had basically remained over the years. The most obvious characteristic, however, was his cold, brown eyes, totally void of any emotion. Able to stare down an eagle, anyone who met him was left with a cold, empty feeling.

Davenport was born in a small southern Michigan town, where he spent the majority of his youth toiling in his father's field. As he grew up, he yearned for a life other than the farm and swore that some day he would be an important figure. He learned in school that the only way to leave the farm was either through sports or the military.

Leaving nothing to chance, he worked diligently at both athletics and studies. If he was going to have to join the military, it was as an officer, not a simple enlisted, so he'd have to get a scholarship to college through either sports or grades.

The young Davenport excelled at football, basketball and track, participating in discus and javelin events. The University of Michigan Wolverines granted him a full scholarship after witnessing his excellence as a linebacker in football. It didn't hurt that he had a 3.8 grade point average to match his athletic talents. In addition to sports, he signed up for the ROTC program, ensuring that if there were a need for him to go into the military, it would be as an officer.

While in the ROTC, he learned of the Navy SEAL (an acronym for Sea, Air and Land) program that was recently implemented in 1962 for the recognized need for unconventional warfare and utilized Special Operations as a measure against guerrilla activity. By his senior year of college, the SEAL program took an interest in him as well, so that when he graduated he was transferred to the SEAL program.

Graduating in 1969 with a degree in Political Science, he went through the rigorous training at Coronado in San Diego, California. The training was to prepare for specifically designed missions - such as reconnoitering an enemy beach from the surf zone, taking down a moving vessel at sea, as well as laying awake in ambush for three days and nights up to your neck in mud. All of this requires a stamina and threshold for pain so enormous that the average man wouldn't attempt it. Only a select few manage to survive the intensity and complete exhaustion endured the training, and Davenport excelled at it. It was quickly recognized that he had an uncanny threshold of pain and endurance, along with above average reflexes, assets that would prove invaluable throughout his career.

AN EAGLE'S VENGEANCE

By

Guy Macdonald

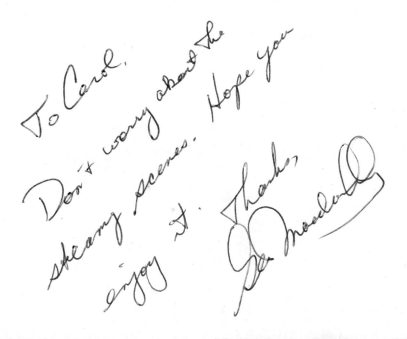

To Carol,
Don't worry about the steamy scenes. Hope you enjoy it.
Thanks,
Guy Macdonald

ISBN: 0-7596-9738-8 (Ebook)
ISBN: 0-7596-9736-1 (Softcover)

This book is printed on acid free paper.

1stBooks - rev. 4/29/02

Davenport was called to duty as the Vietnam War was drawing to a close when he finished training. He was involved in extraction operations, as well as a few special operations requiring weeks in the deepest jungles of Vietnam, behind oncoming North Vietnamese lines. These operations were designed to eliminate key political and military personnel that Washington decided would conflict with future opportunities for negotiations and had been identified for carrying out crimes and inhumanities against the Vietnamese civilian population. Davenport was second in command of a platoon that never lost a casualty, a statistic that the SEALs always regarded as one of their most profound accomplishments, very low casualties considering the intense operations they underwent.

In 1972, Davenport's last mission in Vietnam was to retrieve Prisoners of War. Regrettably, this operation was aborted and one of the team members, Lt. Melvin S. Dry was killed when entering the water after jumping from a helicopter at least 35 feet above the surface.

Throughout the rest of his career, Davenport was involved in many of the SEALs most important missions, many of them classified, either physically with the team or in the planning of operations for Urgent Fury in Grenada, Just Cause in Panama, and Desert Shield/Storm in Iraq. In the early 1990's, it was recognized there were requirements to do something more in relation to CIA activities than the SEALs were designed for. A new unit was developed with volunteers from the various special unit forces like the Green Beret and SEALs, to work with government agencies on terrorist and drug-related issues. Captain Davenport was asked to head the development of this agency. After the devastating bombing of the two World Trace Center buildings in New York, that organization became the forefront of anti-terrorist campaigns first in Afghanistan, and then spreading to various other countries that harbored terrorist groups.

Much to Davenport's dismay, the decision to put him in line for this job was to snub him from future opportunities in the Navy. Although his successes were too numerous to mention, his personality didn't fit well with the upper echelon of the Navy. More than once his stubbornness and loose mouth, as well as his freewheeling personal life, had gotten him into hot water with either public agencies or the military brass. Davenport was his own man and not about to succumb to the pettiness and ass-kissing tendencies of the Pentagon. He wasn't dismayed by the reason behind his selection since he was finally on his own, away from what he termed the "panty-wastes" of the military. He was finally in the one environment he loved, covert operations, normally with the requirement for use of deadly force.

After years of seeing death face to face, normally most of it by his own hand, he had lost any real sense of caring or need for love. The concept of love had eluded him. He was only concerned with his own satisfaction tonight. Currently he was working on fulfilling that need in the hottest nightclub in Washington, D.C. This was the place people came to meet the hottest ladies. A large establishment, it was a converted old warehouse furnished with the latest sound system, lights and gadgets the market had to offer. Costing twenty-five dollars just to enter and drinks twice the normal price at the local clubs, you paid for the ambiance as well as the opportunity to mingle with the fair maidens.

The building consisted of two floors. The main floor played the latest in dance music with psychedelic lights, lasers and a dance floor highlighted by built-in lights which exaggerated the heavy body gyrations. Upstairs was for those who preferred the more romantic setting with soft suede booths, low lights, and easy listening music to set the mood.

Finally able to enjoy a weekend where he could unwind, his main concern was for someone to share his bed.

Having never been married, he was never comfortable in a relationship with one woman for more than a few months, enjoying the variety life had to offer. It had been two weeks since his last fling and he wasn't about to spend tonight alone. Dressed in a tailored gray suit with a maroon satin tie over a light blue shirt, he sat across the table from a stunning woman half his age with the intelligence of an ice cube, his favorite type, not having to bother with boring conversations. They met during a party given by the Secretary of the Navy.

To avoid the stuffiness and idle small talk, they escaped for a quiet dinner at the most expensive Italian restaurant, filling up with linguini and wine. Afterwards she suggested they go to the disco for some dancing and drinking. Not much into dancing, he was fortunate that by the time they arrived at the nightclub, the alcohol at dinner had slowed her pace down some.

Long black hair flowed over a silver gown that left little to the imagination. The abundant breasts screamed for release and it appeared her straps would tear at the seams every time she breathed. With a face that would make most models jealous, she was Davenport's perfect combination of beauty and sensuality without even a hint of intelligence.

Although Davenport didn't go out on actual operations anymore, he still had that wandering spirit in him. Now after spending an exorbitant amount on her for dinner and drinks, he wanted what he felt was his reward; several hours of heavy sex and then send her off in the morning.

"Why don't we get out of here and go off to my place for a few drinks?" he asked her. He figured the three Margaritas she had since they arrived, on top of the wine at dinner, would make her acceptable to anything.

"Okay, suuure." she slurred, looking at him with glossy eyes. Spending most of the night staring at her breasts, he hadn't noticed the eyes. Occasionally he would glance at the long voluptuous tanned legs, which were barely covered by the shortness of the gown, but he was hypnotized by the firm and plentiful melons.

Slowly rising from the chair, he felt the room sway for a brief moment until he overcame the effects of the alcohol and bent over to pull back her chair. Rising, she fell slightly, giving him the opportunity to sample the goods by grabbing her, squeezing her breasts as he steadied her. They were indeed firm and he sensed she was hot with her nipples stiff. Giggling a little, she turned towards him, attempting to focus without success.

"You know what honey, I thing I might be drunk." She said.

Laughing inside, he realized that she was in no condition to resist him as long as he could prevent her from passing out.

Leaving the nightclub, Davenport held her close to his side to prevent her from falling, while giving the valet his car ticket. Looking down at her, he got another look at those splendid breasts when suddenly, she reached up and gave him a deep wet kiss, opening his mouth and sticking her tongue inside while slowly, gyrating her body against his. He could sense the blood flowing immediately to his pelvis and wanted to get into the car before anyone noticed his erection. He knew she could feel it because she began to rotate her hips against it while letting out a slow moan.

When they arrived at his condominium, he took off his coat and grabbed the stereo remote control. Immediately the CD player began to emit classical music from four speakers, inset into each corner of a spacious living room. He decided many years ago, that he was not going to settle for a simple place to live, but wanted the lavish lifestyle he always believed he deserved.

This playground of sophisticated modern stereo equipment, black leather furniture outlined by highly polished brass, glass furnishings and oak cabinets, was always Davenport's starting gate for enticing women to spend the night. It failed only once, but eventually even she returned and fell prey to his trap. Of course, Davenport's selection of women ensured their breast size was higher than their IQ, so it took little to entice them.

When he turned, she was there, staring up at him with those empty glossy eyes, yearning to be taken. Pulling her close he was met by another healthy deep kiss. She slowly gyrated around his crotch, bringing his erection back to life. She stepped back and undid the top of her gown's straps, the dress almost exploding off her body, easily falling to the ground with little resistance. His eyes concentrated on the loveliest breasts that he had ever seen. He had always considered himself a breast expert and this pair deserved recognition in the Breast Hall of Fame. They were firm and stood out, with nipples that pierced the air. As he went to caress them, she moved closer and slid her hands down along his stomach, down along his hips and then towards his crotch. She let out a small moan of approval as she felt his manhood eagerly awaiting her touch and she rotated her hands up and down along the line of his zipper. She moved her hands up to loosen his belt and slid her hand inside. The hands found their target immediately and his eyes rolled back into his head. She knelt down and was undoing his pants when suddenly his pager went off.

He never enjoyed the idea of carrying a pager, especially at moments like these. The Pentagon insisted that all special assistants carry them in case of emergency. He couldn't believe the timing. He considered ignoring it for a half hour to allow time to fulfill the fantasy, but he realized, the thing only went off in extreme emergencies and if he didn't react promptly he'd have hell to pay later.

As she slid her mouth over his erection, his pager went off again and he cursed himself.

"Darling, I'm afraid I have to answer this. Why don't you go into the bedroom and settle in. I'll be right back." Davenport said as he raised her up off her knees.

He watched her butt as she slithered over to the door, reaching out his hands as if grabbing her tight buns. As she got to the door she turned rubbing her hands over her breasts and down her stomach to her crotch "Don't be long honey, I'm hot and wet."

He redid his pants, shoving his erection in as well as he could. He looked at the number on the pager; it was not one he recognized. Normally it would either be the CIA Control Room, White House Chief of Staff, or DEA Chief of Staff's home number. This wasn't one of those. Dialing the number it was answered on the first ring.

"Raven we are glad you called." The voice on the other end said.

"Who the hell is this and why are you calling me at this hour of the night?" Davenport asked, knowing that only a handful of people knew his code name and pager number.

"The who is not important right now. I have a car waiting for you in front of your condo and you need to proceed here immediately."

"Let me get this straight, you are calling me on my unlisted pager, using my classified code name, but refuse to tell me who you are and why you want to see me? Go fuck yourself." This was absurd and he was going to call the Pentagon immediately to see who had given someone this information.

"All your questions will be answered the moment you arrive. Until then I can only tell you that is extremely urgent and of national security."

"Let me tell you, asshole. Unless you're the fucking President I'm not going anywhere. You are using an unauthorized number and I'll find out who you are and hang your ass out to dry." He was just about to hang up the phone when there was a knock on the door.

"Raven, there is an associate of mine at the door to escort you. If you refuse to come with him, then I will unfortunately have to make a phone call to Sundance and tell him about your exploits with his daughter tonight." Davenport recognized the code word for the Secretary of the Navy, David Spears.

"What the hell are you talking about, I don't know the woman."

"That surprises me, his daughter is a rather buxom black haired girl with long sexy legs. She was last seen at a party tonight wearing a silver gown and talking to some military man. We both know she is probably naked in your bedroom so let's skip the dramatics. She has a habit of drinking too much and forgetting where she is. Her father's protection doesn't allow her much of a sex life so she usually seduces someone at her father's parties. I can just imagine the consequences if he were to find out where she is right now."

Davenport could not believe what he was hearing. It all seemed like he had been in total control throughout the evening, when he was actually playing into a woman's hand. He couldn't think of the consequences. The man who controlled all promotions in the Navy, who held his fate in his selection for Admiral next year, would find out that he was just about to begin a heavy night of sex with his daughter. "You son of a bitch. What's going on?"

"The gentleman at the door will see to it that the woman is escorted safely home. You will proceed to the lobby where a limousine is waiting for you outside. Proceed immediately sir." The phone went dead.

Davenport never liked the cloak and dagger business. Following people or conducting surveillance operations wasn't his cup of tea. Preferring quick insertion, swift kills and extraction, the spy movies with hidden organizations that knew everyone's moves were well beyond belief. Now someone knew his every move and was using it against him. He was not about to let someone get the upper hand and decided he would play along to eventually teach them a lesson.   Unfortunately, this was to be the beginning of a deep hole he would be unable to climb out of.

Chapter 1

Opening the door, Davenport found his escort six feet across the hall, leaning against the far wall. The man was of average height and build; dressed in a bland dark blue suit, light shirt and dark blue tie. Davenport deduced that fashion was not his strong point. Evaluating his chances of overtaking the guy was quickly suppressed when he noticed the crease in the left side of his jacket every time he breathed, and his right hand holding onto his belt buckle. The distance between him and the armed man was too much before he would find a bullet with his name on it. The guy was smart positioning across the hall to prevent any impulsive reactions.

"My escort I presume." Davenport said.

The man didn't respond but pointed down the hall to where another man stood wearing the same attire.

"You must be Heckyll and I suppose that's Jeckyll. May I suggest you find a new tailor, the outfits don't do a thing for you." Davenport was thankful he hadn't attempted anything, an easy target for a bullet from the second man.

After taking two steps toward the second man he looked back and found that Heckyll had already entered his condo and closed the door. Davenport wondered to himself how many times these guys had done this, for whatever reason, and what Heckyll would really do when he noticed the voluptuous nude body laying in his bed, before taking her home.

"Well, Jeckyll, your partner wasn't much of a conversationalist, anything you care to say?" Davenport asked.

The man only pointed to the elevator.

"Damn you guys are a lot of fun. I bet you're a real blast at parties."

"Just get into the elevator, Captain."

1

"My God it speaks." The whole ordeal was starting to infuriate him, but he wasn't going to overdo things and would play along with their little game until he found an opening and get some answers.

Taking the elevator down to the lobby, he found a third man dressed like the previous two standing at the entryway. As he proceeded toward the entryway, the guard walked outside and opened the door to a black limousine. He couldn't make out the license plates because of the car's position. He considered making a move on the third guard but the plan was also quickly discarded when the guard moved around the other side of the car. Realizing these men were professionals, Davenport climbed in and surveyed the inside for any options. The door closed and the car immediately left the entryway. The glass between him and the driver was closed, bulletproof he imagined, and he was unable to see the driver through the darkened glass.

He glanced out the windows and noticed the drive was passing near the White House heading towards the center of town. After 12 minutes, the sedan pulled into the entranceway of one of the premier hotels of the city. At this hour of the morning there wasn't much activity and no one at the door. The building rose into the night for 25 floors, each of which contained suites costing over 200 dollars a night.

"You may get out here. Go through the front door and proceed to the elevators. Take the second elevator on the right. In the pocket in front of you is a key. Insert it into the maintenance switch, turning it clockwise, and then press basement. You'll be met at the bottom." A voice said out of the speaker in the front wall before the door automatically opened.

"And if I refuse to go and walk away." Davenport was not inspired about having to go into an elevator with restricted maneuverability and any ability to respond.

"The young lady has not been delivered to her home yet sir. If you fail to make the meeting, her father will receive a call and find his daughter with several bruises, tied to your bed. I'm sure you can consider what would happen next." The voice on the speaker replied.

Not knowing whether it was true or not, he assumed the worst and left the car, walking toward the swivel glass entrance. The hotel lobby was decked out in red carpet with the hotel's logo embroidered in the middle. The glass windows were polarized to keep the sun from heating the lobby and were outlined in gold plating. The lobby was expansive, stretching up three stories with a giant chandelier hanging in the center. Davenport guessed it would take an army of ten men just to lower and raise it. The furnishings were plush antiques of solid oak that were highly polished. Off to his left was the concierge's desk and to his right was the reception desk. On the wall behind the desk were clocks from various points around the world, so that all the visiting dignitaries could figure out the time back home.

A rather pretty young lady was behind the reception desk, fiddling with paperwork, wishing the next few hours would pass quickly so she could go home and get some sleep. The evening duty was usually slow and the only action was watching the guests arrive from various functions, normally drunk or with some female escort provided for them. She took very little notice of Davenport's arrival.

Davenport made his way beyond the lobby to the elevators on the left. He found the second elevator to the right and the door was already open. As he entered, he finally realized he hadn't brought any form of weapon and kicked himself for not thinking clearly before he left his apartment. He inserted the key into the maintenance slot. Although the arrow indicated it should be turned to the left, he did as instructed and turned it to the right. The doors closed and he pushed the button marked B. He positioned

3

himself at the back corner of the elevator so that if there were any surprises when the elevator door opened he would at least have a fraction of a second to react, not that he could do much after that. As the elevator traveled downward, he felt an unusual twinge through his body.

The elevator moved swiftly without making a sound, appearing to go all the way to the center of the earth until it finally stopped and the doors opened. He was poised to react and was met by another man dressed in the same blue suit.

"Jesus you guys need to find new suits." Davenport said, peering around the corner of the elevator "Well, at least you probably don't have to worry about what suit to wear each day, huh?"

"Very amusing Captain Davenport. Why are you huddled in the corner? If we had wanted you harmed, we would have done it a long time ago. Falcon is waiting and will explain everything." The gentleman replied, as he turned and walked away from the elevator.

Walking out of the elevator, the room looked like part of an old warehouse, with dark cement block walls and dim lights hanging from steel beams. There was no sound or exterior light, giving Davenport the feeling as if he was inside a deep cave, like the one they found Osama bin Laden hiding in. He wondered if he actually had gone to the center of the earth. Desks were lined up like a normal office, most of them empty. Computers were on each desk with file cabinets lining one wall. Maps lined the other walls with colored pins marking obscure locations. Unlike the lavish settings in the hotel lobby, there were no comfortable furnishings, only basic desks with uncomfortable chairs. Overhead, cameras were situated throughout the room, each one following him wherever he walked. In spite of his captors, he scratched his nose with his middle finger remembering the poster titled "Last Great Act of Defiance."

His new escort, who he nickname Hopalong because of a slight limp, led Davenport into an enclosed office at the rear of the room, which probably served as a conference room. Along the walls were pictures and maps from around the world with more of the same pins marking obscure locations around the world. There was a long table with several chairs placed around it. In the corner was a small desk similar to those outside. On the wall behind the desk were more clocks like those in the lobby showing the time in major cities around the world. Davenport could hear the whirling of a vent motor, allowing filtered air from the outside to fill the room.

When Hopalong closed the door, Davenport felt like he was inside a bank vault. He went over to some of the maps and pictures but couldn't pinpoint the significance of any of them.

After waiting five minutes, long enough for his temper to grow, the door opened to reveal a large figure in the entrance. In the small light, Davenport could make out an older man who showed the wear and tear of his years. What was left of his hair was wrapped around his ears and strained to reach the top of his head. The face was slightly wrinkled and his shoulders sagged, however, the body seemed trim, missing the usual potbelly normally associated with people over 50. Davenport estimated he was about 55-60 years old, however the eyes contradicted his age. They appeared young and alert, seeming to pierce right through him as if evaluating his inner self. Davenport felt another cold rush through his body, much more severe than in the elevator.

"Captain Davenport, it is good of you to join us." The gentleman said, moving as if floating, toward the corner of the room, taking a seat behind the desk.

"I really didn't have much of a choice asshole." Davenport felt he needed to gain the upper hand and start controlling the situation. "Your security around here is poor,

5

no one even bothered to check to see if I had a gun to blow your head off with."

"Really, Captain, there is no need for obscenity or a short temper. If you had a weapon you would never have made it here. You were checked for weapons in the elevator. Believe me when I say that our security outdoes that for the President. Besides, we have so much to discuss and blowing my head off as you put it would do neither of us any good. Let me introduce myself, I am called Falcon, and I need your assistance in an urgent matter of national importance."

Davenport still hadn't figured a way to extricate himself from the present situation, so he decided to play along, evaluating his options as the old man talked.

"Yeah, well since you got me here, I doubt I'll be able to stop you from talking." Davenport said as he sat down in one of the chairs around the table.

"I know you are a little upset with us at the moment. I would be if I were in your shoes." The man said leaning forward over the desk. "I represent a group of people who are very concerned about the state of affairs of our nation and where it is headed. I have seen your record, and as a patriot who has sacrificed himself on many occasions for this country, I feel you share some of our concerns. Let me ask you a question. After risking your life in some of the worst places on earth, have you really made a difference?"

"What I did for my country is of no concern of yours."

"Captain, there is nothing you have done that I am not aware of. I know of your exploits in Vietnam, Thailand, Iran, Iraq and Afghanistan and the people you have either executed or brought into custody. My question still remains, did any of those incidents change the path of our country for the better?"

"That's not for me to decide. America is doing okay for itself."

"Do you really believe that Captain? Our children are dying on the streets from gang warfare or starvation. Our borders are being infiltrated at an alarming rate. Even after the alarming discoveries of how terrorists lived among us, illegal aliens continue to flood into this country from Cuba, Haiti and Mexico, as well as from the Middle East. The economy still has not recovered since the World Trace Center bombings and is about to be flushed down the toilet while our international friends are starting to turn their backs on us. Now the politicians want to stop the six-year old anti-terrorist campaign and decrease our military forces so they can start spending money on old people who are already dying, providing increased health benefits to everyone including those illegal aliens. This puts an even bigger strain on our economy by taking away important defense contracts and putting more people on the streets with signs reading 'Will Work for Food'. As we slowly decline, other countries including the Middle East and China are building their forces, eventually able to take over smaller countries because we won't be able to stretch our forces to stop them. It is obvious from recent events that the UN and NATO can't stop anything. They are stretched across the entire globe and more and more countries are losing faith in the alliance, refusing to send their troops in support." Falcon rose from the chair and walked over to the maps on the wall.

"Look at the map Captain. Ours is a relatively small country. As we downsize our defenses, the strength of the Chinese and self-righteous Moslems of the Middle East grow. What is to stop them from wanting to stretch their clutches across the lands? They are already rich in their oil supplies while ours are draining. What do we do if the Middle East decides to pull the plug? If Saddam Hussein had managed to continue his trek after invading Kuwait, what would have prevented him from reversing the effects of the blockade by stopping billions of barrels of oil from

7

being exported? We were lucky then and we can't afford to count on luck again."

While Falcon spoke, Davenport was reminded of the old men standing on their soapboxes preaching about all the problems with the world and the coming of the end. "That's very interesting. Have you considered running for office?"

"This isn't about running for office. The only time this country has managed to pull its head out of water was during a war. That's when the people pulled together and became united. This country was at its strongest in 2001 and 2002 after the World Trade Center bombing. Although the people were reluctant to travel and turned a glaring eye at everyone that looked like a Muslim, they were the most patriotic they had ever been. The problem was that the campaign against terrorism didn't have any measurable and visual results that were as easily identifiable as during an all-out war. The nation began to lose interest in the campaign and the aid we were sending to these countries, until they eventually started calling for a more concerned effort at home. Only when this country really feels threatened and can see obvious progress and witness events on the news, do Americans manage to forget their bigotry and greed and rally together, just like in World War II or Kuwait. That's when progress is really made and the economy soars. They didn't pull together in conflicts like Vietnam, Bosnia, or Somalia, because it didn't pose a threat to them. What this country needs is to be threatened in order to regain its pride and ranking as a superpower."

Davenport was growing tired with the sermon. "Do you have some sort of crystal ball that shows the United States being invaded? Get with the program pal, no one in his right mind would attempt to threaten this country or have the resources to try again."

"Have you forgotten, Captain, that a lot of this country had already been sold to the Japanese in the late 1990's? If you look a little harder, you will find that even after the government isolated Middle East holdings and finances, those same countries still control an even larger percentage. We are already being invaded on the monetary market instead of by military forces. With the Middle East already having a foothold and its people scattered all across the continent, they could easily shut us down and start carving a hole. We always thought it impossible for terrorism to spread to this country, but as demonstrated in New York at the World Trade Center, it's for real. Evidence even suggests that a majority of the youth gangs in major cities are funded by Middle East factions."

"You grow tiring, Falcon. Just what has all this to do with me?"

"It's about time the country got a wake-up call. We need a war where the people of America will begin to cry for revenge and force the government to rebuild the armed forces, once again establishing its superiority. With the right provocation in the right place we can stir up the hornet's nest."

"You have gone over the edge pal. I should kill you right now and take my chances getting out of here. There are a lot of people who would be interested in your little stories, who could see to it you are put in a little room with plenty of padding."

"Your first suggestion would not be wise, Captain. Since you left your condo, two weapons have been pointed directly at you and if they had any idea you would do something drastic, they would not hesitate to pull the trigger. Besides, who would you tell? Who would really listen to you? You don't even know who we are and once you left, this place would disappear without a trace and you would be considered a raving lunatic who is ready for retirement. Can't you understand this country is in desperate times? As we speak, the government is considering doing away with your prehistoric organization. Ever since the end of the Cold War and the major cutbacks they don't consider you and your team a necessity anymore. Even in Afghanistan it had limited effect and participation. They want to use the money for more programs that eventually means more money in politicians' pockets. What will you do with your team gone? What will you do on the outside world? Even you are frustrated with the recent downturns in the support your teams are getting in the fight against terrorism."

"What makes you any different from those militia groups you talk about? What possible role could I have in all this?"

"We are not glory seeking weekend warriors that scream about what's wrong with this country and do nothing except make matters worse. There are no guarantees in life Captain and I can only promise that when your part is completed you will enjoy a prosperous future after a large contribution in an account of your choosing." Falcon went on to outline his plan. Davenport sat in awe. The consequences of his plan would be extensive. The absurdity of the plan was almost infallible. It was so offbeat it might actually work. What was being proposed was so simple but held such a dramatic impact on world events. However ludicrous it sounded, Falcon was right in bringing in Davenport because only he could see to the completion of the first phase.

"I have given you a complete rundown of our plan, Captain. All that is required is you to light the spark." Falcon said as he sat down on the edge of the table. "Let me remind you that if you change your mind and discuss this with anyone else, especially government offices, you will not be able to prove it and will spend the rest of your life locked in that little room you so eloquently had set aside for me. Your future would be lonely and short."

"Don't threaten me. You may hold all the cards and leave me with no alternatives but what I want to know is just how profitable will this be for me?"

"Ah, you haven't failed me Captain. I knew there was more than patriotism in your blood. What we have proposed is the amount of one million dollars deposited in a Swiss Bank Account under an alias of your choice tomorrow. When the mission is successfully completed, an additional four million dollars will be added to the account. Would this clear your conscience and allow you to relax comfortably?"

Davenport couldn't believe his ears. Over the years he had prepared to relax comfortably living off a healthy pension and the investments he had mad. This kind of money would make that all seem miniscule, allowing him to move overseas to a nice villa away from everyone where he could lavish in young women for some time to come.

"The figures have a nice ring to them. How can I reach you?"

"There will be no need to reach me Captain. We will be in touch as required. We expect you to carry out the first phase of the plan in two weeks as I detailed. You have very little time so you better get started immediately. One of my associates will escort you back upstairs where there is a car waiting to return you home. You will find a more than ample substitute for the young lady waiting there with my compliments."

As he left the room, he began to consider his options. Falcon was right; no one would believe a word. They would lock him away and his future would be dim. If he carried out this crazy plan he could enjoy a life the way he had always imagined would be there for him and firmly believed he deserved. He had served his country and given everything it asked of him and received so little back, his exploits hidden away in secrecy forever.

During the drive back the condominium in the limousine; Davenport barely noticed the sites of the nation's capital. His mind was swimming with possibilities and obstacles. The biggest obstacle would be getting the team involved and the one man he would have to deal with throughout. Getting the operation planned and started was easy, it was having once again to deal with the team's leader that aggravated him. Regrettably he knew there was no way the mission could be conducted without his involvement, and removing him would raise suspicions, so he'd have to just live with the unpleasantness for the short period of time, recognizing the rewards he'd reap in the end.

The limousine dropped him off in front of his condominium complex and Davenport walked through the quiet lobby and hallways, noticing the disappearance of his three companions from earlier.

As he slid the key into the door, he could hear soft music emanating from his apartment. Opening the door, he noticed the soft glow from several candles lit around the main room. Soft jazz was playing from the stereo, as he spotted a bottle of champagne chilling in the ice bin next to the couch. One hand dangled over the edge of the sofa. As he walked towards the main room, the shadows from the candles danced along the walls to the sound of the music, giving the room a haunting but erotic atmosphere. The entire mood was absorbing, engulfing his sensations and washing away the past events from the evening out of his mind.

Just as he approached the end of the entranceway, a body rose from the couch. Davenport stopped suddenly, his feet cemented in place, as he watched the woman glide across the floor.

Almost as tall as him, with flowing blonde hair and long, lean legs, she was clothed in only a sheer black negligee that hid very little from the imagination. With the aid of the candlelight, he could make out the magnificence of her body, with full erect breasts, strong legs, and trim hips. Carrying a glass of champagne in each hand, she slid in front of him. With only a smile needed, she handed him a glass and they each took a sip.

"About time you got home. I was beginning to wonder how long I was going to have to wait. I didn't want to have to drink the whole bottle before you got here." The lovely woman said as she circled around him. As she walked around him, her free hand moved along his shoulder, down along his back, across his buttocks and hips. When she completed her inspection and returned to meet him face to face, her hand found what it was searching for.

"I see you approve." She said as she moved her hand up and down along his crotch.

Taking him by his hand, she led him towards the bedroom. No further discussion was needed or desired for the remainder of the evening. Davenport was truly in for a night he wouldn't soon forget. Davenport had never experienced a true professional and never one as high-priced as her. The early morning lasted well into the late morning, and when Davenport awoke that afternoon, she was long gone. Davenport began to wonder if the evening's events had truly happened at all, or that it was something in his imagination, until he spotted the manila folder on his kitchen table when he finally went to make a cup of coffee. It wasn't until then that the rush of emotions from the events between the party and returning to his condo in the early morning hours, came rushing back to him. Davenport took a deep breath, opened the envelope and started an adventure that would shake the world.

Chapter 2

At this time of the day, the vibrant pace of electronic activity tended to decrease. Eyes wandered wishfully towards the clock, waiting for the final few minutes of the day to pass. The sounds of fingers busily dancing along computer keyboards became a whisper, as the click of the second hand began to echo in the ears of the masses. Telephones ringing incessantly and papers being shuffled and crumbled were replaced with the clicking of briefcases and carry bags as the workers prepared for the mad race to the parking lot. Normally during the week, all these preparations were futile, as no matter how fast they scrambled to their cars, the freeway would still be backed up for miles and increase their frustration levels. Today, however, on a Saturday, the traffic wouldn't be there and the workforce was not as heavily staffed, so there wasn't a need to get an advantage over anything.

The last final minutes seemed to take an eternity to the impatient, as they clicked off their computers and shoved their unfinished work in the corner of their desk. For those unlucky enough to have to work at the San Diego Union on a Saturday, there was little time to prepare for the night's activities. Most of the Saturday crew was younger, single people, whose only thoughts during the last hour or so were the activities at the local bars and few remaining dance spots. For the luckier ones of the staff, they were more interested in the heavy dates they had arranged for the evening. There would be little time to return home and properly prepare for what the evening held in store.

Before long, the patience ran dry and people started maneuvering their ways to the elevators and stairwells. No one would miss them the last few minutes of the shift, and nothing worthwhile could be started and completed in such short a time. Ten minutes after 5pm, silence reigned throughout the work area. The electric whir of machinery was gone, replaced with the sounds of the ventilation system, trying to circulate the air.

In a small cubicle in the corner, a desk light still flickered, as Kay Cross pondered over her computer terminal. For over an hour, she sat staring off into space, trying to pull words out of the air, but coming up blank. She pulled several pieces of notepaper from the desk and read through them, shuffling them, hoping to unlock something that would magically bring the words she needed to the screen. Sometimes she wondered if possibly, she might be trying too hard, and just needed to start with the basics and expand on them, let the words develop into the story and shuffle them around as necessary.

Spreading the papers out across the small desk, she rearranged them into a particular sequence, and scanned them one last time. Turning her chair back to the computer terminal, she started to type. Basically, she was expanding the small notes into sentences, forming them together into paragraphs and hoping the end result would be the formation of her story.

For the next several hours, she attempted to type the information in, copy and paste from one section to another, and edit certain sections. In between time, she leaned back in the chair and closed her eyes, while she spun the chair around. At one point she walked from the office to the bathroom, meandered into the lounge area and pulled her dinner of bottled water and yogurt out of the employee refrigerator, before returning to her desk. She read what she had so far as she scooped the tasteless yogurt from the container, licking the last remaining drops from the plastic spoon, before tossing them both into the trash bin. After a short inner deliberation, she returned to the typing.

By the time she finished, she looked up and saw that the sun had set several hours ago. Standing up, she peered over her cubicle wall. The glow of her computer created haunting shadows on the walls. Desks were cluttered with notes and folders, collections of the tidbits of information each reporter amassed during research on each story. Eventually they ended up either in the corner wastebaskets, or cluttered nearby, the result of errant shots from disgruntled basketball players. Eventually stories were massaged into the daily newspaper, the result of hours of frustration and sweat ending up in the bottom of bird cages, stuffed in bus and train seats, lining barbecue grills for weekend festivities or gathered at grocery store recycling locations.

Kay stood up from the desk and walked to the window to view the lights of the city. Her long blond hair was rustled and wind-blown, evidence of a hard day beating the streets for a story. A pair of faded jeans and pullover sweater hid a body accustomed to a routine of Aerobics and running. In contrast to the smooth, beautiful face and jade green eyes, her glasses were unflattering, large square rims that didn't fit the face. Usually haunting, the eyes were now bloodshot from staring at the computer monitor for the last four hours.

Starting at the newspaper five years ago, straight out of college, she demonstrated exhaustive investigative techniques. At the university she had uncovered a scandal involving members of the school board who had been extorting money from the school's funds. Making a name for herself, she was quickly hired by the Union. When hired, as with most new reporters, she expected to find that big story immediately and make a bigger name for herself. Unfortunately, the paper had numerous reporters and she was relegated to simple local stories. Spending long days and nights in the office conducting research for fellow reporters and doing interviews, she was growing tired of the minor stories she felt had little significance. With her concentration on work, her social life had come to a standstill. Except for a few office parties, she had not gone on a date, taken in a movie or eaten at a nice restaurant since arriving in San Diego. There were plenty of men asking her out, but she wanted to make her mark in the new world before considering any type of relationship.

Once again, it was another late Saturday night. Her coworkers were out dancing and drinking while she toiled over a story of a woman who lost custody of her child in court to her ex-husband who had been out of work for nearly two years. It was a popular story in town, however it lacked the intrigue and mystery she was looking to cover. Injustice in the courts was common knowledge and the story did little to spark any flames. She wanted a story that would uncover the deepest of secrets, hitting top-level politicians or businessmen with their hands in someone else's pockets, earning her national acclaim. Unfortunately, all newspaper reporters looked for the same story, but very few found them.

Leaning against the wall by the window she gazed at the lights of the city. The building was at the corner of two major highways and she watched the cars scurry along, normally ten miles over the speed limit, off to unknown locations. Along the access roads, nightclub parking lots were jammed and the billboards were lit up identifying local bands that were playing and special drink prices. In the distance she could make out the lights along San Diego Harbor, small boats sailing out towards Catalina Island or just heading off for a weekend fishing trip. She wondered if she would ever get the opportunity to enjoy some of these moments.

"Still looking for that big story, Miss Cross?" Startled, she turned to see a tall black man wearing coveralls, she considered fifty pounds overweight, but would still scare anyone in a dark alley. He was pulling a cart containing cleaning gear and trash barrels. Jim Cartwright had been the janitor at the newspaper for over fifteen years and he had seen a lot of reporters burn out in their early years, spending long frustrating hours,searching for that big story.

"Hi Jim. No, just finishing up a story. I have to get it completed for the Monday edition." Kay was hoping it would be good enough for the front pages, but knew it would end up hidden somewhere amidst the other minor stories in the Local section.

"Miss Cross, if you don't mind me saying so, you need to get out once in a while. Find yourself a nice man and learn to relax. I come in here every night and you're working while everyone else has gone home. I've seen a lot of young reporters in my day that did the exact same thing as you, and they end up overstressed and alcoholics. A pretty young thing like yourself needs to meet someone and spend time at home with a few children to look after."

"Do you mean something like barefoot and pregnant Jim?"

"You know that's not what I mean." Jim said as he emptied trash containers.

"Sorry Jim. All that will come in due time once I get myself established. I have to find out what I can really do before I settle down. I don't want to grow old and keep wondering what could have been."

"Girl, if you don't slow down and take some time for yourself there won't be any growing old or anyone to spend it with. You keep up like this and you'll be asking yourself where has all the time gone." '

I know, but I still have to try. I've worked all my life to get this far and I don't want to stop now when there is still so much more to do."

Kay walked back to her desk and sat down. The screen was half filled with the beginning of her story. She wanted it to be prolific and profound, but the details of the events were not inspiring and it was just another sad emotional story of injustice that belonged more on a soap opera than a newspaper.

Jim carried on with his work in the office, emptying the trash containers and sweeping the floor. He never tried to clean the desks. Reporters were very particular about their desks and any disturbance was considered a sacrilege fearing that something would be lost or out of place.

Most of the notes ended up in little balls, tossed at the wastebasket, eventually swept up by his broom and tossed away. Pages and pages of rough drafts, rewrites and food wrappers were buried under the desks during the day. Jim was never surprised when reporters complained about ulcers, seeing the junk food they digested and cigarettes they smoked all day.

Kay went back to typing on the computer, finalizing the outlines of the story line, eventually realizing that she was only putting words on the paper and they lacked any feeling. A truly gifted reporter's ability to get the reader to absorb the story was based upon how the writer injected feeling into the story. The reader should feel a knot in their stomach or want to jump up and rejoice if the story was worth its weight. Realizing she was getting tired she looked up at the wall clock. It was one-thirty in the morning and she hadn't progressed any farther along in the story than she had been at five in the evening. Figuring she wouldn't get anything constructive accomplished at this hour, she decided to go home and get some sleep, returning in the morning to finish the story before the four p.m. deadline. This would leave her plenty of time for corrections once the editor had a chance to review it.

After saving the story and turning off the computer, she leaned her elbows on the desk and placed her head in her hands, taking a deep breath and exhaling slowly. She started to rub her eyes, but stopped, feeling the pain from their bloodshot condition. Pushing back the chair, she leaned back and stretched out her arms. Feeling the tightness in her muscles reminded her she hadn't worked out in two days and needed to go to Aerobics after completing the story tomorrow. After that she would settle into the apartment's Jacuzzi and relax her worn muscles.

"Goin home, finally?" asked Jim still filling up the trash cans with remnants of the days work.

"I'm not getting much done here anymore. I'll try and finish it early tomorrow."

"Just remember what I told you. You needs to get out and play a little. You know the old saying about all work and no play."

"I'll try to remember that. Maybe after I finish this story I can relax a little. After that I'll have to start working on something a little more exciting."

She didn't know it yet, but just around the corner her wishes would come true. If it didn't kill her first, she'd have that once in a lifetime story. That big break was about to drag her across the countryside, placing her in danger and, if she survived, would allow her to finally consider herself at the top of her class.

.

Chapter 3

The radio suddenly blared into life playing an old Eric Clapton tune. The digital clock read 0800. It was Sunday morning and Lieutenant Commander Greg Morris had no intention of getting up early. The previous evening, he visited his favorite bar for a few sodas and watched another dismal display on the big screen television as the hometown San Diego Chargers lost to the San Francisco 49ers, 36-0, in their season opener. After the game, he stayed to shoot a couple of games of pool with some friends. Before he knew it, he was closing up the bar, talking to a young brunette with long legs. She had just finished a relationship with another man and wasn't interested in any new relationships, but as usual, Greg played the listener. Throughout college he was known as Father Greg for spending more time talking to women on their broken relationships, than actually taking any of them out. He got home around 3 in the morning and after a hard week at work, planned on staying in bed until late.

Since it was Sunday he normally enjoyed sleeping in, even though it was the beginning of the football season. Being on the West Coast the games came on rather early but there were no good games on in the morning. As usual, his mind raced while he was in bed, running through options and possibilities, the previous weeks events and the upcoming week. After a while of tossing and turning, he finally drifted to sleep.

During his first year in the military, the young Ensign Morris was fascinated with the Paint Gun games held in a nearby town, and participated every weekend. Greg enjoyed the thrill of pitting his skills against the locals. Never happy with just playing the game, he usually challenged himself to find new ways to eliminate his opposition in easy fashion. On one such occasion, the owner of the club had called an old friend of his, a Marine Major, to observe Greg's antics, without his knowledge. During the day, Ensign Morris single-handedly managed to subdue 30 people without firing a single shot of his paint gun, smearing them with paint from a play knife. Undeniably impressed, the Major passed his observations to the Colonel on the base that had some friends in Washington, one of them, Commander John Davenport. Before long, Ensign Morris received a call from Commander Davenport. Greg was requested to run through some testing in which he demonstrated his prowess with martial arts, knives, weapons and covert tactics.

After five days of outlasting the best the team had to offer, he was offered a position with a new covert operations unit that was being developed specialize in Anti-terrorist and Ant-Drug operations. The military was taking a new avenue, and the old days of fighting an enemy at sea, had changed to surveillance, long-distance engagements, and participation in Drug Enforcement Operations and Police Actions. This new organization was developed to conduct the type of operations everyone wished we could do but couldn't outwardly participate in. The operations were strictly covert and definitely of the highest security classification. Only a select few knew of the team.

Greg's involvement was classified, and required him to pose as a regular Naval Surface Warfare Officer. It was an awkward position, conducting training at night and on weekends in a remote location in Camp Pendleton, while during the week he was stationed to a ship.

Having never married and with his parents still alive, he was assigned to a ship in California, on the other side of the country from his relatives, living out a dual life. If a mission were to occur, the ship he was assigned to would receive word of a relative either dying or severely ill requiring him to come home for a week. During that week, there would be 3 days of preparation training, a one day transit and no more than 3 days for the mission, allowing a buffer of two extra days if needed.

Training was conducted every Wednesday night, Thursday night and Friday night through Saturday morning, usually ending around noon. He usually spent Saturday night with friends, unwinding and still had Sunday to recuperate, never rising early unless he had an early tee time on the golf course, one of his only other favorite pastimes.

This morning he had no interest in getting to the golf course. He preferred to remain in bed and would later move to the couch to watch the football game or the golf match. Shortly after drifting back to sleep, the solitude was broken by the ringing of the phone. He thought about ignoring it but decided he better answer it. No one ever called on Sunday so it was unusual.

"Greg? Tom. Hey buddy, I got the duty today and just learned that Captain Davenport is on his way out here tomorrow to talk to us. It must be important for the old man to come all the way out here from Washington, don't you think?" Lieutenant Tom Franklin was Greg's second in command and was initially trained as a SEAL before being recruited to the unit. Tom had a unique talent with various weapons and could speak seven different languages, claiming his Italian Mother and Spanish Father had wanted him to be a linguist. Both his parents died in a car wreck when he was in high school and was raised by a distant uncle, a retired SEAL, who lived in South Carolina. He never married and had no ties to the outside world, making him a prime candidate for the team. The team had become his family and nothing on the outside interested him.

"Listen Tom, it's Sunday morning, I'm tired and I'm not interested in tomorrow. Call me tonight when I've had a chance to work out the cobwebs."

"A little too much fun last night buddy. Come on, it's the big man himself coming out here. I bet we have a really important mission to go on. He may even come out here to lead us himself. We haven't been in an operation in over 2 months and I'm getting antsy for some action."

That was the last thing Greg wanted. Although Davenport had recruited him, every time Greg operated with him, they were near catastrophes because of Davenport's stubbornness and ego. It had almost cost them dearly during an operation in Pakistan and he had hoped he wouldn't meet with the "Devil's Angel" as he so aptly called him.

"You're way to anxious Tom. One of these days your enthusiasm is going to get you into trouble." Franklin was an outstanding right hand man but he was too excitable. Too often Greg had to pull him away from fights at a local bar. In the field, Greg kept a tight leash on him to prevent him from storming straight ahead screaming the Rebel Yell. He was afraid Tom was getting too caught up in the assignments and was becoming more a hired assassin than a skilled military man.

"When it does, I'll be right there to meet it head on. Until then you're stuck with me. Anyway, he'll be at the playground Tuesday at oh-seven hundred hours. Don't be late. You'll get your notice tomorrow morning. Be at your best."

"I'll be there. Now let me get back to sleep and I'll see you tomorrow." Greg hung up the phone and tried to get back to sleep. The thought of operating with Davenport nagged at him and sleep was out of the question. He couldn't understand why Davenport would come all the way from Washington D.C. to brief them on an operation. It was highly irregular, unless, God forbid, he was going to lead them. He had been up to date on all the latest news and had heard nothing special.

Since he couldn't get back to sleep, he climbed out of his enormous waterbed and took a hot shower to fully awake and wash away the cobwebs. After drying off he slipped into a sweat suit and walked to the nearby mini-mart to pick up a Sunday paper to see if anything new had occurred overnight.

He returned to his rented apartment after the short walk, feeling a little more refreshed. The apartment was nothing luxurious but it offered him the comfort he required. The furniture wasn't too elaborate; most of it rented colonial furniture except for large oak cabinets that displayed his stereo system and 2 televisions. The cabinets also held his collection of several hundred albums he kept in mint condition and listened to often. After many years he finally gave in to the CD way of music, especially after they stopped making albums or parts for turntables. Music used to be his pastime. He had a guitar on one end of the cabinets and a portable keyboard on a stand to the other side. Greg grew up, like most teenagers, dreaming of being the leader of a rock band. Greg had creative talents that he never fully unlocked, and only managed to play by ear. With age, the dreams faded, and now he only played the instruments to lock the rest of the world out.

The stereo was a collection he amassed over the years on several deployments to Hong Kong and Japan, at the time the latest in technology. The two televisions were set up so that while he was enjoying a show on one, the other was constantly on CNN to be alerted to anything new that happened around the world. CNN was always the first to come out with new stories, even before the Navy received information.

Making himself a bowl of cereal he spread the newspaper onto the table. After weeding out the advertisements, classified sections, and other superfluous sections of the San Diego Union, he scanned the newspapers for any indication of new trouble spots in the world. Nothing different from the usual conflicts in neighboring countries over small stretches of land that he doubted held great importance to call in the team for. The president was pushing the upcoming Peace Agreement and the impact it would have on the entire world's economy, security, and the future for our children.

Morris walked into the living room and turned on the television to see that the Patriot and Seahawks were tied at 0-0. Another thrilling offensive battle he thought. He drifted back to the nagging question of why Davenport was coming and reminisced about Afghanistan where Davenport's brash tactics and excessive risk taking almost cost the lives of two team members. They were sent in at night to extricate a Taliban leader who was reported one of Bin Laden's key executives. The operation was running smoothly until Davenport decided he wanted to take out all the guards rather than slip in silently, grab the general and leave before anyone found out. In doing so, two of the unit's members were caught in crossfire and were almost killed if Greg hadn't spotted the hidden guards and taken them out with his crossbow. Fortunately the mission was a success and marked the beginning of the end for Bin Laden and his terrorist faction.

With his head racing, Greg walked over to the guitar case and pulled out his Epiphone 12-string guitar. Removing the pick from the top of the neck, he slowly strummed a few chords. Easing back on the couch, he played a soft ballad he wrote many years ago while he closed his eyes and tried to turn off the world. While he played, the rest of the world seemed to disappear into darkness. This was the only solitude Greg was ever able to find. It was the only time his mind didn't wrestle with a multitude of ideas, arguments, plans and options. This was the only way he could close out the nearby sounds that filled his ears and clashed with each other.

Chapter 4

While most people were enjoying afternoon barbecues or watching their favorite football team, the President was burdened with clearing another large stack of paperwork from his desk. Dressed in a polo shirt and light slacks, John Lockwood appeared as if he was going to step onto the first tee of the golf course, instead of at his desk in the oval office trying to close out another week and plan the next. He ran his hands through the thick black hair that only had a hint of gray. After the previous President died after a long battle with Pneumonia and the Vice President died of a heart attack, there was an intense election campaign. John Lockwood won the Presidency convincingly. While the stress and long hours would have taken their toll on most men, this President also experienced the loss of his wife to cancer just six months prior to the campaign. Through all this he still kept himself in good shape, both physically and mentally.

From the moment his wife died, he recognized how valuable life was and how short it can be. Part of that is what sparked him to join the campaign. Driven by the memory of his wife, he kept a vigorous regimen of exercise and diet, which included jogging and swimming, as well as walking golf courses rather than using a cart. The eyes remained sharp and the mind quick. The physique returned to its strength and flexibility he had known in college. Standing six-foot-one, he would have been a dominant presence, but it was not his size or conditioning that people immediately noticed. His genuine smile stood out above everything, giving everyone an immediate sense of warmth and down to earth sensibilities.

"Is all this really necessary today?" he asked his chief of staff, Thomas Alexander II. The chief of staff was dressed out in his normal three-piece suit. The son of a prominent lawyer from Colorado, he was the epitome of physical fitness. He routinely found time for a 1-hour workout with a physical therapist. Ever since High School his All-American boyishness was recognized. With blond hair, blue eyes and gentle appearance, he had risen quickly in the political world because of his looks and father's support. The youngest Presidential Chief of Staff ever at only 38, he was the perfect right hand man for the President. He fit right into the political arena. Well liked around Washington, every politician's wife was infatuated with him, although he had never fulfilled any of their dark desires. He always knew the right thing to say and had the answers to all the difficult questions. "I'm sorry sir, but we have to clean everything out in preparation for next week. It should only take another hour. Once you finish with these, we'll go over the next week's schedule."

"How bad does it look?"

"Not as bad as this week, but anything could happen. You will have the time to properly prepare for the upcoming conference."

"We'll need to give as much time as possible to prepare. The planet's future rests on this conference and we need to ensure nothing goes wrong. What do we have the VP doing?"

"The Veep is in New England, meeting with the environmentalists and loggers, to ensure your new Environmental Policy is understood and both will benefit. You know how he feels about this conference and best he's on the other side of the continent."

"You're probably right."

After signing several small documents passed on from Congress, a stack of portraits to be given out to visitors and dignitaries, and reviewing letters from admirers as well as opposing views, he decided putting off sending personal responses to each until later in the day. Although the Chief of Staff would normally handle written responses, the

President felt it was more genuine and even though it took some precious time out of his schedule, it was well worth the effort.

"Okay, let's look at the week ahead." the President said after opening up his weekly diary binder. Looking at the previous week's events, he was always amazed at the amount of changes the weeks went through, evidenced by numerous scribbles, scratch-outs, and different inks used in each day's schedule.

The Chief of Staff walked around the desk and sat in the sofa going meticulously over each day hour by hour. All the meetings the President had to attend, the visitors he had to receive and the functions requiring his presence were covered. Several periods were left open to review documents, write letters, for any unannounced meetings, while leaving some time to relax and conduct his daily workouts.

"I have left Friday open for you to completely review all the documents and possible points that may come up at the conference the following week."

"Have we confirmed where I am staying for this conference?"

"We have been offered a villa on the coast just outside of Acapulco which is used as a summer retreat by one of our esteemed Congressmen. Only a few people will know the location. Even the location of the conference hasn't been released to the press. The Secret Service has already been down to oversee the security arrangements. As recommended, they will be using only the Mexican-American agents to allow them to blend into the crowd better."

"Sounds like a good idea. What is the itinerary?"

"You'll fly down Saturday morning, attend a ball given by the Mexican President that evening. Sunday you'll take a tour around Acapulco during the afternoon and that evening attend a private dinner with the other dignitaries at the Mayor's home. Monday morning will be set aside for meeting all the representatives and short speeches. That afternoon will be set for the formal signing of the treaty. You'll spend the night there before returning the next morning, I figure that will give you a chance for some much needed rest."

"I appreciate that Tom. We've worked long and hard for this treaty and to have all the major powers including the old Russian countries, Korea, Japan and some Middle East countries represented, it will begin a brand new era for the world. People can start sleeping a little easier without the threat of wars or terrorists hanging over their head, not to mention the amount of money that will be saved by each country to be used for more important projects like health care and welfare."

"You don't have to sell me on the program, Mr. President. It's the major companies that supply the equipment you have to convince, along with the military who has been in an ongoing struggles against terrorists, that their campaign is being streamlined and the need to cut back once again, making them feel like a police organization rather than a military force. They have been growing and in the limelight since the World Trade Center and now, just as with the Clinton years, they are being called to make drastic cuts."

"The military firmly goes by the standard if you want Peace Prepare for War. That was okay during the Cold War, but they have to understand the world is changing. I still have the CIA telling me about spies and counter-intelligence when there is nothing left to spy on. Hell, it's been years since that agent in the FBI was arrested for selling secrets to the Russians, and through the investigation, what was considered so confidential was ludicrous. In another year, the old bear that used to be Russia, along with her sister states will be permanent members of NATO. We've had a joint space station in space with many other nations, including our old Cold War foe Russia, since 2001 for God's sake! What does it take for them to see that if everyone is on the same team, there is no opposition? Even the terrorist organizations have been drastically reduced since the early days of Afghanistan and the world no longer supports bombings and attacks on cities they've never heard of."

"It's hard to change the mindset of a hundred years of mistrust. It wasn't that long ago, that we were contemplating an invasion of Korea to prevent them building up nuclear weapons.

Before that we almost went to arms with China when one of our surveillance planes was hit by a Chinese jet and landed on one of their islands. It took a week for us to get the crew back and a lot longer to get the plane back. We were constantly harping at each other over apologies and who was to blame. We invaded Haiti to put the old president back into power and conducted air strikes on Serbia to halt their destruction of Muslims and Croatians. A lot has happened over the last decade and will take some time for it to sink in."

"Well it's about time we stop taking care of the rest of the world, policing all their conflicts, when we should be concentrating on the more important issues of health and economics. Solve those problems and there won't be the need to fight each other over turf wars."

"There are those that feel your methods will only further compound the problem by putting more people out of work and leaving us weakened by a smaller military." The Chief of Staff recalled the recent protests just outside the White House for pro-military supporters and the heavy debates on the Senate and Congress floors from delegates supported by McDonnell Douglas, Boeing and several other major military goods manufacturers who felt the cutbacks would eventually destroy their businesses and put thousand of employees out of work.

"There is no easy solution to any problem, Tom. I'm just trying to come up with the best solution that we can work with to produce results. Building up the military in the present state of affairs is ludicrous. No one is strong enough or stupid enough to take on the United States, especially while I'm the President, and I'm not about to waste taxpayers money on our military getting involved in every minor skirmish around the globe like we used to do in countries such as Somalia and Rwanda."

"Some say we won't be the strongest on the block with you proposed cutbacks, laying us open to some of the growing militaries in Third World countries."   •

"If I didn't know you better, Tom, I would think you were talking me out of my proposals." The President appreciated the young man's inputs and based a lot of his success on their point/counter-point discussions.

"I just want you to fully appreciate what lay ahead."

"Well, I've had enough debate for one day. Is .there anything else we need to discuss?" Seeing there was nothing else, he rose from his chair.

"I have nothing else sir. I'll get these responses done and have them ready for you tomorrow for signature." As the President started to walk towards the door, Tom got up from the sofa and joined him halfway there.

"By the way Tom, do you realize that tomorrow would have been my 25th wedding anniversary?" The President's wife had been his backbone during his years in the Senate, and many of his decisions were debated in their bedroom, with her winning more than half of the debates. He always felt that he won the Presidency strictly on a pity vote and the country's love for his wife.

"My deepest regret's sir. Your wife was a wonderful woman and we all miss her dearly." Tom proceeded down an adjacent corridor while the President headed for the stairs. As he considered the week ahead, he realized that there would be limited time for working out, so he decided to sneak in a short workout this afternoon. At least he had another trip to Camp David planned for the end of the month, a week after the conference to unwind, play some golf and clear his head. As long as nothing major occurred in the world, he could catch up on sleep and might even take in a good book. At least today, he was going to get the chance to watch some football and see if his Redskin's could start out this season with a win for a change. With the schedule for the upcoming conference, he knew he'd get little opportunity to see a game next weekend. What he didn't know is how much his schedule and his life were going to be altered that weekend.

Chapter 5

Five o'clock in the morning came way too early and if she had had enough strength, she'd have thrown the alarm clock across the room when it suddenly burst into life. Having only climbed into bed two and a half hours earlier, Kay looked terrible. Almost falling out of bed, she dragged herself across the hall to the bathroom. Turning on the light, she felt blinded and couldn't bear to stop and look at the reflection in the mirror. She hoped that the shower would bring her to life and set it for a little cooler than normal to help the process along.

Grabbing her purse and keys as she left the apartment, it was evident that even the cooler shower didn't help her wake up. She had already stumbled in the closet trying to get something to wear, spilled her first cup of coffee in the kitchen, and caught her finger in the drawer when getting out a utensil. She hoped the rest of the day would go better after such a hideous start.

Fortunately, San Diego isn't very lively at six on a Sunday morning, so the drive was quick and uneventful, especially since it was still dark outside. Arriving at the office, the stillness and emptiness reminded her of the previous night and her frustrations at writing the article.

The first few hours in the office weren't much more productive than those the night before. It took two more cups of coffee and a fresh donut she picked up on the way into the office to finally get the creative juices flowing. With the caffeine finally taking hold, her fingers began to dance along the keyboard, filling the page with the outline of a story.

After working for six hours since arriving that morning, Kay finally finished her article. She had only a little time remaining to run it by the weekend editor and make the necessary corrections before the 3 p.m. deadline if it was to appear in the Monday paper. The Monday edition was always the most important so the reader would start out the week with something new to think about or return to the conclusion of a story they were left with on Friday.

She walked down the hallway reviewing the article wondering what else could have been said or worded differently. The hallway was quiet since it was Sunday and only staffed with a minimum number of reporters. As she passed some of the offices she could hear a few typewriters playing away as last minute news items were being produced. At the end of the hallway was the editor's office and she knocked lightly and entered. Behind the desk a portly gentleman was stabbing out a cigarette in an already filled ashtray. Scanning a draft front page with thick glasses was Joe Simmons, the weekend editor. He had been with the paper since arriving seventeen years ago, another hard-charging reporter like Kay. A local boy, who had made a small niche in the newspaper world, he never had anything published outside of San Diego, remaining captive to the Union.

The years had taken their toll on Simmons. His once jet black hair had disappeared and his California tan had withered to a grayish white. The chin had tripled over the years adding to the excess baggage around the remainder of his body. Working 12 hour days and most weekends, his long hours at a desk in addition to the two and a half packs of cigarettes he consumed daily, had taken their toll. His jacket was off and his tie was hanging loose with the top shirt button unbuttoned. Even in the air-conditioned room, his shirt was drenched with sweat.

"Scuse me Joe, I have that article for you." Kay said hesitantly. Simmons was the final word on what made the paper and where it was displayed. Although he had taken her on as her mentor, recognizing her talents, he was still devoted to the paper and only allowed the best work to be represented.

"Good afternoon Kay. Another Pulitzer Prize entry?" he said sarcastically.

"Nothing so dramatic. Just the final report on the Melendez story. I've put a lot of hours in it and wanted you to review it so I could get it into tomorrow's paper."

"It's getting a little late for that now isn't it? Let me take a look." He tossed the poster board with the headlines to one side and reached out with his left hand.

Kay handed him the article and sat down on the chair in the corner. Simmons immediately lit up another cigarette and began to read. As he read, Kay noticed that the office appeared to have been hit by a recent tornado. Papers of various sizes and color littered the office with three coffee cups scattered on the desk, all half empty. The coffee pot in the far corner had little coffee left. A distinct burning coffee smell filled the room since the machine was left on, burning the bottom layer of coffee. Near the trashcan, piles of crumbled papers lay scattered about while the can remained empty.

Simmons read through the article, making occasional grunts and jotting down notes. Kay was sure that he would order numerous corrections, forcing it to be held off until the Tuesday edition. After several minutes, he swiveled around in his chair and placed the article on the desk.

"Here you go. I've made some notations on the side. I have a spot available in tomorrow's paper if you can correct it in the next hour and get it down to the printers. I'll call ahead that you're on your way." He thrust the article forward with his right hand, putting out the cigarette with his left.

"Thanks, I'll get this fixed right away." She grabbed the article and proceeded to the door.

"By the way Kay, the boss wants to see you tomorrow at nine o'clock. He has some sort of assignment for you."

"Are you serious? What's the job?" She said turning back towards his desk.

"I don't have a clue. You'll find out tomorrow. Nobody tells me anything around here. Listen. Take a little advice from me. Take some time off to relax. When was the last time you went out?"

"We're not going to start that again are we?" Not long after Kay started working at the paper, Simmons had made several passes at her and asked her out several times. Kay wasn't interested and felt very uncomfortable about it. She finally had confronted him about it, and they had a long discussion and since then had kept a strict business relationship between them.

"I'm not talking about with me. I just noticed how tired you look, and when I saw Jim Cartwright this morning, he told me you were here until almost two a.m. After you make the corrections, get the hell out of here. Go see a show or something."

"I was planning on going to the gym after I was done."

"Oh, that sounds real relaxing. Take it from me. I've been in your position. Blow off a little steam tonight. Get a good night's sleep because you never know what tomorrow will bring, especially with a new assignment. Now get out of here, I have work to do." He made a wave of his hand and went back to his headlines.

Walking back to the office she felt a rush of excitement. Being selected for an assignment, any assignment, especially one by the head editor, was a big step for a young reporter. Thoughts of foreign countries and exotic places started to fill her mind as she strolled with a lively step through the hallway. When she arrived in her office, she sat down and took a deep breath. Thinking to herself, she held back the emotions to regain some reality. It was probably some remote section of California or another nearby state with some inconsequential story she told herself. They weren't going to put her on something extravagant when there were several other more experienced reporters on the staff.

Leaning back in her chair, she gazed at the ceiling, trying to grasp visions in the smoke that still floated above her. It was nice to dream, but one mustn't get too excited about things or the disappointment could be too much to handle, she pondered. In the midst of her dream, she suddenly realized she had to finish the Melendez story in the next hour. Cursing herself she shook the fantasy from her head and went to work on computer. Glancing at the clock she figured she could still get a good work out at the gym before returning home and then open a bottle of wine, change into her swimsuit and soak in the condo's Jacuzzi for a while.

Opening the article, she found only minor corrections. At the bottom was a little note from the editor "Good job, keep up the good work. Enjoy your next assignment."

Kay wondered how Simmons could be such a pain in the ass at one moment and so nice the next. She quickly made the corrections and reviewed her notes to add some details he had requested. It only took 30 minutes to make the necessary revisions. Once completed and printed, she picked up her purse and proceeded to the printer's section. Things were starting to pick up, she thought to herself.

"Well, girl. The door is open, all you have to do is step inside and grab it with all you've got." She said aloud although there wasn't anyone around to hear it. The only problem was making sure you went through the right door and in the upcoming weeks, some of those doors were going to be hitting her head on.

Chapter 6

CDR Joe Bellows was sitting at his stateroom desk, knee deep in personnel evaluations he'd spent the last two days covering with red ink. His desk was piled high with administrative paperwork, most of which he knew he'd delegate to his department heads once they arrived in the morning. He looked at the clock on the wall, a regulation Navy chronometer and noticed it had not been wound, stopping sometime over the weekend. He'd have to mention it to the Navigator this morning. Glancing at his watch, the time read 0545. For the first time in his tour onboard, Bellows was in command. The Commanding Officer departed the day before for two weeks leave. As Executive Officer and second in command, his responsibilities were mainly administrative, but those responsibilities would have to be passed on so he could concentrate on command and operational matters.

As he concentrated on the next set of evaluations, RM1 Wilson knocked on the door and entered the cabin carrying two folded pieces of paper. "Pardon me sir, I have an AMCROSS message that just came in." Wilson handed him the messages and stepped back in a relaxed attention posture.

Bellows hated receiving AMCROSS messages, since they announced the death or near death of a family member of one of the crew. The crewmember would have to be counseled and given permission to go home no matter what the ship was involved in. Fortunately the ship was in a stand-down period for two weeks after just completing four intense weeks of inspections, so the loss of a crewmember would not be too drastic.

He unfolded the message and immediately caught sight of the crewmember's name, Lieutenant Commander Greg Morris, the Operations Officer. Losing a crewmember for a

39

couple of weeks wasn't a problem, but when the Commanding Officer is away on leave and the XO in charge, losing the Operations Officer was severe. Since he was the next down in the chain of command, the OPS Boss would receive the majority of work the XO couldn't handle. Additionally, Greg was one of the best officers on board and nearly ran the ship, even when the Commanding Officer was aboard. The message announced that his mother had been involved in a car accident and was in critical condition in Pennsylvania. Bellows regretted that he had no choice but to let him go home and thought to himself what a way to start his week in command.

"Is the OPS Boss aboard yet Wilson?" Bellows knew Morris was usually the first to arrive onboard every morning, but it never hurt to ask.

"Yes sir, just saw him on my way down here. He was heading into the OPS Office."

"On your way back to radio, ask him to come down to my cabin. Do not tell him why." He initialed the master copy and handed it back to Wilson.

"Yes sir." Wilson said as he left the room. Bellows looked into his cabinet and pulled out his file on officers. He always maintained a complete history of his officers indicating the amount of leave they had taken, schools they attended, professional qualifications achieved, specific items of interest, and for some like Morris a listing of AMCROSS messages received. He turned to Morris' section and noticed that this was the fourth AMCROSS he had received in the last eighteen months which was an unusually high number. Most personnel go throughout a whole career without receiving an AMCROSS. Bellows wondered if Morris' family just had a run of bad luck or a history of health problems. He made a mental note to discuss it with the ship's doctor during the next opportunity. He continued to read through the files on Morris and noticed that he had attained his qualifications for Surface

40

Warfare Officer at a late stage in his career but had completed every other qualification possible shortly thereafter. The most recent was the command at sea qualification, which at that time, was an extremely difficult task requiring extensive study, an 8-hour written exam and once passed, an oral exam in front of a minimum of one Admiral and three Captains. There wasn't anything left for Morris to attain but selection for Executive Officer and eventual command at sea which, based on his record, should be straightforward.

As he read through the files, there was a knock on the door and in walked Lieutenant Commander Morris. As usual the first thing he noticed was that Greg would need a haircut soon. Hair was combed straight back and the length was always on the borderline which someday could come back to haunt him in his career. He made a note to mention it to him when he came back. Other than the hair, Greg was officer poster material. The face appeared to be chiseled out of stone, with squinting hazel eyes, fair skin, and always wearing a smile, no matter what the circumstance. The uniform was noticeably tailor made, form fitted over a body that had undergone an extensive exercise regimen.

Bellows knew Morris was into sports and exercise, seeing him every day during lunchtime returning from either a 5 mile run or a 20 mile bike ride. Morris was a member of the ship's soccer and softball team, excelling at both sports. During the annual Surface Warfare Olympics, Morris was the ship's anchor for the tug of war that they had never lost. Morris would tie the end of the rope around his body, turn and dig his hands and feet into the ground using his strong leg muscles to pull not only the other squad but also his own team with him. He wondered why Morris never joined the SEALs (Sea Air and Land - the Navy's elite special forces) and figured Morris did not have the killing instinct needed.

"Good morning there skipper, enjoying the new responsibilities?" Morris asked in his usual sarcastic humor.

"I'm a little overloaded but coping." Bellows replied trying to figure out a way to break the news to him and realized the only proper way was to just tell him.

"Listen, Ops, I just received an AMCROSS. Your mother was in a car accident yesterday and is in the hospital in critical condition. That's all I know right now. I suggest you make a call home while we try to make arrangements to get you home." He handed the message to Morris. Bellows knew it would take a couple of hours so early in the morning to make the plane reservations and set up transportation.

Morris sat in the semi-plush sofa that needed refurbishing which extended along the wall. He read the message, noticing what Bellows hadn't because he wasn't supposed to, that the subject line held a code indicating it was not a real AMCROSS but a call up for his elite squad to gather at the headquarters. Of course, he was expecting this after his phone call yesterday, but had to play the part correctly to keep the XO from getting suspicious. He placed the paper down on his lap and gazed at the ceiling and took a big swallow.

Turning to Bellows, he said "I just talked to my mother Saturday night. She said she was supposed to go to some Women's function in Cleveland on Sunday after church." To add to the effect, he folded his hands together and rested his chin on them. Morris hadn't quite conquered the ability to shed a tear at will, but did close his eyes strongly as if holding back the tears while taking deep breaths.

"I'm sorry Greg. I wish there was more I could say. I want you to call home while I get the Admin folks to make the necessary arrangements to get you home. I hope everything is okay with your Mom."

"Thanks XO. I appreciate that."

"Do you want the Chaplain to talk to you when he gets onboard?"

"No, that's okay. I'll see the Minister back home when I get there." He crossed his arms and looked at the overhead and closed his eyes to accentuate a feeling of pain and rose from the sofa. "Thanks again. I'll call home and then pack. I'll talk to AOPS (Assistant Operations Officer) and make sure he's up to snuff on everything that's going on, especially next quarters schedule which is due in two weeks to the squadron." Greg turned and headed out the door.

"Let us know if there is anything we can do to help." Bellows said as Morris was leaving, realizing that there was nothing else the ship could do but knew it needed to be said.

When he arrived in his office, Morris dialed up the special phone number set aside to respond to such calls, "Dad, I just received the word on Mom. Is she alright?" he waited the necessary seconds as if receiving a response, and continued, "The ship is making all the arrangements and I should be there by tonight. I'll get a car and go straight to the hospital when I arrive." After waiting for an acknowledgement signal on the other end, he hung up the phone.

He had already packed the night before for an extended operation, had parked his car in the airport parking lot that morning, expecting to be dropped off, and rode his bike into work.

Once dropped off, he would return to his car and travel to the team's headquarters/ operating area at Camp Pendleton. Personnel were required to arrive at night, so he had several hours to kill beforehand.

He spent the next several hours closing out some messages that needed answering and went over last minute details with Lieutenant Steve Myers, his assistant, to ensure everything would be handled properly. He kept running through his head what possible mission there could be, reviewing all the latest political upheavals around the world. He had read the ship's Secret Intel Board that morning and watched CNN but there was nothing significant.

The fact continued to be bothered him that he would once again have to deal with Captain Davenport. The memories of the times he had worked with Davenport and how they had almost turned into disasters would gnaw at him throughout the day. He had to figure a way to control the situation without letting Davenport have the ability to mess up the operation and possible get someone injured or killed. Greg had never had anyone injured in an operation and wasn't about to let Davenport spoil that record.

Chapter 7

Kay pulled her ten-year old blue Honda Civic into the San Diego Union parking lot at seven-thirty Monday morning as usual. Her father had given her the used car as a present when she graduated from college. It had seen better days and keeping it clean was not one of her primary concerns. It still managed to get around town and she planned on keeping it for another couple of years until she was stable enough in her job or it died. Hopefully by that time she'll have saved enough to buy a more prestigious automobile fitting a reporter, probably a Chrysler LeBaron or Dodge Intrepid, although she preferred a metallic green Porsche, which she knew was unattainable.

After leaving the office on Sunday, she had gone to the gym and conducted her normal workout; twenty-four minutes on the bicycle, twenty minutes on the Nautilus equipment, 15 minutes on the stair climber and then thirty minutes of Aerobics. The workout was a lot harder than usual because of the two-day layoff, but she suffered through it knowing she would feel better afterwards. She also realized if she had to go away on an assignment, she may not get the opportunity to work out on a regular basis. Arriving at the apartment at six, she had a large salad and two glasses of wine. Going against all recommendations, she then went to the complex Jacuzzi and soaked her sore muscles for thirty minutes, while the sun set over a nearby hill. By nine o'clock, there was a bright full moon glowing with increased intensity, as she sat on the front patio. Not long after that, she was sound asleep in bed, dreaming of far away places.

Feeling much more refreshed this morning, she walked towards the building with a lively bounce in her step and renewed inner confidence. The male reporters and staff reporting to work at that moment stopped in their tracks as she swaggered by them, dressed in a business dress, complete with panty hose and high heels. No one in the office had ever seen her in a dress before, complete with make-up and hair styled. Many thought she was another new member of the staff. Mouths dropped as she sauntered by, her breasts jiggling slightly as she winked at a few. She was feeling spunky and wanted them all to notice.

When she entered the office, all work stopped. Dave Edmunds, another reporter was about to ask her if he could help her find someone before doing a double take. "Kay, is that you?"

"Morning, Dave. Isn't it a beautiful day today?" She said, sporting a smile highlighted by ruby red lipstick.

"Damn, girl, you look fantastic. What's gives?"

"The boss is going to give me an assignment today and I wanted to give a good impression, that's all. If I went in with my usual attire of sweatshirt and jeans, he might rethink the assignment."

"Well you'll take his mind off work for sure with that get-up. In that outfit you better hope your next assignment isn't at his home while his wife is away."

"He tries that and there'll be a write-up that every newspaper in California will want to publish. I figure it's about time I start looking like a reporter."

"You may want to tone it done just a hair, darlin'. You may look at little too good for these animals in here."

"Thanks, Dave. Anything new happening on the streets?"

"Just the usual stuff, crime and poverty, nothing new. Talk to me later after you see the boss okay?"

"See you at lunch in the cafeteria, if I'm still here." Kay walked over to her desk as he returned to his. Until she finally sat down and settled in, all eyes were glued to her shapely legs.

"Okay guys, the show is over, get back to work." she said to the ogling spectators. Every head immediately turned to their desks and tried to appear busy. It never failed to amaze her that no matter how happily married guys appeared to be, whenever a woman walked by in a skirt and high heels, all attention was diverted in her direction. She wondered if there was a man out there who wouldn't stare but admire both her inner beauty as well as the physical, but she realized someone like that would probably be gay.

****

Captain Davenport was in the bedroom, neatly arranging outfits in his suitcase. He had spent all weekend packing up most of his personal belongings in anticipation of having it moved when the operation was over. Boxes were neatly stacked in every room, filled with mementos, collections of books and several artifacts from some of his exploits. Each was labeled and sealed, containing a list of each item taped on top. After this operation was finished he felt he would not be able to return. With the money set aside for him, he wasn't worried about buying new furnishings at his new destination wherever that would be. All it would take is one phone call and everything boxed would be shipped without question. The real estate company would be contacted later to sell the condominium, when everything was completed.

He laid his uniforms into the garment bag and zipped it up. He wouldn't need much, only a small suitcase and garment bag. For traveling purposes, he usually wore a tan polo shirt and brown pants, with a blue sport coat that currently hung over the sofa in the living room. It was a long eight-hour flight from D.C. to Los Angeles, with connections, where he would rent a car and drive the one and a half hours on the freeway to Camp Pendleton. He anticipated arriving at the team's headquarters late that evening, where he could get a good nights' sleep before starting on the strangest excursion he had ever been on.

Walking back into the living room, he went to the bar and made himself a Bloody Mary. Looking back over his career, each operation was unique in its own way, but nothing had come close to this. The image of the old man who called himself Falcon, especially the eyes, kept popping into his head. Could anything so bold and daring, yet so simple be done and if so, what would eventually be the consequences. Would it lead to a war that the American people would unite for and turn the country around? Was it that easy? The questions kept coming to him and he didn't have any answers. He wasn't a politician or economist, just a simple soldier trying to keep the country safe and sound. Not worried about the effects on his conscience, he wondered if the results would be the ones needed and strengthen the country or would it backfire in its face.

The biggest question that kept recurring was whether or not America could survive a war. The results of Desert Storm and Somalia in some circles were disastrous in a military sense, as too many soldiers were killed by friendly fire. There hadn't been a real war in so long. No one had the experience to reflect upon, only simulated games and exercises on which to base their decisions and tactics. If there was a war, how long would it last and how many senseless lives would be lost?

Davenport figured these were not his problems, as he didn't have any choices in this matter. If he tried to walk away, how long before a bullet would find him, ending up as another soldier's headstone amidst the military cemetery. No one would grieve for him and he would be forgotten in a short time. The team he created would disappear and his achievements would either be buried in some vault or shredded. It was his time to take the money and run. He deserved the good life and would lavish in luxury with women at his beckoning call.

He finished the Bloody Mary and walked over to the couch. Pulling on the coat, he picked up his keys and tickets from the end table, placing the tickets inside his coat pocket. After looking one last time at the condominium, he picked up the phone and dialed the doorman.

"Charles, John Davenport here. Can you send someone up to get my luggage and call me a cab, I'm going to the airport."

At the other end of the phone, the doorman whose full name escaped him, acknowledged and hung up. Opening the door, he remembered back to Friday night and the strangers that entered his life that night. As of that night his life changed. There was no turning back but the personal rewards would overcome any doubt or regrets. It was time to change the world.

****

At ten minutes to nine, Kay walked into her boss's office. The secretary was sitting behind a mahogany desk talking on the telephone. Plants were strategically located around the office, the secretary's weapon to battle the smell of cigar smoke that filtered through the area from the main office. Headlines from old news stories were framed and hung around the walls depicting historic events covered by the paper. Chairs were set up in between the plants for waiting visitors. Kay caught the secretary's eye and was acknowledged by a wave of the hand pointing to one of the chairs.

Pam Reilly had been with the company for twenty-five years, through hundreds of reporters, editors and other staff members. Her hair was a curly auburn with streaks of gray that was normally formed into a ball on the back of her head. She wore granny glasses that rode low on her nose to allow her to see things on her desk close up, while being able to see everything else by looking over the rim of the glasses. She appeared more like a librarian than an executive secretary, walking upright as if carrying a book on her head wherever she went, telling people to keep the noise down. She didn't converse much with the reporters and kept mostly to herself, riding the bus to and from work, rejecting any offers for rides.

"Mr. Jenkins will see you now, Miss Cross." Pam said as she hung up the phone.

"Thank you Pam. How are you today?" Kay said while rising from the chair. She always tried to start a nice conversation that never seemed to go anywhere, but never gave up.

"The usual, there's so much racket around here you can barely think, and the cigar smoke is about to choke me to death."

"Well, try and have a nice day." She wondered why she bothered, receiving only a whispered grunt.

Opening the door to the office she recognized Brad Jenkins sitting behind his oak desk, leafing through a stack of papers. On one corner of the desk sat a computer with wires dangling over the side, leading to a printer along the far wall. Behind the desk were shelves of albums that contained all the headlines from every San Diego Union newspaper since it's beginning. Jenkins rose from his chair, an unlit half-smoked cigar sticking out of the corner of his mouth.

"Kay, come on in." Brad said motioning to a chair by the desk. Brad Jenkins had been with the paper since he began as a reporter, working his way up the chain. He was the most respected of the reporters on the staff, covering most of the major stories ever published by the newspaper during his tenure. His gripping stories captivated audiences, the result of extensive research while providing all points of view. He never took sides with a story, a difficult perspective for most reporters. At 52 years of age, he looked years younger, with only a hint of gray hair amidst the brown locks that were neatly trimmed. Unlike other reporters, he didn't pollute his body with burgers or other take-out food from local grease joints. Instead, he had always brought in his own lunches, normally some form of salad and sandwich. His only real vice was his cigars. Even with busy schedules, he always managed to run 2-3 miles during lunch to keep fit. He was able to find the time for rest and recreation because he was able to write a complete story in one sitting, requiring little changes, while most reporters went through no less than 5 drafts before feeling comfortable with their stories.

"Good morning, Mr. Jenkins, I was told you wanted to see me today." Kay always liked Jenkins because he was straightforward and cared about his reporters. She wondered why he was still single and some woman hadn't snagged this good-looking eligible bachelor.

Jenkins came around to the front of his desk, sitting on the edge. He set the cigar down into an ashtray. "You've been doing a lot of good work around here. I read your series on the Melendez case, especially this morning's edition. I'm very impressed."

"Thank you sir. I really enjoyed doing the research."

"That's good. So, do you think you're ready for some more intensive work?"

"I'm ready for anything."

"Let's hope so. I'm sending Steve Puller off to Washington to cover the groundwork for the upcoming Arms Agreement signing and I think it would be a good idea for you to tag along and help him put the stories together. It still hasn't been announced where the conference will be held, but once it's announced, I want you and Steve to go to the conference location and cover everything regarding it. I also want you to personally interview the President. Do you think you could handle a talk with the big guy?"

Kay had never dreamed the assignment would involve something as big as an interview with the President. She had interviewed lawyers, judges, family service counselors and the Mayor of San Diego but nothing as monumental as this.

"Are you sure you want me to interview the President?" She asked after a brief studdering spell.

"Your interviews during the Melendez case are what made the story. You handled them beautifully, asking all the right questions to get them to commit themselves before they tried to back-peddle and give some politically correct response. Remember, the President is only another man. Besides, the interview is only to dig out the aspects of the Arms Agreement and not about his personal life. Steve can fill you in on all the background information during your flight to D.C. So what do you say? Are you game?" He walked back towards the chair, sat down and placed his hands on the desk, waiting for Kay's response.

"I'm a little shocked. Of course I want to go. When do we leave?"

"You leave at 4 this afternoon, so you better head back home and pack. The paper will send a car around two to pick you up, can you be ready in time?"

"How long do you think I'll be gone?"

"Unknown. The Conference location for next week has not been announced yet, so I expect at least until the end of next week, so plan on ten days."

"That doesn't give me much time to prepare but I'll be ready." Kay rose from the chair and held out her hand. "Thank you for the opportunity, I'll try not to let you down."

He stood up and shook her hand. "Don't let me down. I see good things in you, now go out there and do them." He sat back down and as she was ready to leave the office he called her back, "By the way, while you're gone, take a little time to see the sights and do a little partying. You've been working a little too hard. A tired reporter can't function properly. Always remember that. You need to learn to balance your work with play, okay."

"Yes sir, your only the third person in 48 hours to say the same thing."

"Then we must know what we are talking about. Now get out of here and enjoy your flight." He said, waving his had as his attention went back to the papers on his desk.

****

"Just remember to get our training requests message out next week for our upcoming ISE" Greg said, using the term for 'Independent Steaming Exercises' in which the ship went out by itself to prepare for upcoming inspections. Handing the folder over to LT Myers, he continued. "While I'm gone there should be little to do. Just make sure the repairs on the NTDS (Navy Tactical Data System) are completed."

"I'll keep things on track sir." LT Myers was a reliable junior officer and Greg was confident he could manage everything.

"Stop calling me sir, Steve. I get enough of that from everyone else I don't need to hear it from you. I'm only one step higher than you and after the next Lieutenant Commander selection board that won't be true any longer."

"I appreciate that Greg. Do you want me to call you on anything?"

"Not really, Steve. I'm sure you can handle it. If anything comes up you have a question about, get a hold of the XO and he'll help you out." Greg knew that no one would be able to reach him for at least the next week. He didn't know where he would be, but was sure he'd be out of reach.

"Your ride to the airport is ready for you, sir." Operations Specialist Second Class Petty Officer

McLanahan walked into the office. Although he was only a Second Class petty officer, he basically ran the Operations Specialist division since the chief had retired early and his relief wasn't scheduled to arrive for several months. He was selected for first class petty officer but wouldn't be able to wear the uniform for another month. The Southern Region Weight Lifting champion, his shirt was two sizes too large for his waist in order to prevent the sleeves from bursting every time he flexed his arm muscles.

"Thanks Mac. Tell them I'll be down in a minute." Greg rose from the desk and turned to LT Myers. "I should be back in a week, so don't break anything while I'm gone."

"Roger that. I'll do my best. We're all sorry, Greg. If there is anything we can do to help let us know."

"Thanks, Steve." There wasn't anything they could do for him. As he walked out of the office and headed for the Quarterdeck, he wondered what would happen if something did happen to him on an operation. What would the ship be told? He'd just have to make sure he got back on time.

****

The ship's driver dropped Greg off in front of the American Airlines section of the airport. After leaving the ship, they went directly to his house, where he took some time to make it look as if he was packing for a one week trip home, returning to the car with a full suitcase, filled with clothes he had packed the day before.

"Thanks for the lift. Now quit goofing off and get back to work." Greg said to the young seaman behind the wheel. Everyone on board the ship was aware of Greg's sarcastic personality and that normally he was only kidding.

"Take care sir" the young man said as he put the car into gear and drove off.

Greg went into the terminal and went to the American Airlines ticket counter area. He waited about ten minutes in case the driver got held up and then went up to the second deck to buy a paper and then out to the parking lot, using the cross way over the street.

Arriving at his car, he deposited the suitcase in the trunk since he would not be using it. All of his necessities were packed in a sea bag that was in the backseat along with a strange carrying case. Entering through the back door, he opened the strange case to verify the contents, a crossbow with telescopic sight and thirty arrows of various points, his pride and joy. Made of stock wood and heavy steel, the crossbow was specially made to provide a more powerful pull allowing for greater distance and accuracy. Over the years, several bodies had died without warning when an arrow came from over two hundred yards away unnoticed. Closing up the case he locked the back door and walked around to the driver's side.

Departing the airport he headed north towards Camp Pendleton. Since it was only 3 in the afternoon, he decided to stop on the way. He couldn't arrive at headquarters until dark so he opted for a couple of sodas and shoot some pool at a local club in Carlsbad. Greg was first introduced to the club when his team dragged him there for his birthday two years ago after a mission. Greg had become a regular ever since, becoming good friends with the owner.

As he drove, he looked down at the recent paper to see if the news gave any indication of where the team might be heading. There was nothing new in the headlines that would indicate an operation would be required. Maybe this was just a drill or exercise to tone their skills. He still pondered why Captain Davenport had to come out to see them in action. Maybe an inspection to see if the team was really ready to respond since it had been idle for six months. Another option, one he truly didn't like, was that with the latest cutbacks in the military, the team could be destined for disbanding and the Captain was coming to give them the bad news.

Whatever the reason, he had an uneasy feeling. Never really feeling good before operations, this time the hairs on his neck were tingling. Although he told himself to calm down and quit worrying, he knew that this is what had kept him alive all these years so he'd keep his eyes and ears open.

Chapter 8

A gale force wind couldn't have created more of a disaster than the present state in the bedroom. Dresses were draped over chairs, blouses scattered about the bed, and various other clothes littered the floor in disarray. Two empty suitcases sat on the bed waiting for their cargo. Several pairs of shoes came flying out of the closet, landing amidst the heap of clothes, followed by the sound of disgust. Emerging from the closet, Kay Cross was cradling two purses and another pair of shoes. In contrast to the elegant woman who entered the San Diego Union that morning, she was dressed in jean cut-off shorts and a UCLA college T-shirt. After rushing home and tearing apart her closet, the hair was mangled and the make-up washed away.

The clock on the nightstand read eleven-fifteen. Realizing she only had a couple of hours to finish packing, shower and dress, she began shoving outfits into the suitcases. There was no thought of being orderly, she'd unpack it all at the hotel and sort it out then. She only hoped that she wouldn't forget anything. Whenever she went on vacation, something was always left behind. Thank goodness for hotel gift shops, she thought to herself.

By twelve-twenty she had completed the packing and was piling the remaining clothes back into the closet. It was then she realized she better phone home, since she wouldn't be there for the weekend phone calls from her parents. Closing up the suitcases and setting them into the corner, she walked over to the nightstand and began dialing the phone. Once it started ringing, she lay down on the bed. After three rings, it was finally answered.

"Mom, this is Kay."

"Kay! What's wrong? Why are you calling me on a Monday?" the usual response from an overbearing Mother. Kay adored her Mother who was still teaching Junior High

School after all these years. Fortunately school was off for the week, so she was home.

"Nothings wrong Mom. I got an assignment with the paper this morning and I'm heading off to Washington, D.C." She tried to control the excitement, but like most mothers, she was able to read her thoughts, even through the phone.

"Washington, D.C., huh. That's sounds exciting. What are you going to be doing?"

"I have to cover a story on the upcoming Arms Agreement and might even have to interview the President."

Her Mom began to go on and on about how exciting it sounded, how she was such a big shot now and how excited Dad would be. Kay looked again at the clock knowing she still had to take a shower and get ready for the trip, so she had to cut her mother short.

"Listen, Mom. The paper is sending a car over in an hour and a half and I still have to take a shower and get dressed, so I have to cut this short. I'll call you from Washington this weekend."

"Your Dad will be so excited to hear the news. Just remember that Washington is a terrible place, I hear it's got the highest crime rate in the country, so you take care." Mother's never stop treating their children as kids even when they were over twenty-one and far from home.

"Don't worry Mom, I'll be careful. Say hello to Dad for me. I love you both."

"Love you too." Hanging up the phone she closed her eyes and thought how nice it would be to just lie there in bed and sleep the rest of the day, instead of sitting in a plane for the next eight hours. While lying there she computed the flight hours and realized that if the plane left at four in the afternoon, which was seven in the evening on the East Coast, then she would not arrive in Washington until three in the morning. By the time they got their luggage and checked into the hotel, it would be four o'clock in the morning before she'd get to bed. Not much of an opportunity for sleep tonight. She hoped she could find a way to get some sleep on the plane. Maybe a couple of glasses of wine would help her catch a few hours of rest before arriving she thought to herself.

Finding the energy, she climbed out of bed and went into the bathroom to take her shower. It was then she finally realized she hadn't packed any of her bathroom accessories and sighed, as she had to rush the shower, get dressed and finish packing in the next hour. She was excited about a new assignment, but hadn't planned on having to rush about so much even before it began.

****

It was an out of the way bar, located just outside the city center. Outwardly it appeared as a condemned building, and inside wasn't much different, but the people were common folk and it had a relaxing atmosphere. The beers were inexpensive and the jukebox contained music from the 70's that Greg always enjoyed. Whenever he had the chance, Greg would come up the coast to the bar to relax and swap lies about women with the owner, Steve Foster.

After parking his car behind the bar, Greg walked around to the front and heard a good Journey song blasting away from inside. The moment he opened the door he was immersed in cigarette smoke that seemed to billow out, attempting to escape the confines of the bar. Once his vision was cleared, he was standing face to face with a large rotund man wearing a sweaty T-shirt smoking a cigar. It was evident the man hadn't shaved in the past few days by the stubble that ran across his chin. The wide belly, which sagged over his belt, was the result of his exorbitant appetite for malt liquor. The strings of dark hair were greased back into a pigtail that hung a few inches down his back, the revolutionary that didn't realize the 60's were over.

"Jesus Christ Steve, it's bad enough to walk into this place and get smothered in cigarette smoke. I don't need your ugly puss blowing cigar smoke in my face the moment I open the door." Over the two years Greg had developed a good relationship with Steve Winslow, standing in for Steve on many occasions when he had to run off somewhere or had too much liquor to stand up behind the bar.

"Damn fine to see you too, asshole." Steve turned towards the bar that ran lengthwise down one side of the bar, giving the appearance of an old Western Saloon. Bottles of liquor from various locations around the world lined the shelves behind the bar. As an old Marine, Steve bragged that he had drunk every type of beer produced and could name them all. He had amassed an impressive array of beers from around the world during his 25 years in the Marines and was proud to show them off.

Along the bar, stools covered in red leather pads, which were desperately in need of reupholstering, were lined in a row, with only two occupants. Opposite the bar, in the center of the wall was an old-fashioned jukebox that Steve had somehow managed to get working after seeing it a garage sale. Above the jukebox was an enlarged version of the felt painting of dogs playing pool, which Greg thought fit right into the atmosphere. It wasn't until his second visit that he realized one of the dogs had been repainted to look like Steve. Scattered around the center of the room were small tables with four wooden chairs. Along the back wall and on either side of the jukebox were booths with the same red leather upholstery in need of repair.

Steve walked behind the bar, blowing a puff of smoke out the corner of his mouth, "What'll it be today?"

"Just give me a Diet Coke as always, it's too early in the day for beer."

"What gives with you coming up here on a Monday? Playing hookey from work?"

"No, I have an appointment later today and thought I'd check to see if this place had been condemned or fallen down yet." Greg was always fascinated that Steve was able to make a living off the bar, but every night the place was crawling with locals that considered the bar their second home.

"I keep telling you, it ain't the way it looks, it's the way it feels. When are you going to quick yanking my crank and buy into some of this action."

"Gee, what an offer. I could just see the loan officers expression when I show him a picture of the lucrative offer I have been given."

"Piss off. I got more important customers than you that won't abuse me all the time."

After slamming a can of Diet Coke and a glass with ice in it on the bar, he walked down to the two customers at the far end and started pouring them more drinks. It was then that Greg noticed the four customers sitting at the back booth with cans of beer stacked on the table. He also noticed the young waitress entering the room from the back office, wearing a short black skirt that exposed the finest set of legs he had seen in a while. The T-shirt was engraved in the bar's logo and covered average breasts that, since she was still young, stood erect and bounced with life. Alessandra, who started working in the bar nine months ago, had short blond hair that was cut in a shag, one of Greg's favorite styles, and exposed oversized earrings on her ears.

"Girl, when are you going to come to work dressed?" Greg asked, straining to keep his eyes on hers rather than her legs.

"Hi Greg. Whacha' doin here?"

"I just can't keep away from you, you know that." Greg had always envisioned what it would be like to take her out on a date but never got the courage to ask her. Always kidding around with her, he would always get tongue-tied when it came to asking a woman out. Besides, he was too busy for dates and she was too much a southern California girl for him.

At that moment, Steve came back down the bar.

"Four beers for the booth, Stevey."

"Well, at least someone doesn't think it's too early for beer." Steve reached down into the sink full of ice and beer and pulled four out, propped them on the bar and popped the tops spilling beer in the process.

"What gives with the four in the booth?" Greg said as Alessandra placed the beers on her tray and walked towards the booth. It wasn't common for people to be at the bar drinking this early in the day.

"Well, that's Dave Tibbs in the black shirt. He got fired from work today and decided to share his depression with the other good-for-nothing bums. They're all lazy pricks and I'm surprised one of them lasted at work this long."

Greg glanced back over to the table and watched Alessandra place the beers on the table. The man named Dave was dressed in an old black cowboy shirt with a white pattern sewn on and faded denims that had seen better days. Looking like the proverbial thing the cat dragged in, his black hair was in disarray and had the beginnings of a beard that was in desperate need of a trim. His nose was crooked as if broken in some fight. Even though he was sitting down, Greg could see he was of average size and appeared tougher than he probably was.

Suddenly Alessandra leaped back and Greg noticed Dave's hand fall off her right leg.

"Come on baby, you and me could have a real good time" Dave slurred; puckering his lips, blowing kisses her way.

"Knock it off Dave." Alessandra yelled, turning back towards the bar.

"Don't be so such a hussy, babe." Alessandra stopped dead in her tracks and Greg noticed Dave had grabbed the back of her short dress and was pulling her closer to him. Before he knew it, Steve was on his way to the table.

"Cut the crap, Dave. I think you boys have had enough to drink and better get back home. I'll call you a cab."

"Fuck off, asshole. I'm talking to the lady." Steve flipped his middle finger of his free hand at Steve and yanked Alessandra onto his lap.

Steve grabbed Alessandra's hand and pulled her off Dave's lap and tossed her like a rag doll towards the bar.

"Hey shithead, get your own girl."

"I've just had about enough of you for today, now get your butts out of here and go home. I'm not in the mood today for your shenanigans." Steve turned towards the bar and before Greg could say anything, a bottle of beer went flying from the table and landed dead center on Steve's head. Steve immediately dropped to his knees, reaching to his head with his right hand and the floor with his left. Dave got out of the table along with the other three and walked over to Steve, and kicked with his right foot, landing squarely in Steve's stomach, knocking him over on his back, and landing at the feet of Greg.

"Boys, boys, boys. Is this anyway to treat your host?"

Dave looked up and seeing Greg, laughed within himself, shaking his head up and down. "And just who the fuck are you, asshole?"

"Aw shucks, don't mind me fella's, I'm just an innocent bystander rendering aid to the poor and decrepit." Greg looked down at Steve who had one hand on his stomach and the other on his head. "Now don't you seem to get into some of the craziest fixes? Are you all right?"

Greg said playing the stupid role.

"Look fellas, its Florence Nightingale. Listen shithead, mind your own business." Dave said as the four spread out encircling Greg.

"Well this sort of is my business since I've accepted to be his partner today in this hell-hole." Greg helped Steve to his feet and directed him towards Alessandra who cradled him in her arms and guided him to a barstool.

Without warning, Dave flung a right fist at Greg's head but even if he had been completely sober, he wouldn't have been fast enough to react to Greg's move. Greg dipped his body to the left and grabbed hold of Dave's arm with one hand as it flung by, dragging it behind Dave's back and with his free hand grabbing Dave's head as he smashed it into the table. Lifting him back off the table, he noticed that the nose seemed to be a little straighter now, although it and his upper lip were covered in blood. With his right foot, he kicked behind Dave's legs, dropping him to his knees, and cocked Dave's head back.

"You should be more polite to your elders." Greg said as he brought his face within inches of Dave's. "If there's one thing I can't stand its bad manners."

Out of the corner of his eye, he noticed the movement of one of the other men and kicked out with his left foot, finding his target in the center of the man's chest, propelling him backwards into the wall with a thud and fell face first to the floor. He shoved Dave off to one side and facing the other two.

"The dance floor is open, but I don't think you gentlemen would care to dance, would you?" With that the one on the right lunged towards Greg but found only dead air, as Greg stepped to his left and shoved the man into the pole behind him face first. A slight grunt escaped his lungs and fell to the floor holding his face. Thinking he had the better of Greg with his backed turned towards him, the fourth man began to move towards Greg, but a roundhouse kick met him on his right cheek and he spun towards the bar. Alessandra standing at the bar, grabbed Greg's half filled coke bottle and although aiming at the top of his head, smashed it on the back of his head near the neck, sending the man unconscious to the floor.

"Now, why did you have to go and spoil a good Diet Coke?"

Alessandra looked up at Greg with amazement at what she had just witnessed. Within less than a minute, two men were laying on the floor unconscious, and the other two were on their knees holding bloody faces. Greg walked over to the bar and took a drink from his glass as though nothing had happened.

"Keeeerist. I ain't never seen anything like that before, except in the movies."

"Haven't, Ali, haven't seen anything." Greg gave her a little smile and Alessandra reached up and planted one of the longest, wettest, and deepest kisses he had experienced in a long time.

As she backed away, Greg retreated and flapped his hand across his mouth as if swatting fire from it, then took a deep breath letting it out slowly. By this time Steve was regaining his senses and gazed at the mess on his floor.

"Who the hell is going to clean up this mess?"

"Well you started it Steve, you have to." Greg said with a sly grin. Looking down the bar he noticed the two old men still sipping at their drinks as though nothing happened.

"Well it ain't going to happen today, that's for sure. I'm closing this place up and going home to put a ice pack on my head and alcohol in my stomach." Steve walked behind the bar and took out a dirty towel and filled it with ice, placing it gently on the back of his head, letting out a slight whimper in the process. Steve then proceeded to the phone and dialed.

"Yeah, this is Steve down at the Ricochet Bar on Grant Street. I've had a little problem with four customers I need to you to pick up." For several minutes he had to explain the situation at the bar before he could convince the police station that there were four injured men, the same ones that started the mess, who needed to be taken away, finally slamming the phone into the cradle.

Greg knew he couldn't stay and try to explain what had happened since it would mean going down to the station, answering a lot of questions, and dependant on what time the police finally arrived and got what they needed he'd be late in reporting in.

"Listen, Steve, I can't be stuck here explaining everything tonight. I have very important business to take care of tonight."

"Some hot shot babe I suppose." Alessandra said with her hands on her hips.

"Business, not pleasure, Ali."

Steve leaned over onto the bar, still holding the ice on his head. "I don't plan on pressing charges against these morons and I don't think they'll be in any condition to. I just want the cops to take them away and I'm closing up the shop. Get your ugly ass out of here."

"What time is your appointment?" Alessandra asked, leaning her head to one side. Greg could see her mind at work.

"My appointment is at 10 tonight and it takes me an hour to get there."

"Well, if Steve's going to close up shop, how about I cook you some dinner at my place? Is it okay if I get my ass out of here too Steve?"

"Both of you get out of my sight. Who needs ya'." Steve walked down the bar and talked to the remaining men still sipping their drinks.

"I think I'd like that if you're a good cook. I haven't had a good home-cooked meal in a long time. I live off whatever my microwave can heat up and what I get at McDonald's." Greg contemplated the consequences of not showing up until early tomorrow morning but realized that was impossible. Images of a night with Alessandra were running rampant in his head.

"Well, you're in for a real treat, cowboy. I can really cook." Greg had to laugh at that comment.

"Did you drive to work?"

"Naw, I usually take the bus, I live about 3 miles from here."

"My chariot awaits my lady." Greg bowed and motioned his hands towards the door.

"Let me get my things and I'll be ready in a minute." Alessandra walked towards the back office, Greg staring at the legs and butt the entire stretch. Just as she opened the door, she turned; catching Greg's stare, and gave him a wink and smile as she walked in.

As his mind raced through the gutter, Steve patted him on the shoulder. "Listen, thanks a lot for what you did. There's something strange about you and I can't figure out what."

Greg shrugged his shoulders; "I'm just simple folk, Steve, just like you."

"Thanks all the same. Did I hear you right or did the bottle knock me senseless? You did tell those fella's you were my partner, didn't you?"

"Yeah, I decided to take you up on the offer. If I didn't, you'd end up pissing somebody else off, and I'd lose a good friend and my favorite bar."

"Shit, don't get mushy on me. What did you have in mind?"

"Listen, Steve, when I get back in a week or so, we can discuss it. Right now I have other things on my mind." Greg said as Alessandra walked back into the room carrying her purse and wearing a leather biker jacket.

"Be careful, boy. Don't do anything I wouldn't."

"That doesn't leave much." Greg said as he turned and escorted Alessandra out the door.

As they walked to the car, he could hear the police car as it pulled up out front. He was glad he didn't stick around and have to explain the past half-hour. As he opened the car door for her, Alessandra reached up with both arms and draped them around his neck.

"You are a real gentleman, aren't you? Now do you really want me to cook you dinner or do you just want to cook?" Greg felt her arms push his head forward and her lips meet his, opening them and her tongue dancing with his. After what seemed like ten minutes, she loosened her grip and climbed into the passenger seat.

Closing the door he looked up at the sky and thanked whoever was up there. Not knowing what lay ahead in the next few weeks, this wasn't a bad way to start. Unfortunately, this would be the only bright spot for some time to come.

Chapter 9

Gate guard duty was a lonely assignment, but especially so during the late hours when nothing happened except the blowing wind occasionally sweeping the sand of the beach and whipping it towards the base, clogging the eyes. Monday nights were especially slow because most of the personnel attached to Camp Pendleton remained at the barracks to watch the Monday Night Football games.

Lance Corporal McAllister was leaning against the gatepost, an improper stance for a Marine, but no one else was around and the gate Sergeant was in the back office mulling over some paperwork while catching the last few minutes of the football game. Mac as he was known to his platoon, was staring out over the ocean at the stars when he imagined two of the stars seemed to be growing in size, until he realized they were a car headlights heading towards the gate.

It was 2251, an unusual hour for someone to be entering the gate, Mac thought. Must have been a discouraged Steelers fan since they lost big to Cleveland. Raised in Cajun country in southern Louisiana, he was a true-blooded redneck as well as a true American, which meant Mom, Apple Pie and Monday Night Football. Mac watched as the car neared the gate and was finally able to make out it was a Nissan 300ZX, just as he thought, a foreign car.

When the car stopped in front of the gate, he noticed the man behind the wheel, who had a big smile on his face, holding up an Armed Forces ID card. The top was off the car and some strange ethereal music was emanating from the car radio, not loudly, but with the silence of the night, it stood out.

"What's the matter, buddy? Didn't enjoy the football game?" Mac said as the approached the car to verify the ID card. It was then he noticed the car had naval officer tags on it. "Sorry sir, I didn't expect an officer to be entering the gate at this hour of the night."

"No sweat. Sorry, I missed the game. Normally I wouldn't, except tonight a beautiful woman kept me away. Who won?" Lieutenant Commander Greg Morris was not into the regiment of ranks and forced respect, which is why he like the teams so much, because that's what they were, a team. No worries over rank or prestige, respect was earned without pomp and circumstance.

"Cleveland nailed Pittsburgh 35-3, a regular blow-out." that pleased Greg, a Brown's fan, always rooting for the teams normally considered underdogs every season.

"About time they win the first game of the season. It sure is a beautiful night, isn't it? Sorry you're stuck way out here and not under some tree with your favorite girl."

"We all have to do our time, sir. Besides it's almost over. Have a nice evening, sir." Mac waved Greg through the gate, which wasn't really a gate. Only Lance Corporal McAllister was there to prevent anything or anyone from entering who wasn't authorized. There was a mechanical device to raise a protective barrier, in case the watch felt threatened, but there was little time to get it up, especially if McAllister was standing a good distance from the building and his partner was in the back like tonight.

"You too." Greg put his car into gear and drove onto the base, maintaining the speed limit of 20 mph, although at this hour, no one would be out looking for any violators. Greg wasn't a speed freak like most people who drove sports cars; he liked them for their comfort and the ability to drive around Southern California with the top down.

Mac walked back towards the gatehouse, watching the car drive slowly down the street towards the center of the base, thinking to himself what a strange character. He was also very happy it wasn't some stuffy General or senior Marine who would have ripped out his heart and held it in front of him for being so insubordinate. He had to straighten up for the rest of the watch to ensure that didn't happen. Mac had an impeccable record, and didn't need to tarnish it because of boredom.

Fortunately for him, he held to that oath, because 15 minutes prior to the turnover of the watch a big black car with rental car plates drove up to the gate. Sitting behind the wheel was a man wearing a blue sport coat who held up his ID card and car rental agreement. Looking carefully he noticed the O-6 identification, which meant a full Navy Captain. After verifying his ID card and filling out a temporary car permit, Mac saluted and waved the Captain through the gate.

Mac was scratching his head as he walked back to the gate and noticed his relief entering the guardhouse.

"What's up Mac? Got ants in your head?" the other man said.

"Tonight has been rather strange, Bill. In the past hour I've had two naval officers driving through the gate, one a Captain. It's an awfully strange hour of the night for the pussyfoot Navy to be out." Mac did not really hold a high regard for the Navy since they slept in soft beds and ate a warm meal three times a day. Unlike himself, a member of the United States Marine Corps, the damned finest fighting force on Earth and ready to live off the land and step over anybody who got in the way, which is why Mac enlisted into the Corps.

"Who gives a shit? Now what's going on, it's bad enough my Steelers got beat tonight, I'm not looking forward to standing out here all night and listen to the owls."

Mac shook the questions out of his head; it was none of his business anyway, as he proceeded to turn over the watch.

****

As it started it's decent into the flight path to land into Washington, D.C., the plane hit an air pocket, dropping a good thirty feet and causing coffee to spill and agitating the passenger's stomachs. The sudden drop also woke Kay out of her sleep, which had been continuously disturbed by the rough ride across the country. After running around all day to get ready for the flight, being driven to the airport, waiting in the line to check-in, and three glasses of wine, Sally had been exhausted as well as somewhat drunk and managed to fall asleep before they crossed the Grand Canyon. Unfortunately, the weather across the country was unstable and her sleep was cut short on several occasions as the plane dipped and rose like a boat crossing the English channel.

Kay pulled the compact out of her purse and looked at the results. The hair was out of joint and her eyes were lined with streaks of red, all intersecting at the pupil like major highways on their way to downtown. She fussed with her hair to try and put it in place, realizing it was a hopeless cause. Pulling out her lipstick and make-up, she tried to fix her face up a little to distract observers from her hair.

Steve Puller was sitting next to her sound asleep. Every time she awoke during the flight, he was still there sound asleep and she wondered how anyone could sleep like that. Within minutes of boarding the plane and taking off, Steve had put a pillow under his head and was sound asleep. They had barely spoken since meeting at the airport and only vaguely covered their assignment in Washington. Steve had told her to relax and when they settled in at Washington he would go over everything in detail the next morning.

Steve was of average looks and build. He seemed friendly enough, but Kay wasn't able to determine his true demeanor in the short time they talked. Caught in a crowd, Kay believed he would just blend in and no one would take notice. As a reporter for the Union for seven years he had established a fair reputation, covering mostly political issues and travelling all over the country for campaigns and political issues. Unfortunately, not many people read those sections of the paper, more concerned to read the Sports Section, Comics, Puzzles, Gossip Column and on those stories that uncovered some dirt in any form of business or politics, which Steve wasn't involved in. Steve's articles were generally pessimistic about politics, highlighting the bad aspects rather than reporting on what good might possibly be getting achieved.

Below, Kay could see the lights of a city and reflected back to Christmas days when she was young and her Dad would construct a small village under the tree, with a train set running through the area. At night, the lights of the tree would twinkle and the train would race around the track through a make-believe town with grass, trees, streetlights, park benches, a ski slope up to the base of the tree and a wedding near the Chapel. Those days seemed so far away now as she flew above this unknown town heading for the nation's capital and wondering what the days ahead would be like.

As the plane descended she could make out some of the buildings and realized she was flying over Washington, DC and saw the Lincoln monument stick out to the sky as if pointing a finger to the heavens. Farther on she could make out the Capital building with its white dome reflecting the spotlights into the sky as if searching for answers. Kay pondered the immensity of this city, the power its transcended, and the people that made the decisions for a country that seemed always to be on the verge of a nervous breakdown but managed to overcome it's obstacles and stand tall, although a little crippled.

As a final encore, the plane skipped on the tarmac, once again sending bodies in various directions. Once the plane came to a peaceful ride, Steven suddenly sat up and opened his eyes.

With a yawn, he looked out the window and then at Kay.

"You look awful, didn't you sleep?" he asked as he stretched out his arms ahead of him, snapping his fingers in concert with the sound of twigs being stepped on in the forest.

"You're pathetic. This plane has been bouncing around all night and yet you managed to sleep through it all. I should be grateful that you don't snore."

"After a while you'll adapt to this type of living if you plan on staying on as a serious reporter. You manage to get sleep when you can and shut everything else out. Of course my wife wasn't too thrilled about my habits."

"How does your wife handle you being away so often?"

"She divorced me five years ago saying I was an old man trying to live like a young one."

Kay wondered if she would ever get that way. It had always been planted in her head that the husband and wife were always together and when apart, they grew apart. Her father was always home at night and the family was a tight unit. Realizing that the days when she would worry about marriage were far away, she shook off the thought.

"At least we're finally here and I can get some sleep." Kay said as she picked her purse up off the floor and set it in her lap.

"Not for long, now. We have a busy day ahead starting a nine-fifteen. We need to find out what's going on with this treaty signing and where it's being held. After that we need to get over to the White House and set up an appointment for you to interview the President."

"You're kidding me. You expect me to run around all day on just a few hours sleep."

"Tonight we'll tuck you in early because the next day is even worse. I'll go over the full agenda with you at breakfast at say seven-thirty in the hotel restaurant."

Kay nodded her head grimacing at the thought of getting up and showering for breakfast. Now she wished she had drunk a few more glasses of wine so she would have passed out and slept the whole flight. As the plane came to a stop and everyone on the plane started moving around, even though the seat belt sign was still on, Kay took in a deep breath.

"No time now for regrets. Get what you can and make the best of it girl." she said to herself and shuffled into the aisle like a steer that had been rounded up and were being guided to the slaughter. How fitting she pondered.

****

Greg had driven through the main center of Camp Pendleton and continued on towards the hills beyond. Two miles from the center he turned the car down a side road that was more like a trail than a road. There were no streetlights to guide his way and the road was tricky but he had done it dozens of times. The only regret was that he had to take his sports car down the path. Maybe it was time to trade in the car and get a Jeep, which would be more practical while still providing the open roof.

About two miles down the path at the base of the hills; there was a metal fence with warning signs about the road ending. Suddenly a light shone down from above and would have blinded him if he hadn't expected it. Coming to a stop a young man wearing a black sweater, black pants, boots, black wool stocking cap and carrying an MP-5 suddenly appeared at the car window. "Evening, boss. Expected it would be you."

"Hi Ace. Am I the last to arrive?"

"No, the heavy from the palace still hasn't shown but he should be along soon." He said using the nickname for the Pentagon.

"I guess I won't hear the end of this."

"Everyone was beginning to worry. You are always the first to arrive. What gives?"

"Would you believe me if I told you it was a woman."

"You sir. No way. Must be one hell of a woman to keep you from here."

"You could say that again." With that a gate in the fence opened and Greg was waved on through. "Take her easy, Ace."

"See you later, boss." Ace said before disappearing in the dark.

Greg drove through the gate and spotted the cameras on top of the fence. Giving them a big smile and waving, he turned off his car lights and continued down the path. From the gate, the trail was lit by small red lights that were lined along the way and directed down. Beyond the gate was the center of the best kept secret of the military. Inside the fence were the training grounds and headquarters of Greg's elite team that had no name, no fancy title, and no symbolic acronym that spelled out some elusive predator. To maintain its secrecy, an abandoned part of the base that was previously used for communications, was reconstructed to house the team while still appearing as an abandoned area. In order to prevent detection from overhead camera satellites, the car had to be driven another four miles over the hills guided only by the red lights. For most people it would have been suicidal, but for those that did it on a regular basis it was another drive under the stars.

Greg drove slowly up the winding road until reaching the peak of the hill. Stopping the car at the crest, he got out of the car, remembering to disconnect the inside light, and looked down into the small valley. Under the light of the moon he could make out the shadows of the buildings below. The small quad of four buildings looked like a ghost town. There were no lights to indicate any life and the buildings appeared as empty shells under the moonlight.

Ten years ago, a contract was awarded to a local construction company to build an underground communications center. Once the site was completed, a restructuring of the base was ordered and the plan to use the complex for it's original purpose was abandoned, leaving the entire complex buried. It was deemed too far away from the main base to be of any use and being used to constant changes and waste of taxpayers money, everyone soon forgot about it. Four years later, a plan was adopted to construct a training site in the same location, but by then nobody remembered the underground facility. A different construction company was contracted to build four buildings for classes and offices within the confines of the small valley and work began. Once again, the powers to be decided to alter the plans and the contract was altered just as the buildings were completed. New buildings were to be built closer to the main base, and the building company eager to make extra money, gladly accepted the new contract and built four identical buildings. One year later, the teams moved into the new facility without the knowledge of anyone on the base. Within six months, the teams connected the two facilities.

The inside of the buildings were altered with moveable walls to allow rooms to be changed into different sizes and shapes to match any particular mission. Special windows were installed to let light in but prevent it from going out. Inside the underground facility were offices, a gymnasium, a pool, small apartments for each member of the team, a cafeteria, complete communications facilities, a planning room, and an updated computer network. The majority of the teams work was conducted in the underground facility, while using the buildings for mission planning and training.

Exterior training was only conducted at night for two reasons.

The main reason was that all operations were normally carried out at night. The other reason was to prevent detection by satellites that lingered in the skies overhead. No one was permitted above ground during daylight hours. The site would continue to appear as an abandoned project.

Last year, Greg was given command of the site and the team. At first he was astounded by the complexity of the facility and the ability to continue it's use without detection, but eventually he realized that the Marine Corps kept to their own arena and too much time had passed for anyone to remember the facility was even there. The steel fence that surrounded the area permitted a radius of five miles, preventing anyone from getting within range of seeing the site. Occasionally some stray Marine helicopter pilots flew overhead, but nobody questioned the site.

Greg stepped back into his car and continued his drive down into the complex, guided by the small red lights along the dirt path. All four buildings were of similar construction, each three stories high, with rows of 10 windows across the front. The four buildings were situated with one building to the left, two straight ahead and another to the right. As Greg entered the center of the area, he turned towards the building on the left. Stopping in front of the building, he looked up and knowing the location of the hidden cameras, he smiled and put up the middle finger of his right hand. The wall ahead of him suddenly lifted like a garage door, as if the building had come alive and was about to have him and his car for a late night snack. Greg drove into the building and under amber lights could make out the tunnel that immediately angled downwards. Looking in the rear-view mirror, he watched the wall return to its original position.

Driving down the ramp, he was finally able to turn the lights of his car on. Upon reaching the first level, he could see the large parking garage that housed the team's main vehicles. Motorcycles, jeeps, trucks, and various other modes of transportation were parked in an orderly fashion. Over in one corner, two helicopters that could be folded and crammed into a truck were parked. Greg continued on to the next ramp and reached the second parking level, which was for the team's personal vehicles. Turning right, he parked his car in the first parking spot that had a small sign painted "BOSS". The members of the team told him it stood for Big Old Sorry Sucker. Greg unloaded his gear from the car and walked to the open elevator directly across from the parking spot.

Stepping into the elevator, the door immediately closed and started to descend. Fortunately, the designers didn't install a MUSAC system in the elevator. Several members of the team had volunteered to install music in the elevator, but Greg wasn't into the idea of rap music or heavy metal bursting into his ears each time he used it, so everyone had to sing to themselves as they rode down the three levels.

Reaching its destination, the elevator doors opened and Greg was immediately greeted by a security guard.

"Hell of a way to say hello, giving me the finger, boss." A small, wiry guard named Hank Thompson walked up to him and Greg handed him his gear.

"Thought I was giving the latest password. Que pasa?" Although Hank was small, about 5 foot 6 and 140 pounds wet, he was quick and his dark complexion made it easy for him to pass as a local inhabitant of many foreign countries the missions were conducted in. Born on a Cherokee reservation, he was skilled in knives and was the closest match in martial arts to Greg.

"Just the usual dull routine. I sure hope we get a mission soon so I can get away from this silly duty."

"Everybody here?"

"You're the last except for the big cheese. Any idea what's up?"

"Haven't got a clue. Could be an inspection to see if we still know what we're doing. I haven't seen anything in the papers to warrant a mission, but that never stopped anyone before."

Hank finished his inspection of the gear and handed them back to Greg. "Of course, everyone else is tucked nicely into their beds while I'm standing alone out here. The brief is scheduled for Oh Seven Thirty in the main briefing room. The Captain is about an hour behind you."

Not wanting to face Davenport right away and ruin a perfectly good evening, Greg decided he would turn in and face the music in the morning.

"I guess I'll grab some shuteye then and get started in the morning. See you at the brief."

"Roger that boss." Hand said and went back behind the control panel.

Greg walked down the hall to the left. The hallway turned to the right and at the end was Greg's office and apartment. Not as luxurious as his apartment in Coronado, it still provided a relaxing atmosphere. All the apartments were the same size and offered a small bedroom, bathroom with shower, living room complete with stereo, television and refrigerator. Having the latest in communications equipment also meant satellite antennas providing the added bonus of satellite television for the team to enjoy during their off periods. Unfortunately, during those off periods, the men were usually too tired or impatient to sit around and watch television, preferring to sleep the hours they were offered or do an extra work-out at the gym or pool.

Greg looked at his desk and saw a small stack of papers, deciding to leave them until morning. Walking into his apartment he opted to get three hours of sleep before getting started. Tossing his gear on the floor in the living room, he walked into the bedroom, kicked off his boots and lay down on the bed. Within ten minutes he was fast asleep, caused by a mix of the late hour and relaxation from the few hours with Alessandra.

Chapter 10

Piercing through the drapes directly at its target, the sunlight found its mark like a sniper's bullet, penetrating through Kay's eyelid. Rolling over, she attempted to hide under the blankets. The hotel bed was so nice and warm she didn't want to have to leave. Excuses for not getting out of bed and drudging through the streets of Washington D.C. were racing through her head when the phone suddenly rang. After ten rings she realized the person calling wasn't going to give up, she reached out from under the blankets and probed for the receiver. Finally finding it after two more rings, she pulled the receiver under the covers.

"Hello" she said, the desire for sleep echoing in her voice.

"Kay, where the hell are you. It's eight-forty and you were supposed to meet me in the restaurant ten minutes ago."

"My alarm must not have gone off" she lied. "I'll be down in a couple of minutes. You go ahead and eat; I'm not much of a breakfast person. Order me a coffee."

"Don't be too long. The car is supposed to pick us up at nine-fifteen.

God must really hate me, Kay thought to herself. "I'll be there with bells on, don't worry."

Of course the bells would be the ones ringing in her head from the wine she drank on the plane that still battled with several of her brain cells, she thought to herself.

Realizing it was useless to delay the inevitable, she slithered out of bed, exposing her naked body to the sunlight. She looked across the room to the mirror over the desk with eyes barely opened. The hair was tossed about with reckless abandon and what was left of the makeup she forgot to wash off after arriving at the hotel was streaked across her face. At least the body didn't show the signs of disrepair. The skin was still tight, her breasts still stood out, and the muscle tone was in its proper proportions.

She walked into the bathroom and didn't face the mirror in order to avoid getting a more close up look. What she saw from far away was bad enough. She turned on the shower and tested the temperature. As if to put an exclamation on the morning, there was no hot water and she would have to settle for a cold shower.

"Thanks a lot" she said to the ceiling. "Is it going to get better or are you going to put me through this all day?"

****

At the same time Kay was clearing the sleep from her eyes in Washington D.C., LT Greg Morris was already running around the track in the underground facility at Camp Pendleton. It had become a daily ritual for Greg to start the mornings, except weekends, with a three-mile run, some exercise, followed by a hot shower. While at the facility, he could also enjoy a nice hot Jacuzzi to soothe the muscles and get his body loose. As he finished his run, sweat soaked through his T-shirt, the professional team logo on the front having weathered almost completely. Walking around the track to cool down, he reflected on the previous night. Anyone who walked into the track at that moment would think that Greg was masochistic, as he grinned from ear to ear. Taking slow deep breaths too ease the senses; he considered what kind of future he could have with her. She was beautiful and wonderful in bed, along with other areas of the house, but there needed to be more. There needed to be common interests and the ability to communicate. Greg realized there was no potential for it, especially in his present position, but that didn't mean he couldn't spend time with her and enjoy her company again.

Noticing it was five-thirty as he glanced down at his watch, he had a good hour to finish his workout, shower and sit in the Jacuzzi for a while. Afterwards he would eat breakfast, clear off some of the paperwork from his desk and get to the meeting at seven-thirty.

Completing a rigorous thirty minutes of weights and calisthenics and cleaning off the sweat in the shower, he sat down in the Jacuzzi and closed his eyes. Immediately the images of Alessandra's beautiful body entered his mind, but he quickly shook the images away in order to concentrate on the reason he was here. Normally Greg was able to decipher the mission when the team was assembled based upon the latest news reports or intelligence messages he read on the ship. This time their world was stable, with the usual conflicts in the Balkans, the Middle East or Africa, but nothing that generated enough interest to call in the team.

As he sat there thinking, he suddenly sensed something different. Without warning or opening his eyes he reached up, grabbed a hold of a neck with one hand and an arm with the other, and spun the body into the Jacuzzi. Opening his eyes he saw that it was his executive officer, LT Tom Franklin. Letting lose the grip around Tom's neck, he watched as the head came up out of the water, eyes bulging in surprise.

"What the hell did you do that for?"

"You should know by now that I don't like being snuck up on."

"A simple splash of water would have sufficed. You didn't have to try and drown me."

"Some people need to learn the lesson the hard way. Maybe next time you'll be more careful."

Tom was always trying to get the better of Greg since they first met. Greg wondered if it was just in Tom's nature or that he had to prove something to Greg. Greg always appreciated Tom's talents. An excellent marksman, probably one of the best shooters in the world, he was quick to adapt to a changing situation. Tom's only drawback was his impatience and that he really seemed to enjoy the work. Greg never really enjoyed killing anyone, avoiding it whenever possible, but when necessary, he did it quickly and painlessly. Of course in the war games, where he was noticed, it was only for play that he enjoyed. When it came down to actually killing someone, it wasn't for enjoyment; it was a matter of life or death for a team member or himself. It didn't bother him to kill someone; it came easily, not like killing a helpless animal. He couldn't kill an animal. That was simply murder in his mind. During missions, however, those he had killed were far from helpless; they were soldiers or mercenaries that wouldn't think twice about killing him.

"I'll still get you one of these days, buddy. When you least expect it." Tom climbed out of the Jacuzzi and grabbed his towel off the rack.

"The only time I'll least suspect it is when I'm dead and gone, Tom." Greg walked out of the Jacuzzi and walked over to the towel rack, feeling the cool air that replaced the hot water, bringing new life to all the senses in his body, which were always awake, even when he slept. Since he was young, he slept for short periods of time because he could sense movements around him or hear sounds that were out of place, creating images in his mind. Remembering back to his days in High School, his mother had walked into his room one night and was looking at him as he slept, and without realizing what he was doing, reached up and grabbed her scaring her out of her wits. Even though he continued to apologize, she had kept a distance from him, especially when he was relaxing on the porch or in the family room with his eyes shut. Greg realized back then there was something different about himself, but never knew what it meant until he joined the teams.

After drying off and getting dressed in the locker room, he and Tom walked down to the long hallway to the cafeteria. Breakfast was the main meal on the facility, because for the rest of the day, it was usually non-stop training and drills requiring meals to be light and quick.

"Any idea of why we were all called in?" Tom asked, anxiety dancing in his eyes, awaiting the word to go active again.

"Haven't a clue. I haven't seen anything in the news that would indicate the need for a mission."

"That's not like you. You always seem to know what we're doing before they announce it. This must be really big." Tom was practically dancing down the hallway now, feeling the rush running through his body.

"Don't get all wired up now Tom. It may just be an inspection to run us through some drills or a big pep talk. Just because they called us in, doesn't mean there's something up. We haven't been on a mission for a while and maybe they think we're getting rusty and want to run us through the motions, nothing else." It had been six months since they went to Algeria to silence a terrorist group that was trying to form up from the broken factions across the Middle East.

"As long as it's something. I'm getting real tired of sitting around that office in Long Beach, pushing paper." Tom had been stuck with a desk job at the Long Beach Naval Shipyard, coordinating the shutdown of the base as part of the recent defense cutbacks.

They entered into the cafeteria and found the rest of the team either eating or swapping stories of the past six months since they'd last been together. Thirty men each with special skills, mostly lethal, that if they wouldn't be here, might end up in a similar cafeteria in a prison somewhere. They were good men who straddled on the edge, daring to take risks, few of them doing it for the good of the country, but that didn't matter to Greg as long as they got the job

86

done and kept him alive. It was a mixture of the Dirty Dozen, Kelly's Heroes and Hogan's Heroes.

****

Unlike the spring in Washington D.C. when the cherry blossoms are in bloom and everything seems so alive, the end of fall makes the city appear as death worn over. Kay looked out the glass windows lining the front of the hotel and watched as the people scampered along the streets, hiding under their umbrellas amidst the pouring rain. Cars lined the streets, waiting in the rush hour traffic, which moved only a few feet every minute. The trees in the park across the street had already lost their leaves and skeleton arms sagged downwards, as if finally giving in to the death of the season.

Steve Puller walked up next to her carrying his briefcase and a copy of the Washington Post. A piece of egg was lingering on his right cheek and Sally wiped it away.

"Ready to capture the day, Kay?" Steve looked fresh and alive, wearing a long raincoat opened at the front displaying a dull gray sweater and navy blue Docker pants.

"No, but I guess I don't have much choice do I?"

"Come on, it's not that bad. You'll get used to it."

"I always imagined the capital to be lined with gold, full of diplomats and regal people, not like this" she motioned out the windows.

"You don't get out much do you? Washington is the biggest den of iniquity known to man. The people here are either making decisions that affect each of our lives, either that or their bribing and robbing those same people. The politicians don't care what affect they have on our lives, but how much publicity they'll get out of it and what benefits they'll get from companies they support. Here it's every man for himself and if you get in their way, they'll step all over you."

"They can't all be that way. There have to be some good politicians that are trying to make a difference."

"Sure, when they first get out here, they think they can change the world and convince people with rational thinking. Unfortunately, after they've nearly knocked themselves out with ideals and common sense, the finally realize it's a war and they have to take the gloves off and get down and dirty. Before long, they become the same type of people they had hoped to destroy when they first arrived."

"Don't you think they are making a difference and making the world better? This summit is a sign of better things."

"It's all a part of the game girl. To keep the voters happy they occasionally make some worthwhile decisions, like putting a carrot in front of a horse to pull the cart. They feed us a little, we feel better, and the rest of the time they rant and rave, feed us bullshit, and line their pockets with our tax money. This agreement would have happened years ago, however the government manages to bicker back and forth for ages, until they felt it was time to feed us again. If you still think this a government for the people by the people, you have a lot to learn. Just sit back and listen, but don't just listen to the words, their just lyrical poems written by speechwriters, listen to the feeling behind the words, or the lack thereof. Watch carefully how they carry themselves and when questioned, beat around the bush and give vague answers that hold double meanings."

Kay knew the government had some bad apples. It was her passion to write a story of corruption in government, but couldn't believe that corruption was everywhere. When all the apples are bad, it's hard to tell when something's bad and worth writing about. She wasn't interested in uncovering love affairs or luncheonette gossip, her term for afternoon soap operas; she wanted to cover pay-offs and crime in government.

Steve walked towards the front entrance. "Our ride is here, lets get it together." Outside a young kid in jeans and sweatshirt stepped out of a Ford Taurus parked at the entrance and waved. His hair was tied in a pigtail and a limp cigarette hung out the left corner of his mouth.

"Who the hell is that?"

"That's Tony. He's the photographer who'll be travelling with us. He's a little strange but one of the best of the business. He's sort of a hippy drop-out, but he's not bad."

Kay looked up to the ceiling again. "You're just not going to make this easy are you?"

"What was that?" Steve said as he walked into the rotating door.

"Nothing."

****

At seven-twenty Greg entered the noisy conference room. Standing along the wall and seated in the chairs, the elite team were all coming up with ideas for the purpose of the Captain's visit.

"I tell ya', we're finally going to Iraq and blow Saddam himself away since he's the only sick supporter of terrorism left." said Hank Briscoe, one of the best sharpshooters in the world. "And I get to pull the trigger to send him back to Allah."

"You're crazy Hank, he's old news. I hear it that we're going into Columbia to blow away the drug runners. The Pres is really hot on making good on his promise to cut down drug trafficking." replied Dave Stoddard, the team's radio and electronics wizard.

"Whatever it is, it's about time. My girlfriend was beginning to talk about marriage and that's one battle you can't win. I'd rather go up against a hundred crazed rebels than a woman talking about marriage." said Craig Williams, the team's explosive expert.

Hank Briscoe was the first to notice Greg entering the room. "Hey boss, why don't you tell us what this is all about? You always know what's going on."

Greg walked up the aisle towards the front of the conference room, "The way I hear it, we are going up into space to take on some aliens that are invading Earth. They ran out of room on their planet and want to use ours for their overpopulation. They've sent six starships full of bad-ass aliens and we are supposed to stop them before the world hears about it." Greg tried to maintain a serious composure and the room had gone deafly quiet. "The Special Projects people at Quantico have developed some laser weapons and we are going to be the first to test them out in actual combat in space."

Jim Potter, a muscle-bound Arnold Shwarznegger look-alike from the farms in Oklahoma, with a heart of steel but a brain of ice cubes, stared with eyes wide open, "Whoa, cool. Are we going to get light-sabers also?"

"Feel the force, Jimmy." Greg said smiling. "I'm just kidding. I haven't a clue what's going on."

Everyone in the room started to laugh, including Jim who wasn't sure why everyone was laughing.

At that moment, Captain Davenport entered the room. "Attention on deck" Greg said allowing the small sign of respect to hopefully ease the tension between him and Davenport.

Davenport walked straight up to the podium. "At ease gentlemen."

The conference room was designed similar to a mini-theater, with two large screens at the front, a podium set-up in the middle, and comfortable seats for the entire team. Every mission was briefed in this room because it was soundproof and sanitized to ensure nothing could escape via

AN
EAGLE'S
VENGEANCE

Guy Macdonald

An Eagle's Vengeance

by Guy Macdonald

ISBN 0-75969-736-1

An Eagle's Vengeance is a compelling story set 6 years after the September 11th terrorist attacks. The story follows two significant characters. Kay Cross, a junior reporter for the San Diego Union, gets the rare chance to interview the President of the United States before a Peace Agreement and signing ceremony. Meanwhile, Lieutenant Commander Greg Morris of an elite underground military team believes he is tracking down one of the last terrorist financiers. Cross and Morris become entangled into a nefarious web of events on the eve of the ceremonies, when the media reports that terrorists have assassinated the US President and Vice President. Cross and Morris are suddenly catapulted into a race against time to stop a world war.

To order call 1-888-280-7715 or visit www.1stbooks.com

electrical outlets or ventilation equipment. Each mission had to be briefed three times; the initial planning phase, after the initial training run-through, and finally just before departure to receive the latest information or any changes.

Davenport opened up the pamphlet he brought with him and began the conference without any sort of greeting. "Gentlemen from this moment on you are shut off from the outside world. You will receive no news, no phone calls, no radio or television and you will not be able to leave this facility. We have a lot of work to do in the next week and I will update you on any situation as they occur. We have been given an extremely sensitive mission and I have been tasked by Washington to lead it."

At that moment, all eyes turned towards Greg. Everyone on the team knew Greg's feelings towards Davenport and giving up command of the team to anyone, so they expected an outburst from him. Davenport's eyes were fixed directly into Greg's and a silent war began to wage.

"Do you have any problem with that Commander?"

Although his stomach was turning into knots and disgust was boiling inside, Greg thought it prudent to remain quiet now in front of the troops and set the first battle into place when they were alone.

"No sir, our team is at the government's disposal." Greg wasn't about to admit to giving the team to Davenport's disposal, sensing that another disaster was in the making.

"Good, then we can begin. As you know the anti-terrorist campaign has practically eliminated all factions, thanks in part to a lot of your efforts, but there is still a couple of key leaders that have not yet been apprehended or eliminated."

Hank Briscoe looked over at Dave Stoddard, "Told you so."

Davenport continued, "Recent information has been obtained that one of the most influential of these leaders has been hiding out in a small Central American nation. We have been tasked to drop near his villa and bring him back to the USA to stand trial and once and for all put an end to terrorism. Any questions?"

Every man in the room had several questions racing through their head, but normal practice was to remain quiet until after the planning brief and first trial-run to discuss them. Most questions are normally answered during the first run, those that aren't get asked in the second briefing.

Davenport walked back to the podium. "Good, then lets begin with how this will all be done."

The team spent the next 30 minutes listening to Davenport outline the specifics of the mission and the associated timeline.

Chapter 11

They drove along the city streets amidst the crowded Washington D.C. traffic. Everything seemed dismal and in a rush. The sky was overcast and a slight rain influenced the drab appearance. Traffic was just as miserable as Washington D.C. weather and the people continued to rush along the sidewalks under the protection of their umbrellas.

Being her first time in the nation's capital, Kay wasn't aware of exactly where they were and Steve wasn't about to tell her where they were going. She could only stare out the window and take in the darkened sights. Just as she was about to ask Steve once again where they were headed, she glanced out the window and realized their destination. The car pulled up to the gate and a security policeman walked towards the car. Kay could just make out the White House through the trees.

As Tony talked to the security guard, Kay turned to Steve, "Are you serious? We're going to the White House?"

"They called a press conference today to announce the location of the Arms Agreement signing. We have to attend and hopefully get some answers and find out our next destination." Steve said as he scribbled some notes in his note pad.

"I'm not ready for this Steve. I look like hell. You could have given me some warning."

"Well, if you would have shown up for breakfast you would have found out all the details. Hopefully we'll be able to schedule an interview for you with the man."

"Just as long as it's not today."

After checking the press badges and conducting a mirror check under the car for explosives, the security guard motioned to the shack and the gate opened.

"Any word on where the agreement is going to be signed."

"No, it's been kept quiet, probably for security reasons."

"Wouldn't it be nice to go someplace exotic like Rio de Janeiro or the Bahamas?"

"Don't get too excited Kay, it will probably be somewhere like Topeka, Kansas or Cleveland, Ohio with my luck."

"Anywhere but this dismal city."

"You've never been to Cleveland, have you?"

The car drove up the driveway and was directed to the right where they parked the car amidst vans and trailers where reporters and camera crews scurried about. Kay, Steve and Tony left the car and followed the mass of people into the side entrance where they were directed into the Pressroom. Cameras were lined up along the back wall with cords intermingled in a maze, several people getting caught up in them as they clambered to the few remaining seats. Realizing there were no seats available, they joined the crowd along the near wall and waited.

After several minutes, the Chief of Staff entered the room and proceeded up to the podium. Kay had heard many things about the young politician and his climb up the political ladder, but was surprised at his youth and good looks.

"Ladies and Gentlemen, the President of the United States." the Chief of Staff said into the array of microphones cluttered on the podium. Kay watched Steve pull a small cassette recorder out of his coat pocket, realizing she was totally unprepared for this.

The President walked into the room and Kay noticed how weathered he looked. He didn't appear as fresh and virile as he did on television. The President proceeded to the podium, took out a few cue cards, placed them on the podium and waited for the noise to die down.

"Good Morning, Ladies and Gentlemen. I have called this press conference to announce a historic moment in Earth's history. The signing of the Arms Agreement between all the world's nations is going to be a momentous occasion and the first step in ensuring peace across the entire planet. This weekend all the world leaders will meet in Acapulco and on Tuesday will formally adopt the agreement and begin a new chapter in world peace." The President paused and cleared his throat to one side. "When I took office a year ago, I promised the American people a safer world and a cleaner country."

"My staff worked long and hard to put together a plan that was eventually agreed upon by Congress. Of course there were many who were against this, saying it would leave the country naked, but with this new era across the globe, there will be few factors left to fear. Over the past six years we have tracked down and eliminated the terrorist threat to democracy. Civilized people can once again travel around the world and participate in events without fear. The entire world is a much safer and friendlier place, where people from all walks of life are welcomed and treated the same. I am personally going to Acapulco to sign the agreement. I have fulfilled my promise of a safer world and we are making monumental steps in clearing out drugs and crime in our country. I once again, vow to the American people, that within the next two years, this country will once again stand proud and free, and concentrate on the people and their needs."

Immediately hands began to go up for the round of questions. For fifteen minutes questioned were raised ranging from the arms agreement to health, welfare, and abortion. Time and again the President was eloquent and reiterated the scripted and rehearsed responses provided by the Chief of Staff. Kay was amazed at how the President knew the reporters by their first names, not knowing that a seating chart was displayed on the podium to enable the President to identify each reporter.

"I'm sorry but that concludes the press conference for today." The President said as he closed out the meeting. "I hope to see you all in Acapulco." The President proceeded down the stage and out the door followed by his entourage of aides. The Chief of Staff returned to the Podium and outlined the details of the conference.

Once he completed the details, one reporter stood up. "Where is the President going to be staying in Acapulco?"

"I'm sorry, but that information will not be divulged for security reasons." He made a note of who asked the question to have the Secret Service check on credentials. "Thank you all for coming." he said and proceeded off the stage and left via the same door as the President.

"Not too exciting, is it?" Steve asked Kay.

"Are you kidding me, that was the President?"

"Kay, you had better learn that the President is just another man. The only difference between him and any other man is he's richer, has a big house and driven around in fancy cars. He works hard like every one else but he's restricted in what he can and cannot do. He's just a figurehead that is driven by the strings pulled by Congress and his staff."

Before Kay could respond, Steve proceeded out of the conference room to a desk in the hallway and began talking to the woman sitting there.

"Stevey's a real bummer, huh?" Tony said as he packed up his camera.

"What was that?" Kay said shaking herself out of her daze.

"Steve, he's a real anti-politician. Never says anything nice about any of them. Don't let that get you down none. He really knows his job and the people. If you want answers, he has a way of finding them out."

"Well his personality could sure use some work."

"Yeah, but since his wife left him five years ago, he's been a real downer. You should be happy to be on this assignment."

"I'll keep my judgment for later." Kay said not totally sure after the last twenty-four hours of hell.

"Your judgment on what?" Steve asked as he returned. "By the way, I got your interview set up for tomorrow morning. Try and get up for this one, will you."

"Just give me a chance to get a good night's sleep for a change and I'll be ready early. Why do you think I was put on this assignment?"

"I've only read some of your articles but they didn't appear too bad. Maybe the paper is grooming you to liven up this arena. You'll be a much prettier companion at some of the functions here than the guys from the office."

Initially Kay resented the comment, but realized it wasn't worth arguing about. At least it got her here and a chance to do something important for a change.

****

At the briefing, Davenport outlined the plan of insertion and extraction of a wealthy businessman who made most of his money producing and distributing a large percentage of drugs into America which he used to finance terrorist activities, including the one against the World Trade Center in 2001. He was also connected to money laundering and possibly dealing in acquiring and selling stolen antiquities.

The plan seemed easy. There was normally only ten bodyguards at one time. At night, only four were on station in the vicinity of his bedroom. Six others would be asleep in quarters in another section of his villa, but well within reach to react to any alert. Reliefs would cycle every four hours, normally at eight p.m., midnight and four in the morning. The villa was located one mile inside an eight-foot stone wall. In between the wall were woods that stretched for three-quarters of a mile. In between the woods and villa was open terrain with little cover except for a small pond that stretched from the woods to within 50 yards of the back entrance. At night six Doberman Pincher dogs wander inside the walls and do not get fed until the morning. The front gate is electrified and guarded twenty-four hours a day. The grounds are well lit by spotlights on all four corners of the villa.

The guards are armed with UZI machine guns and pistols but are not overly attentive since they have a tendency to use too much of their product while on duty. Remote cameras, positioned around the grounds and inside the villa are monitored at the front guard shack with ten small screen televisions. The plan called for insertion by parachuting into a small field only two miles from the villa. A submarine would arrive five hours later to recover the team and their captive. The guards were expendable and would be eliminated, making a statement to the few remaining terrorists left around the world. A few less mercenaries in the world wouldn't be missed. If the villa were found to contain drugs, it would be leveled. One team would be utilized to eliminate the sleeping guards, one for extraction and eliminate the guards on watch, and the other to rig the explosives.

As Davenport continued to cover the basic details, Greg watched Davenport as he paraded along the stage, using a light pen to highlight areas on charts and diagrams. Why was this such an important mission to call in the team? With the end of the Cold War and the suppression of terrorists, the military was becoming more of a police force than military force. Now it seemed the teams were becoming the next recruit.

"We're not boring you, are we Mr. Morris?" Davenport said pointing the light pen in Greg's direction.

"With all due respect, Captain. Why have we been chosen to conduct this mission?"

"A legitimate question, Commander. Since things are rather quiet around the planet, the government thought it would be nice to let you earn some of your pay and make use of the millions of dollars they spend on this facility to, how does the commercial go, 'Help take a bite out of crime'. Other organizations and military units will be conducting similar missions on other key members and if it fits into your busy social schedule, Washington thought you might be able to lend a hand. Now that's not too much to ask for is it?" Davenport blurted out in his usual sarcastic manner, coming within a foot of Greg as he finished.

"No sir." Greg said, staring right back into Davenport's black coal orbs. "It just seemed a little odd to use us for such a simple mission."

"Don't take this personally, Commander, but your team has been sitting idle for so long, I'm not sure they're ready for such a mission without weeks of training. Unfortunately I don't have that much time to whip you back into shape. We only have a week to prepare and carry it out."

Greg could hear the mumbling of the team members at the stab at their capabilities.

"My team is ready for any mission you throw at us, Captain." Greg declared as he stood up, letting out some of his frustration on Davenport.

Davenport leaned into Greg's face, "Watch yourself, Commander. Don't fuck with me or I'll wave to you on the ground from the airplane." keeping his voice low enough to appear to be addressing only Greg but just loud enough to be heard by the nearest team members.

As he leaned back, "We'll just see how ready this team is in the next few days. I want the training site set up to simulate the villa by 1930. We'll conduct a walk-through of the villa at 2000 hours. Then you can rest and conduct the first run at 2400. The last satellite pass is at 2300, and we are clear until 0530, so we can work on the plan from 2400 until 0430. The first debrief will be at 0700, right after breakfast. Commander, you and I will go over the detailed plan in one hour in here." Davenport walked up to the podium and leaned over the podium.

"This may seem like a simple mission, gentlemen, but we are dealing with a different breed of enemy. They are not highly trained combat personnel; they are hired killers whose only motivation is money. They would kill their mother for the right price. They are totally unpredictable and if under the influence of drugs, extremely dangerous. Any questions?"

Since there weren't any questions, the briefing was closed and everyone proceeded out of the conference room, except Greg. Each member of the team gave him a raised eyebrow or gritting teeth to signal their understanding with his frustration.

When the room emptied, Greg walked up to Davenport as he descended from the platform. "I would appreciate it if you wouldn't shit on the troops, sir. These guys have been here every weekend, leaving their social life behind, knowing they are doing it for a purpose.

They deserve some sign of confidence."

"What purpose?" Davenport mumbled under his breath.

"Scuse me sir?"

"Quit nurse-maiding them, Commander. I was just trying to get their gumption up so they will try to prove themselves. The world has taken up this peace movement and you should be grateful you still have a team."

Greg couldn't get it out of his head that Davenport was hiding something, but couldn't put his finger on exactly what.

"The team can do this mission with its hands tied." Greg said as Davenport walked to the door.

"Let's not try it that way." Davenport ended the conversation as he left the room.

The nagging hair on Greg's back was sticking straight out and all his nerves were piercing the center of his spine.

Whatever Davenport was up to, Greg knew it meant that along with watching out for his troops, he would have to keep one eye on the Captain the entire time. He was not about to let this mission get out of hand and put them in an in-extremis situation, which Davenport was prone to.

Chapter 12

Sitting in his vehicle, Captain Davenport scanned the terrain through his Night Vision Goggles. Everything was illuminated in an eerie green glow and Hawthorne could make out the details of the building and the surrounding plant life, but no other forms were visible. Since the briefing, the rooms in the building were tailored to exact replicas of the target. The details of the furniture layout were not known, however, boxes were placed to appear as furniture as one would expect furniture in the rooms to be situated.

The basic plan was simple and would allow room for discussion after the dry run. Initially the teams would enter the grounds from the forest at the rear of the villa by the lake. When they reached the lake they would swim to the opposite side and split into three squads. The first squad would scale the side of the house and enter via the roof access. Their mission was to eliminate the primary guards and retrieve their captive. The second squad would enter through the back door and take out the extra guards asleep in their quarters. The third would check the front of the house and then plant explosives in the basement. Timing was crucial as all three teams had to enter the building at the exact same time. That time passed nine minutes ago and Hawthorne still hadn't seen anyone. The entire extraction was to only take ten minutes.

"This is pathetic. We don't have enough time to start from scratch to train these morons. I expected to at least get started on time. Where the hell are they?" Davenport screamed at Corporal Roger Bailey, sitting next to him in the driver's seat.

"I'm sure there must be some explanation, sir." Bailey replied. Bailey was the team's administrative petty officer. He rarely went on missions as his only function was to ensure that the team's paperwork and logistics were handled. In addition to handling the requisitions for paperwork and other sundry items, he was also responsible for ensuring there were enough supplies of food, ammunition, and electronics that were needed if a mission was called. Everyone called him Beetle Bailey, but except for the name, his work was exemplary and anything the team needed was always there.

"I'm going to have someone's ass at the debrief, beginning with Morris's."

"What the hell have I done this time, Captain?"

Davenport nearly fell out of the vehicle at the sound of the voice only two feet to his right. Morris was standing there with the dummy of their captive over his shoulders. Behind him stood the rest of the team, their smiles the only evidence of their presence underneath their black uniforms and ski masks.

"Cheeerist, Commander, don't ever do that, you scared me right out of my pants." Bailey said holding his hand to his chest to make sure his heart was still beating.

"Sorry Bailey." A smile crossed Greg's face as well, knowing it did the same to Davenport as he brushed himself off. "The plan is sound, but we have to assume that not everything will be as placed. We have to take into account the unexpected. Is there any way we can find out anything about the perimeter fences and what might be in the pond? We wouldn't want to swim across water filled with piranha or crocodiles. There will be a lot to discuss at the debrief. Any initial questions from you, sir?"

Davenport didn't know whether to be pissed off or grateful. "Don't be so damn smug, Commander. I'm not sure how you got in and out without me seeing anything, but next time I'll play the captive and we'll see how good you think you are." Davenport climbed back into the vehicle and motioned Bailey to start it. "Briefing at oh-nine-hundred. Get some sleep and breakfast. We'll review the drill and take in any recommendations you think you might have."

As Bailey began to pull the vehicle away, Davenport leaned over the side, "Remember, Commander, I'm still in charge of this mission and I'll be going in there with you."

Greg felt as if someone stuck a knife in his back and twisted it in deep and wide. Right when he was feeling good about himself and the team, Davenport had to pull a dark cloud over him and rain on his parade. It was bad enough to remind him that Davenport was in charge, but to add insult to injury, he was reminded that he had the extra burden of bringing him along. He wondered how anything could get worse. It wouldn't be long before he found out.

****

As Kay sat in the waiting room outside the oval office, she could feel her stomach tighten into knots. Butterflies were fluttering about inside her stomach reminding her of the excitement and anticipation she had when her Dad used to break out the Christmas lights each year and spend one entire day unraveling the streams of lights and cord. Waiting for him to finish decorating was unbearable for a young child. Even after spending several hours reviewing the arms agreement history with Steve after dinner the previous night and working on her outline of questioning that morning, she felt unprepared to meet with the most influential government figure in the country.

Everyone continuously reminded her that the president was only a man, no different from any other. Steve had rambled on during the night about the inadequacies of politicians, especially this president. She couldn't get over Steve's pessimistic attitude towards politicians. Throughout her studies, the professors had reminded her time and time again that a reporter must keep an open and unbiased mind. The key to a good reporter was to question everything and provider the readers and listeners to all sides of the story, without trying to influence your own particular opinion. Politics and the legal system were the hardest areas to report, her professors lectured. There were so many sides to each story that a reporter had a tendency to get caught in the whirlwind and succumb to taking sides. They advised her that when a reporter reached that point, it was time to switch to another area of reporting or retire. She wondered whether or not it was that time for Steve.

Arriving thirty minutes before the scheduled interview, she underwent tight scrutiny by the security personnel. Her records were reviewed, purse inspected three times, passed through two metal detectors and answered more questions than she had scheduled for the interview. With past security breaches including disgruntled voters firing at the White House, or the time in the first month of his term when a drunken female infatuated with the President attempted to climb over the White House fence to see him, Kay could understand the tighter scrutiny but believed they had gone a little overboard.

Finally led to the waiting room, she found two secretaries scurrying through stacks of papers, answering telephone calls and running in and out of the oval office. She estimated one of the secretaries to be thirty-five years old and the other over fifty. Each one wore plain looking below the knee dresses with their hair turned into a bun at the back. They reminded Kay of librarians and wondered whether one of the earlier first ladies had been uneasy with pretty secretaries and revealing dresses and initiated this dress code to keep their husbands eyes on the business of the country and away from any distractions. She was sure that this was a particular concern of Hilary Clinton during her husband's eight years in office. Every time one of the secretaries or one of several well-dressed men paraded into the oval office, Kay caught a glimpse of the President sitting in his chair behind the desk, gesturing orders or handing over papers for the secretaries to retype or send on to another office. The secretaries desks sat in the two corners away from the door, covered with stacks of paper and books. A window separated the desks and Kay could make out the familiar parade grounds were the President commonly arrived in his one of his helicopters. Along the walls were pictures of past presidents and other leaders signing historic documents or shaking hands that marked specific events in the country's history. Several dying plants adorned the shelves along one wall, evidence of the lack of attention caused by higher necessities.

"The President will see you now, Miss." The elder secretary said as she returned from the oval office.

"Thank you." Kay said, startled out of her reflections and feeling her stomach tighten even more.

Proceeding through the door opened by the secretary, Kay was immediately taken back by the size of the oval office. After all the movies she had seen and pictures of the furnishings in many women magazines, she had expected the room to be much larger. Instead the room seemed somewhat cramped. Across from the President's desk sat two small sofas facing each other across a coffee table. There was just enough room between the desk and the sofas and between the sofas and fireplace for one person to pass. Although she imagined the furniture to be expensive they were not what she considered comfortable. The sofas could barely hold three people and the cushions were paper thin, possibly due to the many people who sat in them over the years. Along the walls were bookshelves filled with volumes of books that appeared to have been placed there a hundred years ago and never moved. On either side of the President the two flags, the Unites States flag and that of his office stood erect and reminded her of the many speeches past presidents had made over the years.

The door closed behind her and she could sense the silence created by the soundproof walls and bulletproof glass. As she stood there dumbstruck and awed the President walked over to her from behind the desk.

"It never ceases to amaze me how every person that enters here for the first time has that same look. I believe I had it the first time I entered it too." the president motioned Kay towards the sofas. "Please have a seat, Miss, um, I don't recall the name."

"Kay Cross, Mister President."

"First we can start by doing away with the formalities and you can start calling me John. Is it all right if I call you Kay?"

"Certainly."

"Listen, Kay we don't have a lot of time, I have another conference in about fifteen minutes so have a seat and I'll try to answer some of your questions. Can I have one of the secretaries get you a cup of coffee or anything?" The President walked back behind his desk and sat down in the big black chair that looked like the only comfortable item in the room.

Kay sat down on the sofa shaking her head no and found that her assumptions about the lack of comfort were reinforced. She tried to adjust to a comfortable position but found it useless.

"Forget it Kay. That couch is meant to be uncomfortable so my staff members won't fall asleep on me while I pontificate." the president said with a grin.

The President's smile was warm and sincere and started to untie the knots in her stomach. After all the criticism about the President Steve had expounded on her the night before and stories of the man being harsh and cold-hearted, Kay was surprised to see him so friendly and easy-going and felt much more at ease.

"I must apologize Mr. President. I haven't really started out on the right foot."

"Don't be silly, Kay. Most of those in your field act the same way their first time here. Some have fainted, thrown up on me or tripped and broken something. I like reporters during their first few visits here. They have fresh new ideas and respect the office. After some time they become unruly and walk in here like they own the office. Now start calling me John or I'll end the interview."

"I'll try, John."

"That's better. Now you're from the San Diego Union if I recall. What kind of questions do you have for me?"

"As you are aware, I'm here on account of the upcoming arms agreement. There has been a lot of criticism on the upcoming signing in Acapulco. Many politicians and voters believe you are weakening the country by signing this agreement. They have little faith in the other countries being so expedient while we leave ourselves defenseless. How can we be sure that one of the countries doesn't drag their feet or maintain some sort of stockpile which could eventually be used against us after we have eliminated all our systems?"

"You get right to the point, don't you?" the President swung in his high-back leather chair to look at the Eastern wall. "Some of the people feel that this leaves the country vulnerable, but a part of the plan provides for close monitoring by all of the countries involved. Status reports will be compiled by inspectors every month on the progress. Representatives from each country will review and compare these reports at the end of each month and amend the schedules as necessary to ensure that no country will have an advantage. It is imperative that the time schedules are maintained. Any country that falls behind on their schedule must forfeit ten million dollars for each violation to the Humanitarian Council, which would be used for supplies to undeveloped countries around the world. The onus is placed upon the countries themselves to prevent them having to contribute these funds."

"How much money does eliminating these systems save this country?"

"Billions of dollars that will be channeled into other programs and reduce the country's deficit."

"What programs will benefit from these savings?"

"Initially we have planned to reallocate these savings to boost the anti-drug program, education system, prison improvements and welfare programs. The majority going to fighting the drug problem and improving our schools."

"What about the military? With this reduction in our countries defense system, isn't there a plan to redesign the military to take up the slack?"

"The beauty of this program is that our national defense systems are not reduced. If all the countries heavy weapons systems are removed, then we all maintain an even par with each other. We continue to reduce the military, eliminating some of the non-essential programs and revamping the emphasis of the military to a national asset rather than so much an international one. We will continue to deploy overseas to maintain a global presence and diplomatic ties as well as support NATO and international exercises, however a large chunk of the military will be used to eliminate the influx of drugs into this country by sea, land and air."

"That mustn't sit pretty in the Pentagon."

"The Pentagon needs to understand that there is no enemy anymore. Even after the Cold War the world took a different aura with countries cooperating rather than being secretive. The Space Program would have died without the international input it had over the last ten years. The new enemy was terrorism by groups of religious fanatics that didn't even receive backing from the religions they professed to be driven by. Over the last six years we've eliminated their infrastructure and support. Now there is little left in the world except for the ongoing battles across some borders and within our own nations with crime, medicine, drugs and poverty. These are the new enemies the international community must face, and we each have to deal with them individually. In order to do that, we need this agreement to allow us to refocus our efforts."

"There are still many people in Washington and in companies that provide services to the military that are opposed to this idea. What will companies like McDonnell Douglas do now that they won't be developing and constructing equipment for the military?" Kay asked.

"Many of them will be funded to assist in the deactivation and destruction of the weapons systems. Funding will also be provided to them to divert their research towards bettering today's society. We have a lot of problems in our own backyard that require much of their technology.

We need to find ways to improve farming, cleaning out our seas and air, space exploration, alternate energy resources including those for transportation, telecommunications, and a number of other programs we tend to neglect while trying to create a more powerful defense. Many of the systems we use in our weapons can be immediately transformed to these problems. Additionally, the military won't be entirely eliminated and we need to continue to improve on them while emphasizing their new roles in coastal and anti-drug defense."

"While many of the voters approve of the agreement and the trend towards world peace, many of them are military and defense contractor personnel who will end up out of work. When the presidential elections come up again, the full impact of this agreement will finally be evident to them. How do you see your party's chances for in the next elections?"

"Over the last six years since the World Trace Center bombing, our economy has seen drastic ups and downs with many people being forced out of jobs. Our unemployment rate is nearing the worst the nation has ever seen. By having the current defense contractors refocus their efforts on improved technologies to battle the problems we have at home, there more opportunities for people to work. There will be more occupations to choose from in the future and government funded training will be provided to those military personnel affected to help them fit into these growing fields. I feel very confident the American people will understand that to achieve such a worthy goal, everyone will have to suffer a little to grow. It's as the saying goes, no pain no gain. This plan is designed to grow quickly with as little pain as possible for everyone. In the long run everyone will gain and America will be a much stronger country economically as well as physically."

The President rose from his chair and walked over to Kay. She couldn't get over his calmness and began to wonder if it was all for show. He seemed so carefree and friendly. Was it a mask he put on for the press Kay wondered? He sat down next to her and leaned back on the couch.

"Kay, I don't conduct business concerned with how it will affect the next elections. I took this office to serve this country and make it stronger and safer. The people will have to decide if they feel that I have accomplished that to their satisfaction. I am doing what I believe is right and in the best interest of the people. If they are not satisfied that is their choice and the beauty of our governmental system."

"What's next after the agreement is signed?"

"We make the streets safer for everyone. We eliminate the drug problem, put away the criminals and improve the education of our children who will carry this country on into the future."

The next ten minutes went quickly, covering topics on welfare, the space program and U.S. support to other countries. Throughout the interview, Kay felt the President was straightforward and frank. Unlike what Steve had told her, he was covering specifics and not beating around the bush, as Steve put it.

After a while, the President smiled and rose from the couch. "I'm afraid that our time has run out and I have to go to another conference. It has been a real pleasure talking with you. Are you going down to Acapulco for the signing?"

"Yes sir."

"Have you ever been to Acapulco before?"

"No. I'm really looking forward to it."

,"Acapulco is beautiful during this time of year. It's way too hot during the summer. I look forward to seeing you there." He opened the door to the secretary's office and motioned to the younger secretary. "See to it that Miss Cross is given a personal tour of the White House before she leaves, okay Lucy." He turned back towards Kay, "You haven't been on a tour before have you?"

Kay rose from the couch and walked towards the door. "No I haven't. This is my first time to Washington and I've only had enough time to see the Press Room."

"Terrific. Lucy will take care of you. You have a few days left before we all have to be in Acapulco, so be sure to take in the sights of our wonderful capital."

"I sure will. Thank you so much for allowing me the interview. It has been a real honor to talk to you and get your insights."

"My pleasure. I hope we get the opportunity to talk again. Next time come up with some easier questions like what are my hobbies and my favorite authors."

"I'd like that."

"Right this way Miss Cross." Lucy said as she proceeded out the door into the hallway.

As Kay left the office she was still overwhelmed by the President's demeanor. Why did everyone make him out to be rude, egotistic or elusive? Was the interview only a guise to impress a new reporter? Everything about him seemed sincere and genuine. Whether it was or wasn't, he seemed to have all the answers and knew where he was going. The big question was whether or not the American public would understand and agree that they should have to make some sacrifices to get ahead. The country had been struggling in the recent years and although they had pulled together in 2001 and 2002, the intense patriotism slowly abated since then and people were reverting back to their selfish and rude "Me" generation again. The protests and opposition of the United States involvement in Vietnam, Iraq and Somalia were evidence to the fact that people didn't want to make sacrifices anymore and wanted everything handed to them on a silver platter. Would this President be able to sell this to the public any better than previous Presidents had? Would he be able to win them over like he had her? Even more important was whether or not he could win the support of the companies and military that was going to be affected by this agreement and the politicians that supported them.

Chapter 13

After three days of intensive training the team was finally getting a break. Greg had convinced Captain Davenport that Friday would be set aside for weapons cleaning, organizing the equipment and putting final touches on personal gear. After the morning rehearsal and debrief, each member was left to themselves to gather their thoughts and organize what they needed for the mission. That afternoon the gym was filled with team members working out and relaxing in the saunas. During these periods it was normal to find each person reflecting on their past and present, locked away inside themselves. There was very little conversation or the usual pranks that prevailed throughout the week.

It was now five-thirty in the evening and everyone was gathered in the briefing room. Up to this point the date of the mission had not been mentioned, but most knew it must be close if they were called to this special meeting. After a day of reflection and solitude, the conversation returned the moment they entered the room, spreading rumors of when the mission was to start. The memories of childhood days, family and friends had been reviewed each knowing that during the mission, these memories had to remain forgotten. All attention had to be focused on the task at hand and survival of each member of the team.

The doors to the briefing room opened and Captain Davenport entered with Greg trailing behind. After a week of putting up with Davenport, Greg appeared frazzled and tired. While the others pondered their lives, Greg was locked in a room with Davenport fine-tuning the mission and unsuccessfully trying to talk Davenport out of going on the mission with them or at least having assigned himself to the squad that would take the terrorist supporter out of the house. Greg was to lead the squad in and go with the third squad to secure the area and plant the explosives, which did not make him happy. Greg was the leader of the squad and he continuously tried to convince Davenport that it was his position to lead the extraction force, not the Captain's. Although Davenport didn't show it, Greg felt that the Captain wanted the glory position so he could brag to the Generals and Admirals that the mission was only successful because of his role.

Davenport walked up to the podium and Greg took a seat to his right in the front row.

"Good evening, gentlemen. I want to congratulate each of you on a good week of rehearsals. I must admit I had my doubts about your capabilities, but I see they were unwarranted and you are ready to do business." Greg wondered why Davenport was suddenly turning into Mr. Nice Guy, which troubled him, even further. It was like the snake leading Adam and Eve to the apple.

"Tomorrow morning we will conduct our last rehearsal. After that we need to put all our gear in ready status and be prepared to fly out Saturday at 1800 hours and conduct the mission during the early hours of Sunday. We drop within three miles of the target at 0230 and need to be in and out of the house no later than 0400 for a 0500 pick up on the beach. Get all the rest you can tonight and tomorrow. Expect to be back here by Sunday afternoon if all goes well. We'll stand by for further orders when we return. As I've said before, I can't tell you the location of our drop for security reasons but maps of the surrounding area between the drop zone, target and the beach will be handed out during the flight. It's relatively good ground and we do not foresee any contact with locals or hostile factions. Are there any questions?"

"Yes, sir. Any chance we can stay a little longer and pick up some local soo-vee-nears." Jim Potter called out in his usual Oklahoman accent bringing a laugh to most of the team.

Greg expected an outburst from Davenport outlining the sensitivities of the mission and the need for serious thinking and was shocked at the reply.

"Son, if you don't make it to the pickup point on time you can get all the souvenirs you can find before the local government or drug cartel members hunt you down." Davenport closed his binder and leaned onto the podium.

"Gentlemen, Operation Final Vengeance will close the book on terrorism and launch the beginning of a change in the world. We've spent the whole week preparing. It's basically an easy extraction with little or no resistance. I can't make any promises of what you can expect when you return, but you will know that you were responsible for making America a better place. There won't be any parades or banquets in your honor. Nobody in their right mind would let you into their homes if they knew you, anyway. You'll have to be satisfied that this is a giant achievement and if done right, will make a difference. Briefing at 0200, rehearsal to commence at 0230. Since there are no more questions get a good nights sleep and I'll see you in the morning." Davenport stepped off the podium and walked out of the briefing room.

Greg was still stunned by the change of character for Davenport. As the rest of the team left the room with their chests out and boasting amongst themselves, Greg scratched the back of his neck feeling his hairs even stiffer than the first brief. Something was out of the ordinary and he couldn't place it. Davenport was sounding more like a politician than the perverse mercenary he always appeared to be. Greg had expected Davenport to be insulted by a mission so simple and without some form of firefight, instead he seemed amused by it, almost satisfied.

****

Interviewing the President seemed like a relaxing period compared to the remaining part of the week. They raced from one building to another, met governors and senators, attended press conferences hosted by almost everyone who wanted to make their statement about the upcoming arms agreement. For most of the time, Kay was just a passenger, watching and listening to Steve as he drilled politicians and sweet talked secretaries. It amazed her at how everyone he talked to called him by his first name. There were no introductions and he didn't need an appointment to talk to anyone.

At nights, Kay didn't see much of Steve. After dinner he would take off in a cab and not be seen again until the next morning. She worried about him, thinking he may have a drinking problem, but Steve was always raring to go early in the morning. On the other hand, she thought, maybe he had some lady, or a few ladies, lined up each time he came to Washington, and would spend the night with them. She thought about talking to him about it, but figured it wasn't her business and he'd probably get uptight about it.

After three days of rain, dark clouds, and cold nights, the weather finally broke and sunshine became the norm. It figures, Kay thought to herself, the sun would come out the day they were leaving. They were at Dulles Airport, awaiting their afternoon flight to Acapulco. After the horrible flight from San Diego, Kay was relieved to see that the flight would land in Acapulco at five in the evening. At least she would get in at a decent hour and get a full night's sleep.

They planned to settle into the hotel that evening, take a drive that night to the site where the arms treaty would be signed, wait at the airport for the President's arrival and his usual speech. That evening they would attend the Conference banquet and ball. Sunday they would to try and interview a few of the dignitaries scheduled to attend the conference. Monday was set aside for attending all the festivities of the ceremony. Tuesday was the big day and Kay knew that meant crowded spaces and hundreds of reporters from around the world, in all facets of the media business, trying to get the best vantage point and the best coverage. It was times like these that Kay was beginning to dread. The last four days were bad enough, pushing their way through waves of reporters attending press conferences and standing outside the White House.

"So how did you enjoy our country's capital, Kay?" Steve said as he sat down next to her at the airport gate. They still had an hour before their flight, but Steve was very particular in getting to the airport early so that his luggage was checked in and, so he believed, was guaranteed to arrive at the next destination.

"It's not all the glamour and prestige I once believed it to be. In fact, it seemed somewhat chaotic."

"That's politics. The epitome of chaos in order. One hand doesn't know what the other is doing and blames everything on the other. They are so pompous and pig-headed that they fail to hear each other talking. Most of them say the same thing but argue about the other one being wrong."

"It does seem a little out of control but the country has been doing all right so far."

"Listen Kay. You have to turn off that patriotic stand for your country bit and start looking closely at what is really going on around you. This country isn't just a little out of control; it's gone over the edge. Look at the statistics. Unemployment is at an all time high. The amount of homeless is multiplying faster than rabbits. The rich are getting richer and the poor poorer. We are in a country in which a 21 year old kid, who didn't finish college, is earning three million dollars a year to sit on the sidelines sixteen weeks a year for a football team. Meanwhile, a mother with three children has to work two jobs earning barely enough to feed them because a drunk driver killed her husband. We have kids in elementary school hooked on drugs and dying in our streets from gang wars, yet we spend millions of dollars to find out why mice eat cheese. Hundreds of illegal aliens are crossing our borders every day from Mexico and Cuba and we are fighting over whether we should support their education and health, while our own children graduate without being able to read. Our government is squabbling over how much a pay raise they should get while hundreds of people a day are getting laid off. We supply aid to starving countries around the world, while ten children in our own country die each day from malnutrition."

"You make it sound like the end of the world."

"I may not be far off. At least it may be the end of America, as we know it. Japan owns half our country and most of the rest belongs to the Middle East. Our country is on the edge of fiscal and economic disaster. This country needs a big-time wake up call and signing this arms treaty does nothing but weaken us even further. Everyone thought the bombing of the World Trace Center in 2001 was going to wake up this country, but the patriotism and dedication only lasted a few years. We're even worse off now than were getting before the incident. Something's going to happen soon and America better be ready to stand up and take account of itself or we're going right down the toilet."

Kay just stared at Steve. The blood vessels on his neck were ready to bulge and his face was beat red. Like the old men standing on the boxes in Central Park, he was lecturing to no one and pointing to everyone. Kay had never seen Steve like this. In the short time she had known him he tended to be very opinionated but it always was orated in a satirical, comic sense. Now he was preaching and prophesizing, almost like the politicians he was referring to. He was becoming one of them without realizing it.

"You're beginning to sound like a politician yourself, Steve."

With that she received an icy stare. "I will never be like them. I, unlike the overfed, overpaid and under-worked gluttons in Washington, strive to make things better. I'll get the people to open their eyes and see where we are going. Americans don't want to believe their world is in peril. They want to be pampered and feel they are safe in their homes, warmed by the fire in the fireplace and sipping wine. They will soon begin to realize what's going on and hopefully it won't be too late." To Kay it felt as if Steve were staring straight into her soul. He was pointing his finger at her and the people in the airport. He took a deep breath and stood up from his seat. "Just watch and see, young lady."

With that he took off down the terminal hallway and disappeared into the men's room. As she turned she noticed several people staring in her direction.

"Too much coffee." she tried to explain as she got up and walked to the gate window. She stared out across the runways and wondered if Steve was really going over the edge. She thought about calling the office and talking to Brad Jenkins but realizing the time, she knew Brad would be in conference over the day's stories so she decided to hold off until they got into Acapulco. What really bothered here was she was beginning to wonder if Steve was right. Was the country in such disarray? She remembered all the homeless people she saw in Washington, D.C. over the last few days. The Union's office was not in town and she never had reason to go there so she didn't notice them in San Diego so much. She saw the occasional man standing at the corner with the sign "Work for Food", but the number she saw in the country's capital was alarming to her. What was it that Steve thought would happen that would send the country in fear? Why was he so hyped up about this arms agreement? She figured she would just have to wait and see.

Chapter 14

On the weekends in Southern California, when the moon is full, young lovers converge on the beaches and hills to bask in the glow and snuggle in tight embraces. Tonight was completely the opposite. There was no glimmer of a moon over the hills of Camp Pendleton, and the overcast skies made it completely void of light. It was nights like these that people who camped out began to envision the glowing eyes of predators peering out of the woods.

At first glance, Greg began to imagine the same feeling when he spotted two small soft green globes off to his left looking in his direction. Once they started to close he realized it was the faint glow of the Night Vision Goggles worn by Hank Briscoe. With Greg's ability to see and sense things in the dark, he could just make out Hank slowly working his way towards him, weaving around trees and bushes to hide himself.

"Quit skulking around Briscoe and get over here." Greg said, kneeling down behind a large tree.

"Jesus Christ, boss. I could barely make you out with these confounded things yet you knew who I was without them. I sure could use a set of them cat-eyes of yours. I hate these fucking machines." Hank whispered as he knelt down beside him.

"Don't be so impressed, Briscoe. I smelled you before I saw you. Don't wear that disgusting aftershave tomorrow or they'll have alarms off before we even land."

"Har-de-har-har boss. Maybe you should leave this job and get your own stage show in Las Vegas."

"Is everyone in position?"

"Yeah. Team one is about ready to scale to the roof. Team two is in position by the back door. Our team is standing by awaiting the signal."

"Good. As soon as team two enters the back door, we hightail it into the basement."

"Boss, how come you're here with us and not on team one?"

"The Captain has sole responsibility for team one. He wants me to make sure that their backs are covered until the pickup."

"Seems pretty shitty to me."

"Just as long as we get it done right and no one gets hurt is my concern."

"Shit, this is cake walk compared to our other assignments."

"It never pays to be careful. Now get the team ready. We go in two minutes."

As Hank crept back to his position, Greg thought about his comments. He didn't want to alarm any of the team with his sense of wariness of the mission. Something just didn't seem to fit into place and having Davenport along for the ride didn't help matters. He couldn't get over the nagging questions of why his unit was used for this operation and why all the secrecy. They had never been involved in a mission in which they weren't pre-briefed on the location or the complete details of their target made available. This was the first mission in which they were sequestered like a jury from radio, television and newspapers. He couldn't imagine why a simple mission to extract a terrorist financier was that much more sensitive than the extermination of some Third World leader or politician.

To have Davenport thrown in to lead the mission made it that much more unbearable. The team had been in Somalia for two weeks prior to the Marine landing, laying the groundwork by providing intelligence and surveillance information without him. Why was it necessary for him to be in on this mission? The worst part was the manner in which Davenport treated the mission. After the first day,

123

his concentration was not on the specifics of the operation, but the political aspects of it. After each debriefing, Davenport would expound on the necessity to rid the world of terrorists once and for all and make the streets a safe place. This was not the usual manner for a military man who had seen and contributed to death around the world, from the jungles of Vietnam, to the palaces of the Middle East. Greg expected him to be irritated from having to participate in a seemingly political operation rather than a military one. Instead he appeared to be almost at peace with it, as thought it was his last hurrah. He wondered if maybe this was Davenport's last mission and he was only involved to get one final hurrah before retiring. After one of the briefings he questioned Davenport on whether the Captain was considering retirement, but the topic was quickly brushed aside.

Putting aside his frustrations he returned to his team and looked down at his watch. In fifteen seconds, the first and second team would be entering the building. He held up his hand, fingers extended as the rest of the team looked over at him. Ten seconds later he began to pull each finger into his palm, signaling the last five seconds of countdown.

When the team reached the steps to the side entrance, Greg stopped holding up his right fist. The team clung to the building walls as if they were a part of them. Greg pointed two fingers at two of the silhouettes he could make out in the dark, pointed down the stairs and then moved his fingers in a scissor motion to tell them to proceed down and check the door. The two figures disappeared down the stairs and within seconds one reappeared at the top twirling with his right hand giving the all clear signal.

Greg twirled his right index and middle fingers in the air and then pointed them down the stairs. Without question or hesitation the remaining team members proceeded quickly down the stairs and entered the building.

Although six men rushed towards the building, not a sound, not even the slightest whisper of the wind being disturbed could be heard. While on the roof, six men entered the building and six others were slipping in the back door, the evening solitude was not broken.

Once his team was inside the basement, he held both hands up in the air and put his right index finger into his left fist and the team went immediately to work, rigging charges. Although never briefed, it was standard procedure for the team to rig explosives for a remote detonation as a precaution in case the team met resistance on the way out, as a distraction and destructive demonstration to aid in their escape.

The team had five minutes to rig the explosives and return topside to cover the first and second teams departure from the building. Within four minutes each member signaled his rig was completed and returned to the entranceway. Greg pointed to Hank with his right index finger and then made a circular motion followed by closing his fist and pulling down, the signal to take the team up and secure the area for departure.

Once he gave the signal, Greg turned and went throughout the basement, for a last minute inspection of the placement and rigging of detonators before he would depart. As he got to the last set, he noticed the toggle switch on one charge was set on automatic rather than remote and changed the setting. If it had been the real operation, Greg would never have been able to leave the basement and the teams inside would have been turned to ashes, because automatic setting immediately set the timer for sixty seconds.

Pissed off, he left the basement reminding himself to give Scott Dempsey a good ass chewing afterwards, along with a healthy reminder to the rest of the team. He wasn't going to mention it at the debrief for fear Davenport would lose his cool and make them do it again, delay the mission, or leave Dempsey behind. Neither one of the choices was acceptable to Greg, especially having to complete the mission with one less person.

When he reached the top of the stairs, he glanced at his watch. Four minutes and thirty seconds had passed since they started. He moved along the wall and turned the corner to the back of the house and watched as the second team departed. Ten seconds later, the first team, led by Davenport proceeded out the back door. The second man of the first team was the team's biggest, Peter Coleman, nicknamed Conan, because of his enormous size and strength. At six foot four, he could have been a pro-football defensive lineman, harassing quarterbacks instead of risking his life, but he couldn't cut the grade at Nebraska University and had to quit school. Fortunately for the team, he joined the Navy and was recruited into the team. Coleman was carrying a large sack over his shoulder like it was a rag-doll, however it had been filled with sand and rocks to match the expected weight of a 250-pound man. The rest of the team followed him out, covering his back and once they were fifty yards from the building the third team proceeded into the woods behind them.

Inside the woods, the teams regrouped. Greg's team was to take up the rear and transport the terrorist, who they recently learned was going by the name of Estoban. The first two teams would clear the area ahead to the beach, which was supposed to only be two miles from the house. If resistance was met by any of the forward teams, two alternate routes were established with back-up pickup locations along the beach, two miles apart, one to the south and one to the north. If the first team met resistance, the second team would lead the rest to the northern pick-up. If both of the forward teams met resistance, the third team would proceed alone to the south pick-up. Once at the beach, an infrared signal indicating their location would be sent out from the beach to the recover team sitting a half-mile off the beach.

Instead of proceeding farther into the woods, the teams turned and headed back towards the teams headquarters on a 2-mile path laid out by Davenport. From the minute the teams proceeded to enter the area within 100 yards of the building until they reached the headquarters, no sounds were uttered. Although the members of the team would act like clowns and criminals every day, during any mission or rehearsals it was strictly business. Unfortunately for Greg he knew that the moment they entered the headquarters they would be back to normal and wish he could keep them outside for a while longer.

****

Kay expected to find Acapulco with run down buildings, cheap hotels, beat up cars with the chassis lowered as far as possible, and street vendors marauding the car every time it stopped, just like Tijuana, Mexico, which she had visited numerous times while living in San Diego. When they left the airport and drove to the hotel she was surprised but pleased to find lavish hotels and expensive cars. The street vendors were still present but not in such large quantities as she experienced in Tijuana.

When they got to the hotel, a letter was waiting for Steve at the hotel. He read it while they checked in and then informed her that he had to make some calls and that she was free for the day and could use the time to sleep in and see the sights. Spending the remainder of the day walking around, Kay picked up some small souvenirs and post cards for family and co-workers.

By nine that evening, Kay had drifted off to a deep sleep while reading one of her favorite romance novels. At seven the next morning the eyes remained closed, but instead of her body still lying in the bed, she was submerged in a steaming hot bath, filled with bubbles provided by the small bottle that lay empty on the bathroom floor.

Lying there content and at ease, she reminisced about the past week. The excitement about being given the opportunity to cover this story, the exhausting plane trip to Washington followed by an endless day with little sleep, the discussions with numerous politicians that didn't seem to know which way was up, the enjoyable interview with the President along with the parties and press conferences that closed each day. The most disturbing part of the trip was the final days with Steve. His demeanor had shifted dramatically and he was more outspoken and pessimistic about the country's future and the people that ran it than during the first few days. The episode in the airport returned to her and she recalled his sudden outburst or rage, the peak of a building tension, which finally burst through the core. Fortunately, he had calmed down during the flight, spending it asleep as he did during their flight to Washington. While they drove to the hotel he was friendly and peaceful, as if the previous events hadn't occurred. Once he opened the letter at the hotel, however, he became preoccupied and she never saw him again that night after they checked into their rooms.

Clearing her thoughts, she started to recall the book she was reading the night before, of how the main character, an independent and successful female attorney, had met a man on one of her business trips. The man was the usual dark and handsome type that are only seen on the covers of romance novels and blue-jean advertisements. Recalling the previous nights chapters, her mind began to dream about the powerful love scene on a hotel patio.

Slowly Kay's hands slid down her neck and over her breasts. With the middle finger of each hand she drew circles around her nipples that became erect at the sensitive touch mixed with the steaming bath. She pinched each nipple between her thumbs and index fingers, then held her breasts in her hands and pushed them together, letting out a slight gasp. While her left hand remained on her left breast, her right hand slowly caressed her stomach on its way down. Her legs parted allowing her hand to slide between her thighs as she slowly began to caress herself. As she moved her hand, her head began to sway back and forth and her mouth opened slightly. Leaving her breast, her left hand rose to her face and she slid her index finger into her mouth, sucking on it as it slowly retreated. In a short time, the pace of her right hand increased, as did her left index finger, as it moved in and out of her mouth. When the pace of her right hand began to move even quicker she finally had to grab hold of the edge of the bathtub with her left hand. More and more gasps sprang from her lips and her whole body splashed in the hot tub, sending waves of water onto the bathroom floor, as she envisioned the man from the novel making love to her on a balcony overlooking the people below.

After almost two minutes of this pace, her left hand took one final flex on the tub and the arm stiffened while a long low guttural moan drained out of her mouth before all motion stopped. Her body lay there limp for several minutes, her eyes rolled in the back of her head. As her eyes slowly began to open, glossy and distant, she tried to recall how long it had been since she had made love to a man. This was not a normal occurrence for her but the hot water and the previous nights story had awakened the need within her she had shelved for so long. She wondered if she would ever find that man of her dreams that would unlock those things inside her she kept hidden over the years. Little did she know that her question would soon be answered but the circumstances would not be one in her dreams.

****

Sitting behind the large oak desk piled with papers, one wouldn't believe that this office was thirty thousand feet in the air aboard Air Force One. A converted Boeing 747; the insides had been gutted and compartmentalized to accommodate the President and his staff. It almost appeared that the office onboard the plane was large than the Oval Office. At least the furniture was more comfortable. On the right side of the plane was a brown leather couch that provided more cushion than the one at the White House. On the other side of the plane, two brown plush leather chairs were set for discussions and visitors.

The President reached over to the intercom and pushed the button and within seconds the Chief of Staff arrived.

"Tom, I've made a few amendments to the speech for Tuesday. See that Andy gets these fixed." the President said as he handed the brown folder across his desk.

"No problem, sir. Anything else?" he said reaching across the desk.

"I want to go over this new Welfare Bill with you that Congress just dreamed up, but first I'd like an update on what the Vice President is up to while I'm gone." The President leaned back and propped his feet up on the desk.

Tom sat down in one of the leather chairs in order to maintain eye contact. Sitting in the couch meant he would be looking only at the bottom of the President's shoes and he had to see the expression in a persons face to understand the true meaning of their discussion.

"Well, while you are in Acapulco, he'll be taking a trip to Vermont to that Wildlife Protection Agency festival that you were supposed to attend. He is scheduled to return Monday night for several visitors to the White House on Tuesday, such as the winner of this year's national spelling contest and the leaders of the United Auto Workers from around the country. Since he's been involved with them over the years it's the perfect opportunity to keep them on our side by having them visit the White House and get their pictures taken with him."

"Has he been fully briefed on all the major issues? He's been away for over a month now and is probably not up to speed with the latest developments."

"I personally updated him on all the issues Friday. Each of the agencies will be briefing him today on their issues so he'll be fully in the picture."

The President was always pleased on how Tom kept a hold of the full picture. He never missed a detail and was always one step ahead of everyone else. The President wondered how much longer it would be before Tom Alexander would be running for President himself and then assumed Tom was enjoying the power the position gave him without him having to be in the limelight. The Chief of Staff avoided media coverage as much as everyone avoids someone with the flu. It was clear that Tom wanted to control the government without having to succumb to the indelicacies of actually running for office.

Tom wasn't the type to cuddle up to babies and mothers or lower his esteem by eating a greasy burger in a diner with some factory workers just to win some votes. With Tom it was either you listened to what he had to say or you didn't. If you didn't then the hell with you and get back to the end of the line. Politicians were a strange breed, the President thought. They lessen themselves, lie to themselves, and do stupid things to please the voters. A smile came to his face as he reminded himself that he was a politician also.

"What so funny, Mr. President?" Tom asked noticing the grin.

"Nothing, something funny just came to my mind. Now, about that new Welfare Bill."

While they talked, the President kept wondering about his Chief of Staff. He was like the company's foreman who made everything work and got the job done, but it was the Manager of the plant that got all the credit and limelight as well as the bad. While the manager sat back in his office, watching all the workers while flirting with the secretary, the foreman was down on the floor, getting dirty with the rest of the workers, repairing equipment that went awry, waking up the lazy employee that got drunk the night before, and evaluating the product at each stage of its construction. Whenever the Manager had to give a briefing to one of the company executives, he would call in the Foreman and ask him about the product, the employees, the production figures and other pertinent questions so that he would come off knowledgeable in the sight of his superiors. When the Manager had a good Foreman, the manager kept getting pay raises and was seen positively in the light of his peers. Just like the President, getting all the knowledge from a good Chief of Staff so that he looked good in the public eye and kept atop the rest of the politicians and bureaucrats in Washington.

The President wondered where this type of person eventually ended up. Would he be happy being a Chief of Staff for the rest of his life? Where else on earth would he have the powers he enjoyed now?

It wouldn't be long before he got the answers to those questions and found out just how wrong he was about him.

.

Chapter 15

Amidst the darkness a low guttural hum barely broke the silence of the night. Not visible to the naked eye were the infrared lights along the makeshift runway and inside the aircraft's cabin. With the aid of night vision goggles, the fat whale-like appearance of the C-130 sitting amidst the deserted field of Camp Pendleton was still difficult to see. Engineered with specially designed engines to quiet the sound, the aircraft landed undetected in the backlands of the Marine Base to pick up its late night passengers.

Greg walked over to Captain Davenport, respectfully but grudgingly saluting.

"We're ready to board, sir. All the gear is aboard."

Davenport inched up the left sleeve of his ninja-style black uniform to gaze at his watch. "Twenty-one fifty-five, right on schedule." Greg glanced at his watch to confirm the time. "Get the men aboard and let's get this show on the road."

Greg returned to the men huddled to the right of the aircraft and with his right index finger pointing to the sky and circling twice, motioned them to board the aircraft. Without hesitation they rose from their hunched positions and scrambled aboard the aircraft. After every man was aboard Greg lifted himself into the hatch and peered back. Even in the darkness he could make out Captain Davenport momentarily glancing down at the ground as if in prayer before he made his way to the aircraft. Once Davenport was aboard, Greg closed the hatch and put on the helmet and adjusted the mouthpiece.

"We're ready to roll." He said into the microphone. With scarcely a whisper, the engines revved up and the team could feel the forward momentum as the aircraft sped along the matted-down field towards take-off speed. Greg glanced at the men sitting along the sides of the aircraft and had to laugh as some were taking the time to fasten their safety belts. Even the bravest of men still had a fear of flying. It wasn't long before the nose of the aircraft begrudgingly lifted off the ground and began their ascent and southerly flight.

Once the aircraft leveled off at thirty thousand feet, Captain Davenport undid his safety belt and proceeded forward into the pilot's cabin. The rest of the team attempted to find comfort in the belly of the steel whale, some checking their gear for the umpteenth time, some leaning back and catching a few hours sleep, while others stared off into space, thinking within themselves, trying to quench the natural human tendency to let the unknowing cloud their judgment, instilling doubt and eventually fear.

As the rest of the team went about their normal pre-mission flight traditions, Greg went over the next twenty-four hours. Correlating the time between take off and the time required for insertion, Greg estimated that the plane would have to be in the air for four and a half hours. Adjusting for the aircrafts speed, Greg tried to pinpoint the location of the mission. The flight didn't seem long enough to him to be far enough into Central America to areas such as Columbia to conduct an anti-drug lord mission. A Boeing 747 could barely make it inside the borders of Central America at best, and this beast didn't have nearly the flight speed, even if it was barely loaded.

Several other things continued to nag at Greg as well. Why all the secrecy of the destination? Why the isolation from television and newspapers? Why did the aircraft fly onto a makeshift runway in Camp Pendleton instead of the normal boarding at Mirimar Air Base? The most troubling of all was Captain Davenport's disposition throughout the whole affair. Recalling earlier missions that Greg had the displeasure of serving on with him, the Captain was always outspoken, obnoxious, overbearing and self-centered. Over the past week, Davenport was quiet and remained locked in his quarters except for the briefings and training. Even during mealtime, Davenport ate meals in his quarters. Only twice during the week did Davenport call Greg into his office to discuss some minute details while shrugging off Greg's questions concerning the mission.

When Greg questioned him on several points of the mission, Davenport would respond with a 'Work out the little details yourself, Commander' or 'we'll cover that later'. Unfortunately later never came. During previous missions, Davenport would oversee every minute detail, ensuring that no one 'slipped up'. Greg wasn't sure if Davenport was just getting too old for this game or simply had no interest in it. Especially disconcerting was the inattention given to the withdrawal procedures. Normally, this aspect was given a high priority. It was as if Davenport thought a limousine would pick him up just outside the gate of the villa and take him home. There were no contingency plans made in case the boat didn't show at the beach. Contingency plans were an integral part of every mission and Davenport said there was no need for them. Resistance would be light if any and the boat would be there and then ramble on about some inane aspect of the mission.

While Greg wrestled with his questions, Davenport returned from the cockpit and began handing out slips of paper. On two laminated sheets were charts. One sheet contained the chart outlining their insertion point to the villa, the other from the villa to the beach. As well as Greg could see, there were no other residences within the areas, just woods and the villa. As he glanced over the chart something seemed missing. Jungle, there wasn't any jungle Greg thought to himself. If they were going into Columbia or another Central American country, he expected to see some form of jungle instead of woods. The hairs on the back of Greg's neck stiffened and he could feel an uneasy twinge crawl up his spine. Had he watched too many Hollywood movies to think all of Central America was in the jungle? He remembered Panama and the jungle that seemed to infest the entire territory.

After Davenport finished handing out the maps, he sat down by himself towards the front of the cabin. Instead of his usual pompous aura, he seemed withdrawn, staring off into space as if he was in some faraway paradise soaking up sun. From that point on until just before they departed the aircraft, he remained motionless, eyes focused on a point outside the aircraft. The rest of the team either slept or kidded amongst themselves like school athletes on their way to a sporting function. No one talked about the mission; they believed it brought bad luck.

Throughout the flight, though, Greg continued to question and evaluate. Nothing seemed to fit and he couldn't shake the haunting feeling that something wasn't right. He couldn't pin it down to one particular thing. Whatever it was, Greg knew he would have to be extra careful and keep a keen eye out to protect the team as well as himself.

****

Inside the ballroom, the lavishly dressed ensemble of diplomats and dignitaries danced, drank and mingled. The pomp and circumstance at the airport for each arrival had died, the flamboyant and dull speeches had subsided, the lavish dinner was consumed and now it was time to relax. The Mayor of Acapulco had outdone himself in preparing the gala. Even while his country continued to struggle with an economy that was always on the brink of destruction the gala was equal to any diplomatic reception before it, champagne flowing, the finest food and a small band. Here was the moment when diplomats and politicians almost became human beings. Here they could unwind and speak their minds without the throngs of reporters and lobbyists.

Only a select few reporters were lucky enough to receive invitations to the after dinner party. Surprising Kay the night before, Steve presented one of those invitations to her. Expecting some sign of celebration he was amazed to see the look of dismay on her face. Not prepared for any type of function and packing as lightly as possible she hadn't brought any formal dresses and wouldn't forgive Steve for not giving her some early heads-up. In an unusual act for her, she awoke early the next morning and set out for the stores as soon as they opened. In two hours she finally found a gown using up a large chunk of the available credit on her VISA card. When she returned to the hotel, she immediately gave the bill to Steve and told him the paper had to pay for it. For the rest of the day she prepared herself, spending the afternoon in the hotel beauty salon getting her hair done and foregoing the day's events at the airport, locking herself in the hotel room to complete the renovation. When it was time to leave, she met Steve draped in an overcoat, hiding what lie underneath.

The moment they arrived at the Mayor's house, she took off her overcoat and handed it over to the servant at the door. Steve's mouth opened wide. Kay stood there adorned in an elaborate white backless gown. Clinging gingerly from straps over her shoulders, Steve's imagination ran wild as he imagined the body that lay beneath. Normally seeing her in jeans and safari jacket or a women's business suit, he wasn't prepared for this. She had spent the afternoon in the hotel beauty salon to get her hair done. Foregoing the day's events at the airport she locked herself in the hotel room to complete the renovation. Not one for women with mounds of make-up, he noticed that Kay used very little and of what she did use only faintly highlighted her natural beauty.

"Close your mouth, Steve, you look like a baboon." Kay said as she slid her hands down her sides to smooth out the gown.

"Excuse me, my name is Steve Puller, have we met."

137

"Amelia Airhead, know cut the shit and get me a drink. Champagne or a gin and tonic."

"I am really impressed, Kay. You look fantastic. I think you overdid it though with the gown. With all these horny diplomats here without their wives, you'll be busy slapping away a few hands."

"That's why I came with you Steve. You can be my Knight in Shining Armor and save me from these vicious dragons."

They walked into the ballroom and stood there absorbing the atmosphere. The smell of money and power infested the room. Servants busily scampered around the room carrying trays of drinks and hors d'oeuvres. Men in tuxedos and women in long-flowing gowns maneuvered around the room to meet the influential. In one corner the band played some soft music that was barely audible over the voices. Dark skinned women in gowns accompanied many of the men, many of them half the age of the dignitaries. Professional women were Kay's guess, serving the wishes of their countries President to attend to their every desire, no less.

"I was hoping I would get the opportunity to see you again, but didn't expect it on this occasion. You look extremely ravishing tonight, Miss Cross."

Turning, Kay was pleased as well as surprised to see the President standing at the bottom of the steps holding out his upward turned hand. Glancing over at Steve, she was amused to see the bitterness and disappointment in his face.

"Thank you very much, Mr. President." She said, placing her hand in his and walking down the stairs.

"You'll really hurt my feelings if you don't start calling me John. This is a festive evening and there's no room for such formalities."

"I'm sorry, John. I'm not used to such important gatherings or being in the midst of so many important people. This is my associate and mentor, Mr. Steve Puller from the San Diego Union."

"Sir." was all Steve said, shaking hands while looking elsewhere.

"Steve Puller. I believe I've read some of your articles. You don't fancy politicians much, do you?"

"I can think of better professions." Steve replied, his attention drawn.

"It's alright, Mr. Puller, you're not the only one who thinks poorly of us."

Kay noticed that the President didn't request Steve to call him by his first name and she could feel the electricity building.

"If you don't mind, Steve, I'm going to steal Kay for a while. Why don't you enjoy the delicious appetizers by the far wall, the shrimp is excellent."

Answering with a grunt and questioning eye, Steve disappeared amidst the crowd.

"I hope Mr. Puller's views on politicians aren't shared by you, Kay." the President said as the walked along.

"I'm still open-minded, Mr. Pres...I mean, John. He's been covering Washington for a lot of years and this is only my first time. It will take me a little more time and a few more visits to the capital to develop such a deep uneasiness towards politicians and their business."

The President grinned. As they walked he nodded his head or shook hands with people from the crowd, introducing Kay to some of them. After each one, he would share some humorous bit of trivia on each one that made Kay laugh.

"In hopes of not being too forward, I wonder if you wouldn't mind cheering up an old man and have the pleasure of a dance with me."

"I would be delighted, although I must warn you, I'm not well practiced on the dance floor."

139

"I find it hard to believe that you aren't the envy of every man in San Diego." he said as he led her out to the dance floor. The band played a version of a Phil Collins song.

"Unfortunately I don't take the time to get out much."

"Take a bit of advice from someone who's been there, you can't spend the early part of your life chasing after the golden ring without taking some time off. Before you know it, the best part of your life is gone and you'll wonder where it went."

"I seem to be hearing that type of advice a lot lately."

"Well, maybe it's time you listened. Don't become another one of those casualties of the baby boom era, fighting to get to the top and find yourself there all alone. You seem to have the brains and you certainly have the looks to get there."

"I don't plan on getting there on my looks, sir." she said taken back slightly by the chauvinistic remark.

"I didn't mean that in a bad way. I meant you carry yourself well and that gets noticed. What I mean is that if you want true happiness when you get to wherever it is you want to be, save some time for yourself and enjoy. If you don't your only choices will be divorcees and dirty old men like myself."

"I wouldn't say that someone like yourself is a bad choice."

"I'm used goods young lady. You need someone fresh and alive who can take you places and share in your dreams."

"Right now there's no place I want to go and my dreams don't involve a man right now." Kay said smiling inside remembering the hot bath she had the day before. "Besides, I don't think I'll meet any of them tonight."

"Sometimes I dread these parties, but seeing you here has made it much more enjoyable."

"Mr. President, if I didn't know any better, that sounds like a come-on line." She said, fanning herself with her right hand, imitating that she was feeling hot like a southern belle on a hot August night.

"One can never tell." The President said with a smile. "It's just nice to be able to come to one of these parties and not have to talk politics. Of course, if a photographer captured us at this moment, there would be wild stories spreading across every supermarket tabloid tomorrow."

Kay began to look around the room to spot anyone with a camera.

"Don't worry, cameras are not allowed in here and although you weren't aware of it, the entranceway has a metal detector and X-ray that checks everyone when they walk in.

"You mean they could see through my gown?"

"Just looking for metallic objects, nothing obscene. With this much brass in one place, special precautions have to be taken."

"Doesn't all this Secret Service protection bother you?"

"It takes away a lot of the privacy most people enjoy, but it's a small price to pay to try and help this country, as well as the world, to get better."

The music stopped and they both walked over to a table and sat down.

"Listen to me, I'm beginning to sound like a politician again." The President said as he waved to a waiter carrying a tray of champagne.

"I'm curious though. We see it in the movies all the time, but is it really necessary to have armed guards at your side everywhere. Look at tonight. You're not surrounded by any guards." Kay said waving her hand as if circling the room.

"It may not appear that way to you but they are there. Besides, this palace has it's own special security forces. With all these dignitaries in one place you have to provide the security while allowing them the comfort of feeling free of it."

The waiter delivered two glasses of champagne and wandered off towards another table in which several men dressed in flowing white robes attempted to get his attention.

"Take that waiter for instance. He's probably one of the security personnel armed to the teeth under that outfit."

"Will we ever be free of terrorists and crazed activists?"

"My dear, the terrorist problem as we have known it is pretty much a thing of the past. The real concerns are the assassins and mercenaries that will kill anything for the right price. Lee Harvey Oswald wasn't a terrorist or anyone else who has attempted to assassinate the president. Those involved in the Oklahoma City bombing weren't terrorists, just someone upset with the system. We know terrorists as someone who attempts to create fear and make us unsure of what we are doing. Assassins are not preoccupied with those type of things. Assassins are just plain greedy or have mental problems. It's unclear what goes on in the mind of an assassin or the things that drive him, be they political or otherwise. The big key is money and who is going to pay them and why."

"You mean like the theory that Oswald was a dupe for the Russians because they couldn't handle President Kennedy's strength?"

"There are a lot of unanswered questions behind a lot of events in history. Think about this for a minute. Consider what we are about to do here in the next few days. Nations from around the world are signing an agreement to abolish weapons that threaten each other. Think again of what that will do to several big companies who manufacture these weapons and how those in charge will see it as a direct attack on them. They don't look at what options are open to them; only that money has continuously flowed into their pockets when things are left alone. The men that run these companies are very powerful and influential, especially with many politicians. They will not lie down easily if they feel their power is being stripped away. There are many ways they could have stopped this from happening. Anyone of these men in this room could have been assassinated or had families threatened or whatever to stop them. Accidental deaths are a common occurrence around the world and many of the countries represented here were established on terror and murder. Consider the assassination of the Presidential candidate in Mexico, favored to win the election. As the investigation digs deeper, there are indications of government involvement. I could name several other such circumstances but this is not the time. I'm sorry to carry on but I don't want you to think that everyone in America is strongly behind this deal. There are many at home who would just as soon see me replaced in order to maintain the status quo. Some won't want to wait until the next election."

Kay sat in disbelief at what she was hearing. To her, these were only stories that you saw in the theater. Government corruption, political assassinations, Mafia style murders, all these were just wild imaginations of novel writers and worn out reporters trying to make a story. Now the President of the United States was telling her that these were all realities of the world. Was she that naive to think that ours was a perfect world in which the best man won the election. Was she gullible enough to believe that the dirt and slander printed on the pages were a wild story, created by one man, instead of hints or clues planted by a corporation or organization to get someone to think twice?

"Do you really think that someone would go as far as murdering their country's leader just to maintain their business? It sounds a little too Hollywood for me."

"Kay, as a reporter you must know that somehow stories slip out about someone's past or their present involvements. Where do you think they come from? Are reporters really good enough or have the resources and time to find out these things? Do you think your editor would give you the time needed to conduct extensive research on someone just to find out he had a relationship with some girl back in college and got her pregnant? Who do you think the undisclosed sources are? Do you really think Oswald had enough reason as an ordinary citizen to assassinate the President and think he would get away with it? Why was he murdered before he could stand trial? How could he have planned so far in advance to know Kennedy would be coming down that street and the building empty on that particular day? Those details weren't known until just days prior. You also have to ask yourself how does someone become so powerful to gain control of big business? Do you really think they get there because they are nice guys and have earned it? Each of them has fought and scratched their way to the top by stabbing people in the back, stealing deals from others and influencing others into agreements. When you get used to that way of life it becomes natural. To stay on top you have to be just as vicious and conniving. These type of people hate to lose and will stop at nothing to win."

"But once the agreement is signed they've lost."

"Listen, this isn't the type of conversation I intended to have with you tonight. How about we go up for another dance and change the subject." the President stood up and placed his hand out.

Kay didn't want to end the conversation but wasn't about to say no to the President. She took his hand and they proceeded out to the dance floor amid several other dignitaries. As they danced the President chatted about the memories of his days in Montana but Kay couldn't shake the recent conversation from her mind. Throughout her life she believed that although big businessmen she had met through her family were pig-headed and unfriendly she couldn't imagine them considering murder or any other form of violence to get ahead. She suddenly recalled but couldn't remember the name of the movie with Robert Redford as a book reader discovering the deaths of his co-workers, being chased by unknown assailants as he uncovered a deep political corruption scheme. To her it was just entertainment, the imagination of a gifted writer. Was it possible that things like this did occur without anyone knowing? Who was Deep Throat and why did he talk to the Washington Post (another Robert Redford movie she remembered) without letting anyone know his identity?

The rest of the night she danced and talked with the President but their initial conversation was never brought up again. When the President finally said goodbye, she couldn't help but look at him in a different way, as if he were a marked target. She felt sorry in a way for the man she had come to respect in such a short time. She wondered if she would ever get the chance to talk with him again and finish the discussion.

Chapter 16

For the first time since he handed out the laminated charts, Davenport rose from his seat and walked into the cockpit. Greg glanced down at his watch, 0215, which meant they would be commencing their insertion in the next 15 minutes. As he glanced around the compartment, the men were quietly conducting last minute checks on their gear, except for Conan, who always managed to sleep the entire flight during a mission no matter what type of aircraft.

A few minutes later, Davenport returned and put his headset back on.

"We reach the drop zone in seven minutes." Davenport indicated looking directly into Greg's eyes.

"Seven minutes, aye." Greg acknowledged. With two clicks of his right hand, he got the attention of the rest of the team except for Conan, still asleep. He pointed to Briscoe and motioned with his right thumb towards Conan. Briscoe put a left elbow into Conan's arm, barely moving the massive pile of muscle. Eerily the only movement was the opening of the eyes while the rest of his body remained still. Once he had everyone's attention he held up six fingers to indicate the time remaining until drop. Everyone on the team acknowledged with a thumbs up signal and began putting their gear in order in preparation.

At the three-minute point the yellow light over the compartment door lit indicating time to prepare for departure. Greg clicked twice again and held up three fingers and then motioned with his index finger rising into the air for everyone to get out of their seats and into position. Tom Franklin sitting on the other side of the door opened the door to the blackness of the night sky. The evening was overcast which meant no glow from the stars or the moon. Very few lights were on in the dense villages

146

below. In such darkness, a man wasn't sure if he was going up or down with no horizon to guide from. Hidden in the black void was the unfamiliarity of the ground below, never visible until just before landing on it, which meant the body had to be alert throughout the jump to hit and roll.

Greg pointed to his eyes and everyone conducted a buddy check on the man in front of him to make sure the gear was strapped down properly. Greg turned and checked out the gear of Davenport who seemed preoccupied and distant, not really acknowledging Greg's presence.

Once completed the time seemed to go by slowly waiting for the green light. In what seemed like minutes but only lasted 25 seconds, the light changed green and Greg pushed the first man through the opening. In a matter of 20 seconds, the entire team of 20 had departed the airplane and it began its slow turn to head back to the North. Jumping at 30,000 feet allowed the aircraft to remain undetected to anyone on the ground, but it also allowed the team time to adjust their decent to keep the team relatively together. At the 2,000-foot mark everyone deployed his chute. At that height the decent was slowed just enough to allow a sensible landing without serious injury but didn't leave them defenseless and open for discovery for a long period of time.

Gazing around the group, Greg checked to see that everyone's chute had opened. He counted out 19 before he looked at his parachute to ensure it was fully open. In less than a minute they were on the ground. Once they touched ground, three team members dug a hole for everyone to stash the parachutes and cover them.

Within five minutes of departing the plane, the team was gathered together and into their three-mile trek. As they maneuvered through the woods, Greg still couldn't understand why, if they were in Central America, they were walking through woods instead of jungle. The air was cool and a slight breeze was blowing, which was not the climate for growing drugs of any kind. It suddenly dawned on him that maybe the reason for all the secrecy was the fact that Estoban was on a holiday excursion and they weren't in Central America after all. That would explain the short flight and terrain. Thinking to himself he began to understand the sensitivity of the mission if in fact they were in Mexico instead of Central America to extradite a key terrorist figure that was linked to the drug cartels. If the Mexican government ever got wind of such a mission, the political downfall would be disastrous, especially when their government is already in turmoil with their economical problems. It still didn't explain why it was kept secret from the team. It would have been more beneficial to let them know where they were going so they could take the necessary precautions for just such a mission. A firefight would be avoided at all costs to risk later publicity. With the team thinking they were in Central America, a firefight would not be as critical and a few extra lives taken would mean nothing, especially if they didn't think they were Columbian police or military.

With this new possibility rummaging in Greg's head, he would make decisions based on them being in Mexico vice Central America. He would be unable to verify their location with Davenport since communications were limited to hand signals from the moment they left the airplane, so he decided to wait until reached the safety of the submarine before letting off some of that steam built up inside over the last week on Davenport.

Taking the precautious route to remain undetected, it took the team 30 minutes to cover the three miles to the exterior of the villa's walls. That still left one hour to scale the eight-foot wall, cross through the woods, across the pond, enter the house, eliminate the guards and grab Estoban. Four ropes with anchors at the end were tossed over the wall and within one minute the entire team was on top of the wall. The first four men to reach the top were able to scan the woods for movement with the aid of their night scopes. Giving the all-clear signal, the team leaped to the ground and cautiously moved through the woods to the edge of the open terrain. Greg pointed to the four snipers on the team, then pointed at his eyes and put his hands together by the edge of his head as if sleeping. The snipers began to search the grounds for the Doberman Pinchers and once spotted, were tranquilized quickly and silently. Greg always found it ironic that a team that didn't hesitate to kill a man, took the time and humanity to tranquilize animals. It was determined long ago that the animals were not the enemy and not accountable for their actions. Greg looked at his watch, 0325, five minutes ahead of schedule but the hardest part was yet to come.

****

"You and the President seemed to be getting rather chummy." Steve remarked with a disturbing tone as they left the palace.

Ignoring his comment, Kay pulled her coat tighter to protect herself from the cool wind that whistled in the night air. The party seemed to go on all night and when she finally looked at her watch it was three in the morning and many of the guests were still drinking and talking. Fortunately for her and the rest of the guests, the first events of the day were not scheduled until eleven o'clock. At least she'd be able to get some sleep before a tedious day of speeches and formal proceedings. After the President left, she spent the rest of the evening enjoying some dances and light conversations with some of the other diplomats while trying not to sound like a reporter.

"So what did you and lover boy have to talk about?" Steve remarked again after they got into their car and began to drive off.

"Nothing special" she lied. "We just talked about some of his boyhood memories and his family. He misses them and wanted to spend a little time dancing to get away from all the diplomatic hoop-tee-doo."

"Well if you ask me it didn't look good?"

"No ones asking you, Steve!" Kay responded upset with the tone of the conversation.

"Listen kid, I..." Steve was cut short by a finger pointing in his nose.

"I'm not your kid. I'm here as an associate reporter, not your daughter. Don't be giving me advice on who I should be talking to or what I can be doing with them. If I decide to dance with the President of the United States or anyone else it is none of your concern."

"Whoa. Calm down Kay. I was just going to mention that, uh, it didn't look good for the President. You should know that, uh, politicians and reporters are not a compatible equation."

The remark didn't seem very sincere to Kay. It appeared he was backtracking to cover himself.

"Let's be honest with each other Steve. I find your approach to politics and politicians in general abhorring. I'm sure there are a few bad apples in the bunch but there are more than enough of them who are really try to do their job in the best way they know how. I can't understand your disgust with them, especially the President. He's a sincere, honest man who thinks this is the best way to go for his country and there are a lot of people who agree with him, including me. But with all that aside, we are reporters. We are supposed to be indifferent and just report the facts. Everything you've preached to me over the past week is based on here-say and innuendos. You have yet to shed one piece of evidence that indicates the world will be worse off with this agreement. I'm sure some will be upset with it, but if you recall democracy is based upon the wishes of the majority, not the richest."

"Feel better now that you have that off your chest?" Steve said taking a right on a deserted road that seemed to stretch for miles. "Now let me tell you something. I've been in this business covering politics since you were in grade school. Yeah, I've seen some good politicians come and go, but the majority rules business is a load of crap. Spend some time in the hallways of Congress someday. Sit at the bar of some of the fanciest restaurants there and keep an eye on who comes in and out. You need a wake up call young lady. The majority doesn't rule, it's whoever's willing to spend the most money to convince, or should I say contribute to a politician's fund in order to get them to share their point of view. When was the last time your Congressman asked you how you felt on an issue? Your congressman is being wined and dined by representatives from every major company across the states. His campaign funds are getting fatter from contributions from some of these major companies as long as he's willing to support them. Don't you ever wonder how some of these people get into office when their issues are so contradictory to yours and most of the people you know? It's because he's got the most money in his funds to get on T.V., put ads in the papers, visit all the key points in the state to be seen. If you ask most of the voters, they couldn't tell you where the person they voted for stood on any issue. Why did they vote for him then? Because he's the name they saw the most on TV or heard about. So don't tell me you know all about politics just because you danced with the President. They got where they are because they have a way of hypnotizing people and showing how vulnerable they are while stealing you from behind. Don't fall into their trap so easily sweetheart. Step back a few paces and really look at things before you start spouting off."

Unable to reply, Kay stared out the car window at the blackness of the night. She couldn't get over the similar comments the President made about big business and their quest for power. As they drove along, she noticed there were no streetlights and the headlights did very little to give someone a good view of the road. The area seemed unfamiliar to her and although she couldn't make anything out in the darkness, it didn't appear like the route they took to the palace.

"Steve, is this the way we came?"

"No, I didn't want to get caught up in the traffic of everyone returning to their hotel from the party. This road will get us back faster anyway."

"How can there be any traffic at three-thirty in the morning?" It didn't seem reasonable to Kay that there would be that much of a traffic jam from a few people leaving the party.

"If you recall the Arab delegation had left a few minutes before us. The Arabs are very keen on security so their convoy consists of eight cars with 10 motorcycles travelling well under the speed limit. They won't let anyone pass and you can't get within a half mile of the convoy. I for one don't want to crawl my way back to the hotel."

"Sorry, I didn't realize." Accepting the excuse, Kay closed her eyes and leaned her head back on the chair when the car began to vibrate excessively.

"What the hell is that?" she asked looking at smoke billowing out of the front hood.

"I don't know. I better pull over and take a look." Steve steered the car to the side of the road and pulled it to a stop. "Open the glove compartment and see if there is a flashlight in there."

Opening the glove compartment stacks of paper erupted from its hold along with a small pocket light.

"I'm afraid that's all there is."

"It will have to do. Stay here while I check it out." Steve said, unlatching the hood from inside the car, opening the car door and moving to the front. There was no argument from Kay. Better to stay inside a warm car than stand out in the blowing cool wind at three-thirty in the morning.

Steve opened the hood and a billow of smoke came out as if a volcano had just erupted. The light of the pen-light moved around the front of the engine for several minutes before Steve appeared at Kay's door. She rolled down the window.

"It appears we blew a hose. I'm going to call Tony on the cellular to get a hold of the rental company and have him come out here and pick us up. I'm afraid we are going to be here for a while."

"How long is a while?"

"I figure at least ninety minutes. It will take me a while to get Tony, then he has to get a hold of the rental company and it's at least a half-hour drive out here to find us. You might as well crawl into the back seat and get some shut-eye."

"I think I'll just lean the chair back and sleep here." Kay said. As she leaned the car seat back she thought to herself, another perfect ending to a perfect evening. Unknown to her the ending was far from reaching her.

****

It ended up only taking 45 minutes to get over the wall, through the woods and across the small pond. During the crossing of the pond, one of the team almost drowned, finding a sudden drop off. Fortunately, there wasn't a sole in the back of the house, mainly due to the guard going inside for a cup of coffee to remain awake. The dogs would be asleep for another two hours, which wouldn't matter much since the team would be heading for the beach in another half hour.

At the moment they had left the security of the woods, Greg had an itchy feeling that someone was watching.

Before leaving the woods, he conducted a thorough scan of the back of the house and surrounding areas and discovered nothing, yet he couldn't escape the nagging feeling that something wasn't right. In the complete darkness, he knew that the team was undetectable, even with night detection devices, and considered his uneasiness was due to over anxiety and uneasiness with having Davenport around. During any mission, Greg always considered the worst-case scenario and was extremely careful. However, this time his sense of foreboding was unusually strong and he couldn't decide whether he was just being overly careful or was letting present company get to him.

Without waiting for the allotted start at 0400, Davenport gave the signal to commence. Unable to vocalize his opposition, Greg had to get his squad into position. As in the previous week's training, he gave the appropriate signal to the squad and they moved to the side of the villa and waited for the main team to enter the building. With his NVGs stowed in their pack on his back, he was still able to detect the silhouettes of the squad scaling the wall to the roof amidst the lights of the villa. Once they were on the roof, he held up his hand awaiting the second squad to enter the building. With the commencement beginning early, the advantage of using his watch for a 0400 entrance was null and void and he had to rely on his senses and cat-eyes. Within seconds he spotted the second squad scale the steps to the back door. Sticking two fingers towards the direction of the villa, the squad immediately moved to the side of the house and began the task of rigging the basement full of explosives. Greg waited at the top of the stairs and once the team was inside, moved to check the front of the villa.

On his way forward, Greg could make out a slight whistle coming from the front of the villa. Moving along the wall he made his way to the forward corner as the whistling increased. Placing the MP-5 at his side, he waited until an image began to appear at the corner. Without warning, the unsuspecting guard who was staring into the sky became an instant lump of flesh as Greg grabbed him from behind and snapped his neck. Greg grabbed the legs of his victim and moved him back into the shadows. He took one glance along the front of the villa for anymore guards, and once satisfied no one else was there, he lifted the body over his shoulders and made his way back to the stairs, carrying him down into the basement. By the time he arrived the squad had finished laying the explosives. The mixture of C-4 and Pentaerythritol Tetranitrate (PETN) was extremely volatile and the team was carefully finishing the final stages of rigging. Extremely sensitive, PETN was used as a detonator for big explosions. Worse than Nitroglycerin, it had been packed with extreme care along the trip with lubricated padding. The PETN was rigged on a small spring, which allowed it to fall onto the C-4 when Greg activated the electronic trigger. Alone it was enough to destroy the villa, but in conjunction with the C-4 would cause considerable damage. within 500 yards in every direction.

Laying the lump of flesh in one corner, Greg began to check the progress. No one gave any indication that they noticed his extra baggage as he came into the room, each attentive with the sensitive task at hand, however, each one had sensed his arrival and were ready to react if it hadn't been their leader. As Greg moved from one station to another, he received the thumbs up signal from each man, indicating their rig was complete. Greg checked each and activated the electronic receiver. Pleased to see that all the rigs were completed flawlessly, unlike the last training session, he began to head out of the basement. Just before he stepped out of the basement, he stopped and turned. Removing the NVGs from his bag, he took a scan of the entire room. Expecting to see some form of drug laboratory or weapons, he was surprised to find only antiques and a workshop, equipped with wood working machinery and tools. Everything in the basement was neat and tidy, clothes hanging on a rack along one wall, throwbacks from twenty years ago. Continuing to glance around the basement, he came upon the guard he had eliminated a few minutes earlier. Even in the green glow of the NVGs he could make out Hispanic features, however the guard was clean cut and dressed in clean clothes, unlike what he expected. Expecting a hired mercenary, he figured the body to be covered in three day old facial hair and wearing dirty clothes, but he found that even the boots seemed smartly polished and fairly new. Immediately the hairs on the back of his neck began to pop out of their roots. Feeling something was incredibly wrong, he hurried up the steps and to the rear corner of the villa to find his squad ready to cover for the departure of the first and second squad.

Just as Greg made it to his squad, the first members of the other squads began to emerge from the back door. Hunched down low in a protective stance each man dispersed in an arc outside the door to cover the remaining members. Greg counted as each men left the villa, and once Conan left the door with a body over his shoulder, he noticed there was one man missing, Davenport. 'Where the hell was he', Greg thought to himself.

Before Greg could finish asking himself the question, the sky lit up and it seemed as if all hell broke lose. Gunfire erupted from every corner of the woods. Even with the protective suits each man wore, they only provided cover to certain sections of the body, leaving areas open for the bullets to tear the flesh and penetrate. Conan hadn't taken two steps before bullets began riddling his body, some reflecting off the body armor on his chest and stomach, while several tore through his arms and legs, while another found its mark directly in the center of his forehead. As if a tree were falling, his immense body leaned backwards, falling atop the body he carried. Greg dove to the ground and tried to return fire. Within seconds each member of his team was either dead or injured trying to find cover. Without thinking, Greg made his way along the ground to Conan's body, pushing the large lifeless form off the second body with his legs. Looking down at Conan's package, Greg noticed that it was still breathing and then spotted something he hadn't seen in several years on the man's ring finger and a sudden chill went through his body.

At that moment, bullets began to dance around him from behind. Greg looked back to find Davenport standing on the steps firing directly at him. None of the bullets from the woods were aimed in Davenports direction, and Greg noticed Davenport screaming something into a hand-held walkie talkie. Without waiting to ask any questions, Greg grabbed the body by the shirt collar and began a dash for the pond while remaining low. As he made his way to the pond he reached into his pocket and grabbed the transmitter. Within 25 yards of the pond, he felt the tear of a bullet enter into his left arm and right thigh. Ignoring the injuries, he continued onto the pond setting each of the detonations in standby for the main switch. As he reached the pond, he leaped into the pond, activating the electronic detonator while glancing back to find the whereabouts of Davenport.

Unfortunately Greg didn't notice Davenport at the steps during the quick second of flight, but as he entered the water, the earth shook, as the entire villa seemed to leap off its foundation at the force of the explosion. The fireball extended over the pond and into the woods, charring everything and everyone within the first 50 yards of the woods. Trees ignited as if they were paper, spreading the fire even farther into the woods. The guard at the front gate, who didn't figure into the team's plan for elimination, was added to the statistics when he became engulfed in the fireball, 400 yards from the villa. The large steel gate bent slightly with the force of the blast and remained warped once the flames welded it into a permanent bow.

Nothing inside the concrete walls surrounding the villa was spared. Within fifteen seconds every form of life was incinerated. Within two minutes the fires had ceased as fast as they had begun. The trees of the forest singed and crackled from the intense heat, but no living sound was heard. It was as if Hell itself had opened up and swallowed the entire area into the bowels of the Earth.

Chapter 17

The band was playing a sweet cacophony of melodic sounds as she danced amidst the clouds. Having dozed off while they waited for someone to come, Kay felt as if she was floating on air. Dancing with a handsome man she had never met before, she felt free, as if nothing could touch her. Slowly the mist began to build and the stranger began to fade in the distance, enveloped by the clouds. Just as the stranger began to disappear, she could hear him call to her for help. He stretched out his arms and she suddenly became aware that he was not dressed in a tuxedo but some other black outfit, dirty and stained. Suddenly the wind picked up and the mist was blown aside. She felt the ground begin to shake and the world around her collapse.

It was at that moment that she awoke to find the sky as bright as day. The car was shaking violently and the windshield was cracking in several places. In order to escape any injury by broken glass she struggled to open the car door, which seemed to push back at her from the strong gust of wind. Just as she managed to pull herself clear of the car, the front windshield shattered, sending broken glass into the front seats, ripping large gaping holes in the upholstery. Fighting against the wind she worked her way to the back of the car to shield herself, almost being lifted into the air along the way. At the rear of the car she found Steve huddled down to defend against the wind.

"What the hell was that?" Kay asked kneeling beside him.

Steve shrugged his shoulders, "You've got me. It felt like an earthquake."

Kay peered over the top of the car. "I've been in a few earthquakes in my time and have never seen the sky light up like that at the same time." she said pointing towards the end of the road.

The air temperature began to dramatically increase, even more than the normal sultry heat of Acapulco. The ground stopped shaking, as the wind seemed to settle. Standing they both gazed down the road to see the trees glistening from hot cinders that settled in the dry leaves.

"Do you have any idea what's up the road?" Kay asked turning to Steve who just shrugged his shoulders. His face seemed intense and concerned but not like she expected. He didn't appear concerned for anyone's welfare but as if something had gone wrong.

"Maybe we ought to walk up there and see what's going on or if anyone needs any help? she said, beginning to walk down the road.

"I don't think that's such a good idea. We ought to just remain here and wait for Tony to arrive and help us with the car."

"Aren't you worried that someone might be hurt up there?"

"I'm sure there's nothing we can do to help. I don't want to leave here and miss Tony."

Kay walked stomped back to Steve with fire burning in her eyes. "What kind of reporter are you? Doesn't your instincts demand that you go and investigate what happened? Don't you want to be the first to arrive at something big happening? Aren't you the least bit interested?" she asked walking directly up to Steve and staring him straight in the eyes.

"No!!" Steve replied. "I'm not about to go walking down a deserted road in the middle of Mexico to find out its some sort of government confrontation, gang warfare or family feud gone wrong and end up getting shot for being in the wrong place at the wrong time. I'm a political reporter for a city newspaper. I don't work for CNN, risking my life to get my picture in someone's living room. Now shut the hell up and get out of my face." He said pointing to the rear of the car.

Shocked at the sudden outburst, Kay retreated to the rear of the car paralyzed. This was the third time that Steve had gotten upset and raised his voice at her. Once before at the airport and now. 'What had gotten into him' she thought to herself. She couldn't believe that he was always like this. This was not the same person everyone lauded about when she learned about her assignment with him. They said he was highly respected at the newspaper. A friendly person and a wonderful teacher.

As she stood there wondering what to do next the sound of sirens pierced the air. Looking out over the barren territory, she wondered how someone could have reacted so fast to an emergency in such a place so far off the beaten track. Back in San Diego, it would have taken the police a good ten minutes to respond to a fire or 911 call downtown during the middle of the day, let alone someplace outside of the city or in the middle of the night. This place seemed a hundred miles from anything and glancing down at her watch noticed it was only four in the morning and already some emergency unit was almost on top of the scene.

She looked back at Steve who was standing near the front of the car looking into the woods as if searching for someone. If he was looking for Tony, why was he looking into the woods, she asked herself. Besides that, where was Tony, she wondered. It had been at least an hour since Steve said he was calling him. An evening that started so peacefully and serene at the Presidential palace had turned into a nightmare, and it was only just the beginning.

****

Gasping, Greg's head broke through the surface of the water and inhaled the hot air, which immediately burned his throat. The stench of burning flesh and wood filled his lungs and nostrils. As the first large breath entered his body, it quickly departed as he vomited from the nauseous odor that penetrated his inner being. He had been in hellholes before and witnessed death of several different varieties, but he had never experienced such a gut-wrenching aroma as that caused by the vaporization of everything and everyone within a quarter mile of his location.

Realizing he was still holding onto something with his right hand, he pulled it clear of the water to reveal the waterlogged and lifeless body at the other end. The head was covered by a black cloth bag and the rest of the body was clothed in expensive silk bed wear. Wrapping his arms around the limp form, he made his way to the edge of the pond where he could sit half-in half-out of the water. When he could sit upright, he brought the body across his lap and checked the neck for a pulse. Although weak, there was a pulse, however the breaths were very short and raspy, a mixture of water in the lungs, the charred air that lingered over the area, and the drugs the team had put in him before they carried him away to ensure he remained still and silent until they arrived back at the base.

As he sat there gathering his breath in short strokes to limit the stench from entering into his system, he gazed around. Lumps of darkened forms were scattered everywhere. Where once stood his proud team, there now lay charred lifeless objects, wisps of smoke rising from each towards the sky. Along the edge of the woods were more clumps that reminded him of charcoal after an afternoon barbecue. All that remained of the villa was a pile of rubble that extended out towards the woods from a crater at least five feet deep.

Hanging his head down as if to cry, there was no emotion in him to allow that. After several missions and training, he had lost his faith in religion so there was no prayer offered up for his friends and companions. Only anger that he had no other alternatives when he watched his team get struck down like little targets in an amusement park booth. All that remained was a sense of rage for the removal of something dear to him and the inability to have done something to prevent it.

As he regained his composure, he pulled the bag away from the head to discover an unimaginable nightmare. Lying on his lap, barely alive, was the President of the United States.

Immediately his head began to spin trying to comprehend the depth of betrayal as the initial rage now increased ten-fold. The picture was becoming even more vague than before. Somehow, somewhere, the mission Davenport had led them to, extracting a terrorist key figurehead, turned into a firefight that led to the death of his team and now to discover that their captive was instead the highest political figure in the United States.

Suddenly the pain from the bullet wounds in his arm and thighs, the stench of the air and the weakness from the entire event disappeared and his entire being came alive. Climbing out of the water he dragged the President to a clear area and pulled out a small oxygen bottle that each member carried with them to allow them sufficient oxygen to escape an area, lasting up to two minutes. He strapped the mask across the President's face and switched the valve to the 'on' position.

As the oxygen went to work, Greg looked around the clearing again in hopes that someone else might be alive. It didn't take long to realize that it was fruitless to believe anyone could have survived the blast. As he surveyed the bodies near the woods, he could barely identify the uniforms, but knew from what little he could see that it was military. It was then Greg's mind began to work on what he had to do next. While he started formulating a plan he immediately sensed the sound of sirens in the distance, increasing in intensity as they approached. The first thing he had to do was to put as much territory between him and this area as possible and try to unravel the mystery that was rapidly evolving. Not knowing the reasons why and who was behind this, he needed to time to patch himself up along with the President and get some answers before he confronted any policeman, who once they discovered the destruction would shoot first and ask questions later of anyone found nearby.

Lifting the President over his right shoulder without concern for his own injuries, he quickly headed into the woods knowing that it was going to be difficult getting an unconscious President over the back wall but he had to keep as far from the road as possible.

As he struggled with the body over his shoulder, he continued to come up with questions that needed answering. Hoping that the military would be so perplexed by the amount of death and destruction at the villa would allow him enough time to get clear and begin his new quest of discovery.

****

The sound of sirens grew closer to the villa. Amidst the ruins that used to be the holiday retreat of a U.S. Senator, the piles of wood and bricks continued to smolder. The only sound was the crackling of residual fires that tried to stretch out to surrounding areas only to find there was nothing left to burn. Moments after Greg fled into the woods a pile of charred wood began to stir as if erupting from within. The pile grew in size until the wood gave way and a steel door appeared, smoke billowing from within. During the days of uneasiness with the Russian and Cuban threat, an underground bomb shelter had been added to the villa grounds and forgotten, except for blueprints that were not provided to Greg's team.

As if rising from the grave, Captain Davenport, covered with soot and grime, emerged from the hidden fortress. Keeping alternative open for anything, Davenport had planned to use the shelter in case things got out of control, so he kept the information on the shelter to himself. Barely escaping the lethal blast, he scrambled into the underground protection to find that the shelter did not provide as much protection as he had hoped. The force of the detonation sent shockwaves that nearly crushed his eardrums and the intense heat had turned the shelter into an oven. Exhausted and barely able to breath, he finally emerged when he estimated the danger had passed. Coughing up soot to clear his lungs, he inhaled deeply, undisturbed by the stench and heat. A participant in the wanton destruction and killing of entire villages in Vietnam with napalm, he had experienced far more than this.

Struggling to gain his footing and clear his head, he scrambled over to the pond to revive himself only to find the heat of the water unsatisfying. Before he was able to clear the cobwebs from his head, voices began to emerge behind him.

"No move señor." a voice with a strong Mexican accent demanded.

Davenport remained on his knees realizing there wasn't enough time to grab his weapon and turn. While he contemplated his alternatives, the figure of a Mexican policeman appeared to his right holding a pistol in both hands.

"I guess this isn't Club Med, is it?" Davenport asked trying to gain some time to recover his strength and find a way to overcome the policeman. As he arose from his knees he could hear movement behind him. Turning his head slightly his hopes of disabling the lone policeman and disappearing into the woods vanished. Behind him stood at least twenty policeman and military personnel, guns raised uneasily and ready to fire at the slightest sign of danger.

"Señor, my name is General Ruesta." Said a man emerging from the crowd of policeman, walking to within ten feet of Davenport. His English was much more refined than the initial policeman's, possibly educated in some U.S. military schools. "As you can see you are at a slight disadvantage and escape is impossible. You and I have a lot to talk about. I am interested, why are you standing here amidst this disaster?"

Davenport stood there motionless and speechless, trying to consider his alternatives. Looking around he got his first real look at the devastation and wondered what went wrong. Ruesta motioned with both hands for his men to lower their guns. Circling Davenport he investigated the blackened form, impressed with the size and attire.

"It appears that you are not just a simple farmer, nor are you a Mexican citizen. Perhaps you could tell me your name?"

"Jose Greco."

"Very amusing, señor. I am a very patient man and we will have a lot of time to find out the answers." Motioning with his right hand, five men dressed in military attire moved to Davenport. After disarming him, two men grabbed his hands and handcuffed them behind his back. "I apologize for the barbaric treatment, but you have given me no other option. When I finish here we will have a chance to sit down and talk." Again he motioned with his hand and the five men pushed and prodded Davenport towards the front of where the villa used to stand and to a large truck parked amidst the rubble. One of the guards opened the rear door and just before Davenport was forced inside, the area suddenly grew dark and quiet as a guard slammed the butt of his rifle against the lower part of Davenport's head, knocking him unconscious.

Chapter 18

An hour had passed since the horde of vehicles drove by Kay and Steve with sirens blaring. Vehicles ranging from Jeeps and police cars to armored personnel carriers, each with machine guns manned, whistled by at high speed never once bothering to notice the stranded car. What puzzled Kay was there were no fire trucks. Thirty minutes later, one of the armored personnel carriers raced by heading back in the direction it had originally come. Although the glow from fires had quickly subsided on the horizon, it was odd that there were no local firemen rushing to the scene. It almost appeared to her as if there was a war going on and the cavalry was responding. Leaning on the front right of the car, Steve had taken very little interest in the parade of military forces.

"Why didn't you try to wave any of those vehicle down for some help?" she asked walking back towards the front of the car. For the first time she noticed that he was no longer wearing his jacket and wondered what the belt along the back of his shirt was for. When she got to the front of the car she got her answer. Steve quickly turned in her direction and she stood there staring down the barrel of a handgun.

"You're getting to be a regular pain in the ass. I told you to stay at the back of the car."

As she stood there she was transfixed on the small hole at the end of the barrel and couldn't move her feet. Every sort of emotion began to run through her and she could feel her heart pulsating as if trying to escape from her chest.

"I told the paper to leave you in Washington and I didn't need you here. Now I have to think of a way to get rid of you before I leave here."

"What the hell are you talking about? What is going on?" Many more questions were running through her head but she couldn't sort them into words.

"Afraid I can't answer that right now. Now get your ass in the car and stay there." Walking over to her, Steve waved the gun as if pointing towards the car. Grabbing her left shoulder with his free hand, he spun her around, jabbed the gun into her lower back and pushed her towards the side door. Just before reaching the door he stopped and the gun slowly lowered from her back.

"Excuse me ma'am, is this man troubling you?" A voice other than Steve's asked from behind her. Turning she found Steve standing motionless, arms at his side, with a handgun against his cheek. Over his left shoulder a dark face that appeared to be covered in dirt was smiling at her. Standing there with her mouth wide open the face appeared familiar to her but she couldn't figure out from where.

"If you don't mind, lay the gun gently on the hood with two fingers." LCDR Greg Morris said as he moved towards the opposite side of Steve. Steve laid the gun on the hood while his eyes strained to his side trying to locate the stranger. "Very good, now for our next performance, how about dropping to your knees and placing your hands underneath your knees."

Steve began to lower but without warning swung out to his left to find empty air. A split second later, the back of the Greg's hand holding the gun found its mark against the left side of Steve's face which let out a bone crushing crack as if a wooden slat had been broken. Steve's body followed the force of his head as it reeled to one side and he fell face first onto the hood. An instant later, Greg's right leg went between Steve's to push them apart and returned the gun to the back of Steve's head.

"You don't listen very well, do you? If you and I are going to get along, you have to learn to listen to what I say. Now be a good boy and let's try it again."

As Steve struggled to get to his knees, he turned and faced Kay, exposing a severe cut across his left cheek and blood seeping from his mouth. Without thinking she began to walk towards him and from out of nowhere she was suddenly staring down another gun barrel.

"If you don't mind, I would prefer that you remain back a few steps until I can figure out what's going on here." Greg said barely looking at her as he searched along Steve's body with his free hand.

"He's bleeding."

"He's lucky to be alive after that move." Greg said as he returned the gun to the back of Steve's head. "Would either one of you like to tell me just who the hell you are and what the hell you're doing here?"

"We're reporters from the San Diego Union, here to cover the signing of the Arms Agreement and were on our way back to the hotel from a reception when the car broke down.

We're waiting for our cameraman to come out here and give us a ride back."

"Do reporters normally carry guns and push each other around with them?"

"I don't have any idea why he is carrying a gun. Were you involved in that explosion down the way?"

"For now, I'll ask the questions."

Greg stared down the street towards the site of the explosion and then towards the woods in the same direction Steve had earlier. When he turned back, she couldn't get over the fact of how familiar the face looked. She could always remember names and faces but knew she had never met him in person and was puzzled as to why it was so familiar.

"Do you have anything to contribute to the conversation?" he said as he leaned down towards Steve placing his left hand on Steve's shoulder. "If you're a reporter, why are you carrying a gun and prodding this lady around?"

Steve's silence was rewarded when Greg's hand slammed the right side of Steve's head against the side of the car, adding to the pain.

"We are never going to get along if you don't talk to me. I have very little time to wait for an answer."

Wincing from the pain, he turned his head towards Greg and painfully grinned at him. "Your time is much shorter than you think, asshole." Attempting to overcome the intense pain in the side of his head, he reached out again for the stranger dressed in black. Steve grabbed the gun, but with a sudden move, the gun turned back towards Steve and went off, the bullet finding it's way down Steve's neck and through his heart, ricocheting off his spine, creating havoc to Steve's internals.

"Damn it." Greg said as Steve's body limped to the ground like a sack of potatoes. At the same time Kay screamed, never truly experiencing death face to face. She had reported about people losing loved ones and been to her grandparents funerals, but had never watched as life came to an abrupt halt.

Within seconds her scream was silenced by Greg's hand over her mouth. Directly in front of her eyes were another set of eyes that seemed so distant and lifeless. There was no pain or sense of loss in them from Steve's death.

"I'm going to remove my hand and I want you to shake you head if you will promise to remain quiet." She nodded her head and he removed his hand.

"I am not having a good day so I would like some honest answers."

"I'm Kay Cross, and I'm a reporter at the San Diego Union. I'm telling you the truth, we were here to cover the signing of the Arms Agreement."

Greg stared at her and sensed the woman was truly frightened. Something was really wrong but after the incident at the villa, nothing was surprising.

"Where the hell are we?" he asked.

"Excuse me?" Kay was stunned by the question. This man appears out of nowhere, throws Steve around like a doll, points a gun at her and Steve and then Steve is killed by it and he doesn't even know where he is.

"Where the hell are we?" he replied.

"Just outside of Acapulco."

If the woman was telling the truth, Greg began to understand why it didn't seem like they had flown all the way to Central America. It still didn't explain why in the middle of nowhere he finds the President of the United States where he was supposed to find a key terrorist figure and end up losing his entire team.

"You say you just happened to be here when your car broke down."

"That's right. Steve pulled the car over here and said we blew a hose. Smoke was billowing out of the front."

Greg motioned for Kay to follow him to the front of the car. He opened the hood and found a distinct smell that wasn't from an engine, but a small smoke bomb used in drills to add reality if they got caught in a burning building. Walking to the driver's side he opened the door and found the keys still in the steering wheel. Turning the keys the engine immediately started.

Dumbfounded, Kay couldn't believe what was happening. "I saw smoke coming out of the hood when he opened it."

"You are either a tremendous actress or you really don't know what's going on. A device was placed under the hood to let off smoke to give it the appearance of being broken. What were you and this guy, Steve, talking about before I got here?"

"He had been pretty uptight lately, and when I asked why he didn't flag down one of the vehicles that raced by here towards the explosion, he pointed the gun at me and talked about how he told the paper he didn't need me here and now he had to figure out a way to get rid of me before he got back. Just what the hell is going on? Why was he carrying a gun and why are you here?"

"I'm afraid I don't know all the answers to that and I'm not in a trusting mood right now. The big question is whether to leave you here or take you with me for fear that you will tell everyone what happened here."

"You can't leave me out here."

"Taking you with me is not a great option either, however I do need to get out of here and I can't really do it alone. Come with me." Greg said, grabbing Kay by the arm and heading back into the woods.

"Where the hell are you taking me?"

"I have a package out here that I can't leave behind and I can't leave you alone up there for fear that you will race off to whoever is down the road."

When they reached the edge of the woods, Kay noticed the body lying against one of the trees. When Greg lifted him above his shoulders she was amazed to find the man who only hours ago she was dancing with.

"Jesus Christ, that's the President. Who the hell are you?"

"Right now I'm the only one who can save him. Someone decided that he shouldn't be the President any longer and didn't want to wait for the elections. Now let's get the hell out of here."

With everything that had happened in the past few hours, the stress was beginning to take it's toll on Kay. Having not slept for almost twenty-four hours and being exposed to total confusion for the last hour, she could barely stay erect. Just before she was about to pass out, she felt the stranger's arm catch her and she suddenly felt a surge of strength as if it passed from him to her. She turned and looked into the face and eyes and it suddenly dawned on her where she had seen him before. Standing in front of her was the man from the dream she had while sitting in the car just prior to the explosion. The man who faded away from her on the dance floor was now holding her up and guiding her back towards the car.

****

High atop the Hilton Hotel in Acapulco, the lights were off in the Presidential Suite except for a desk lamp in the corner. The dim light created shadows, which danced along the expansive interior, hopping from plush leather sofas to oak cabinets that were the trademark of the hotel.

Dressed in satin pajamas that bore the Presidential seal, the Chief of Staff had a tight grip on the phone receiver, turning his knuckles white. Although it was only five o'clock in the morning, he appeared as if he had just walked out of the shower, hair neatly in place, with his eyes wide open.

"You've got to be shitting me." Thomas Alexander said as he slammed the phone back into the receptacle. Breathing heavily the blood vessels in his neck bulged with rage. Slamming his fists onto the crafted oak desk he uttered obscenities at the wall and the shadows that danced upon them, using words he hadn't expressed in ages.

After a brief 2 minutes of lost composure, quite unfamiliar for the Chief of Staff, he gained control of his emotions and picked up the telephone, punching four numbers. The phone was answered on the second ring.

"Carmichael, get your ass out of bed and get in here."

"What's the problem, sir?" A timid voice answered. Andrew Carmichael, the Secretary of Defense, was a retired Air Force lawyer appointed to the post after the sudden death of his predecessor. It had taken quite a lot of convincing of the President by the Chief of Staff to get him the position. Carmichael was not a forceful type, more conniving than knowledgeable, like most lawyers Alexander thought. Alexander classified him as a squeamish fox, afraid of his own shadow, but able to tear a gash out of the back of your neck when you weren't looking. Unfortunately, he was unable to use those tactics convincingly enough to get the President to call off the Arms Agreement. The President was not very happy with Carmichael, which caused the SECDEF to maintain a safe distance most of the time.

"Don't ask questions." Alexander replied, slamming down the telephone again, nearly shattering the receiver. Rising from his chair, Alexander walked over to the window, hands clasped behind his back, fingers entwined so tightly they were turning pale. Gazing out over the Mexican capital at night, his eyes were fixed in an icy stare, not concentrating on one particular item but stretching beyond the horizon.

"Yes sir?" Carmichael half-stated, half asked as he entered the large office moments later, closing the door behind him. Dressed in a similar pair of pajamas, he barely looked alive, unlike Alexander. The satin attire was wrinkled, with his hair askew, he wore a worn out robe and was in desperate need of a shave. Gingerly stepping across the plush carpet towards the desk Alexander glanced at the pathetic creature's reflection in the window.

"You're one for two." Alexander stated without turning, still staring out beyond what the eyes normally saw.

"What do you mean, sir?" Carmichael asked causing Alexander to spin around and slam his open hands onto the desk.

"I mean, you lethargic mouse, that our egotistical, self-centered glory boy failed.

Although you managed to see to it that the Vice President meant his untimely demise in a car wreck tonight, your plan for the President was blown up, literally."

"That's not possible." Carmichael began to say but was immediately cut-off by a wave of the Chief of Staff's hand.

"It appears that your Davenport failed to plan properly. As the Mexican soldiers you convinced were going to break up a gang of terrorists began to gun down your expendable team of GI Joes, an explosion in the villa tore the entire countryside into a barbeque."

"So what."

"It appears Davenport survived the incident by diving into an abandoned old bomb shelter at the villa before it was torn from its roots. He's now sitting in a Mexican Army Jail."

"So we take care of him some other way."

"Unfortunately, you moron, one of our agents has already contacted him and learned even more depressing news. Just before Davenport leaped into the shelter, he spotted one of your lean, mean, fighting machines pick up the President and dive into the villa's lake as he set off the explosions."

"And he survived?"

"We've searched the lake and found nothing except a set of footprints leading out of the lake towards the woods. That means this boy hero and the President are probably still alive and undoubtedly going to try and find their way back to Washington."

Carmichael sat in the chair, arms clinging to the armrest as if he was riding a roller coaster. Alexander could see him shaking in fear but also noticed the look in his eyes, which meant his brain was already at work on a sly scheme.

After a moment's pause, Carmichael stood up and started to pace the floor, his hand rubbing at his chin and his head gazed down at the floor, the picture of a man deep in thought. Alexander was about to comment again, when Carmichael suddenly turned and faced him.

"What would you say if we went ahead and announced the death of the VP and President anyway?"

"Are you insane?" Alexander screamed, pounding his fist once more on the desk.

"No, hear me out." he said as he sat back down in the chair. "We announce their deaths, as planned that they were the result of concurrent terrorist attacks by Iran in retaliation to the full embargo we placed on them for positioning their missiles at the Straits of Hormuz and conducting nuclear testing. But we add a new twist. We also say that the CIA has uncovered evidence that, as part of its plan, they intend to insert a duplicate, an imposter who looks and acts like the President and will claim to have been saved from the terrorist ploy. The imposter intends to assume the Presidency and attempt to reduce our forces in the area. We also state that we were able to positively identify the body of the President by his dental records. The moment the President tries to show his face, everyone in the country would try to kill him and save us the trouble. In the meantime, we tell Davenport that he doesn't collect his money until he finishes the job properly. After which we put an end to him."

Alexander fell back into his chair stunned. He knew Carmichael was crafty, but this was so simple he wondered why he didn't think of it. As the country ran around trying to be the first to hunt down and kill the imposter, he would be able to assume the responsibilities of the Presidency. It was only a year ago that he convinced the President to establish a change to the law and convince the Congress that the Chief of Staff should be next in line for the Presidency if both the President and Vice President were incapable of continuing their duties.

"Get on the phone to the Press Secretary and fill him in on the details. I want this announced immediately so that the moment the people wake up on the West Coast and have their first cup of coffee, they'll hear the word of their new President and start gearing up to eliminate this so-called imposter. Also get Davenport out of that jail and on the trail of our so-called hero. He trained him; he should be able to find him. Also inform everyone that the Arms Agreement signing is postponed and get Air Force One ready to head back to DC this morning."

Without a word, Carmichael leaped from the chair and headed out of the office.

"Get a hold of everyone on the staff here and tell them to be in my office in 30 minutes." Alexander told Carmichael as he reached the door. "Now that I'm the President its time to start getting back to business and move on to the next step."

After Carmichael left the office, Alexander leaned back in his chair and a large grin began to stretch across his face. The wheels were in motion, he thought to himself, and before long the country would be back to its rightful place, the power and strength returned to a nation that had been dormant for too long. There was nothing left standing in his way, and he taken the next step towards fulfilling his goal. Unfortunately for him, there were a lot more steps that would prove much harder.

Chapter 19

Almost immediately, Davenport could sense the strong stench of urine and sweat. Although his eyes weren't yet open, he felt confined, bringing back bitter memories of Prisoner of War training school in the back woods of California. The smell was similar and what seemed like far away sounds of moans and snores were immediate indications that he was somewhere he preferred not to be.

As he opened his eyes and saw the rusted iron bars, chipped concrete and dim lights, the reality of where he was came to light. The morning's events at the villa, the encounter with General Ruesta, and a meeting with one of the "Falcon's" messenger boys after he initially came to began to resurface. Gazing through the small opening on the outer wall, he guessed it to be early afternoon and cursed himself for allowing the butt end of the rifle crash upon the back of his head. Feeling the back of his head he felt the resultant bump while the splitting headache pounded at his temples. Regrettably, he was supposed to be on a first class flight to Switzerland by this time to collect his money and begin a new identity, not sitting in some rat infested Mexican jail. Then he began to think about Morris and the sight of him leaping into the pond carrying the President's body. How pathetic he thought to himself. Morris couldn't even have imagined who it was he was trying to save. Reaching over and squashing a cockroach that was crawling along the floor, he wondered why General Ruesta was so interested in seeing him. He had assumed that the General would have been a part of the plan and should have expected to see Davenport there. He evaluated the facts surrounding the morning's events. Too many bullets were landing in his vicinity to be considered stray shots and no one acknowledged his commands on the hand held radio he was given to direct the Mexicans. Something wasn't right in Denmark, he thought to himself.

While he pondered those questions the door across from the cell opened and in walked General Ruesta, looking frustrated and upset. The guard opened the cell door and stood back, his rifle raised precariously in Davenport's direction. Walking in, the General stared at Davenport for several seconds before saying anything.

"I'm interested, senor. You don't look much like a terrorist, a little old to be running around with rebels. Why don't you tell me what you are doing here and what happened at the villa."

It appeared to Davenport that his questions had been answered. General Ruesta considered him a terrorist instead of an American officer. Davenport wasn't about to divulge anything to this backwards toy soldier but would use him to gain his own information.

"You can't always judge a book by its cover, sonny." he replied imitating an eighty-year-old man.

"Don't play games with me, senor. I am in no mood. My government wants answers to a lot of questions. Now why did you try to kill the American President in my country?" Davenport decided to use the dumb boy routine until he got some answers of his own.

"I don't know nothing about no President. I was out looking to score some good Columbian Gold and told that was the best place to go. All of a sudden I'm caught up in some major gun battle and thought it was some drug war."

"Interesting clothes for a drug buyer."

"You can never be too careful when in a strange land."

"You will rot in this cell and be screaming for my assistance before long, I can assure you, if you don't answer my questions." Davenport could tell Ruesta's patience was wearing thin, the blood vessels on the General's neck swelling and his face bright red.

"I don't know, this is almost better than the hotel I was staying at."

Just as it seemed that the General was about to swing at Davenport, another soldier came rushing into the room calling his name. Ruesta walked over to him and the soldier whispered something in the General's ear. The soldier was rewarded with a blow that knocked him clear out the door. Ruesta began screaming obscenities at everything and the soldier with the gun stepped back a few steps to avoid the same retribution.

Ruesta walked back into the cell and Davenport prepared to defend himself and teach the General a valuable lesson.

"I think you would have preferred answering my questions and remaining here my friend. Unfortunately, the American government is not the least bit happy about the death of their President and you are to be handed over to them. Some very unfriendly people are outside to meet you and if I were you I'd keep an eye over my shoulder. I have a feeling you may not make it back in one piece, which really doesn't upset me, although I'd prefer to be there in person to watch you suffer and die slowly. Of course if you were to tell me what is going on, I could convince my government to keep you here a while longer and safe from that Yankee retribution."

It was apparent that Ruesta was not happy about losing his star witness. Had he been able to break Davenport, which was not likely, he would have been the hero of his country. If he were to lose Davenport to the Americans, it would be a major blow. Davenport's only chance of getting out of this mess was out in the open where he could attempt an escape.

"You know, I would really hate to have to leave these plush accommodations and your warm personality, but I have a date tomorrow night and she has much better legs than you do."

Ruesta swung with his right hand to hit him but was met by Davenport's left arm and in the same movement; a right hand quickly wrapped itself around his neck.

"Tell your lackey out there not to get any ideas. The instant I hear a gun shot your larynx would be crushed and although he'll probably get me it will be after you've already started your journey to hell ahead of me. I grow tired of your games and although I hate to be a poor guest and leave the party so early I think you'll understand."

Ruesta's eyes were in shock and for the first time he felt fear. There wasn't much action for Mexican soldiers except for exercises. Officers merely gave orders and made life miserable for everyone but have never faced real danger. Even though he was a General, the pseudo Army that he commanded never saw any life threatening events other than driving through downtown traffic. For the first time in his drab existence, he was witnessing what it was like to face death at the hand of another man. Unable to speak with the grip around his throat he just nodded and waved the guard to relax.

"Now why don't you introduce me to my escorts and get me the hell out of here." Davenport said as he let loose of the grip on Ruesta's throat.

Ruesta rubbed his neck with his hands and stomped out of the cell, Davenport following with the guard bringing up the rear. It took Davenport a couple of seconds to adjust his eyes to the midday light when the entered the main office before he noticed that one of his escorts was the same man that visited him earlier in the day. A smile came across his face as he believed that Falcon had sent his messenger boy to spring Davenport and he could get back on about his business, but just as fast the smile went away as he pondered the other possibility. It was possible that the General was right and Falcon didn't want any loose ends. The messengers could be here to see that Davenport never got a chance to tell someone of what really happened at the villa. Somehow, no matter what the reason they were here for, Davenport concluded his best option was to get clear of them at his earliest opportunity.

Ruesta spoke briefly with the two men and then stormed off towards the end of the room, pushing soldiers out of his way as he marched through the door like a young child who didn't get his way.

The two escorts grabbed Davenport by each arm and almost carried him out of the door. When they got outside, the one who visited him earlier in the day climbed into the back seat with Davenport.

"I have a message for you from Falcon. You missed the target. The President is still alive and if you want to see the rest of your money, the job needs to be finished. Falcon does not appreciate failures."

"What do you mean he's still alive? Nothing could have survived that blast."

"It appears that the man you saw diving into the pond with the President on his back somehow did manage to survive and carried the President off before the Mexican Army arrived. There was no trace of either of them at the villa. Falcon assumes he's on his way back to Washington. Once there you'll immediately be linked to the attack since your boy hero who's aiding him will undoubtedly point you out as the leader. He must not be allowed to return to Washington. Falcon also wants to know why you had to destroy the villa and why you failed so miserably."

Davenport's rage began to erupt. All his plans for a sweet and luxurious retirement were destroyed because of Morris, the same man who almost ended his career years ago. Somehow, Morris had managed to not only survive the explosion, but also managed to avoid the barrage of bullets from the Mexican Army, rescue the President and clear the area before General Ruesta and his bloodhounds arrived. Now some fancy pants wanted explanations for something he knew nothing about. All of this began to eat away at Davenport and he swore to himself that he would see to it that Morris would pay for all the aggravation he had caused.

"I'm sure Morris set off the explosives as he took off into the pond. It's standard operating procedure to rig explosives in case trouble is experienced on the withdrawal. Changing that part of the operation would have raised suspicions. I never though anyone would be able to set them off if the Mexican's had done their job properly. Now get me back to California if you want this ended." Davenport declared, coming face to face with his escort.

"We're headed for a flight right now, however the flight is for the Texas/Mexican border. If the President plans to go to Washington, he'll try to cross there."

"No he won't. Morris is a lot smarter than that. He'll need to get to familiar ground first and evaluate his options. He'll first head to San Diego to hide and develop a plan. He's a creature of habit."

"He won't get far. We have agents all along the border and he'll have a hell of a time getting past them."

"Shit." Davenport cried out. "You'll be lucky they're not all killed. Nobody is going to get to Morris before I do. Anyone who tries is going to have more than he can handle. I discovered and trained Morris. He managed to eliminate or imprison an entire group of Seals during a POW camp drill single-handedly and finished it off by taking me prisoner the moment I arrived. A bunch of redneck self-declared bounty hunters will only get themselves killed."

Falcon's messenger boy reached into his pocket and pulled out a cellular telephone. Contacting the pilot he alerted him to the change of plans and the need to file a new flight plan. After he finished he put the phone back in his jacket pocket and leaned forward to pass the information on to the driver.

"Everything is arranged. We'll fly into San Diego. We'll have a car standing by and head downtown where you can pick up whatever supplies you need. There's a change of clothes for you on the plane."

Davenport just shrugged his shoulders and glanced out the car window as they drove on towards the airport. As the Mexican scenery passed by, Davenport began to review his options and develop a plan. Unlike Morris, Davenport wasn't familiar with San Diego and looking for Morris would be like looking for a needle in a haystack, however, he also knew how Morris' would think, especially with his options so limited. Morris would need a safe place to hide and he only hoped that Morris would go where he thought he would allowing Davenport the opportunity to take care of him and the President before one of Falcon's foolish clones tried.

****

Although he knew he had little time to spare, Greg knew he couldn't be seen driving in daylight for too long. They had driven as far as he thought safe until they reached Manzanillo, a small town along the coast and a good day and a half drive from the border. Arriving before noon, Greg had Kay check into a run-down hotel so that he could collect his thoughts and consider his options while waiting for the effects of the President's drugs to wear off. Once they entered the room and put the President on one of the beds, Kay quickly fell asleep on the other bed. Not really wanting to drag Kay along with him he knew he had no other options at the present.

While he contemplated what to do, he turned on the television to see if there was any news on the incident. Flipping through the various Mexican shows he finally found a news broadcast. Having taken Spanish in High School and stationed in San Diego for 8 years, a haven for illegal Mexican aliens, he had a fair understanding of the language. The news rambled on about several conflicts around the world and then was immediately cut-off for a special announcement. What they announced nearly caused him to fall out of his chair. From what he could translate, the newsman announced the deaths of both the President and Vice President of the United States who were killed in separate incidents. The U.S. government believed both to be terrorist attacks by the Iranian government in protest to the recent embargo placed upon them. Not able to fully understand, he believed the announcer mentioned a plan uncovered by the CIA in which Iran had inserted an imposter who was going to claim to be the President and had been saved from the attack. The imposter was believed to be heading back to Washington and may be accompanied by another terrorist claiming to be a military member from the Special Forces that had rescued him. Fortunately, for Greg's sake they didn't have a picture on the screen of himself.

A large reward had been offered for any information leading to the capture of these imposters.

A picture of a man Greg recognized as the White House Chief of Staff appeared on the screen. The newscaster then announced that Thomas Alexander III had assumed the duties of the President and would be returning to Washington immediately, the Arms Agreement having to be postponed until the matter was resolved.

Turning towards the body lying on the bed, Greg began to question whether or not he had rescued the real President or the imitator the news had just reported. After all the strange happenings over the past week with Davenport; ending up in Acapulco instead of some Central American country, being told they were going to capture a key terrorist figure, and ending up with what he thought was the President of the United States, Greg wasn't sure what to believe anymore. Glancing over at the other bed he questioned what part the so-called reporter played in the picture. The two reporters so close to the incident and her companion trying to kill him led him to wonder if she had some connection in the whole affair. The hair on the back of his neck was standing on edge again and Greg pondered just walking out the door and disappearing somewhere. Unfortunately he had nowhere to go and it wasn't in his nature to just abandon the President if it was really him. Deciding that the only option open to him was to keep this information from them for now, he would use the short amount of time he had available to find out as much as possible about the two of them, and verify their true identities.

Having met the President once before when he visited Greg's ship on a cruise when the President was a Senator, he figured an imposter wouldn't know certain small items from that visit that the real President would. Greg had worked closely with the Secret Service agents on that visit to provide security and had spent quite a bit of time talking with the President one night. The girl was a different story and he wasn't sure how he was going to get to the truth about her existence and would have to watch her closely throughout the coming days, before he found an opportunity to let her go.

The other real problem he faced was where was he going to take them. With news being spread about someone impersonating the President, every Tom, Dick and Harry would be out to earn that reward. After the way the country bonded together against terrorism after the World Trade Center bombings, the patriotism would once again grow dramatically and everyone would want to be the hero. It would be impossible to travel by day and they couldn't go straight up to the White House gates and demand to be let in. There had to be a way that he could return to the states and keep the President under wraps until he could find a way to convince someone of importance that this was the real President, but first he had to learn the truth himself. If it wasn't the real President, he'd turn him in himself.

What really puzzled Greg, was why the Chief of Staff had assumed duties as the President. Remembering back to his days in school and the incident with Alexander Haig, he thought that the Secretary of State or someone along that line was next to assume the Presidency.

Greg turned off the television and sat back in the chair. Closing his eyes he tried to collect his thoughts since they were racing faster than an SST. Almost immediately, the image of Davenport standing at the door of the villa just as Greg was avoiding the barrage of bullets.

It seemed to Greg that the only way to start putting the pieces of the puzzle together was to start with who had given Davenport the orders to take the team on this mission, if there was such a person. It seemed unimaginable that Davenport could have put this whole thing together by himself. Although Davenport was egotistical and power hungry, Greg couldn't believe that this whole mess was planned solely by Davenport. It seemed unlikely he would have anything to gain and wouldn't have allowed himself to get caught up in the middle of it and end up among the smoldering ashes. If it had been, then the story of the President's death didn't make sense, along with the simultaneous death of the Vice President, which also appeared too coincidental. The only other option was that someone else had planned all of the events, including the death of the Vice President, using Davenport and the team as pawns for a bigger purpose. The question was, what was the bigger purpose and what had they hoped to be gained.

Since the President would be out for several more hours, Greg figured that he would have to start with the girl and find out what she knew. Opening his eyes and looking at her he realized she was exhausted and wouldn't be able to provide anything helpful for a while. Turning, he caught his reflection in the mirror and realized how bad his own condition was. Looking down, he saw the dried up blood on his pant legs and sleeve and figured the first order of business was to clean himself up and somewhere along the line find some clothes other than his team gear.

Rising from the chair he felt his muscles tighten. The ordeal of the last 12 hours, including the flight from San Diego, the trek to the villa from the drop zone, carrying the President through a hail of gunfire and diving into the pond, carting the President away from the villa and the encounter with the girl and her companion were taking their toll. After removing his gear, he took an inventory of his body to uncover the extent of damage that he had incurred. The wound on his arm wasn't deep and would only require bandages. The injury to the leg, on the other hand, was more severe. The bullet had gone clean through the thigh. Luckily, he thought, he wouldn't have to dig out the bullet; however, the wound was a prime candidate for infection from all the dirt and sweat it had been exposed to over the last six hours.

Greg walked into the bathroom and turned on the shower. Remembering how bad Mexican water was for them, he hoped it was only bad for drinking and wouldn't make the wound worse. Hoping to use hot water to kill the bacteria, it was barely lukewarm. Taking a few deep breaths, he sat down on the edge of the tub and pulled the nozzle over the wound. Almost immediately the pain shot through every nerve in his body. Closing his eyes, biting down hard and grasping the edge of the tub, it took all of his strength not to scream out. Taking control of his senses and continuing to breath heavily, he endured the sensation for the few minutes he considered was enough to clean the wound. When he was finished he examined the wound and found that the bullet had gone clean through without damaging the bone or arteries. While washing off the wound on his arm, the nerves were brought back to action again but not as bad as the first time. He used one of the skimpy hotel towels to dab the wounds dry.

Returning to the bedroom, he broke out his first aid kit and used the cleansing agent and disinfectant on the wounds, finding just enough material to bandage both. Unfortunately he would need to change the dressings regularly. In addition to finding some more bandage material he would also need to obtain some different clothes. Of course, he realized he had no identification or money and wondered if the woman would have enough available money on her. Believing that most women used all their money and credit cards to purchase clothes, he didn't hold much hope in that. Looking at the dress she was presently wearing only seemed to confirm his theory.

Sitting back down in the chair, he closed his eyes and between the stress of the mission, the confusion of the situation and the pain of cleaning his wounds he fell asleep. As he slept the image of Davenport continued to haunt him. For the few hours he managed to sleep, they were restless ones, his mind struggling through images of Davenport.

Chapter 20

Sensing the slightest change in his surroundings, Greg awoke to find the reporter Kay sitting up in bed. As she stretched, her arms reached towards the ceiling and Greg finally got his first real look at her in the faint light. Although her dress was wrinkled, it didn't hide the slim figure underneath. The breasts were of average size but full, rhythmically moving with every breath, straining the material of the fancy gown, which barely covered them. The legs were long and slender, kept firm from rigorous aerobic exercises Greg assumed. While most men would have stared at those particular aspects of her body, Greg was drawn more to the smooth silky hair and delicate face. Although she wasn't the type found on the cover of glamour and fashion magazines, there was a simple beauty that was echoed by the hypnotic green eyes.

After several seconds of stretching, she reached down with both hands to clear the sleep from her eyes when she suddenly noticed Greg staring at her. Surprising to her was that it wasn't a sensual stare but as if he was judging her. Looking down, she noticed her dress was wrinkled and attempted to straighten it and her hair.

"Good morning...or should I say good evening." Greg finally said after looking at his watch, which read seven-thirty in the evening, six hours after he heard the news report.

"You're not catching me at my best uh, what is your name by the way?"

"Not to sound like a dime store novel, but let me ask the questions for a while." He said considering where to begin.

"Is this going to be an inquisition? Don't you need a bright light shining in my face mister secret man?"

"Sorry to disappoint you, but things are a little out of kilter for me now. Before I reveal anything to you I'd first like to find out who you really are and what role you play in all this. You have to admit that it is rather strange to find you out in the middle of nowhere, conveniently close to the events of this morning, accompanied by someone who was very intent on seeing me dead."

"Not any stranger than having you sneak up out of nowhere, right after a large explosion, kill the reporter I was with and then whamo, reveal the President of the United States unconscious in the woods."

"Fair enough. Now can you tell me again what you were doing in a deserted area of Acapulco this morning?"

For the next twenty minutes Kay went over the details of the past week, her assignment by the San Diego Union, the trip to Washington D.C., the interview with the President, the trip to Acapulco to witness the signing of the Arms Agreement, the gala party the previous evening, her discussions with the President and the events on the road leading up to Greg's appearance. Watching her eyes as she talked, Greg could easily see that she was telling the truth. If not she was one of the best in the business. Tears would come to the edge of her eyes each time she talked about the President, yet she held them back. If she was acting, Greg figured she would have let the tears flow for effect.

"I read the San Diego Union quite often, what type of stories do you write?" Greg asked.

"Mostly hard-luck stories. My most recent story was about a lady who the county decided her two children were better off with her out-of-work ex-husband."

"I've read that. The Melendez story if I remember right. That was a pretty good story."

"Thank you." was all Kay could say, stunned that someone she met outside of the office had actually read one of her stories, remembered it and complimented her on it.

"Inteviewing the President seems a big step from Melendez after such a short time with the paper, isn't it?"

"I was rather amazed myself and a little scared, but if you want to get ahead in the business you have to take advantage of the opportunities."

"Well maybe this is another one of those opportunities." Greg said as he got up from the chair and walked over to the President's bed.

Leaning back against the wall, the impact of that statement hit her. As a reporter the first rule was not to wait for the story to come to you but to go after a story. Caught up in the intensity of the previous twenty-four hours, she never even considered that this may be the story she had been looking for, the one every reporter yearns for his entire career.

Looking up she watched as Greg sat down on the edge of the President's bed. If she wasn't mistaken, it appeared that Greg was conducting an inventory on the President.

"How much do you really know about the President?" Greg said turning his head towards her.

"I've only met him twice in person. Once during the interview and the other at the party. He appeared caring and in control, although he seemed somewhat paranoid."

"Paranoid?"

"During our conversation at the party, he sidetracked once and talked about assassins as well as the dangers of powerful people. He talked about how the signing of the Arms Agreement would affect a lot of major companies in the U.S. and worried about what the people in charge of those companies were capable of and consider doing."

"Have you ever met his Chief of Staff, Thomas Alexander?"

"No. Why do you ask?"

"Just curious. Did the President appear any different the night of the party then during the interview?"

"A little more relaxed since he wasn't in the Oval Office, but he was still as charming and gracious. What is this all leading to?

At that moment the body that lay next to him began to stir. Remembering the effect the drugs would have, Greg knew the assumed-President would have a severe headache and remain groggy for several more hours. It was then that Greg thought about some other possibilities that he hadn't previously considered. If the earlier news report was right, whoever may have planted the imposter in the President's place had gone to a lot of trouble and could conceivably have replaced the drug as well. This option seemed unlikely unless someone on the team was involved. If somehow it had been replaced, than the imposter might only have been stunned by the explosion and awoken hours ago. If so, he would have over-heard everything he and Kay had just discussed. The complexity of the situation and possibilities began to overwhelm Greg.

Assuming the proper drug was really used, the only real opportunity to verify that it was the real President would be to question him while he was still groggy. On the other hand, if it really were an imposter and the drug replaced, then questions would be answered as rehearsed. The only real playing card Greg held up his sleeve was the one evening off the coast of Bosnia when he and the President spent some time together and the specifics on his interview with Kay, something an imposter would not know about.

Deciding that he would question the would-be President on other matters in the mean time, he propped the body into a sitting position, propping some pillows behind his back. This was done for two reasons, one to get the blood flowing to the brain and alleviate some of the effects of the drugs, mainly the oncoming splitting headache. Secondly, to look into his eyes as he talked. Learning long ago from his mother that the eyes are the only clue to whether a person is lying or not, a lesson he had learned the hard way while he was growing up, he was able to ascertain the emotion the eyes couldn't hide.

"Five dollars says his first words are where am I." Greg said as he smiled towards Kay and rose up from the bed, walking towards the sink to pour the would-be President a cup of water. Realizing again where they were he stopped halfway remembering the old adage about drinking Mexican water. Walking back towards the door, he took the canteen from amidst his pile of gear and walked back towards the bed. Sitting next to the would-be President he unscrewed the top. Grabbing behind the President's neck to support the head, he lifted the canteen to the President's mouth and slowly let some run inside. Anticipating the next moment, Greg leaned away and as expected, the man began to cough and spray water across the room. The eyes opened abruptly and Greg could still make out the drug-induced haze in the man's eyes. That was a good sign, Greg thought to himself. If the man were an imposter and the drug replaced, the eyes would seem clear and alert.

"Take it easy, sir. Just relax and drink some of the water." Greg said leaning the head back as he poured some more water into the mouth. This time it was accepted.

After a few swallows, the would-be President opened his eyes again and attempted to work through the haze to distinguish the man in front of him.

"Where am I?" was all the man could ask just as Greg had anticipated.

"Told you." Greg said at Kay. "Sir, you are in Mexico. Can you tell me who you are?" The first question Greg wanted to ask while the man was still in a stupor.

"John." he replied, pausing for a second and looking directly at Greg's face but it was clear he couldn't make out any distinct features.

"John, what?" Greg asked. The man squinted his eyes attempting to focus.

"Um...I'm afraid I can't remember now." he replied. Instantly Greg knew he was lying, but not sure of what. By not giving his full name it meant that the man could be the

President protecting himself in unfamiliar territory, or an imposter under the effect of drugs and not recalling what he was trained to answer with. If it had been an imposter without the effects of the drugs, he would have rambled off that he was the President.

"Well, have some more of this John." Greg said handing the canteen over to the man. Motioning for Kay to follow him, he rose from the bed and walked towards the door. Since the first question didn't reveal anything, he decided on a different approach.

"I want you to talk to him and see if he recognizes you."

"Why on earth for."

"Just humor me."

Grabbing Kay by the arm, they walked back towards the bed where the man was finishing another gulp of water. Holding one hand to the side of his head, it appeared he was trying to shake the cobwebs out of his head, literally, as he shook his head and pushed against it.

When Kay sat down next to him the man looked up and his eyes grew. He almost began to say something, his mouth opening slightly, but then abruptly he looked around the room, trying to keep from looking at her. Greg was positive that he recognized her and was trying to not let on. This was another good sign, Greg thought. If it really was the President and unsure of his surroundings, believing he was in danger, he might assume that Kay was also in trouble and didn't want to acknowledge their acquaintance and put her in jeopardy.

"Sir, it's me. Are you okay?" Kay said as she put her hand on the side of his face.

The would-be President turned back towards the outline of Greg. "Who are you people and where am I?"

As Kay was just about to answer him, Greg put his hand across her face to prevent her from giving her name, even though that move would look bad in the President's eyes. If Kay had said her name, the imposter would immediately acknowledge knowing her. Greg preferred that the man reveal her name instead.

Smiling at her, Greg shook his head and motioned her back towards the other bed.

"I'm sorry but I'm afraid I can't indulge that information right now" Greg said. "There are too many things going on right now and until I can determine who you are, I'm afraid that all I can tell you is that you are in a Mexican hotel."

"I want to leave."

"Be my guest but I'm afraid you are in no condition to do so." Greg replied stepping back as the man attempted to raise himself from the bed. After spending almost fifteen hours asleep under the influence of a harsh narcotic, the body was not as willing as the mind and the man's legs quickly gave way, immediately slumping towards the floor and falling into Greg's prepared arms. It was a moment Greg had hoped for. If the man were an imposter he would have play-acted falling but the body would have been preparing itself for the impact of the floor. This body gave no indication of it and was like a tree that had just been chopped down by a lumberjack's axe.

"I suggest you lay back for a while until you're feeling a little better." Greg said as he lowered the would-be President back on the bed, returning him to a sitting position.

When Greg began to pull away, the man grabbed hold of each side of Greg's face and stared at him as if trying to recall the face. After a few seconds the man let go and fell back against the pillows, closing his eyes.

"Who are you? You look vaguely familiar, but I can't place where." The man said with his eyes closed. Greg could tell the man was making every effort to get control of his senses.

"Is that so?"

"Haven't we met before?"

"I was hoping you could tell me." It was the only way Greg was sure that the man was truly the President.

"I can't recall, but it seems like a while ago." the man replied.

"Well, hopefully it will come to you." Greg said, depressed that he wasn't going to get the answer he had hoped for.

Greg walked back to the sink and ran some cold water. Leaning over he poured some water into his cupped hands and splashed it on his face. Looking into the mirror he could see the weariness in the eyes. Stubble was already forming on his face, and the eyes were red and puffy.

The hair looked greasy and severely out of place, which in most cases he would find disturbing. His hair was his pride and joy, able to let it grow in College once away from his parents and their preferred crewcut. Some remnants of ash were evident on his face and hair. Desperately in need of a shower, he was afraid that in the few moments he would take to have one, Kay and the man would be out the door not knowing that there was a contract out on him that every man and child would be out to fulfill. If it really were the President then he would need Greg's protection. If he was an imposter, then there was a great deal of danger that in someone's haste to turn him in, somebody else would be killed or injured, possibly even Kay. Greg was not going to let that happen while he had the chance. He would turn the imposter in. After that, then what, Greg thought. It was a question he hadn't begun to face and would keep it away for now until this was cleared. Greg's life was in as much danger as the man sitting on the bed. It was his team that had been lied to and sent into Mexico, supposedly to cover the murder of the President. The answer to who was behind it and why was yet to be considered, but that too would have to wait.

"I suggest you get a few more hours sleep until dark and then we will have to get back on the road." Greg said to

Kay. Tears were settling into the corners of her eyes as she stared directly at the man sitting on the bed. Not sure if the tears were from the fear of not knowing what was going on or from seeing the President in his present condition, Greg began to feel somewhat sorry for her. If she truly was an innocent pawn in this game, than the whole affair must be unbearable for her.

"What is going on?" she said looking at Greg with puppy dog eyes. Greg wished he could tell her.

"I wish I could tell you. Just relax and get a few hours of sleep."

At that moment the man's eyes opened and he sat straight up.

"I remember, it was onboard that Navy ship I visited in the Adriatic over the Christmas holidays right when I was Senator. You were involved in working with my Secret Service team." The man declared. A huge weight began to lift off of Greg's shoulders, but he had to make sure.

"Very good, sir. We watched Alabama and Washington play their bowl game." At that the President swung his head towards Greg.

"What the hell are you talking about? It was my Alma Mater, BYU against San Diego State in the Holiday Bowl. We played cribbage and drank that disgusting Fly Juice or whatever you called it." This was truly the President, Greg realized, having lied to see if the man would correct him.

"Yes, sir. And it's Bug Juice. Sorry I had to lie to you but I had to be sure."

"Most disgusting thing I ever drank."

"I think you said it about twenty times that night also."

"It's Greg isn't it? I'm sorry but I seem to have forgotten you last name."

"That's all right, Mr. President, its Greg Morris." They shook hands and the President looked over at Kay.

"Kay, I'm sorry, but I didn't know what was going on and didn't want to put you in any danger." he said. Kay came over beside him and they clasped hands. "Now what the hell is going on and what are you doing here with him?"

"I'm afraid you'll have to ask him, sir. He brought you to me and won't tell me anything."

"I'm sorry sir, but how well do you really know this woman."

"Well, I've only met her twice, but I'm a good judge of character. She's a hell of a fine lady who needs to take some time off from work." With that Greg saw Kay's first smile since he met her.

"Whether I like it or not, I'm getting some of that time off now, just not the way I had planned."

"How well do you now the gentleman she was with, sir?" Greg asked inquiring about Steve Puller.

"You mean that reporter Puller?" the President asked. Greg nodded. "Never met him in person until last night but I didn't care much for his articles. He constantly slammed the government and its politicians. I can't say that every one of them is a rose, but we're not all bad apples. So what is going on?"

"I'm afraid sir, that we've got a real problem." Greg spent the next hour outlining everything Greg could recall, from the day he arrived at Camp Pendleton to the present. The President sat back and listened, occasionally rubbing his chin and staring at the ceiling, contemplating every word that Greg said. Throughout the dissertation, Kay sat with her mouth wide open, not believing what she was hearing. Occasionally Greg would have her fill in with the time she was with Steve in Washington, his outbursts about politics and the events after the party where Steve pulled the gun on her before Greg arrived. Greg was relieved to finally be able to relate the story. It was when he related the news story Greg heard on the television that the President seemed extra concerned, tapping his index finger on his lips. To an outsider, it would have sounded like a fairy tale, as it did to Kay, but the President seemed to accept all of it.

Chapter 21

When Greg finished the details of the past week, the President leaned back and closed his eyes. While he sat thinking, Kay and Greg looked at each other wondering what would happen next. Outwardly, the President looked as if the news was routine, however, looking into his eyes throughout the conversation, Greg could see the mixtures of hate, frustration, confusion and remorse inside. Each emotion trying to gain control, while the President wrestled within himself to control and properly evaluate them. After such intensive news, it was clear that the effects of the drug had quickly washed away, his mind concentrated on the matters at hand.

"You say the news actually reported both mine and the Vice President's death." The President said, looking up with squinting eyes.

"Yes, sir. The Vice President was killed in a car crash in Vermont that was supposedly caused by a terrorist plot, along with your death." Greg replied.

"Then if they were wrong about my death, it may be possible that they were wrong about his."

"It's possible but very unlikely. The news showed a scene of the crash. The body was identified by his wife. The only verification of your death was through your dental records but no pictures of the scene. Since you are here alive, it has to be some sort of cover-up. There was nothing left of the area when I left there except ash and charred bodies. It wasn't long after I carried you out of there that sirens and military vehicles were on their way, as Kay said. That left no time for someone to plant a cover."

"Why then?"

"I can only assume that someone in our country wanted you out of the way, possibly to prevent the Arms Agreement from being signed. Somehow Davenport is involved but I don't know if he was tricked into it or planned it. Although he's clever, he's not powerful enough to have managed your announced demise and the death of the Vice President. I had always wondered why there was so much secrecy about the planned drop sight and the mission. I'm sure that either someone convinced Davenport he was really going after a key terrorist figure and used him and us as a ploy, or Davenport knew all along. I'm not buying into the story about terrorists, since I'm the supposed terrorist group that blew you up."

"Well at least the Chief of Staff has taken charge."

"Forgive me, sir. I'm a little confused on that point. If memory serves me right, isn't someone like the Secretary of Defense or someone like that to take over if something should happen to you and the Vice President?"

"We changed that a year ago. The Chief of Staff convinced me that if something should happen to both of us, which seemed absurd at the time, then the best person to temporarily assume the duties would be the one who is the closest to me, namely the Chief of Staff."

"I don't mean to be rude or anything sir, but how much do you trust the Chief of Staff?"

"Implicitly, why?" the President responded, sounding taken back by the question.

Knowing he was treading he still had to be completely open and not leave any options out.

"Let me go over one scenario for you. The Chief of Staff convinces you to change the rules to allow him to take over the presidency. One year later, the unthinkable happens and now both you and the Vice President are declared dead and he's sitting in the oval office." Seeing the President's face turn red, he knew that it was not an option he preferred to hear. "I'm not saying this is the case but it is a possibility and we should be extremely careful."

The President stood up and tried to steady his legs and stretch his muscles. Looking back at Greg, he glared at him for a few seconds and then looked up towards the ceiling.

"Tom Alexander has been with me this entire term and has stood by me through it all. He and I may not agree on a lot of things, but we manage to come to an understanding on every issue, each of us considering the other's opinion. I can't even fathom him doing something like this." He said looking back at Greg and returning to the bed.

"I'm just saying we need to be careful. If it's not him it has to be someone else who is very powerful with a lot of connections. I'm not wrong in assuming that you will want to return to Washington and clear up this matter, am I?"

"You're damn right I'm going back!" the President said with emphasis.

"Well, with everyone in the country out gunning for someone claiming to be the President who survived the explosion, I think it's prudent we take it one step at a time. It is not going to be easy to get you back without someone taking pot shots at you. We can't just book an airline and fly to Washington, step up to the front gate and demand entrance."

After much discussion, Greg and the President agreed that they would let Greg figure out a way to get the President back. With darkness only a couple of hours away, Greg told the President and Kay to get a little sleep before they checked out of the hotel and got back on the road.

With some of the drug still in the President's system, it didn't take long for him to fall back asleep and Kay followed shortly thereafter. Neither slept very well after learning of the news, but they did manage to rest.

While they slept, Greg sat back in the chair again and contemplated their next move. 'A fine mess you've gotten yourself into' Greg thought to himself. Instead of sitting back in his office at Camp Pendleton after a simple drug lord extraction while awaiting further orders, he was now trying to figure out a way to get the President of the United States back to Washington without either of them being shot or arrested as terrorists. His only hope was to get them someplace safe in the U.S. while he figured out a way to get the President back in office.

As he contemplated all the obstacles and possibilities, he managed to drift off and sleep for a short while. During his sleep, though, he was hounded by the same vision of Davenport standing in the doorway of the villa screaming into a walkie-talkie. Although he didn't trust or like Davenport, because of his Rambo-approach to everything and Greg's fear he would get someone on the team killed or hurt, he couldn't forget that Davenport led them into this mess and the entire team was dead because of it. What Greg couldn't understand is why Davenport wasn't running for cover or firing at the people hidden in the woods; unless Davenport was indeed involved in the plot and was trying to finish the President off, not realizing the blast that Greg was about to set off.

The image of Davenport's grin on the steps, kept racing through his mind until he awoke forty-five minutes later, his body soaking wet from perspiration. Greg glanced at the time on his watch and got up from the chair to look through the curtains and verify that it was indeed night-time. Not having to worry about either of them leaving now, he decided to take the next few minutes while they slept, to get a shower. He needed to wash the soot and blood off his body and refresh himself so that he could remain awake throughout the evening's ordeal.

Greg knew that from this moment on until the President was sitting comfortably in the oval office, that sleep was going to be a rare event. While most people took a shower at the end of the day to help them sleep, it had a different effect on Greg, awakening his body and mind. Greg started every morning with a shower - along with a Diet Coke that he wished he had right now - to get the blood flowing.

After his shower he replaced the bandages and remembered he needed to pick some up at a convenience store during their drive tonight, if one was available. A change of clothes was also necessary but didn't think a place would be open at night. A little more refreshed and alive, he returned to find the President and Kay sitting up in their beds.

"I was hoping you were going to clean up sooner or later. Did you leave any hot water for the rest of us?" Kay said comically, trying her best to ease her tensed emotions.

"I'm afraid that there wasn't much there in the first place."

"That figures. After everything else why should there be any hot water." Kay replied rising from the bed and closing the door behind her in the bathroom.

"Kay is quite a woman. In the short time I've known her, it's quite obvious she has a lot of character and chutzpah."

"I'm afraid we've haven't had much to say to each other. I was really unsure of who she was or her role in all of this. Somehow she got mixed up in something she was unaware of. I have a feeling that her associate, the other reporter, was involved in all of this."

"Just because they were nearby."

"I watched them for a few moments before I approached. He was not interested with anything about the car. During the whole time he was staring into the woods and not down the road, like someone waiting for assistance. I think it's rather odd that a reporter would be carrying a gun, fake a breakdown, be loitering as if waiting for someone to come out of the woods and then turn the gun on his associate. If I'm right and he was mixed up in this, this is a whole lot bigger than I care to imagine. We will have to be leery of anything and anyone."

"Aren't you being a little paranoid?"

"Sir, it's my business to be paranoid. Something kept nagging at me while we were preparing for this mission, telling me something was wrong, but I didn't react. Now my entire team, friends of mine, are dead, and everyone in the United States is out to see to it that I'm either killed or put in prison. They believe you are an imposter, and anyone seen to be aiding them will also be considered a terrorist and an extra target. I'm not about to make the same mistake by blindly trusting anyone."

"That's a sad way to go through life, son."

"Maybe, but it's safe. That's why when we get back on American soil, the first thing I want to do is see to it that we let Kay return to her home."

"Is that because you are concerned for her safety or because you don't trust her."?

"Both."

"Then allow me to add some more fuel to your fire if I can continue on your way of thinking. If she is in danger, won't she still be in danger if she returns and everyone wonders where Steve Puller is? How is she going to answer the questions? Whoever may have been working with Puller will come after her for answers. If she is an accomplice in all this, isn't she more of a danger to us by letting someone know what we are up to?" The President said, leaning back on the bed.

This was something Greg had not considered. The only thought was to get her out of the way so it was only himself and the President. He didn't figure anyone would be aware of her part in all this or care anything about her. Killing her was out of the question if she wasn't involved. As the President pointed out, separating her from them was a severe risk to them as well as to her. Sitting back in the chair, Greg wrestled with the idea of dragging her along on the escapade and finally decided that bringing her along was a necessity. At least she could provide them some sort of camouflage, making it appear like a family travelling together. Greg wondered if he was going to regret that decision in the days to come.

****

Suffering through a lukewarm shower, Kay still felt refreshed after removing the day's wear and tear from her body. As she stepped out of the shower, she looked at the wrinkled gown hanging on the doorknob and wished she had something else to change into. Realizing there wouldn't be an opportunity for a while to pull into a mall and buy some more comfortable clothes, it suddenly dawned on her that there were two suitcases of clothes and accessories of hers still at the hotel in Acapulco. She hadn't realized until now that someone would have to be asking questions on where she was. She wondered if anyone would have gotten concerned enough to start looking for them or had Steve made arrangements for them to disappear since he mentioned killing her the previous night.

Toweling herself off she stared again into the mirror and was disgusted at the image that looked back. Without make-up and her hair wet and stringy, she wished she had her make-up bag at least. Then again, she thought to herself, who the hell was going to see her in the middle of the night driving through Mexico.

After dressing and running her fingers through her hair to try and give it some sort of normalcy, she happened to notice the bloody bandages stuffed in the wastebasket as she opened the bathroom door.

"Jesus Christ." she exclaimed feeling her stomach lift. Fortunately she hadn't eaten all day there was nothing there to stir up.

"Are you alright." the President asked, the first to notice her leaving the bathroom.

"There's a pile of blood soaked bandages in the wastebasket." She declared looking at the President.

"Are you injured?" the President asked.

"Nothing I can't handle for now, however, sometime tonight we need to try to pick up some more bandages." Greg replied so not to alert them.

"How bad is it?" the President asked.

"The worst of it is over and they are properly tended to. I just need to make sure I change them occasionally to prevent any infections."

It was evident to Greg that Kay was sincerely concerned. The same look was on her face as when they first met, as if she knew him from somewhere and felt sorry for him. The look puzzled him and also made him nervous. This was not the time to get softhearted and warm. Until this was over, Greg would have to remain cold natured and alert, without emotion so that his mind was clear to respond to what may lie ahead.

"Sir, are you interested in a shower?" Greg asked trying to change the subject.

"If anything, just to shake the bats out of my head. Someday you'll have to tell what drug you used so I can put it the coffee of all those TV journalists who continue to harass me with stupid questions. No offense." he added smiling at Kay.

"None taken, sir. That's why newspaper reporting is better, because we can just make up the stuff on paper, rather than trying to do it on the spur of the moment." Kay and the President shared a brief laugh before the President went in to take his shower.

"Just who the hell are you really?" Kay asked once the President was out of the room.

"My name is Greg Morris." he replied.

"No I mean who are you really? You were talking to the President about drug lords, missions, extractions, and all other sorts of stuff you hear about in the movies. Are you with the DEA or some other government agency? I'd hate to think you're one of those slime balls in the CIA or something like that."

"I'm not one of the slime balls, but what I am may not make you extremely happy either."

"Why is that."?

"Since I'm all that's left, I guess there's no harm in telling you, but it's just between you and me. This is not a newspaper interview or something you'll eventually publish." Greg was not about to divulge anything in particular, but the concept itself was damaging enough if someone found out what he did for a living.

"Why, are you going to tell me it's in the preservation of national security or something like that?" If only she knew Greg though to himself.

"Something like that. Do we have an agreement?"

"It doesn't appear that I'm going to be able to write for the paper for a while, so there's no reason to worry."

"I have reason enough to worry. You'll be back to reporting again someday and none of this can be repeated. Do we have an agreement?"

"Yes." Kay replied begrudgingly. "What's the big deal."?

"The things that I have been involved in are not what you would normally consider legal. Although I am in the Navy and appear like any other officer onboard a ship, it is only a cover for what the government had trained my team for."

"You're not going to tell me you're Rambo are you?" Kay said sarcastically. Greg was not amused and stood up walking directly at her until he stood a few inches away from her.

"You better wake up and smell the smoke. You may cover your small injustices to man in your paper, but you couldn't even fathom the injustices caused around the world." Kay stepped back until she reached the bed and sat down, her mouth wide open in amazement at the sudden unexpected outburst. Trying to control his temper, he grabbed the chair and pulled it closer to the bed, directly across from her.

"I'm sorry. After losing some of the people I had the highest respect for, I take what I do very seriously. They risked their lives on numerous occasions, so that others may live theirs a little easier. I'm not Rambo, but I am...or was involved in a special team that conducted covert operations for the government."

With that he went on to explain without being specific, the team's involvement in extractions, rescues and surveillance around the world in what would be classified as non-friendly territory. So as not to completely turn her off, he didn't mention the several times the team had to go into those same areas and kill someone or some group. That he thought would be a little too much for her to handle.

"I'm sorry." She said. "I only thought those kind of things were movie material. Stuff to make stars out of Stallone, Willis, Segal and Chuck Norris famous. What made you do something like this"?

"First off, their lives are a lot more glorified. I did it because I believed and still do that I made the lives of many suffering people a little easier to cope with and hopefully saved some lives that might have been lost otherwise. I was good at it and although some might think it illegal, it still seemed right."

As Kay lingered on this revelation, Greg got up and looked outside the window again. The room was silent except for the shower running and the President whistling as if he was in his shower at the White House. Looking back at Greg, she couldn't shake the image of him she had in the dream, slowly slipping away in the mist. Who he was and what he was about still wasn't clear to her, but deep inside she felt protected. In a way she felt sorry for him, and wondered why she had the dream just before he entered into her life. It would take her a while to figure out the meaning of it, and hoped it wasn't a premonition of things to come.

Chapter 22

After checking out of the hotel, they headed north along the Mexican coast. For the first several hours, the drive was uneventful. There was no elaborate scenery, only barren countryside with little or no sign of life. When they had driven for four hours, they pulled alongside the road so that Greg could take over the driving duties, providing everyone a chance to stretch their legs. Filling up with gas at the gas station near the hotel, Greg figured they had another hour left before they would need to stop at a gas station. During the drive they noticed a few gas stations operating and Greg hoped there would be one open ahead, stopping at the next one available.

While they sat along the empty roadside, Kay was amazed at the vast amount of stars in the sky. Without the distraction of city lights and only a sliver of the moon glowing, the naked eye was permitted to take full advantage of the wonders the sky could offer.

"I've never seen so many stars in the sky before." Kay said as she turned. Looking for Greg she found him a few steps away from the car staring out across the countryside.

"Stay here for a few minutes." Greg said turning back towards her.

"Where are you going?"

"I'll only be a few minutes." With that Greg took off into the darkness.

"Just where in the hell is he going?" she said turning to the President who was lying back on the hood of the trunk, staring at the stars.

"I wouldn't worry about him." the President replied still looking off into the sky. "Isn't the sky beautiful at night? I remember as a boy sitting in the backyard of my grandfather's farm in the country and staring up into the sky. I dreamed of being an astronaut like John Glenn then.

211

He was our national hero and I was fascinated in what was out there."

The President shifted to one side of the hood so that Kay could lie down next to him.

"I dreamed of being an actress. I guess most girls do. Growing up in California there was always some celebrity around and movie theaters were spread all over. My parents would take me to the movies and I wanted so much to be like Meryl Streep or Sally Field."

"What stopped you?"

"I wasn't very popular in high school and never got any parts in the school plays. I spent most of my time reading. I wanted to know about things, what made them happen and how it affected everything. When I saw "All the President's Men" and what the reporters did, I figured then and there I wanted to be a reporter. I joined the school paper and enjoyed interviewing people and writing the stories. It wasn't long before I was hooked."

"Rather ironic that you developed your career interest while watching a movie about political intrigue and here you are wrapped up in all of this."

Kay looked up at the stares while letting the last statement sink in. The coincidence was almost spooky. The event that started her into reporting had led her directly to this moment, a participant in what could be the biggest political scandal of all time. She thought back to the moment she was assigned to cover the Arms Agreement and what she had said to herself about going through the door that had just been opened. Imagining the assignment to be nothing but a learning experience, she was now having another door opening for her and she needed to start taking advantage of it.

"You're right. Here I am worried about what may happen to me and forgot the first thing I was taught as a reporter, to take advantage of every opportunity."

"You can't blame yourself. I'm not really sure I can even come to grips with what is really happening. The whole event seems incomprehensible. I had envisioned someone possibly trying to assassinate me, but was never really worried because the Secret Service seems to always have things covered. I had become rather complacent in that regard. Now I'm not sure how I can get back alive and convince people of who I really am."

"What made you decide to be President?" Kay asked.

"When I got over the desire to be an astronaut, I became intrigued with the law. My high school history teacher spent a lot of time covering how law had changed the land. I wanted to be a part of something that would make things better. I didn't study law to be an attorney covering murders or divorces, but rather on the development of laws. I wanted to help create laws that would make things better for people. My grandfather suffered through some hard times as a farmer and it eventually killed him trying to get by while the laws held him back. While I was in law school I reviewed a lot of the current laws and sent numerous letters to congressman and senators on ways they should be changed. Just before I graduated I sent a letter that the senator became very interested in and took to the Senate. The law was eventually passed and after graduation the Senator hired me to his staff. It wasn't long before I became involved in the hustle and bustle of the nation's capital and wanted to remain a part of it, improving as many laws as possible. When the Senator decided to retire I decided to try and run for Senator figuring it was my only way to keep improving things. I just want to get this country where it belongs, where it's safe to go out at night and believe in itself, like it used to."

Kay had expected a simple answer and was amazed at how much the President opened up to her. Although she had only known him for a short time, she felt a deep respect for him and his ideals. Politics were not an important aspect of her life as she grew up and she wasn't even sure she voted during the last election or who she voted for if she did.

As she was about to ask him about losing his wife, a lump of something falling between her and the President startled her. Without a sound, Greg appeared in front of them wearing a worn out set of coveralls and shirt.

"Hopefully these will fit you Mr. President. We don't want you parading around everywhere in your pajamas." Greg said as he folded his gear in his arms.

"You scared the daylights out of me!" Kay screamed. "Can't you whistle or something before you approach?"

"Sorry, it's habit."

"Where did you get these?" the President asked.

"There's a little farmhouse over there that had them hanging on the line."

"You mean you stole these?" Kay asked.

"I've borrowed them. If we survive this, I'll return them. As the Marines would say - adapt and overcome. We needed clothes and since I don't think we'll find a clothing store open at this hour, I went for the next best thing. Now here's a simpler dress for you. If you prefer to go around in that outfit for the next several days I'll gladly return them."

"What are you going to do next, rob a bank?" Kay asked, afraid to hear the answer.

"I am not a criminal, Miss Cross. Hopefully you have enough money to get us to San Diego. Now do you want it or not?"

"I might as well." She said holding out the dress. It was a simple pattern dress that had seen better days but appeared more comfortable and fitting than the gown. "If you don't mind I'll change inside the car while you wait outside."

"Don't take long. We need to get moving. I figure we have about another six hours of darkness left before we have to find someplace to rest and out of view. Hopefully we'll find a gas station in the next hour to fill up."

"This really beats it. You really hate me don't you?" Kay asked looking up at the sky as she walked to the side of the car.

"What was that?" Greg asked.

"Nothing." she replied and stepped into the car and changed clothes.

****

After forty-five minutes Greg was getting concerned about their fuel. Looking down at the gas meter, the needle was getting dangerously close to the E mark. Suffering through the explosion at the villa, the confrontation with the reporter, and hearing the news on the Mexican television station, Greg did not want to have it all come to an end because they ran out of gas. Making a mental note to never letting the gauge get below half a tank, Greg kept driving through the deserted highway hoping that the decision was not too late. A few miles later they found a gas station with a small convenience store attached. Greg pulled the car alongside the gas pump and breathed a sigh of relief.

"Miss Cross, could you go in and pay for the gas. Also see if they have any bandage material." Kay nodded and proceeded up to the store.

"I'm going to make a pit stop." The President added as he left the back seat.

When he received the signal from Kay, Greg began to fill up the tank. After the tank was full, he screwed in the cap and proceeded to the rest room on the near side of the store. The President was still inside, so he stood in the dark on the side of the building when he noticed a car drive slowly into the station and park on the far side of the building. Moving to the front corner of the store, he watched as two men came out of each side of the car wearing long jackets.

In the faint light Greg could see that both were Mexican. The hair on the back of his neck began to tingle again. The men walked slowly into the store, surveying the area before they entered.

Moving along the front of the store, Greg looked in through the window and saw Kay by the refrigerators at the back. One of the men went to the far corner of the room while the other walked towards the register. Each man was of average height and sported scraggly beards. Even though they were wearing long jackets, Greg could see that the man by the register had a better build while the other man was overweight. Within seconds both men pulled out shotguns and the man by the register began to scream in Mexican at the attendant. Kay screamed as well, dropping her sodas on the floor. Without hesitation, Greg proceeded to the front door.

"Hey honey, did you get the bread?" Greg said as he opened the door, looking at Kay. Noticing the same look on her face she had when he killed the other reporter, he winked at her and flashed a smile to ease her nerves.

The man by the register began to scream in Mexican for him to get down on the floor and Greg gave him a puzzling look.

"What's going on here?" he asked, staring the man in the face. Pointing the shotgun at Greg's head, the man walked up to Greg, bringing the barrel within inches of his face. A move Greg had hoped for.

"Hey Gringo, you stupid or somethin'?"

Greg looked down at the floor as if noticing something, which diverted the man's attention for the split second he needed. When the man glanced down, Greg grabbed the barrel of the shotgun and slapped at the end of it, quickly removing it from the man's hands. Before the man could react the barrel was now pointing directly in his face. The man's eyes grew wide in disbelief and he froze in place.

"How stupid can you be? That's one of the oldest tricks in the book." Greg said smiling.

Suddenly Kay screamed again and Greg saw the other man grab her and put her in front of him as a shield, pointing the gun at Greg. The man started screaming at him in Mexican, waving his gun around.

"I'm getting real tired of people pointing guns at me. This is four times in two days and it's getting boring." Greg began to lower the shotgun with his left hand to appear as if he was going to drop it, while his right hand reached behind him at the knife he kept on his belt. Never planning to use it he always kept it handy as a habit.

Greg stared directly into Kay's eyes as he lowered the gun. In the next instant he spun the gun around and smashed the butt end against the first man's head, who immediately dropped to the floor.

"Down on the ground Kay." Greg screamed as he threw the knife with his right hand at the second man. A second after Kay's body began to fall; the knife penetrated the man just below the throat. The man fell backwards into the refrigerator doors, dropping the gun in the process.

As he walked towards Kay, the first man began to stand and Greg kicked out with his right foot, catching the man on the left cheek, knocking him into the register desk and unconscious. By the time he reached Kay, the second man had pulled the knife out and was yelling at Greg in a mumble, blood spurting out of his mouth. He tried to raise the knife as if to strike at Greg, but received a foot in the stomach that felt as if a bat had been thrust into him. Looking up from his hunched position, the last thing he saw was the bottom of Greg's shoe as it found its target directly on his nose, splintering it in several places. The man's body fell like a sack of flower, a heavy thud echoed in the store as the head met the floor.

As Greg reached down to pick Kay off the floor, he noticed the amazement in her eyes mixed with the fear of the previous few minutes.

"It sure doesn't look like anything is going to be easy for us." He said smiling as he lifted her off the floor. At the same moment she reached her feet the President walked in through the front door.

"What the hell?" was all the President could say as he spotted the two men sprawled on the floor.

"They were trying to overcharge me for the gas." Greg said.

"Are you for real?" Kay asked staring into Greg's eyes. "One minute I'm in the middle of a robbery and the next you nearly kill two men without even thinking twice and then joke about it. There's not even a sign of feeling or remorse in your eyes."

"You seem to have a habit of getting guns pointed at you, Miss Cross." Greg said.

"Will you stop calling me that, you make me feel like an old lady!"

"Sorry. Did you find any bandage materials?"

"Yes." she said as she walked to the register. At that moment they both noticed the desk clerk standing there frozen in fear, not knowing whether or not she and Greg were going to rob him as well. Greg leaned down by the second man and picked his knife up, cleaning it on the man's jacket. The clerk began to ramble on in Mexican while waving his hands.

"What the hell is he saying?" Kay asked Greg.

"He's telling you to take the stuff and get the hell out of his store. He thinks you plan to rob him too."

"Well I'm not a thief like someone else we know." she said and dropped some pesos on the counter, picked up the supplies and walked to the car, while talking to herself.

Greg and the President looked at each other and smiled.

218

"She sure has a lot of spunk in her." the President said. Both men proceeded out the door to the car. When they arrived at the car, Kay was sitting in the front seat still talking to herself.

"Are you alright." the President asked her as he sat in the back seat.

"In the past forty-eight hours, I've had my life threatened twice. Each time, John Wayne here has shown up. Why is this happening to me and who the hell are you?" she asked looking again at Greg.

"I guess I'm your knight in shining armor."

"This isn't funny, damn it. You've killed one man, severely injured two others, stolen clothes off some poor farmer's clothesline and got me on some wild trek across Mexico. I just want to go home."

"Listen, Kay. Like it or not, you're involved in this ordeal. I would love to leave you behind, but I think there's something you need to know. Whoever went to the trouble of killing the Vice President and President has a lot of power and since I think the other reporter was involved it's beyond imagination who else may be involved. It seems likely these people will go to any extreme to see to it that the President doesn't make it back alive. If they managed to get to you, your life would be in serious danger and the President and I are not about to let that happen. Although I would like to say that it's because we don't want to see you get hurt, my main reason is that they may be able to find out from you what we are doing and put us both in worse danger. I'm afraid you are stuck with us until this is over. At least when we get to San Diego I can get you somewhere safe until we get the President back in Washington."

"You really have a way of charming the women, Greg." The President said.

Kay just stared out the front of the car, trying to hold the tears from falling. This was not what she had expected when she was given this assignment. At the same time, she still couldn't shake the image of Greg in her dream and what it meant.

"Well, we should have about another four hours of darkness left. As soon as it gets light we'll pull over and find a place to stay. We should be able to get across the border tomorrow, but driving across will be extremely difficult and I have a better idea. For now, why don't you both get some rest." Greg said as he started the car and proceeded back onto the highway.

Closing her eyes and leaning back in the seat, the image of Greg disappearing into the mist and crying for help reappeared to Kay. She couldn't shake the emotion she felt and confusion the image created.   When the image disappeared, she began to think about what Greg said about who was behind all this. During the next four hours she dwelled on the question but couldn't come up with any logical conclusions.

****

On any normal day, the sun stretching its fingers over the top of the Mexican mountains would have been a glorious sight for lovers and dreamers. Unfortunately for the driver and two passengers in the car, it was a signal to get off the road and find a place to stay until darkness. Throughout the night they closed the coastline and when dawn approached they neared a small fishing village the was snuggled at the foot of some hills, the shadows cast by the rising sun, creating a breathtaking scene that would have been adored by artists.

The coast was lined with simple homes cluttered with the fisherman's trades. Nets, ropes buoys and baskets decorated the homes, something one normally sees in an old post card. The village was quiet and appeared deserted but Greg knew that was because the fisherman had started their craft before the sun rose, out in their boats early. Driving off the main road, he worked his way along the curvy streets to the waterfront. Looking out over the small harbor, Greg found what he was looking for.

"I don't think we're going to find a hotel in this place." Kay said, leaning up against the passenger door, her head cradled in her right palm.

"I have something else in mind." Greg replied as he got out of the car. "Wait here." he ordered and walked off towards the small marina.

"What the hell is he up to now?" Kay asked, looking at the President.

"Beats me." The President just shrugged his shoulders. "Maybe he's going to see if he can get us some fish for breakfast."

"You're not serious?"

The President smiled and closed his eyes as he leaned his head back against the door.

After ten minutes Greg returned, climbing back in the car and turning the engine on.

"Where the hell have you been?" Kay asked.

"We need to find a place to park this car out of the way."

"That isn't an answer."

"I've found our way back to San Diego."

"In this town." Kay shook her head and then looked up into the sky, as if pleading for answers, knowing she wouldn't receive any as usual.

Driving about 50 yards Greg found a small overhand in the hill and parked the car underneath.

"This looks like a good place." Greg said as he looked around.

"A good place for what?" Kay asked.

"To leave the car, we won't be needing it any longer." Greg got out of the car and started for the marina.

"Let's go folks, we're wasting time." He said looking back at the car.

"I'm not going anywhere until you tell me where the hell we're going." Kay said as she folded her arms and stared out the front of the car like a frustrated child.

"I bet you were a real pain in the ass on family outings." Greg said, getting a snicker out of the President who was climbing out of the back seat and an icy stare from Kay.

"You appear out of nowhere in the middle of the night, you kill Steve, drag me and the President into a hotel in some unknown town, and you've been traipsing us across Mexico without any hint of where we are going. I feel like I've been kidnapped. I'm tired of being paraded around without knowing what we are doing."

"Let me lay it on the line for you, Missy. Someone has tried to kill the President on foreign soil using American soldiers. My whole team is dead, charred flesh because someone went to a lot of trouble to cover up something. I intend to get the President back to the White House without one or all of us from being killed. If, God forbid, we somehow get split up and whoever is behind this finds you; it would be better for all of us if you didn't know what I am planning. Right now, I want to get back into the United States without having to cross the border in case somebody is there looking for us, which I'm sure they are. Now don't make me have to forcibly drag you along. Once I know we are in a safe place, we'll hopefully be able to figure out a way to get back to Washington."

"Come on, Kay. I know it's not easy, and I don't like it any better than you but Greg is our only option in getting back alive. We need to trust him." The President said as he opened her door.

Kay stepped out of the car and looked at the President with sad eyes. With all that had happened since the ball, she felt as if she would just scream. The President put his arm around her and she felt as if she was back in her father's arms.

"Thanks, Kay. Hopefully, Greg knows what he's doing and it will be over before long." the President whispered in her ear knowing she needed some comfort and support.

They left the car behind and caught up with Greg who was standing at the edge of the marina glancing around. After a few seconds, he walked down the marina and threw his gear onto a blue and white fishing boat that had seen better days but looked better than most left at the pier. Climbing aboard, he held out his hand to pull them both aboard. When Kay and the President were on safely, Greg disappeared towards the rear of the boat. A minute later he peered over the edge of the deckhouse.

"Sir, would you mind casting us off?" Greg asked.

"What?" the President replied, not sure that Greg actually wanted them to undo the lines to the pier.

"Cast off. Undo the lines to the pier."

The President went forward and undid the lines, followed by the ones aft when the boat suddenly came to life. The engine gurgled and struggled for several seconds, rattling the entire boat and sending Kay banging against the bulkhead. Within a minute they were pulling away from the pier and heading away from land. Greg looked out and saw that the majority of the fishing boats were working to the north, so he maneuvered the boat to the South to open up the distance.

By the time they were out of sight of the other fishing boats, Greg headed southwest and turned up the engine as far as he thought they could go without a strain. When the ship straightened on it's course, Kay and the President arrived in the deckhouse.

"Where is the crew?" Kay asked, afraid of the answer.

"We're all here." Greg replied, leaning back and looking aft. "Isn't the sea a calm and serene place? Here you can sit back and reflect, clear the mind."

"Oh Jesus Christ, did you steal this too?" Kay screamed, bringing her hands up to the side of her face.

Greg just leaned his head to one side, raised his eyebrows and smiled.

"You're a rather resourceful type, I must admit that." The President said with a laugh.

"He's nothing but a common criminal. First someone's clothes and now a boat."

"In case you forgot, we're already considered fugitives. All of America thinks I'm an imposter from Iran. The man's just doing what's necessary."

"Why don't you two go down and get some rest. We've got quite a trip ahead of us. Who knows when we'll get another chance. Who knows, you may even be able to get a tan today."

"Good idea." The President said. "Come on Kay, you look like you'll fall down if you don't lie down. Why don't you go down and get some sleep and then when you wake up, start putting some of that story together."

Kay followed the President down the ladder and into the crew compartment, which needed a lot of work. Deciding it would be cleaner and cooler to sleep topside, they grabbed some pillows and blankets and went back up.

"Do you really think Greg knows what he's doing?" Kay asked the President as they laid the blankets on the deck on the forward part of the boat.

"After what I saw this morning at the gas station and what you've told me so far I think we're in good hands. I just hope we can figure a way to get back to Washington and convince everyone that I'm the real McCoy. Compared to the last few days, I'm afraid this is probably the easy part."

When they finished preparing their makeshift beds, they laid back and stared into the sky. It didn't take the President long to fall asleep, but Kay kept staring into the vast blue sky, void of any clouds, and wondered if the President was right. Looking up at the deckhouse, she caught a glimpse of Greg standing at the controls and she wondered again who he really was and what the dreams meant. Before long the exhaustion and stress took their toll and she too was fast asleep.

Chapter 23

No different than a week earlier, the secretary's office was still the same. Lucy remained busy, trying to decipher the scrawled handwriting as she typed it into the computer. It wasn't visibly apparent that anything had changed until the intercom from the Oval Office erupted with the voice of Thomas Alexander.

"Lucy, get Carmichael in here." He bellowed, the intercom shaking from the vibration.

"Right away, sir." Lucy replied, rolling her eyes. Picking up the telephone, she dialed in the correct three digits and after three rings, heard the voice of the Secretary of Defense answer.

"Sir, the President would like you in his office." Lucy said and heard the frustrated grunt on the other end.

A few moments later, Andrew Carmichael entered the waiting room, looking weary and wrinkled. It had been three days since the Acapulco incident and the pace that Alexander had set to change things was taking its toll. The bags under his eyes demonstrated the lack of sleep he'd had while his hair looked as if he just walked through a wind tunnel. Prior to the past few days Carmichael had walked with shoulders front and back straight. Today he was hunched over slightly, the shoulders drooping.

Ever since Alexander took office, Lucy had noticed a steady decline in the SECDEF's personality and demeanor. Every morning Carmichael was summoned into the Oval Office, and usually three more times during the day. Today was no exception.

As was normal practice, Lucy logged the SECDEF's arrival and smiled at him as he entered through the barely noticeable door in the wall to the Oval Office.

"Good morning, Mr. President." Without a smile in return or even an acknowledging grunt, Carmichael walked through the door closing it behind him. Lucy just shook her head and went back to the daily routine of shuffling paper and deciphering the scribbled notes of the President.

****

"Any news?" Alexander asked the moment Carmichael closed the door. Thomas Alexander III was in his glory, sitting in the high back leather chair behind the large desk. The monumental pace over the last three days weren't evident in his appearance. Alexander maintained a steady schedule of working until 2 in the morning and starting at six, yet always looked as if he had spent eight restful hours in bed. The shirt was neatly pressed and his hair was in perfect order.

"Still nothing, sir." Carmichael said as he walked over and plopped down in the sofa in front of the fireplace, his full weight falling into it since the muscles in his legs were drained.

"Jesus Christ, Andy, it's been three days now. We should have heard or seen something. These people couldn't have vanished."

"We have people stationed all over the border, at every harbor and every airport. There's no way they could have gotten through without being noticed. Since this thing started every car crossing the border has been checked and anyone getting off a plane from the south is checked under the guise of looking for the terrorist imposter."

"What about the other one?"

"As far as we know, he's still in San Diego. As I told you yesterday, he somehow managed to slip away from his two escorts and we continue to look for him as well."

"They're imbeciles." Alexander said banging his fist against the table.

"He nearly killed them in the process. Both of them are in the hospital. One needed twenty four stitches and a cast for a broken arm, the other one is still in a coma and he's not expected to last too much longer."

"I want them found." Alexander said getting up from his chair and walking over to the window that overlooked the front garden. "Things are starting to take shape and we don't need them screwing it all up. Do you understand?"

"Yes, sir." Carmichael said leaning back into the sofa while his eyes rolled back.

"What about our progress on Phase II?"

"As we planned, Congress just returned from their vacation period and they have started their discussion on the issues. We can anticipate a vote by Monday. The Senate will then take up the matter and should be able to vote two days later."

"That's over a week away!" Alexander screamed as he turned towards Carmichael.

"We can't move much faster than that without raising eyebrows. We have to let things take their normal course and follow the procedures. When the votes are finished you can approve them, and they'll become law by that Thursday. We've waited this long, we can wait another eight days."

"I don't want to sit here and wait while they're still on the loose. Every day we delay and he's out there, is another chance for something to go wrong."

"There's nothing he can do to stop it. No one is going to believe a word he says and the moment someone sees him, they'll do anything to turn him in."

"He's not alone. His guardian angel won't make things easy."

"He'll just be another casualty. He's got nowhere to go."

"You just get it resolved. I want everyone in here this afternoon." Alexander waved his hand and Carmichael recognized it was time to leave, thankful it wasn't worse than it could have been. Rising from the sofa and heading towards the door, his relief was short lived.

"You better not fuck this up, Andy. So far the only problems have come from your end. I don't need to warn you of the consequences if you screw this up, but I assure you it will be slow and agonizing." Carmichael looked back; sweat beating down his forehead, but Alexander had already returned to his chair and was engrossed in a stack of paper. There was no response expected or desired. Dejectedly, he turned and walked through the door, returning to his office to try and figure some way of finishing things.

****

A gentle breeze was blowing and Kay awoke to the sound of the water as it splashed against the side of the boat. Sitting up in the bed she looked out the small porthole to see the sun as it was setting. Or was it rising, she thought to herself. During the past several days she had lost track of time and wasn't sure if it was morning or night.

The moment they had left the coast she drifted off into a deep sleep. When she awoke several hours later it was dark and she felt nauseous. The boat was swaying from side to side as well as from front to back. Never having been at sea before, she was unable to adjust herself to the tempo of the waves and was suffering from her first case of seasickness. Her equilibrium had been thrown out of kilter and her stomach felt as if it would explode. Although she hadn't eaten anything substantial the twelve hours prior, what still remained had screamed for release. After several more rolls she couldn't hold back anymore and leaned over the side of the boat and vomited into the dark sea. Hanging over the edge for what seemed like an eternity, she regained herself and rolled onto her back. Looking up she noticed a faint light above and found Greg still standing at the wheel, smiling as he looked at her.

That night she wasn't up to any of Greg's criticisms or remarks so she had rolled back over to her back as if she hadn't seen him. Looking up she noticed the vast array of stars in the sky. Gazing at them in awe, she began to wonder about Greg, who he really was, what he was about and why he was involved in all of this. At times he came across as tender and caring. At others, he seemed like the ultimate nightmare, the kind of person you don't want to meet in a dark alley. There was no in between she thought. His personality ran from one extreme to the other at the drop of a hat. She remembered the first time she saw him on the deserted road and how his eyes seemed so empty and cold. Since their night in the hotel though, she was captivated by his green eyes, which seemed to dance in the light. He wasn't what one would call handsome, she thought, but there was something unique that made her feel warm and safe inside.

It didn't take her long that night to fall back asleep. The next day she woke with a calmer stomach, but not completely adapted to the environment. The rest of the time she spent talking with the President, sleeping or enjoying the sun. Finally adjusting to the feel of the sea, she began to enjoy these moments, underneath the crystal blue sky that remained cloudless the entire time. Everything was so complacent to her and the events of the previous days seemed so far away. It was as if she was in a different world away from the rat race she knew in San Diego. She could get used to such a relaxing and contemplating way of life.

After realizing that the sun was indeed setting, she laid back and let her mind float free as the peace and tranquility enveloped her. Memories of her younger days in school and the simplicity of life she used to enjoy with her Mom and Dad. Engulfed in the serenity of it, she was suddenly startled back into reality when the President grabbed her shoulder.

"Greg says we need to go topside." The President said.

"What's going on?"

"I don't know. He just asked me to get you. Have you slept alright?"

"Beautifully. Don't you find this so relaxing and comforting? I was just thinking of home when I was younger and everything seemed so right again."

"The sea is a powerful place, young lady. Some men could spend their entire lives at sea while others are overcome by its simplicity and lose their own identity."

"Tell the master I'll be up in a minute. Let me wash up a little and get the sleep out of my eyes."

"You shouldn't be so hard on him, Kay. He's only doing what he thinks is right. I'm putting my life in his hands and don't think they could be in a better position. In fact, he's quite a guy if you get to know him. We've had a lot of time to talk."

"I don't disagree with you, sir, but I just find him so difficult to deal with at times."

"I'll admit he lacks some people skills, but be patient." With that the President left and closed the hatch behind him.

Rising out of the makeshift bed, Kay walked over to the washbasin and splashed some water into her face. As she raised her head, she caught her reflection in the small mirror and was happy to see the beginning of a good tan. The life seemed to be back in her face and she had to smile. Although her hair was in desperate need of a beautician, she felt good and renewed.

When she opened the hatch she noticed that the sun was just about gone and the moon was barely visible. A few stars could be seen coming to life in the sky and there was the sound of birds in the air. Greg and the President were on the upper deck by the wheel talking and she climbed the ladder to join them.

231

"Greg was just telling me that we will be going ashore soon." The President said walking over to her and helping her onto the deck.

"Where are we?" She asked, attempting to make out the shadowy coastline.

"We're along the California coast, just north of San Diego." The President replied.

"Aren't you worried about someone seeing us at the dock?" She asked looking at Greg.

"I'm afraid we aren't pulling into any dock." Greg replied without turning.

"Excuse me." Kay said as both she and the President stared back at him.

"You're right. I'm sure someone will be keeping an eye out on every port to see if we try to go in that way. We can't risk pulling in." Greg turned and faced them, holding on to the wheel with his left hand.

"So why the hell did we take the boat?" Kay said frustrated. All the relaxation and serenity were dissipating rapidly and she began to feel trapped again.

"I know a place where we can pull the boat up close to the shore and then swim in. It will only be a mile from where I intend to take us. We'll go in after dark with the lights off so no one can see us from shore."

"Are you insane? You want us to swim ashore? In the dark?" Kay screamed, holding her head in her outstretched fingers.

"It's the only way we can get to safety. Any other way we risk being seen by either the people behind this scheme or some gung-ho glory seeker recognizing the President and try to take us in or kill us."

"I can't believe this. Why don't we just keep on sailing along the coast and stop in Washington or Canada?" Kay had been able to lock away the entire episode with the explosion, death of Steve, the hotel interrogation, driving in the middle of the night stealing clothes and breaking up a robbery, to stealing this boat and now all those emotions were flowing back, one right on top of the other, smothering her.

"Sir." Was all Greg said as he looked at the President.

"We can't wait to get somewhere else. I need to get back to Washington before things really fall apart. Whoever is behind this has something else in mind, and it won't take them long before they get whatever they're after. The longer we stay out here the less the chance I can prevent it from happening." The President explained as he placed his hand on her shoulder.

"Besides, it won't be that much longer before they discover the car and the missing boat and put the puzzle together. They'll be looking for us before too much longer." Greg said returning to the wheel and staring out ahead of the boat.

Sitting down in a chair, Kay put her head in her hands and shook her head left and right. She wanted to go back down below, sleep and put it all behind her again. This couldn't be happening to her. It had to be a dream and she wanted to wake up and find herself back in her apartment, never having left for Washington, D.C. or Acapulco. She knew that was impossible and this nightmare was real and she had to pull herself together.

"I'm sorry sir, I just can't believe all this." Kay said, staring up at the President.

"It's okay. Greg tells me that once we're ashore we'll be close to where he feels is the safest place for us."

"Listen, Kay. I know this isn't easy. I'd rather be on a golf course than here. Once we are ashore, this should be all over for you and it will just be the President and me the rest of the way. You'll be able to stay there until this all blows over and I'll come back and get you when it does."

"You play golf?" The President asked.

"Yes, sir. Ten handicap."

"We'll need to play when this is over. As you know I'm an eight."

"I'd love to."

"Are you two crazy? We're out here running away from God knows who and you're setting up a golf match?" Kay stood up and walked over to Greg.

"What happens if you can't come back? What happens if someone finds you and hauls you in or even worse, manages to kill you? What am I supposed to do? I don't even know where we are going?"

"You'll be able to keep up with the news there and if you see something like that then you know it's safe to come out. I'll show you how when we get there. There's no place safer in the country and you won't be far from San Diego, so you can get your life back on track."

"Why doesn't that make me feel any better?" Kay asked as she looked up into the sky. The President walked over to Kay and put his arm around her.

"We've gone this far Kay and we have to keep going and see the whole thing out to its completion."

"I just don't like the idea of sitting around and waiting for something to either happen or not happen. If something were to happen to you, how am I supposed to live with that? I won't be able to write or say anything about it without people putting me in a straight jacket. Keeping it all inside will just make matters worse and it won't be long before I really will need that straightjacket and a rubber room.

"The we'll just have to do it right so you can write all about it and get the Nobel Prize for Journalism. I'll be happy to attend the ceremony."

"Hey, if we don't make it, you can write it as a novel and make lots of money." Greg said comically.

"How can you be so flippant about this? Don't you care about anything? Kay responded angrily, her eyes fixated on Greg who could feel the daggers coming from her.

"I care about getting you two safely ashore and in a safe place. Then getting the President back into the White House. As for anything else it will have to wait until this is over before I worry about them."

The tension in the air was unsettling and the sudden quiet pierced the anxiety even further. Frustrated and angry, Kay realized it was futile to continue to argue about it and went to the lower deck. When Kay went forward, the President walked up to Greg.

"Women!" Greg said shaking his head.

"Maybe you should take it a little easier on Kay. She's just scared and unsure of what is really going on." The President said staring towards the coast.

"She's a grown adult. She needs to get out of her shell and see what the real world is all about."

"Unlike you, Greg, she's not used to running around the world in the dark, not knowing what's ahead. The biggest concerns in her life are what story to write, what sales to attend, which outfit to wear each day, and what food to cook. She's not naïve to the facts of life and the harshness it holds, but it wouldn't hurt to let her know what's going on with us from time to time, rather than being kept in the dark. Just makes the unknown that much scarier."

"I'm not even sure what's going on, are you? I'm concerned that if I tell her what we are going to do and we get separated, whoever finds her will surely be able to find out what we are up to. As you said, she's not accustomed to this type of work and we can't afford to put her in that position. I know you are in a hurry to get back to Washington, but until we can figure the best way to do it, we are going to have to stay at this location. We can't afford to go unprepared and wind up in jail or a morgue. Sorry to be so blunt sir, but the facts are the facts."

"Parts is parts, huh?" The President said using an old Navy adage. "I have a few ideas in mind."

"So do I, but until we get ashore and in a safer place, let's save them. When we get some rest, cleaned up and something to eat, then we can try to put things together."

"Can I suggest then, that while we are waiting for dark, that I take over the wheel for a while so that you can go down and talk to Kay. She really needs to feel as though she has a grasp on what's going on and a friendly word of assurance from you would really help. Having you two at odds doesn't help matters, and we all need to be a little more relaxed and thinking clearly."

"I'll do my best."

With that, Greg went down below and the President took over the helm. It was a moment the President relished. Steering a ship as it gently rolled along the waves. Darkness was still over an hour away but the sky was already turning orange and the effect on the coastline was breathtaking. The President reminded himself that he would have to buy a boat and return here some day to enjoy the freedom and tranquility of it again.

Chapter 24

Greg wasn't known for his tact and articulate style and he knew it. His was a life of action and deeds, not words. This inability to gel in with a crowd and start up a conversation was the key reason Greg remained a bachelor. For Greg, leading men on a mission was ten times easier than standing in front of a crowd giving a lecture and a hundred times easier than walking up to a strange woman to ask her to dance. The few women he had met and had some form of a relationship with had been introduced through mutual friends. Relationships never really lasted though since the women normally became very suspicious of his sudden departures and extended absences. Greg always found it amusing that he was able to fool the ship during missions but was never able to fool a woman. Lying was easy with a man but a woman makes a man feel guilty, even when he is telling the truth.

As he walked down below to see Kay, his stomach began to rumble. Having gone on missions into unknown territory with his life depending on his reaction at every corner, he never felt fear or apprehension. Never pondering over his next move but relying on instinct and a sixth sense of danger, it seemed natural covertly sneaking up on someone and slicing his throat or sticking a knife into his skull behind the ear and scrambling his brains. Now, standing above the ladder leading below to Kay, his mind began to race about what to say and how to react. This was strange territory for him. Here the enemy wasn't an object or person he could easily manipulate, but his own inadequacies.

It took Greg a minute to gain his composure and block the uneasiness. Reminding himself that he had to keep his mind on getting the President back to the White House, he shut out the apprehension like someone would shut off a faucet. The eyes turned black and empty for a few seconds before regaining color.

When he reached the bottom of the ladder, he found Kay with her head in her hands leaning over a table made of old slats strapped together and nailed to wooden stumps. Having never gone below until now, Greg was amazed on the relatively clean condition it was in. Although the furniture was mostly makeshift items and seemingly uncomfortable, everything had a proper place and was neatly stored in shelves on the walls. Navigational equipment and charts not used on the upper decks were neatly packed and folded. Expecting to find beer cans in every corner and pieces of fish in every crack, Greg found the floors and walls to be clean and well preserved.

"I guess I should apologize for my recent behavior." Greg said feeling an apology was the first matter of business, not expecting the reaction.

"Don't come down here and patronize me you, you, you sadistic insensitive shit. I don't know who the hell you think you are, but I've had enough of your rude and macho-man bullshit."

Kay said, standing up and looking directly at Greg. Bringing all her courage to bear and letting off some of the frustration that had been boiling inside, she walked straight up to Greg and swung to slap him across the face. Unfortunately, without thinking, Greg reactively caught her hand in mid-air. The force of the sudden stop nearly broke her arm. It took tremendous effort for Greg to prevent himself from taking the next step and tossing her across the room.

"What the hell?" Why'd you do that?" Not fully understanding what brought on the sudden outburst he was even more surprised for what happened next.

Kay suddenly broke out in tears and fell to her knees. Everything that had happened to her since the party in Acapulco had finally peaked and her emotions went into

238

overdrive. The up-and-down roller coaster between fear and relief, the intensity of the situation and the lack of control she had were more than she could bear. The world was slowly closing in on her and she felt as though there was no way for her to fight it anymore. To make matters worse, the confusion of the man standing in front of her and the dream she had of him before the explosions complicated matters.

Greg could never really understand women nor their emotions and sudden mood swings. This was another case of normal woman behavior, he thought, complex and ever changing. Having learned to shut out emotions almost to the point that he had forgotten what they were, he didn't know how to deal with Kay's present position. The first thing he needed to do was to get her off the floor and back at the table. At the moment he picked her up he suddenly found Kay's arms wrapped around him and her head buried into his shoulder, another moment he hadn't anticipated. Not knowing how to react, his hands dangled at his side while he pondered what to do.

"My God, you really are empty." Kay said as she stepped back from him as if she were afraid of catching a disease. Kay lowered her head, wiped the tears from her cheek and returned to her chair by the table.

"You really don't feel anything do you?" she asked Greg looking up with big round puppy-dog eyes.

"I'm not sure I understand your question." Greg replied as he walked over and sat down across the table from her.

"Just this moment, when I had my arms around you I felt as though I had my hands around a vacuum, cold and empty. What kind of a person are you?"

"I'm just like everyone else."

"You are far from everyone else. I knew that the first moment I saw you. The moment you appeared from behind Steve, your eyes were like black holes. The night at the gas station, the moment you walked into the store you had the same empty look. When you killed Steve and severely injured those thugs, it was without any sense of regret or hesitation. When I reached out for you just then, you didn't even react by hugging me. Yet, at other times I've noticed how green your eyes are. It's as if you switch them on and off like a light switch. How can you do that?"

Looking into her eyes Greg sensed both fear and sympathy. It was evident that she was confused but he could also sense her inner strength. It was wrong for him to think of her as just another simple-minded woman. By taking a swing at him she demonstrated her desire to overcome and take control of things. After all that they had been through, he was amazed at how much she still remained in control, except for the recent outburst. It was then he began to realize just how things might be to her. Risking your life and trekking across unknown territory is standard routine for Greg but not for Kay. At that moment he decided that it was time to put all the cards on the table and hope that she could handle it.

Greg sat down at the table and began to relate the story of who he was, what he did for a living and why they were in the terrible mess they were in. He didn't go into details over particular missions. As he talked, Kay tried to understand but knew that asking questions would be inappropriate. Knowing that she was already in an unstable condition, Greg tried to relate the events as easily as possible without sounding defeatist.

While he related the events of the past week, he began to feel apprehension at their possibilities. He knew there was little possibility of them succeeding with the tremendous odds that were stacked against them. The entire United States population believed that their President was dead and that terrorists were attempting to take over the country by replacing him with an imitator. There was no one that he could think of that he could talk to and convince them otherwise. Greg didn't have many friends as a result

240

of his covert position and the friends he did have were all laying dead in Mexico. Any attempt to convince someone of the outlandish and inconceivable truth would be extremely difficult. Who would believe that someone in the government would concoct such a devious plan? Politicians were known by many to be underhanded and some were downright unethical, but nobody would believe that they had purposely planned to kill the President and take over the government.

Pondering that thought, Greg wondered who could be powerful enough to pull off such a plan. It couldn't be by just a few people. There had to be someone else behind the Secretary of State, he thought. In order to kill both the Vice President and the President there had to be a larger organization of people pulling the strings. Greg also contemplated the other question on why someone would go to all this trouble. There had to be something more than just taking over the Presidency. Someone wouldn't go to all this trouble just to gain the White House. The President wasn't so powerful that the Secretary of State could change things fast. With all the red tape and congressional melee that everything had to go through for approval, there had to be some other underlying purpose.

"Hello, is anybody in there?" Kay asked. Startled, Greg realized that he had been so entrenched in his thinking that he totally blacked her out.

"I'm sorry, what were you saying?" Greg asked, regaining his composure.

"You were talking about the mission in Mexico to apprehend some terrorist and found the President instead when you drifted off into la-la land. Why would you be sent on a mission to apprehend the President?" Greg could tell that Kay was getting frustrated with his explanations and the lack of information.

"That's what is bothering me. It was as if we were supposed to fail and the team along with the President killed in the process. Right before I leaped into the pond with the President, I spotted our superior officer standing in the back entranceway, yelling into a radio but he wasn't talking to us. He wasn't shooting at the people in the woods, but looking directly at me with a sheepish grin on his face. He wasn't aware that I would actually set off the explosives and blow the entire building and surrounding area to kingdom come."

"Your superior officer?"

"Yeah. He was the one who ordered us on the mission and was hell-bent on going with us. It was unusual but that does happen. Every time he has been on a mission with us it has always been plagued with problems, but not as bad as this. It's as if he was intent on seeing the President dead. At least he went up with the explosion. Nothing survived it. When I got out of the pond, the entire area, including all the people in the woods, was charred to ashes."

As he said it, Greg was amazed at the possibilities. Captain Davenport had to be a part of the scheme. Although he never liked or trusted the captain, he couldn't believe that it was possible for him to be party to killing the President and the Special Forces unit he had established just so the Secretary of State could assume the Presidency. It just heightened his awareness that there was something far more reaching in this whole ordeal, but he couldn't put his finger on why.

"So what do we do now?" Kay asked, her puppy dog brown eyes ready to break into tears again.

"First thing we have to do is get to a safe place. I have to see the news to find out what is happening and figure out how to get the President back to Washington and into the White House without getting him killed in the process. Everyone believes that the President is dead and that there is a terrorist plot to implant an imposter in his place. The news I saw in that hotel in Mexico said that they had found the President's body amidst the rubble."

242

"Well, I can assure you that he is not an imposter." Kay said standing up.

"Relax, I know that. I met him several years ago on a ship and only he could have remembered the conversation we had. The problem will be convincing someone that the President is really alive and someone in the government arranged to have him killed."

"I can't believe I'm caught up in all of this."

"I'm sorry. I was trying to find some form of transportation when I stumbled upon you and your friend on the side of the road. I couldn't just let him kill you, now could I?"

"That's not very amusing." Kay said emphatically. Her eyes were locked into Greg's who could feel the daggers being projected from them. "I don't know what came over him. It was my first big assignment and I had never worked with him before. I was there as a sort of an apprentice."

"Well, you're getting an education. When this is over you'll have one hell of a story to tell." With that remark, Greg could see the wheels turning in Kay's head. He needed something to take her mind off their present situation and get her hopes up, even though he didn't have much himself.

"That's if I live through this."

"When we get ashore and come up with some way to get the President back to Washington you are staying there where you'll be safe. I'm not going to risk any more lives than the President and mine. You'll have plenty of time to work on a great story."

"And if you don't make it, no one will believe my story."

"Then we better make it. I wouldn't want you to lose out on a Pulitzer Prize on my account." With that Greg stood up and started out the door. Before leaving Kay to her thoughts, he turned and saw her staring off into space.

"Just make sure you spell my name right." He said and went topside.

Kay sat there for a while and pondered what Greg had just told her. It all seemed so conceivable. This was supposed to be the highlight of her career, embarking on her first real assignment. It was supposed to be a simple coverage of the peace signing and ended up a nightmare. Now she was on the run with a paid assassin and the President on an ordeal that no one would believe.

Perplexed by Greg's split personality, she continued to wonder what type of person he was. The constant shifting from empty black holes to heavenly green eyes plagued her. It was hard for her to imagine someone who could go between an uncaring killer to a passionate and caring individual. Kay couldn't decide if he was a hero or a madman on the loose. She was captivated by him but also afraid of him. A person like that could lose control of himself at any moment and be extremely dangerous, yet she couldn't escape the dream she had the morning she met him.

It was then she was startled by the sudden silence when the engines stopped. At that moment, she felt as if time stopped. Unsure of what they were about to face next and where they were going, she tried to gather her emotions and regain her composure. Wiping away the earlier tears and pulling her hair back with her fingers, she got up. Whatever was to come next, she knew she had to prepare herself for the worst and hope for the best.

Chapter 25

Not having realized it, Kay was suddenly aware that the sun was setting to the west. Looking out over the water, the sea seemed to come alive, echoing the vibrant colors of the sky. It was a sight she would remember for a long time to come. The clouds were a mixture of red and purple while the sky was a somber dark blue. The light of the sun seemed to reach out in branches as the rays picked their way through the clouds reminding her of the skylights in Las Vegas as they pointed into the sky. The sun was just beginning to touch the horizon and looked like a large tangerine orange falling into the water.

"If you watch closely, as the top of the sun meets the horizon you can see the green flash." Greg said, busily working with something in his bag.

"Green Flash?" The President asked looking over to Greg while walking over to Kay.

"Yeah, the green flash." Greg said as he approached the doorway to the deck below. "As the last bit of yellow of the sun meets the blue of the sea, it appears like a burst of green light just as the sun sets. Of course it's a lot easier to see with binoculars. You need a clear horizon in order to bring it out, it doesn't work in rough seas."

With that, Greg disappeared below.

"I think Greg has been at sea too long." the President said as he put his arm around Kay's shoulder. "Are you okay."?

"I'll be alright. I just needed some time to get my head back on straight again." Kay said as she continued to stare at the wondrous beauty of nature, void of the skyscrapers and smog.

Within minutes the sun disappeared over the horizon, but the dazzling colors of the sky and clouds took longer to disappear as they faded into the night sky. Staring out to the west for almost fifteen minutes, Kay was amazed at how brilliant the sky looked when there wasn't the futility of civilization restricting the view. As the sky darkened, it turned into a blanket of stars. There were more stars in the sky than she had imagined or ever witnessed. The clouds had all disappeared and the sky appeared to be a solid black sheet with millions of tiny holes letting in a spot of light. It wasn't until Greg reappeared from below that Kay looked to the other side and noticed that they were along some coastline and she could make out the lights of cars moving speedily down some highway.

"Where the hell are we?" Kay asked.

"If my calculations are correct, and the coastline does look right, we are along the California coastline just north of San Diego. This is where the pleasure cruise ends and we move to the next phase of our vacation destination." Greg said and then regretted his glibness when he caught Kay's eyes rolling into the back of her head. "I'm sorry. What I mean is, that this is where we have to go ashore and go to a secure place I know of."

"Are you sure there's a safe place to get ashore?" The President asked, searching along the coastline, which was about a mile away.

"It's dark, but sandy and flat. I forgot to ask earlier but are either of you afraid of swimming?"

The President shook his head from side to side while Kay's eyes burst open wider.

"We'll never make it. You can't expect us to swim all that way to shore" Kay said.

"It's a little less than a mile and I'll be helping most of the way. We don't have any other choice. Unfortunately our beloved boat here doesn't have an inflatable boat that we can use to row ashore so we have no other alternative. We'll wait a couple of hours until it's completely dark and then go ashore. There are two life preservers I brought up to keep you afloat. We'll take it nice and slow in getting ashore. It should take no longer than 30-45 minutes."

"This is insane. You expect us to swim a mile in the dead of night, and then traipse ashore soaking wet. We'll stand out like sore thumbs." Kay said throwing her hands into the air. "Mr. President will you please talk some sense into him."

"Listen, when we get ashore you'll have to stay close to me. There is a path that we have to take to get to where we are going and we won't be seen by anyone. Once there I can guarantee you warm beds and a hot meal. We'll get a good night's sleep and then tomorrow work out what we're going to do next."

"I'm afraid we don't have any other options here, Kay. We'll have to trust him on this. I have all the faith in him that we'll be safe and he knows what he is doing. This is what he is trained for." The President said to Kay. "Besides, I could use a good swim. I haven't had a good bath in several days and probably stink to high heaven. My family is well known for the excessive body odor. The water will do some good. And as I've told you time and time again, stop calling me Mr. President."

With that, Kay smiled. Here the President of the most powerful country in the world was telling her about his family's body odor. She couldn't get over how calm and relaxed he made her feel. Even in the midst of adversity, the President always seemed to know the right thing to say to make her feel better.

"Well if the salt water doesn't work, there'll be hot showers where we are going. There's also a bathtub for the lady, a Jacuzzi and a steam room. In a few hours you can relax and be refreshed. Regrettably the masseuse is out of town so I can't offer you a massage."

The President laughed and walked over to Greg. "Just where the hell are you taking us?" he whispered.

"To my unit's headquarters. You probably aren't aware of our facilities at Camp Pendleton, nobody is, not even the people at Camp Pendleton. At least there we can get some rest and figure out how to get you back to Washington and convince everyone you are the real President. I have a few ideas, but a good night's sleep will allow us to think clearly and evaluate our options. I'll also need to get some gear because I have a feeling this will not be easy."

"What about Kay?"

"I think it best that we leave her there, where she is safe and keep an eye on what's going on in the news. We'll establish some communications to allow us to keep in touch with her and find out what is going on in the news. The hard part will be getting across the U.S. without being seen by too many people. If someone sees us there's no telling what may happen."

"Just what are you two whispering about?" Kay said as she walked over to them.

"If you must know, it's been several years since I've been swimming and I was just asking Greg to keep an eye on me tonight." the President said. Greg was relieved and impressed by the President's comments. He really didn't want Kay to know exactly where they were going until after they arrived. Knowing the President would maintain his silence no matter what, he worried that if something went wrong and Kay got lost tonight, she may end up in the wrong hands and be forced to give up their location. Although he regretted it, it was best to keep Kay in the dark as long as possible until he was sure she was safe.

"Well I suggest you sit back and relax, maybe even do some stretching exercises to prepare you for the swim. I make it 6:30 in the evening, so we should plan on leaving at 8." Greg said and went back below deck.

"Are you sure we're doing the right thing?" Kay asked the President.

"All I know is that Greg has gotten us this far and he's the only one that has any chance of getting me back to the White House. From what I can ascertain about him, I couldn't be in any better hands. I know this is toughest on you, but it won't be that much longer until we're safe. You have my word on it."

"That's good enough for me. I don't know what it is about him, but I think I'm glad I'm on his side." Kay said as she sat down on the deck and started stretching. "I haven't had a good workout in almost a week. I just hope my muscles are up to this."

The President sat down beside her and tried to work the stiffness out of his joints as well, knowing that even though he maintained a good exercise regimen, he was not prepared for a mile swim.

"Well, maybe we'll be lucky and some dolphins will come along, take pity on us and pull us ashore." he said smiling.

There he goes again, Kay thought. Finding a way to take her mind off the situation and elevating her spirits.

****

At the same time, it was 9:30 p.m. in Washington, D.C. and Thomas Alexander II was sitting in the Oval Office awaiting the arrival of his Secretary of Defense, Andrew Carmichael. The time was growing short and things were not moving along as fast as he had expected. It would be three more days before Congress would take a vote while the preparations to put the plan into effect were not yet all in place. As he fumed over the long list of items that still had to be accomplished, Carmichael entered the room.

"You asked for me?" Carmichael said as he approached the chair positioned across from the desk.

"Has the press been notified of my press conference tomorrow?"

"Yes. The media is having a field day in how you are going to handle the President's assassination. There are more theories in the newspapers and on TV than there are members of Congress."

"Good. I want to keep them guessing."

"You mean you're not going to announce your plan tomorrow?" Carmichael asked, feeling the weight of the world falling on to his shoulders. It wasn't unusual for the new President to make changes without notifying him, but a change like this would severely interrupt the plan.

"Everything is as planned. I just want them scavenging throughout the night before they put their stories out for tomorrow's papers. What I am concerned about is the latest on finding our lost friends." Alexander said as he stared through Carmichael with glaring eyes, looking like he'd leap over the desk and strangle him if it was bad news.

Carmichael swallowed. "I'm afraid we haven't heard anything. It's as if they left the planet. All the highways, airports and borders are being watched. We have notified every state and city law enforcement agency to be on the lookout for them. We have people everywhere and no one has reported anything."

Alexander fell back into his chair. "Well what about our bird dog? Any word from him?"

"The same. He disappeared as well."

"Well you better find him. I don't trust him and I want him to complete his job properly and close out this chapter."

"I really don't think he'll leave. He's not about to let his boy get the better of him. He's rather pissed off about his apprentice beating him at his own game, and he won't stop until he's tracked him down."

"I don't want to hear what you think. You find him and keep that loose cannon on a leash. I don't need him running around shooting at people and blowing things up. This vigilante of yours has already screwed things up and I don't want him making matters any worse. Not now."

Alexander spun around in his chair towards the window overlooking the grounds and Carmichael knew that was a signal that the meeting was over. Standing up, he thought about saying something else, and decided it best to just leave.

As he walked out the door, Alexander spun around again in his chair. "And you better get on top of what else we have to do before I give my speech. I want everything in place before Congress calls for a vote."

Carmichael knew it was fruitless to interject anything and left the office, feeling the heat of Alexander's stare surge through him.

Alexander got up from the chair and pulled the drapes over the windows. Sitting back down he reached into his bottom right drawer and pulled out a rectangular steel box. Laying the box on the desk he inserted a key and opened it. Inside were several small notebooks and a cellular telephone. Pulling out the telephone he called up the number placed in the phones memory and waited while he walked to the center of the room. After three rings a familiar voice answered.

"Falcon, this is Nightshade."

"Of course it is, who else would be calling me on this phone?" Falcon answered.

"Cut the wisecracks. Things are not getting done as planned. We are behind schedule and I still have our friends on the loose and Raven unaccounted for."

"Everything is on schedule. I've taken the liberty of personally handling some of these matters and the rest is in progress. Everything will be in place on time. As for your friends, I'm surprised they've made it this far. I'm sure it won't be long before they are handled. Raven can take care of himself."

"Raven is a nutcase. We should never have paid him until this was over. He could screw the whole thing up by creating his own war on the streets with this commando of his."

"Trust me. I never intended on Raven being paid. He can't retrieve any money without the appropriate code word for the account. Something I simply forgot to mention to him. When the task is finished, Raven will be also."

"Tomorrow is all set. Once I announce our plan there won't be anything to stop us."

"The people are hungry for revenge, my friend. We've been complacent long enough. It's time for this country to reclaim its rightful place in the world. Call me the moment anything new develops. I'll personally look into the other matters. We have a meeting scheduled for tomorrow night to lay the groundwork for the final phase. By this time next week, the world will be a different place."

"Just make sure our friends don't screw things up."

"Who would listen and believe them. Goodbye Nightshade."

With that the line went dead. Alexander went back to the desk and returned the phone to the box. Jamming it back into the rear of the drawer he turned and looked back onto the White House lawn. Falcon was right; by next week the world would be a different place and Alexander would be right there on center stage, conducting the symphony and returning the country to its proper status.

Chapter 26

Darkness quickly engulfed the small boat that sat lifeless in the calm sea. The sky was a canvas of black inundated with more stars than there were people on the planet. Like a tiny speck in the vast emptiness, only one body moved on the deck of the boat. Moving effortlessly, Greg was busy at work, tending to last minute details. Off to one side, two heads on top of life preservers bobbed on the surface of the water, staring quizzically at his antics. After a few moments, Greg slid into the water and swam towards Kay and the President. When he reached them, Kay quickly grabbed his shoulder.

"This is definitely a bad idea. I'm never going to make it all the way to the shore." She said breathless as she paddled to stay in place. "Can't we move the boat closer so we won't have to swim so far?"

Greg grabbed her by the shoulders and turned her back towards the boat. Her mouth quickly dropped to her chest, amazed at what she was witnessing. Slowly the boat was disappearing into the black sea.

"Consider it incentive." Greg said with a sly smile.

If she had the energy, Kay would have swung her hand sharply against his face, however, with the majority of her body underwater and the life preserver restricting her movement, all she could do was glare at Greg and say, "You're such an asshole."

"I've been called much worse. Really, it wouldn't take someone long to spot the boat and ask questions. We can't allow anyone the opportunity to ascertain where we are hiding. I rigged the boat to sink as fast as possible and we needed to do it this far out so it won't be seen from the sky by a passing airplane. Out here the water is over a thousand feet deep, whereas it quickly rises closer to shore."

She took one last glance as the mast of their escape boat slowly slipped below the surface of the water.

Greg turned to the President. "Let's get this phase of our trip over with and get you both ashore and into more comfortable surroundings. The easiest way is to swim backwards. The preserver will keep you afloat and it won't take much of a kick." With that, he laid back, took hold of each life preserver and started kicking backwards towards the shoreline. Both the President and Kay were amazed at how effortless it was to move quickly through the water. As they drifted back, Kay once again was astounded at how many stars were in the sky when there were no lights. In the dark there was no perception of depth or distance and it looked as if you could walk completely across the galaxy stepping from one star to another.

After about 20 minutes of gliding across the sea, Greg abruptly brought them to a stop. When they turned around, they could see the shoreline much closer than they expected.

"We're lucky that the sea is as calm as it is, but there's still a lot of under-current as the tide moves in and out. From this point on, we will go in face first, and be ready for the surf to pull us towards the shore. You'll need to get rid of the life preservers, or you won't be able to overcome the under-tow taking you back out to sea. I'm sure you've both bodysurfed in your life. Once you feel the ground under your feet, push yourself ashore as fast as possible." Greg said as he helped them undo their life preservers.

"Then what?" Kay asked as she tried to figure out the snaps on her preserver.

"Once on the beach we'll meet and you'll follow me." Greg responded.

"Follow you where? There's not a damn thing out here." She snapped as she looked at the shoreline to see nothing but more darkness.

"Ahhh, that's my special surprise." Greg said, still not willing to give her much information until they were safely in the underground complex.

Kay just rolled her eyes, realizing it was fruitless to press further. Once settled though, she was definitely going to give Greg a piece of her mind.

****

The loud ring of the phone suddenly broke both the silence and Andrew Carmichael's brief rest. Andrew was sitting in his living room, his dry and weary eyes closed from reading piles of reports during the past several hours. He looked over at the antique clock above the mantle. The time just barely after 9pm. Cursing under his breath, he grabbed the phone.

"Who the hell is calling at this time of the night?" He growled.

"Sorry sir, but I figured you'd want to hear immediately." The timid voice on the other end of the phone answered. Carmichael recognized the voice as that of Tom Shepherd, one of the 10 special investigators he had in Mexico trying to find evidence of the missing President and his rescuer.

"You found something?" Carmichael asked as he sat up in the bed.

"We learned of a boat that was stolen from a remote fishing port. Just outside of town an abandoned stolen car was discovered. We think they've taken the boat and might be headed back to the U.S. Coast." Shepherd responded.

"How long would it take for them to get to the coast?" Carmichael inquired.

"At best rate, they could have arrived in San Diego tonight. Once we discovered the boat we immediately alerted the port authorities in San Diego and up along the coast with a description of the boat and to contact us immediately.

"Good. Let me know the moment you hear anything." Carmichael pondered on the latest news. Before hanging up, he thought of one further step. "Tom, from what I know of these characters, they're pretty sly. Get the authorities to search along the coast just in case they try to get ashore in some other manner. They wouldn't be foolish enough to pull right into a main port for fear of being recognized."

"Yes sir, we'll get on it first thing in the morning." Shepherd replied.

"No. We can't wait until morning. If they could be in San Diego tonight, I want them out there immediately. We can't waste any time." Carmichael snapped back.

"Yes sir. We'll get on it immediately. We'll let you know if we find anything."

"Good. Get yourself up to San Diego and coordinate things from there. Call me the moment you hear anything."

With that, the conversation ended, and Carmichael hit the receiver button. By this time he was sitting on the edge of the bed. He dreaded that he had to call the Alexander on this, but if he waited until morning, he knew the screaming would be much worse than it would be for waking him up.

After one ring, the phone was quickly answered. "Yes?" Alexander inquired.

Startled by the speed it took for the phone to be answered and how alert Alexander sounded, Carmichael just shook his head. "Sir, this is Carmichael, we have some news on our terrorists."

Thomas Alexander II, the newly crowned President, was sitting up in the bed, papers scattered around, including news reports on the President's assassination, the potential steps the new President was going to take, and the affect everything was having on the stock market. Once Alexander got involved in a project, the hours were insignificant. "This better be good news."

"Pretty good. The investigators found a stolen boat in a remote port in Mexico with an abandoned stolen car not far from the dock. We believe they're going to try to get to the coast by boat." Carmichael said without much conviction. "We've alerted all the Port Authorities and we've started a search up and down the coast to see if we can find them."

"When do we expect they'll reach the U.S. coast?" Alexander asked.

Carmichael took a deep gulp; afraid this was going to come up. "Well based upon the time the boat was discovered missing, they could have made it to San Diego by today, but we had already notified the Port Authorities."

The silence at the other end of the line knifed through Carmichael. He could just imagine the veins on Alexander's neck swelling to the bursting point. He tried to find words to subdue the moment, but Alexander was the first to break the silence. "Andrew, if they slip through our fingers and get ashore, I assure you that your fingers will never be able to hold anything ever again." With that, the line went dead. Carmichael let his head fall back as he closed his eyes. This job was not going to get easier he thought.

****

Exhausted and out of breath, Kay collapsed on the beach. Soaking wet, covered with seaweed and every muscle in her legs aching from her toes to her upper thighs, she suddenly realized that she wasn't in as good as shape as she thought she had been. She couldn't believe she was lying on a California beach, soaking wet, and wasn't on a vacation, getting a tan, and reading the latest Danielle Steele novel. Instead she was running from God knows who, caught up in some elaborate political conspiracy, one of the greatest news story and the inability to put it in print.

Rolling over on her back, she took a deep breath and wondered if there would ever be any sanity in her life again. Suddenly she felt a cold hand on her shoulder and her nerves came completely alive and she leaped up. If she had any more energy, she'd have screamed.

"Kay, it's just me." the President said.

Gasping for air, she reached over to him and welcomed his soft embrace. "I can't take much more of this."

"I know what you mean. Every muscle in my body aches. If I ever get back into office, I'm definitely going to expand my exercise program."

"Where's our Guardian Angel?" she asked.

"I don't know. I'm still trying to figure out if all my body parts are still here."

"What the hell are we supposed to do?" Kay tried to get to her feet.

"We're going to take a nice healthy stroll and then a nice hot shower and climb into a warm soft bed." Greg said as he appeared out of the shadows without any warning.

The President gazed at Greg, wondering how he wasn't even breathing heavy and moved so effortlessly. "Does this place have room service?" The President quipped back.

"I'm afraid management has really cut back at this locale, so we'll be on our own. You don't even have to make your own bed if you don't want to."

"Sounds great. The White House formalities were really getting to me." the President laughed.

"Everyone ready?" Greg asked.

"Ready for what?" Kay asked. "From what I see, it's sheer cliffs, how do you expect us to get up those. I can barely move my legs as it is, you can't expect us to be mountain goats now."

"Trust me. The Morris magic is just a short walk away." Greg smiled as he raised his eyebrows and led them towards the cliff walls.

"Somehow that doesn't make me feel any better." Kay said.

"Oh give the guy some credit Kay." The President said as he put his arm around her. "He's gotten us this far. You're back on solid ground and still in one piece."

"When I get to a hot shower and soft mattress, then I'll give him all the credit he deserves."

In a couple of minutes they reached the edge of the cliffs. The President and Kay gazed up and as they came back to the base, they noticed that Greg was nowhere to be found.

"Now where the hell is he?" Kay ranted.

"Now you see me, now you don't." Greg said as he magically appeared out of thin air from the wall of the cliff.

"What the hell?" the President gasped. "How'd you do that?"

"It's a hidden passage we have from the complex to the beach. We've had to use it several times upon return from missions. It doesn't have much light, but it's only about a two-mile hike into the complex. There you'll have all the amenities you need. Now just take my hand and follow me." Greg said as he took Kay's hand and proceeded through the darkness of the wall.

Chapter 27

Although she couldn't see a thing, Kay could smell the damp, musky air of the tunnel that they had entered. There was nothing but complete darkness and the stench of old plant life soaked in seawater that permeated the air. The cold dampness surrounded her and seeped into her muscles and joints, magnifying the pain that already consumed her. Suddenly the sounds of the ocean faded and then a light thud. She felt like a caged animal with the walls converging on her, until the darkness started to fade and small lights began to flicker along the walls of what appeared to be an endless tunnel. Fortunately the lights came on slowly, dim at first, allowing her eyes to adjust.

"Welcome to my home away from home." Greg smirked. "Nobody knows this place exists and we're not far from those showers and soft beds I promised you. We'll be able to rest and then consider our options and plan out how to get you back to the White House, Mr. President."

"I'm impressed." The President said. "It's amazing the secrets that even the President doesn't know about."

"It's not the Hilton, but I think you'll be more than pleased. We'll be safe here while we contemplate our next move."

"Yeah, that's what they say in the movies and then suddenly the world crashes in on them." Kay said, as she felt the cold chill climbing up her spine.

Greg didn't want to let on to both of them that he had an uneasy feeling as well. The hairs on the back of his neck were tingling again. Greg couldn't shake the feeling that something was waiting for him, which he shook off as ludicrous since he was safe in their underground complex, far away from any dangers that lurked across the countryside looking for them. Still, his intuition had never been wrong before, so he was going to keep on his guard just in case.

"Well in 30 minutes you'll be soaking in a hot tub or shower. I'll try to prepare something for a late dinner, before we all get a chance to sleep to recover from the past few days' ordeals. We're deep underground and miles away from anyone." Greg said as he began to lead the group down the long tunnel.

The walls were smooth and slick, the rocks worn away by man and the moisture of the salt air. The ground was a mixture of sand and dirt that covered a hard rock surface, making it easy to walk in silence. The stillness of the air and the lifeless silence, broken only by an occasional drop of water onto the floor and the shuffling of their feet on the sandy surface, brought an eerie feeling to Greg's two guests. The President smiled hesitantly, remembering the Haunted Mansion ride at Disney World, half expecting to see a ghostly image slither out of the wall towards them. Kay, however, had her hand clenched tightly around Greg's arm, her fingernails digging in. Greg smiled; shaking his head at how naïve and uncharacteristic Kay was to other women he had been with.

Most women he had spent time with had a soft exterior but tougher interior, remaining independent and somewhat daring. Kay on the other hand, tried to give the impression she was tough, but inside she was nimble and frail. He'd never heard a woman whine so much except for the comedies on prime time television. Yet, he was attracted to her in some strange way. There was something in her eyes that indicated something else was locked away deep inside and a sensuality that had yet broken free. Greg shook his head and wiped the thoughts out of his mind, remembering the task at hand and the uneasy feeling he had, the farther they went down the tunnel.

****

Twenty minutes after they started down the tunnel, the lights began to fade and darkness slowly slipped in, making it more difficult to find their way. Greg wondered why the lights weren't operating properly and just a bit ahead seemed to be out completely. He turned to the President and Kay and huddled them closer, as if that were possible, since they seemed to be riding on his back through most of the tunnel.

"Seems we have a slight mechanical problem as the lights seem to be out ahead. Hold on close. We're almost there."

"Forget to pay the light bill?" the President asked trying to sound calm, but feeling himself a bit uneasy.

"If we did that's your department's mistake and when you're back in office you can correct that problem." Greg smiled as he nodded his head. He could sense how tense they both were and just wanted to get them into the complex and relaxed, but the hairs on the back of his neck were standing straight up and every nerve in his body were sending off signals of danger. Something just wasn't right.

They walked a little farther until the tunnel was completely void of light. The tunnel had numerous bends in it, to keep the light from reflecting to the outside through any unforeseen cracks. Since the lights in this area were out, there was no way to see what lie ahead without Greg's cat eyes and familiarity with the tunnel. He knew the tunnel just had one more bend in it before the complex, but something deep down inside told him that there was something waiting for him. He found it hard to believe but wasn't taking any chances.

"Mr. President, I want you and Kay to stay here for a few minutes while I go up ahead and try to find what's wrong with the lights. It's a little treacherous around here and I don't want you slipping and falling." Greg lied as he placed Kay's hands in the President's. "Sit here for a while until you see the lights come on. You might want to keep your eyes closed until you sense the lights come on our you'll get blinded."

Assured that they were sitting down along the wall, Greg moved up to the bend in the tunnel. Kneeling down he slowly peered around the corner. Trying to focus ahead, something seemed out of place. Then he noticed the two small flickers of green light in the middle of the hallway, floating in mid-air. It probably wouldn't have caught his attention if they hadn't suddenly moved. Greg suddenly realized what was happening and knew it would take every ounce of strength and wit to overcome this obstacle.

****

He had seen them moving down along the tunnel in the surveillance cameras. Things were working out just as he planned, and the ordeal would be over before too much longer and he'd be basking in the sunlight of a tropical beach, living off the interest in the money he earned. He stared down the tunnel through his night-vision goggles, waiting until the right moment when he'd catch them completely off-guard, turn on the lights to blind his impetuous Lieutenant and laugh as he silently and quickly placed a bullet in each of their hearts. Captain Davenport snickered at his cunning and ingenuity, anticipating that Greg would find some way to get them back to the complex. He'd been waiting two days, resting comfortably in the confines of the modern facilities that he oversaw from it's beginning. Now he was going to close it down permanently, and finally live the good life after years of kicking around foreign soils, fighting un-printed wars, and putting up with the political ass-kissing of the Washington arena. It was his turn and he was going to bask in it.

Suddenly he saw Morris appear from the corner, standing there and looking back down the tunnel. An evil smile stretched across Davenport's face as he turned off the night vision goggles and lifted them off his eyes. Reaching over to the light switch he closed his eyes and with his other hand raised the Barretta pointing down the tunnel. He'd give Morris a few more seconds before he'd flip on the light switch and blind the incoming group.

"Time to die folks." Davenport laughed as he flipped on the light switch. He opened his eyes to find his targets but only found an empty tunnel. In the brief second of shock, he suddenly felt a sharp pain in his stomach as the wind was quickly pressed out of his lungs.

Morris had timed it to perfection. Once he saw the two green lights fade, he raced towards them, rolled and ended up kneeling in front of the form when the lights came on. He had closed his eyes in anticipation of the lights coming on, and thrust his fist deep into Davenport's mid-section. Opening his eyes, he grabbed the arm holding the Barretta with both hands that had lowered at the force of the punch. He rose to the standing position with Davenport at his back, wrenching it outwards, and bringing his knee up to the wrist of his would-be assassin, causing the gun to fall effortlessly to the floor. Without hesitation, he thrust his left elbow back into Davenport's chest, propelling the man backwards.

Davenport reeled backwards, still trying to fill his lungs with much needed air, as his back found the wall. Before he could react, Morris had spun around and the bottom of his right foot found Davenport's cheek with a crushing force, sending him to the floor.

Morris went to kick Davenport, like a soccer player kicks the winning goal, however Davenport caught it in his arm and twisted the leg. The action caused Morris to lose his balance and spin to the ground. Quickly picking himself back up he found himself face to face with his former mentor, still trying to fill his lungs with sufficient air.

"So, the student thinks he can beat the master?" Davenport gasped.

"Oh, quit sounding like a Kung Fu movie. I half expect Grasshopper to slide in and take the pebble out of your hand." Morris responded, taking a defensive stance.

"Enough talk. I've got a tropical beach calling my name, and don't want to waste anymore time toying with you." Davenport said before attempting to slash his right foot against Morris' head, which was quickly met by a block.

****

When the lights came on, Kay and the President both stood up and waited patiently for Greg to return. Hearing noises they slowly walked to the bend in the tunnel and were amazed to see the drama unfolding at the end of the tunnel. Morris was engaged in a fierce battle with an older gentleman, each trading kicks and punches, blocking many of them, but each getting through occasionally.

Blood was evident on both faces and fists, feet and limbs flying through the air faster than they could keep track. Out of the corner of his eye, the President noticed the gun lying on the ground. He quickly moved towards it and picked it up, however, there was no way to use it with the two bodies moving so quickly.

Suddenly Morris received a kick to his mid-section that sent him flying through a glass wall that shattered around him. Before he could stand up, Morris found the top of Davenport's right foot against his cheek. Both the President and Kay watched as Greg's bloodied face was met by the kick, and his body flew back against an exercise bench. The weight and bar went falling to the floor as Greg tumbled onto the floor. The exercise room was full of exercise equipment, mats, weights and various weapons the teams used for practice.

Davenport casually walked up to the bloodied Morris, smirking, feeling triumph within his grasp. Grabbing Morris by the throat, he lifted him up, seeing the determination still in Morris' eyes, and for a short moment felt sorry such a good soldier had to die, but the sentiment was short lived. Reaching down to his side he pulled out a long knife, and prepared to drive it into Morris' heart when a shot rang out and the bullet splattered into the wall near Davenport.

"I think that's quite enough." The President shouted, the Barretta pointing directly at Davenport.

Davenport's eyes shifted to the President and he grinned. "Wait your turn Mr. President, your time will come shortly."

The brief distraction was the moment that Morris needed. He knew it would only be a matter of seconds before Davenport would hurl the knife towards the President and the struggle would be quickly over. With the last bit of energy he had in him, he leaned back and smashed his left foot into Davenport's chest, sending him hurling backwards. As he fell backwards, Davenport tried to regain his composure enough to throw the knife at Morris. Just as he was about to release the knife his chest began to singe with a sharp pain as his body came to a sudden stop. The knife just dropped to the floor as Davenport tried to breathe, but every muscle in his body became limp and unusable. He couldn't raise his arms and could barely breath. He glanced down to see a spear sticking straight out of his chest. Looking up, he found Morris walking up towards him. With one last bit of energy, he grinned at the damage he did to Morris' face.

"Falcon will not let you succeed in getting him back you know?" Davenport gurgled out of his mouth, along with some blood.

"What the hell are you talking about?" Morris asked.

"Some......thing......you'll......find......out......soon
......" but Davenport never finished the sentence. His eyes
rolled backwards and his head dropped down to his chest.
Greg fell to his knees and before completely passing out,
felt hands holding him up and saw Kay's sparkling eyes
staring into his just as the room went dark and he collapsed
from the injuries and sheer exhaustion.

Chapter 28

With just the simple movement of a finger, the seas came into focus through the powerful binoculars. The improved vision still didn't help locate anything out of the ordinary in the calm seas. The sun wasn't expected to rise for another 4 hours, so the only light available was from the partial moon that gave the sea an iridescent glow.

Leaning over the railing on the bridge wing, Tom Shavers, Lieutenant Junior-Grade in the U.S. Coast Guard, lowered the binoculars and rubbed his eyes. It had been a long sleepless night. After a full day of paperwork, he had gone home for a good night's rest, but before he had a chance to climb into his warm bed, the phone rang calling him back for an immediate ship's departure on a search mission. The ship was delayed in leaving port by two hours while the Engineering department corrected a minor problem with the Diesel engine. It was now three-thirty in the morning, three hours after leaving San Diego harbor, and he had just taken over the bridge watch. Because of the delay he only had a chance for a brief two-hour rest before he was back on the bridge for the three-hour watch.

"Nothing on the radar scope, sir." The young Petty Officer said from the small doorway that led to the bridge.

"And nothing visually." Tom replied. "It would have been a good idea if we had some general idea of where this ship was located."

"Well, from what I heard, every boat we have is out to sea. It must be some important boat."

"Probably some politician's kid took Daddy's boat out and got lost after partying too much." Tom laughed with the young Petty Officer.

Tom turned back to the vast body of water and returned to scanning the emptiness. He wondered how long they'd be out looking. At least the weather forecast called for clear weather over the next several days, so if there were something out there, someone would have to see it. Suddenly the silence was broken as a Coast Guard helicopter flew less than a hundred yards from the ship, speeding over the water at the same level as the bridge wing. Tom smiled, waved, and thought what a bunch of hotshots helicopter pilots were.

At the same time, unbeknownst to the young LTJG and the Coast Guard crew, 150 feet below, the small boat that previously carried three passengers, continued to drift towards the sea bottom. Had the Coast Guard vessel launched on time, they would have arrived at the same spot to find the three passengers going over the side of the small boat before it began to sink slowly beneath the water's edge.

****

Kay stared at the limp form on the table. She and the President managed to find the medical facilities near the weight room. They hauled Morris' bloody body to the examiner's table shortly after he collapsed unconscious from the battle with Davenport. She then looked up at the President with empty eyes.

"Now what the hell do we do?" she asked. "I'm not a Nurse."

"Well we could at least clean him up and let him rest." The President said as he checked the shelves for towels and medical supplies.

Kay looked at the blood that had dried up above Morris' right eye, just below his nostrils, and across his left cheek. After seeing Morris' handle the thugs at the gas station, she never imagined she would see him in this condition. She found herself feeling empty inside and helpless. The man who appeared out of nowhere to save her from an almost certain death on a remote Mexican road by killing without any remorse or thought, whose cockiness and self-confidence was almost repulsive, and treated her with such insignificance, was now lying unconscious in front of her and she was experiencing such deep feelings for him. Throughout their ordeal, the conflict within her continued to build. She detested him for his ideals, everything he stood for, and his treatment of her, but she felt a strong pull towards a man who plagued her in a dream that she had since she was a teenage girl.

"Get his clothes off so we can get him cleaned up." The President said as he started to wet some towels and put dressing and bandages on a tray.

Kay continued to stare at Morris in a foggy daze, unaware of the President's comments. The President walked up to her and startled her as he touched her shoulder.

"Are you with us?" the President asked.

"What?" Kay replied.

"We need to get his clothes off and clean him up."

"I think I'll leave that chore to you."

"Okay," the President said, "I'll get his clothes off, you wet some towels and bring the tray over here."

Kay walked over to the sink, still a little distant as her mind battled within itself.

She ran several towels under the faucet, while she stared off into space. When she finished, she gathered up the towels and rolled the tray to the table. She gazed back to table and suddenly felt the air escape her lungs. Morris' body looked as if it was carved out of stone, highlighted by muscles and veins as if painted on an artist's canvas. A small towel draped across his hips, there wasn't an ounce of fat evident across a washboard stomach and powerful legs.

"Uh-hum." The President cleared his throat trying to get Kay back to the real world. "Can I have one of those towels?"

Kay shook her head and woke up from her surrealistic dream. "Sorry."

"Cut some of that tape into strips and stick them to the tray."

The President worked diligently to clean the caked blood off Morris' face. After 30 minutes he finished bandaging the cuts and putting ointment on the bruises and old injuries from the firefight at the Mexican villa.

"There's nothing else we can do for him now except let him rest, which we need to do as well." The President said looking at the weary reporter. "Our best bet is to try and get some sleep and see how he's doing in the morning."

"Maybe we should keep an eye on him for a while?" Kay asked with sincere concern.

"He'll be fine. The injuries are not that severe and we both could use some rest. I don't know about you but I'm exhausted."

"I guess you're right." Kay said as they walked out of the Infirmary together and looked for the sleeping quarters.

"What are we going to do about that guy in the exercise room?" Kay suddenly remembered the corpse still propped up in the weight room with a spear sticking out of his chest.

"Leave him there until Greg wakes up and figure it out then. I don't think he'll be going anywhere." The President said with a smirk.

"Oh that will make me sleep so much better." Kay replied.

"Sorry, was just kidding. Get some rest and we'll figure out our next step when we wake up."

"Okay." Kay said, wondering what the next day will bring, unaware that the adventure had only just begun and she'd need this rest to survive the next couple of days.

Chapter 29

Even at seven in the morning, the activity was as chaotic as Wall Street during the peak of a Bull market trading period. People shuffled from one room to another carrying stacks of paper and computer printouts. Military guards stood rigid at entranceways and staircases, like statues, in spotless uniforms. Andrew Carmichael wondered if there was ever a moment of quiet inactivity in these hallowed halls of the White House. Every time he had been inside, even on holidays, no matter the hour, the semi-orchestrated melee consistently played out.

Carmichael entered the President's outer chambers, greeted immediately by the Executive Assistant.

"Good morning, Mr. Carmichael. The President is waiting inside." She said as she reached beneath the desk and pushed the concealed button, which was quickly followed by a soft click and the hidden door cracking open slightly in the wall.

Carmichael pushed the door open and cautiously strolled into the Oval Office. Alexander was sitting behind the desk, which was one of the most recognized pieces of furniture in the country, from the numerous television addresses given by the previous President. Alexander was busy striking out sections of some bill that he wasn't pleased with, giving the Senate and Congress something to keep them busy while he continued to finalize the plot that started months earlier. Although he had only two hours of sleep, he looked well rested and immaculately dressed. He didn't even look up at Carmichael as he entered.

"Any news?" Alexander asked as he continued to scribble on the pad of papers.

"Nothing. The search started ten hours ago and no sign of the boat." Carmichael said as he walked towards the desk.

"Any word from our infamous Captain?" The Alexander inquired as he motioned with one hand for Carmichael to take a seat.

"Not a word. I'm concerned about what he's up to."

"Captain Davenport is either dead or is finding out that his bank account has not grown as expected."

"That's what concerns me. What if he's learned he's been double crossed and tries to get revenge?"

The Alexander laughed. "Who's he going to take revenge on? He has no idea what's going on and who is involved. The word is already out that, if he magically appears, he is a threat to the country and to use extreme prejudice to eliminate our worthless pawn. He's no use to us anymore. With all the publicity regarding the terrorist plot to imitate the President, there's little chance they'll get very far, but we'll need to have all our resources in a high state of alert."

Alexander stood up and walked around the table.

"I don't want anyone asleep on this. We've made enough mistakes on this already. Or should I say, you've made enough mistakes already." Alexander said as he circled Carmichael like a vulture surveying its prey.

"I've been extremely patient to date, but we're getting too close to our goal to have someone screw this up. Anything goes wrong, I hold you personally responsible, so you'd better be on top of this from here on out. I have Air Force Two fueling up as we speak to take you to California and oversee everything." Alexander's face was right next to Carmichael's, poised like the vulture ready to take that first taste.

Carmichael could do nothing but gulp. He dreaded the fact that he had to suddenly pick up and head to California, but he also realized it would create a greater distance between him and Alexander. Being across the continent from the lunacy was the one silver lining behind that dark cloud that had been looming over his head since a few days ago.

"I want progress reports three times a day and called whenever you have something important." Alexander said as he walked back behind his desk. "Two days from today, all the pieces will be in place and Congress will have no alternative but to support the bill."

"Yes, sir. I'll see to everything." Carmichael said as Alexander went back to scribbling on the papers in the middle of the desk. There was no recognition of Carmichael's remarks; just a steady silence that indicated the conversation was over. Carmichael got up out of the chair and walked towards the door.

"Don't return unless our friends are history." Alexander said without looking. Carmichael left the room and wondered if he'd ever see the Oval Office again as he walked down the coveted halls.

****

Kay woke up in the darkness completely dazed and confused as to what day it was and where she was. Hoping it had all been a bad dream, she turned on the light only to have that dream quickly evaporate. The bare walls and lack of windows brought to life the nightmare she had been suffering since leaving the ball in Mexico. Her entire body ached and her head pounded. She needed a long hot bath to get rid of the salt that infested her every pore and the dirt that coated every wrinkle in her body.

Kay got out of the surprisingly comfortable bed, feeling the cold of the tile on her feet, which sent a chill through her body. She threw on her filthy clothes they stole from Mexico and decided to try to find a shower. Walking down the empty corridors, she felt completely out of place. Everything seemed so surrealistic. She missed the comfort of her warm bed and bathtub that were less than a thirty-minute drive away.

She found an open door and walked inside to find a huge pool and smiled as she spotted the Jacuzzi on the other side near the showers. She walked around the pool to the Jacuzzi and saw that the heat controls were set to one hundred degrees and the jets were already activated.

Her muscles begged to feel the soothing relief from the hot water as the jets beat upon them. She walked into the shower room to find towels on a shelf. Things were finally looking up as she undressed by the lockers that reminded her of her high school gym days. The water was warm and refreshing, as she used the soap on the small trays. She could immediately feel the wear and tear of the past few days slip away and sink down the drain.

Believing that she was completely alone, she threw the towel over her shoulder and headed towards the Jacuzzi. Stepping out of the shower room, she suddenly froze as if her feet were in cement and couldn't move a muscle.

"Well, this is quite a way to start the morning." The voice of Greg Morris echoed from the Jacuzzi, bouncing off the walls of the vast arena.

Greg had regained consciousness a few hours after Kay and the President had left him in the Infirmary. He had already showered, put on a new set of clothes, fired up the rest of the equipment in the complex, put food out in the kitchen to cook up for breakfast, and taken a look at the latest news on CNN. Having achieved all of this, he felt it was time to loosen up the body and tend to his wounds, so not realizing that anyone was awake yet, he activated the Jacuzzi before going into the gym next door to do some stretching exercises. He returned to the poolroom just as Kay was starting her shower, unaware that she was there, removing his clothes and climbed into the hot bubbling water.

Kay was speechless and couldn't even move to cover her body up. Her mind was telling her to slither back into the shower, but the body was not cooperating.

"Oh quit worrying. The body is a wonderful thing and it's not like I've never seen a woman's body before. You definitely have nothing to be ashamed of that's for sure." Greg said, realizing the insensitivity in his words and how that probably only made her feel more embarrassed.

"I'm sorry, I didn't mean it like that. Just relax and enjoy the Jacuzzi. I'm sure your body could use it and there's plenty of room for both of us." He said trying to sound like the perfect gentleman but failing miserably.

Kay finally recovered her senses and threw the towel around her body. Greg just smiled at her.

"Kay, there's nothing left to hide now, so just get in the Jacuzzi and enjoy it. It really does help. If it makes you feel any better, I won't watch." Greg said as he turned his body and looked the other way.

"You are such an asshole." Kay said, completely embarrassed by her current position.

"I've been called much worse." Greg replied. "Now get in and quit worrying."

Kay stepped to the edge of the Jacuzzi, and while keeping a constant eye on Greg, stepped into the water, letting the towel slip away as she lowered herself in.

"See that's not so bad." Greg said turning back towards her. "I'm hurt that you haven't even asked how I was feeling."

"By the sounds of things, you are already feeling much better." Kay said, seeing the bruises and scars on his face, shoulders and arms, some new, some old. What captivated her more were the beautiful hazel eyes she first noticed had suddenly turned a bright green. She was hypnotized by his eyes, as if drawn into them.

"I'm not feeling too bad considering the last few days. How about yourself, how are you holding up?"

"Sore, tired, frustrated, hungry, mad and have a throbbing headache." Kay responded.

"Well, after this Jacuzzi and a good breakfast we'll hopefully take care of most of those problems. We can spend the morning trying to recuperate and decide how I'm going to get the President back into office."

"Do you think we have any chance?" she asked.

"Honestly? I give us one chance in ten. We have the whole country believing he and I are nothing but terrorist impersonators. On top of every would-be American hero trying to kill us, there's whoever is behind all this gunning for us as well. I don't know what Davenport was referring to, but the pieces all point to a slew of people and we don't have a clue as to who they are. Even if we do manage to get him there, we still have the problem of convincing a nation he's the real McCoy."

"Won't they know to look for you here?"

"There are very few people who know about this place. Even the President wasn't aware of it. The big problem is I don't know if Davenport told anybody he was waiting for us here or not. With his ego, he probably didn't and was going to brag when he brought us in, but we can't be too sure."

Kay leaned back with her eyes closed, as the jets sent the hot water hard against her legs, waist and back. With the soothing sensations enveloping her body, she was no longer thinking about being naked with Greg. All her nerves and senses were coming back to life. She pondered over the last few days as she stretched out her legs. Suddenly she felt a twinge as one of her legs brushed against his, not realizing how relaxed she had become. Quickly she moved her legs off to one side and breathed heavily. Opening her eyes, she immediately looked into his deep green eyes, which seemed to look deep into her very soul.

"Maybe this isn't such a good idea." She said, reaching over for the towel. As she tried to stand up, her weak legs gave way and she fell forward into Greg's arms. Her body just melted into his, feeling the security of his arms, shoulders and chest. Trying to recover herself, she reached out again to gain her balance, only to find it on his left thigh. She looked back into Greg's eyes and was completely overcome. Whether her fall was accidental or unconsciously calculated, they were face-to-face, body against body, surrounded by hot surging water that just multiplied the hidden feelings. It was no surprise that their lips met in a warm kiss that she believed were only shared in movies or romance novels. Passion surged their souls, as tongues danced with one another, hands exploring each other's arms and backs, bodies squirming against one another.

Overcome by the fire burning inside her, Kay tilted her head back, allowing Greg to kiss and nibble along her neck and shoulders. Without thinking, she arched her back and rose, exposing her breasts to his moist lips, feeling them around her erect nipples, sucking gently as his tongue played with them. His hands held her waist tightly as her whole body tingled with electricity she only dreamed was possible. As he began to kiss back up to her neck she lowered herself, her legs straddling Greg, feeling him slowly enter inside her, effortlessly. She clenched Greg tightly as he filled her so completely.

There was nothing else in existence for either of them at this moment, but the emotions that erupted within them. Like molten lava, the heat moved higher and hotter within them, while their bodies melted together. They moved in harmony, each thrust feeding the fire, kisses deep and intense. Leaning back again, she took him in even deeper as his mouth and moist lips returned to her breasts. Her hands tightened around his head, fingers sliding between his thick hair. The sensations even more intensified by the vibrating hot water caressing their bodies. It was hard to tell whether the water or their bodies were hotter, but each probing of Kay's inner being by Greg's erection stimulated every nerve within.

Kay could feel each nerve converging to her hips; building with a ferocity she had never felt in her life. Simultaneously she could feel Greg grow harder and hotter within her. Their bodies locked into an inseparable hold, until their passion reached an indescribable crescendo, their bodies melting into one, flowing together, sharing a moment rarely felt between two people.

Feeling lighter than air, Kay held Greg tightly as if she'd fall forever if she let go. Both breathed heavily, their chests locked together, sensing each other's heartbeat. It took what seemed like an eternity for each of them to fall back down to Earth.

As Kay suddenly came back to life, passion was replaced with fear and insecurity. She suddenly realized that she had just made love to a man she appalled and barely knew. She was still straddling him and holding him within her, their fluids flowing together inside her. The intensity of the sensation was beyond description, but the sudden fear almost made her sick. The conflict within her just reached a higher plateau.

"My God, what the hell have I done?" She screamed. Although she had never felt more fulfilled or like a woman, her stomach was also twisted in knots from the turmoil of making love to a man who slipped in and out of her dreams while in reality aggravated her to no end.

"If you don't know, we're in serious trouble. As far as I'm concerned, it was the most intense sensation I have ever experienced." Greg said as his hands moved from her waists up along her body.

Kay pushed away from him and leaped out of the Jacuzzi, grabbing the towel and racing off into the shower room. Tears began to flow uncontrollably from her eyes. She collapsed on the wooden bench, her head in her hands. Greg got out of the Jacuzzi and followed her into the shower room. Seeing her in this condition confused him to no end. Greg never did quite understand women, and this completely took him by surprise. He knew he felt something for Kay. He wasn't sure what it meant, but after this was sure there was something pretty intense.

"What is wrong?" Greg asked, trying to figure out what was wrong with her. Greg had always been able to figure out what his enemies were thinking, how he could manipulate what he knew and take advantage of the situation. But that was always with men and never had to face the complex emotions that raced to extremes at a moment's notice, like in a woman.

"Get the hell out of here and leave me alone." Kay cried without raising her head from her hands. She didn't want Greg to see her in this condition. She felt weak and insecure, more so than she had ever felt before.

Isn't there anything I can do? You have to agree that this just indicated that there is something going on here."

Greg's words didn't help her. Now he was coming across as a normal human being with emotions and feelings, yet she still remembered that night on the dusty road when he killed with no remorse and a cold emptiness in his eyes. This just compounded the conflict, especially with the feelings she experienced as she watched him lie limp on the infirmary bed, blood covering his face.

"There is nothing going on here." She lied. "You took advantage of my weakened state and got your jollies off."

"Is that what you think? Well my dear, you could never be more wrong. I believe it was you who fell into me, I didn't bring anything on." Greg began to walk away. "I'll never figure you women out."

Greg stopped and then turned back towards her. "If you can't see that there is something going on between us, then I feel sorry for you. I have some fresh clothes for you. I'll leave them in the hall and whenever you want breakfast, it will be ready in the cafeteria just down the hall. I'm going to check on the President and start looking at what we're going to do next."

"Damn!" Greg screamed as he turned, shaking his head as he walked back into the pool area.

Kay just felt sick inside, her stomach twisting into knots. She couldn't handle this conflict that welled up inside her. Like a tidal wave, the tears began once again to flow effortlessly. She returned her head to her hands and just fell back into her deep despair wondering if she'd ever be able to understand what was going on.

Chapter 30

The distinct smell of bacon grew stronger as Greg walked down the hall towards the kitchen. The closer he got, the aroma of eggs and coffee grew stronger, tantalizing his senses and making his stomach growl in anticipation. It had been several days since they all had a good, hot meal. Now after his invigorating episode with Kay, Greg's energy yearned for the richness of solid food and protein.

Opening the door to the kitchen, the scents engulfed him, causing him to instinctively lick his lips. Behind the expansive counter that ran along the middle of the kitchen, the President was moving pans across the range with such grace and ease, it almost appeared as if he was born there. Hands were moving effortlessly from one pan to another, scrambling eggs and flipping bacon. Next to the grill, toast was stacked on a plate while the coffee pot was full of rich, dark coffee.

"Someone in here would make someone a great wife." Greg said as he walked towards the refrigerator. Startled, the President almost dropped the skillets.

"Please make some type of announcement or sound when you enter a room with me in it. . It's very disheartening." The President said, returning to his cooking.

"Sorry. Sure smells good." Greg leaned over to take a big whiff of the delicacies in the pans.

"Well, you know as well as I do, that bachelor's either learn to cook or die on fast-food and microwaves." The President replied.

"You got that right. After week's of McDonald's and Taco Bell, I had to learn to cook or grow to be 300 pounds." Greg replied as he pulled a Diet Coke out of the refrigerator.

"Don't you want a cup of coffee?" The President asked as he slid the bacon from the skillet to a sheet of paper towels on the counter. After moving the pan back to the oven, he pulled half of the paper towels over the bacon and dabbed out the grease. Gingerly, he took the pan with the eggs in them, and carefully slid them onto a large plate on the counter.

"Afraid I don't drink that nasty stuff. Never really enjoyed the smell or the taste. This is my one bad habit in life." Greg said as he waved the can in the air. "My veins are filled with DC, not blood. It gives me all the charge I need to get the day started."

"Well don't say that to Kay. She believes you don't have a heart and that would just add fuel to the fire." The President said with a grin.

"I think I already added enough fuel this morning that would put any college bonfire to shame." Greg said dejectedly.

"God. Now what have you done?" The President asked as he wiped his hands off on the towel and put two plates on the counter and some silverware.

"Never mind. Just hand me some of that bacon and eggs. I'm starved."

"Sometimes I wonder about you. You'd almost think you two were married the way you both banter back and forth."

"That's not even funny, sir." Greg said as he angled his head and stared down the President.

"Maybe, but there is something going on between you two. I can see it in the way you look at each other."

"That's what I was just trying to tell her, but she's as bull-headed as they come. Anyway, I'm tired of spoiling a good meal. Let's drop this subject and get on to more important things, like how we're going to get you back to D.C."

"What did you have in mind?"

"I have a pilot friend, who might be able to fly us back there. He's a retired Marine, and we're sort of partners in a club he owns outside San Diego. I can call him this evening and try to arrange for him to fly us out there tomorrow morning, early."

"The earlier the better. I was watching CNN this morning and Alexander has the government looking at granting him authorization to declare war on the terrorist's who reportedly killed the Vice-President and me. I'm not sure what Alexander is up to, but we need to get back before Monday, when they plan on making a vote."

"I can get you there, but the bigger problem is what do we do when we get there. You are not going to be a receptive face."

"We need to get in touch with Senator Bellows. He and I go way back to college. If there's anyone I can trust, it's him."

"And then what?" Greg asked, finishing off a piece of bacon.

"I'll work that out with him. But I'll need your help. We have to find a way to convince the Senate of what Alexander is up to, and get this vote cancelled. CNN is already predicting a 90 percent affirmative vote with the entire nation screaming for revenge."

"I think I know of a way, but it will depend on what happens when we get there. This is really excellent. Sometime you'll have to let me cook up my specialty, Shrimp Jambalaya, for you."

"I'd like that. Now tell me about this so-called partnership in a club?" The President said with a smile.

Greg went over his relationship with Steve Winslow and the club. The two of them sat and talked around the table like nothing was going on around them. They took advantage of this moment, realizing it might be the last chance they'll have to relax and enjoy a good meal together.

****

"Nothing. The Coast Guard and Navy have both been out along the northern Mexican coast to San Francisco." Carmichael said into the cell-phone as he stood at the end of Pier 6 at San Diego's Naval Base. "We've had helicopters and search planes out all night and morning. Several boats have been inspected but no sign of them."

"Keep on searching. They are either still out there or already ashore. We've got to put an end to this once and for all." Thomas Alexander II screamed through the receiver.

"They'd be foolish to risk showing their faces in public. Maybe the decided to go into hiding since you declared they were terrorists and headed down to Central or South America" Carmichael suggested.

"I know John Lockwood. He won't give up his Presidency without a fight. He's too damn stubborn to know when he's beaten."

"We have every spot along the coastline filled with agents where ever it's possible to bring a boat ashore. They won't get through." Carmichael said, trying to reassure Alexander, but mostly trying to reassure himself.

"They better not. You're life depends on it." With that remark the line went dead, an ominous sound that sent chills up Carmichael's spine.

****

John Simmons, editor for the San Diego Union, and reporter Dave Edmunds sat in their office focused on the television set. CNN was covering some of the debate in Congress over the decision to retaliate against the terrorists. Congressman Todd Davies, the republican from California was at the podium.

"Members of Congress. John Lockwood was a firm supporter in the fight against terrorism. President Bush pledged that he would not negotiate with terrorists, especially after the World Trade Center bombing in New

York. The mighty sword of American justice was handed over to President Lockwood. Six years later, we applauded our efforts and believed that terrorism was finally put to rest. We didn't have another successful terrorist incident on American soil, until now. Now, a whole nation has taken terrorism into its womb. It has hit this nation at its core while we rested on our laurels, and we cannot stand idly by and let these actions continue any longer. It's time to act now - swiftly, without remorse, without prejudice, and decisively. President Lockwood and Vice President Pollard's strengths and determination will be the backbone of our nation." Rounds of applause rang throughout the room.

"Somebody sure rattled his chain." Edwards said. "Congressman Davies has never been this outspoken before on anything."

"I know what you mean." Simmons said. "I've never seen him this animated before."

"Do you really think we'll go to war over this?" Edwards asked, leaning back in the chair and pushing the mute button on the remote. The beginning of speeches were usually great, but they tended to drag on endlessly afterwards.

"It sure looks that way. From the reports I've received from Capital Hill, the Pentagon has brought everyone in and they are feverishly working over operations and contingency plans.

All leave has been cancelled for the Marines at Pendleton and sailors at Mirimar, Coronado and Thirty-Second Street Naval Bases. I've noticed ships pulling out of San Diego harbor at a feverish pace."

"I hear that Alexander himself plans on addressing the Senate on Thursday. They expect over a million people to be present during the funeral procession of Lockwood's casket tomorrow in D.C."

"Job security my friend. Everyone's buying up newspaper's like they're going out of style, just to catch up on the latest events."

"That's for sure. By the way, have you heard anything from Kay or Steve yet?

"Nothing. Nobody's heard a word from either of them. They never checked back into the hotel the night of the assassination. They were last seen at the banquet."

"Weird." Edwards said, before sitting back up and turning off the mute button to hear the CNN reporter talk about the search for the terrorist imposter of the President. If only he knew that Kay was watching the same CNN story not far away.

****

Kay sat in awe at all the coverage on CNN, realizing that she was caught up in the middle of it. Listening to the reports of the President's assassination and the debate in Congress was bad enough. Hearing about the search for the terrorist impersonating the President was too much, since she was a part of it. Fear started to build inside her, finally coming to the fact that her life really was in danger. She hadn't faced it directly until that moment.

Suddenly the caption above the CNN reporter caught her attention.

"Two San Diego Union reporters are still missing in Acapulco." The reporter said. "Steven Puller and Kay Cross have been missing since the Arms Conference ball last Saturday night, and are suspected to be linked to the President's assassination. Both were last seen, as taken by this video camera, occupying much of the President's time during the ball. They're coincidental disappearance has been directly linked, as their rental car was discovered two days ago in a small Mexican village and a boat stolen."

Kay's heart sank into her stomach. She wasn't upset that she was being linked to the assassination, but that her mother and father might be listening. She could just see them crying. She could see their neighbor's looking at them differently as the parent's of the President's assassin. Her concerns were not for herself, but with her loving parents, who unexpectedly, were now caught up in this horrifying event.

"I'm sorry you had to see that. Maybe it's time we had a long talk." Greg said as he entered the lounge where Kay was sitting.

"My God. My parents......" was all Kay could say.

"I know. But you must understand something. The people involved in this are doing everything in their power to find us, no matter who it involves." Greg walked over to the chair next to her.

"Why? What the hell is this all about?" Kay cried out. "I hate you. You got me and now my family involved in this."

"Listen. Let's get one thing straight. I didn't drag you into anything. I could easily have left you there in Acapulco. What would you have said to the Mexican authorities when they found you and your dead partner so close to the President's villa? Believe me, you'd be dead right now. Whoever is behind all this would have silenced you, probably in a Mexican jail. I took you along because I was concerned about your safety. Believe me or not, I'm not the ogre you make me out to be."

"Yeah, right. You drag me on this trek with you, then when I'm at my weakest, you take advantage of me." Kay said as she glared at him, tears welling up in her eyes.

"I never planned that or expected it. It happened. Whether unconsciously or not, we both got wrapped up in the moment. You can hate me forever for that if you want, but it won't do either of us any good right now. You may not believe it, but I felt something there. I just can't let my feelings enter into anything right now. My number one priority is the President. When this is all over, if you want to hash it out with me and take it out on me, that's fine, but it will have to wait. Right now, the President and myself need you to get a grip on reality and work with us. I wanted to leave you here until this was over, but with the latest news and the potential that Davenport told someone about this place, you're going to have to help us."

"Do what?"

"I believe that the Chief of Staff is behind all this. I'm not exactly sure what, but I also know he's not alone. I also believe the reporter you were with was also somehow involved, so it's pretty wide spread. With Captain Davenport involved, this gets pretty messy. I'm not sure what we're up against, but right now I don't know who to trust. You and the President are the only ones I trust right now and we have to get him to D.C. and find a way to get him back into office. I can't do it without you."

Greg got up out of the chair and started pacing around. He thought better on his feet and needed all his wits about him in talking to Kay. He was torn on whether or not to take her along, but he could use all the help he could get. She might slow them down and leaving her as a casualty would be acceptable, except for the fact that he was feeling something for her.

"I won't lie to you. This won't be easy. Wherever we go, we run the risk of being identified and somebody either alerting the authorities or trying to steal the glory for themselves by killing us on the spot. I'm sure every government agency and police department is on the lookout for us and told that we are dangerous. They won't hesitate to shoot us on sight."

Kay just sat there taking it all in. Everything was coming together in a whirlwind. What started out as her biggest thrill had turned into a nightmare she couldn't have imagined. She was hunted, her family was humiliated, her

289

life in danger, and her only safety was through a man who lived in both her dreams and reality, wrestling with her emotions.. It was all too much for her to bear.

Just as she was about to cave in, the President walked in. Seeing him brought some relief to the madness. The stark reality was, that he was the one with the most to lose or gain. The man she had come to know and admire in such a short time was the one who had the biggest cross to bear. Her conflicts were insignificant compared to what he was facing.

"How are you holding up my dear? The President asked as he sat down next to her and took her hand.

"Better now that you're here." Kay replied, clenching his hand, feeling his strength and commitment surge through her.

"I know how hard all of this must be on you. But I trust Greg and if we are going to make it, we need to trust and rely on each other."

Kay rested her head on his shoulder and felt so secure and warm. The whirlwind was subsiding and the softness of his voice subdued everything, just like her father did when she was a girl, late at night, waking up from a bad nightmare.

"I know, sir." Kay said.

"How many times do I have to tell you to call me John?" Kay looked up and saw the smile on his face, which brought one to hers.

"That's better. You are so much prettier when you smile." The President said, wrapping his arm around her and hugging her close.

Kay sat up and looked at Greg, who had a hint of a smile on his face. When she looked at him like this, he almost seemed human and personable.

"We'll get through this." Greg said as he walked towards them. "But we are running out of time and need to move quickly."

"What do you have in mind?" Kay asked, almost sensing anxiety at what lay ahead.

"I'm going to contact a good friend of mine who will hopefully fly us to Washington. Once there though, we are open and vulnerable. We'll have to travel at night and rest during the day. We need to get the President to Senator Bellows and convince him this is a sham, in order to stop the Senate from giving Alexander the power to take the nation into war. How we do that we haven't quite figure out yet."

Greg walked over to Kay and knelt down in front of her.

"Do you have any experience with guns?" He asked.

"No. I've never even held one in my hands." She replied hesitantly.

"Well, I hate to tell you this, but you're about to go through a crash course on weapons. We don't know what we are going to run up against in Washington, but we need to be prepared for anything. Today I'll go over some of the basics with you and let you spend some time practicing."

"Practicing? Where?"

"We have a practice range in the complex. Tonight we'll get a good night's rest and try to leave before sunrise tomorrow morning. We won't get much rest during the rest of the week, so get as much as you can today. We'll be moving around at night and resting during the day." Little did he know just how much moving around they were going to have to do.

****

Kay walked into the training room to find Greg spinning around, kicking and punching bags with such dexterity and speed, that she was suddenly frozen in awe. Only the night before he had been lying unconscious on the medical table, covered with blood. Now he was moving around as if his body had totally rejuvenated and healed. In his hands, were some type of knives, that looked as if they were part of his body, moving gracefully in harmony. Suddenly, his body twirled at the dummy, and in a split second, his hands moved through the air, the knife slashing across what would have been the neck area, and the top of the bag sagged, then, dropped off completely. The image almost sickened her.

Suddenly realizing that Kay was in the room, he stopped. He was barely breathing heavy, although the intensity of his movements would have worn out most of the people she saw at the gym.

"Sorry, just getting in a bit of a workout, to loosen up." Greg said as he laid down the knives and grabbed a towel.

"How do you do that?" She asked, her mouth still open wide.

"Well, someday, maybe I'll show you. Lots of years of practice. Right now we need to start slow and concentrate on you learning how to fire a weapon. Some other time we'll teach you how to use your body as a weapon for something up closer.

Greg spent the next couple of hours showing Kay how to hold, load and aim pistols and machine guns. He showed her how to move around with a weapon in her hand, how to fire at the bulk of a target rather than a specific spot, and how to stand when it went off.

Confident that she understood the basics, he turned on the target range, handed her a Barretta pistol, and several cartridges.

"Now just concentrate on the biggest mass. Don't try to stare down the barrel at the target, just point it towards the center and compensate after each shot."

Kay loaded the weapon and fired the first shot at the paper target, roughly 50 feet away from her. The bullet went off to the right and Kay went reeling backwards. She hadn't expected such a kick. The vibration went right up her arm to her shoulder.

"You're holding the gun too tight. Hold it like you were holding an animal. Just enough to keep it from getting away, but not enough to strangle it. Try it again." He said as he moved her back into position. "The first time is tough, you're never ready for the recoil."

Kay fired off another round, expecting the kick this time, and it hit the chest of the silhouette. Kay jumped excitedly at hitting the target.

"Yeah, yeah, yeah. You hit it. Now let's see how you do a little farther away." Greg said, shaking his head.

Kay managed to hit the target about 60 percent of the time at various ranges. She was feeling more comfortable with every shot and began to experience a sense of power she hadn't felt before.

"Okay, one last test." Greg said as he walked her to another booth. When he turned on the light, Kay almost leaped out of her skin at the sight of the object in front of her. Hanging from a target hook was the body of Captain Davenport.

"My God, you have to be kidding me." She uttered.

"Shooting at a paper target is one thing. When you have to do this the next time, it will have to be at a real person. I need to know that you can actually pull the trigger at another human being."

"I can't do this!" She exclaimed, feeling her pulse rate increase dramatically.

Suddenly the body started to move closer, and after a little rigging, Greg moved Davenport's arm up that held a weapon. Greg fired off some shots. Kay was scared to death. Everything was happening so fast.

"Shoot him!" Greg screamed. "Either you shoot him or he'll kill you, me and the President." Davenport's body came closer, and the pistol was aiming right at her. "Shoot him!" Greg screamed in her ear.

Without thinking, Kay raised the gun up and fired directly at the lifeless body. One shot after another until she emptied the cartridge, her finger still pulling the trigger after the gun was empty. Greg grabbed her and the gun.

"It's over. Take a deep breath." He said, taking the gun away from her. He realized that panic might be a problem, but at least she finally took that first shot at a real body, something he's seen many a man fail to handle.

"I'm sorry I had to do that. But I can't afford to have you freeze up later on. If it comes to it, you and I both need to know that you can fire at something living if it's necessary."

Kay slapped him across the face without warning. Tears welled up in her eyes, mostly from fear. Greg dropped the gun on the table and grabbed both her arms that began to swing wildly in his direction.

"I hate you. I hate you." She screamed as she tried to swing.

Greg pulled her closer and wrapped his arms around her. Her hands continued to hit him in the back, each time with less force than the previous one. Finally her arms stopped and the tears flowed.

"I am truly sorry. It's going to be a lot worse when it's for real. When bullets start flying, you have to instinctively be able to fire, without any consideration other than your own safety." Greg loosened his grip on her and she stood back. He could sense the fear and not anger in her eyes, but knew it would subside. "At least you hit him with every shot."

Kay turned to look at the body, and noticed the ten bullet holes that hit directly into his chest.

"Pretty good shooting, if I do say." Greg said trying to get a smile out of her, but again, failing miserably. "Listen, go get some rest. I'm sure the President is whipping up something good for lunch. We have a long road ahead of us, but at least the first part to Washington will be uneventful.

Greg couldn't have been more wrong.

.

Chapter 31

Outside the air was crisp and clean, the sunshine beaming through the clouds, with birds chirping as they sat upon the telephone cables strung from pole to pole. Inside the air was musky and stale, the only light coming from overhead lights that needed replacement in several spots. Music from an old Led Zeppelin song played on the jukebox. Just the way Steve Winslow loved it. Let the commoners live it up in the California sunshine and sweet smell of the ocean, he thought. Steve preferred the aroma of a good bar, the musk of day old beer staining the tables and floor, the lingering smoke from cigars and cigarettes hanging overhead, along with the mixtures of perfume and aftershave.

Steve was busy restocking the bar when the phone rang. The bar wasn't going to open for another two hours and he wondered who in the world would be calling.

"Hello?" He answered as he squeezed the phone between his shoulder and ear so he could continue to stock the bar.

"Someone hasn't killed you yet for messing with their wife?" The voice on the other end asked. Steve recognized the voice instantly.

"Jesus Christ. That's a voice I hadn't expected to ever hear again. You face is on every newscast and post office wall." Steve said as he froze in his steps. "How's the terrorist business?"

"Hazardous to one's health." Greg replied. "Hopefully you don't believe everything you see on television."

"Hell, I think I've been on the other side of the news enough to know that half of what they report is just plain fiction. What the hell is going on?" Steve said as he put aside the bottles and leaned against the bar.

"It's a long story. I'll tell you about it someday, but first I need a favor."

"Gee, and I thought you were calling because you wanted to tell me you missed me. What is it? Need someone to rob Fort Knox or steal a submarine?"

"Do you still have that broken down old thing you call an airplane?"

"And the horse you rode in on buddy. You want a favor you better talk nicely about my Lou Lou Belle." Steve said with a smile, as he pulled over a pad of paper and grabbed the pen by the cash register.

"I need you to close up shop for a few days and fly me and a couple of passengers tomorrow morning."

"Dare I ask where you want me to fly you to, or can I assume from the news you have a specific destination planned?" Steve said as he fumbled around in an old cigar box with business cards piled in it.

"Good guess. How long would it take you?"

"We'd have to fill up once, but shouldn't take more than 12 hours."

"Need I remind you that this needs to be extremely discreet? We can't land in any busy airports. Someplace nice and secluded."

"Boy, there are a ton of out of the way airstrips all across this country, and I've been to quite a few in my days. You know me. I prefer the simple life. The better bars are in the smaller towns." Steve replied. Finding what he was looking for, he unfolded a piece of paper and laid it on the bar.

"Good. We need to leave before sunrise."

"Hell, it's a slow crowd usually tonight, so I'll close up the place early. I'll have her up and running by five am. How's that?"

"Perfect. We'll see you then."

"By the way, what the hell did you do to Alessandra? She ain't stopped askin' about ya since you left." Steve asked.

"Some secrets are better told over a beer. Say hello to her for me."

"Yeah right. I ain't going to be waiting around for you, so be on time."

"We'll be there. You just have Lou Lou revved up."

"You got it." Steve said as he heard the line go dead. He laid the receiver down and finished scribbling some notes on the pad. Glancing at the unfolded piece of paper on the bar, he took a deep breath and started dialing the phone.

****

"Mr. Carmichael on the phone for you, Mr. President." The voice of the secretary said over the intercom.

"Thank you." Was all that Alexander said.

"This better be good news for a change." Alexander said after picking up the phone. Alexander leaned back in the chair and twirled around to look out the big window behind the desk.

"Yes sir. I just received information on our three friends and exactly where they are heading. We're making arrangements to fly out tonight and intercept them."

"How the hell did they get ashore? Why don't you just pick them up tonight?" Alexander screamed, the force vibrating the phone in Carmichael's hand.

"Well, sir. We don't know if they are ashore, as we don't really know where they are. All we know is where they're headed and when they'll be there."

"I want this done clean and simple. No more mistakes." Alexander demanded. "I don't want word of this getting out to anyone."

"It's almost perfect. It's in a very remote spot, so no one will ever hear about it or get in the way." Carmichael said confidently, feeling much better about himself and not having to look Alexander in the eyes.

"That's what we thought about the beginning of all this. We wouldn't be in this mess if that would have gone as planned." Alexander said with a growl. He knew that before long, he'd have to do something about Carmichael. He didn't have the fortitude or tenacity for this job and his carelessness had already cost the organization plenty. He was well aware of what would happen to someone if they fell out of Falcon's graces.

"Nothing can or will go wrong. By tomorrow night, the whole mess will be cleaned up and you'll have the world praising your Presidency." Carmichael responded, knowing that he was spreading it a little thick. "We can make the morning headlines on how we dealt with and put an end to the terrorist's scheme." Carmichael was hoping to play to Alexander's ego, but he was failing miserably.

"I don't want this announced anywhere. I don't want someone to start saying that we've resolved the conflict and lose our chances on the vote. If the nation sees that it's all over, the sympathetic types will claim that revenge has been achieved and the nation will lose their passion to see justice. Once we're in the driver's seat after winning the vote, then we can make some declaration about finding the terrorists and putting an end to their plans. Meanwhile, we'll be bringing this nation back to its long-lost status as the world leader.

"Any word on our Captain?" Alexander said as he turned the chair back towards the desk.

"Nothing. He's either dead or left the country."

"Well he'd be better off dead. If he left the country, he'll get a rude awakening when he checks out his bank account." Alexander said with a grin stretching from ear to ear. He loved how easy it was to manipulate people.

"But what if he finds out he's been cheated? He won't take it sitting down."

"Who cares? Once the issue with our three friends is resolved, we'll report to Interpol that our beloved Captain has been found to be a part of the terrorist plot. If he's alive, he'll be arrested and we'll see to it that he doesn't talk to anyone."

"Yes, sir."

"You call me the moment it's over. Then get back here so we can finish this up." Alexander said before he hung up. Leaning back, he turned the chair back around and gloated as he gazed through the window. He was confident that within a week's time, the whole project would be completed and nothing could stop it.

****

Greg took one last walk through the halls of the complex. He wasn't sure if he'd ever see the place again. Meandering through the corridors, he reminisced about he past few years here, the people he'd worked with and became friends with. Normally in the Navy, the officer and enlisted ranks didn't mingle, but in this setting, where each member relied and depended on one another, that trust developed into friendship that went beyond camaraderie.

Greg was a personable leader. Even on the ship's he served, the crew had respected and liked him, but they never dared get too close to him. He treated his people fairly and tactfully, rarely ever raising his voice or demeaning someone in private and most definitely not in public. Greg was a motivator without being pushy and overbearing. He set the example and his dedication was evident. Most people, who worked with or for him, respected him for his honesty and infectious positive attitude.

With the team, it was a little different, in that each member was a particular cog on the wheel. Although he was the leader, he was also an integral player in the team. They each had a job to do. Greg was the planner, motivator and guidance, but it was quite often that the team would be broken down into many smaller parts to work different aspects of the job. The Petty Officers became team leaders and Greg the overseer. Even though he called the shots and gave the go/no-go on every aspect, it wasn't what would be ruled as management/employee relations. The team respected him for seeing that, for getting input from everyone, and not holding himself above anyone else.

Now they were all gone. As he walked into the pool area, he remembered the day before Captain Davenport arrived and Tom Franklin tried to sneak up on him in the Jacuzzi. Walking through the gym area, he saw flashes of Peter "Conan" Coleman stretching his oversized muscles on the weight bench or picking up team members with one hand. Entering the Cafeteria, he could hear Hank Thompson and Dave Stoddard arguing about some aspect of the American Indian and their struggle through the ages. The place was still alive with their voices and deeds.

Nearing the end of the complex, he turned around and took one last glance. In his head he was saluting his fallen brothers and friends. Outwardly, he closed his eyes and lowered his head for a few seconds. Looking back up, he grabbed the stack of bags he packed earlier, turned towards the President and Kay, and motioned them silently into the elevator. Tossing the bags inside, he went over to the wall and one by one switched off the lights to the complex. As the last light went off, and only the glimmer from the elevator shone in the hallway, did he open his lips.

"Goodbye, my friends. Rest in Peace." Greg said. With that he entered the elevator and pushed the button to the parking area. No one said a word all the way up the elevator.

****

301

The Humvee bounced along the dirt road that led out from the complex. Greg didn't even take a look in the rearview mirror to see it one last time. He kept it in his mind that some day he would return. They made it through the gate marked 'Restricted Area' and proceeded down the roads of Camp Pendleton.

"Aren't you worried about somebody seeing us?" Kay asked, lying on the hard floor in the back next to the President. This is not the kind of ride she expected after hearing how expensive this truck was on the consumer market.

"Not hardly. Getting off the base is a lot easier than getting on." Greg said as he made the turn onto the road that led towards the gate. To be sure, he had worn an enlisted cammie uniform and pulled the cap down lower on his forehead. As they neared the gate, a Marine stepped out of the guard shack and stood in the center of the gate, holding up one hand for the vehicle to stop.

Greg was surprised to be stopped, but with the recent announcements of military leave being cancelled and personnel on alert, he wasn't completely unprepared. He slowed the vehicle and stopped just shy of the guard, making him walk towards him and keeping the back of the vehicle out of the light.

"What's up, Sarge?" Greg asked in a Texas accent as he stepped out of the vehicle, both hands behind his back.

"No one leaves the base without authorization."

"My damn CO called me and said his car were broke down and I had to drive all the way out to his house at the crack of dawn to pick him up and bring him to the base. I'd much rather go back and have a good breakfast and let you tell him I can't leave." Greg said, continuing his deep Texas drawl, keeping his head tilted slightly.

"I don't know anything about that. Let me check with the dispatcher." The Marine said as he walked towards the shack.

"You'all do that." Greg said following close behind.

As they entered the guard shack, Greg pulled the pistol out from behind him and fired one shot into the back of the Marine and then fired it upon the other guard sitting a the counter. At this time of the morning, Greg knew there'd only be two guards and very little activity. The pistol fired small tranquilizer darts that they'd used in numerous missions since they barely made a sound, except for the soft release of air. The drug quickly entered the blood stream, rendering the individual unconscious for 10 minutes. More than enough time to get away and get to the airfield.

Greg caught the Marine in mid-fall and sat him down on the chair next to his partner. He pulled the darts out and laid their heads and arms on the counter to appear as if they had fallen asleep. He next pushed the button to open the gate before walking out of the shack.

Surprisingly, a vehicle arrived at the gate just as he walked out of the shack. Greg looked at the driver who was waving his identification card out the window. Walking around he stared at the driver who let the window down. Greg instantly noticed it was a young Marine lieutenant behind the wheel, and quickly saluted.

"Where's your regular uniform, soldier." The young Marine asked.

"We've been running a surprise security drill, sir. The regular Marines are getting debriefed inside. Go right in, sir." Greg answered and in the finest manner, came to a formal Marine attention and saluted.

"Carry on soldier. Keep up the good work."

"Yes, sir." Greg replied with a smile as the young officer drove off.

"What the hell's going on?" Kay whispered from the back as Greg returned to the driver's seat and drove through the gate.

"I gave them something to think about, so they're sleeping on it." Greg replied.

"Jesus Christ. You didn't." Kay bellowed.

"Of course not. I just tranquilized them. They'll wake up in about 10 minutes with a big headache. They'll be in quite a bit of trouble for falling asleep on the job, but they'll survive." Greg said with a smile as he turned off the road and onto the highway heading into San Diego.

It was a short drive to the remote airstrip. At first glance, the place was abandoned. Nobody was moving around and only a few old, dilapidated planes were parked in a row along a flat field. The field was rarely used, save for an occasional crop-duster or plane streaming a banner for some sporting event or over the beach. At four forty-five in the morning, it was a ghost town. Greg parked the Humvee by the rusted hanger, and offloaded the bags. He looked around the airstrip and noticed the blinking flashlight off to his left.

"Let's go." Greg said to the President and Kay.

"Where? I can't see a thing." Kay moaned.

"Follow me. Our first class flight is just over here." He said as he pointed towards the silhouette of a plane in the dark.

"Damn, I like a man who's prompt. Shows fortitude." Steve said as he grabbed one of Greg's bags. The contents rattled metal on metal and the weight of it almost pulled his arms out of their sockets.

"What the hell you got in here?" Steve asked, holding it with both hands and lifting it into the back of the plane.

"I can never go on a trip without all my essentials. Toothbrush, hair dryer, dress clothes, and an occasional side-arm." Greg replied with a smile. "Good to see you my old friend."

304

"You sure are somethin' pal. Mornin, sir." Steve said holding out his hand to the President.

"Good Morning, yourself." The President replied, admiring the friendship the two shared.

"We're flying in this thing?" Kay asked disgustedly.

"Hey, don't you go putting down my lovely lady until you see her in action." Steve said as he threw another of the heavy bags into the plane. "She'll get you wherever you need to go and give you a hell of a ride the whole way."

Steve turned to Greg. "Where'd you get this set of legs?" He whispered.

"You don't want to know." Greg said rolling his eyes. "If you want her, you can keep her."

"Asshole." Was all that Kay said as she climbed into the plane.

"Plenty of fire in that one. Bet she's a joy to have around." Steve said elbowing Greg. "Allie's going to be pretty jealous."

"Don't rattle her cage or you'll have more than you can handle, my friend."

"Well, let's go. Everyone onboard and we'll high-tail it outta here." Steve said as he climbed into the plane and held out his hand to bring Greg aboard.

"Thanks, man. I owe you one." Greg said as he climbed aboard. Steve pulled the cord by the doorway, pulled the door up and turned the handle to lock the door securely.

"I'm sorry, but the stewardess called in sick today, so you're on your own." Steve said as he walked into the cockpit.

Before long the plane started to move forward, rolling along the bumpy field and vibrating, as is the ground was experiencing a 7.5 earthquake. Steve turned the plane to face down the long strip of field. Pushing down on the brake he pulled the throttle down some more, to rev up the engines, and then let go, sending the plane barreling down the runway.

"Fasten your seat belts and hold onto your britches. And away we go." Steve bellowed as the plane picked up speed, aiming towards the cliffs that dropped off towards the beach. Kay hung on to the seat with every muscle, staring out the cockpit window, her mouth dropping to her chest. She looked over at Greg, who was leaning back, his eyes closed as if he was asleep. Kay just shook her head and closed her eyes, afraid that the plane was going to fall off the edge of the cliffs and into the ocean. About 200 yards shy of the cliff, the plane angled upwards, the wheels bouncing off the ground, until they were completely airborne.

"Yeehaw." Steve screamed as he banked the plane hard left and headed off to the east.

Chapter 32

In the sky, the body feels a sense of detachment from the hustle and bustle of the world. Normal flights would glide along the sky, above the clouds, allowing the passengers to sit back and dream about better times and places. Regrettably, this flight wasn't so smooth. The President tried to find a relaxing position but the plane shook and rattled throughout the flight, bouncing his body from one side to another. Kay hung on for dear life, watching pieces of the plane flap dangerously, giving her the impression that the whole plane would soon come apart into little pieces and be scattered about the countryside below.

Up in the cockpit, Steve was calm and relaxed, letting the autopilot steer them on a northeasterly heading while he watched the farmlands pass below. Greg sat in the copilot seat, oblivious to the passing objects below or the vibrations of the plane. He continued to run through his mind the options that lay ahead of him. It was second nature for Greg to play devil's advocate with himself, running through different scenarios and balancing the positives against the negatives for each alternative. There were so many things that were unknown.

They had flown for about 5 hours and had recently passed the Nebraska border. Steve had continuously announced each landmark and state border throughout the flight, as if his passengers were interested while they tried to keep their teeth from chattering and their heads from hitting the ceiling.

Greg was getting rather curious about Steve's unusually high spirits. At first he passed it off to Steve's love of flying and adventure. The more the flight when on, however, the harder it was for Greg to comprehend why Steve was being so blatantly happy. It wasn't like Steve to be so uplifting and amusing. He was normally rough and rude on the outside, lambasting everything from politics to religion. His humor was normally more of a sarcastic nature, at best abrasive and callous. This wasn't the Steve he had come to know the past few years and the curiosity was once again causing the hairs on the back of his neck to tingle.

While Greg gazed out the window to the right, he still noticed that Steve was adjusting several knobs on the panel. During the past 30 minutes, unbeknownst to Steve, Greg had noticed him out of the corner of his eye or in a reflection in the window, consistently adjusting the controls. Greg also noticed that the objects on the surface of the Earth were slowly getting bigger. It was barely distinguishable, but still enough to increase the severity of the tingles on Greg's neck.

"I'm going to go check on how the others are doing." Greg said unfastening himself from the copilot seat.

"Okay, buddy." Steve said, waving his right arm in the air.

Greg walked back and sat down next to the President.

"Sir, something isn't right." He whispered to the President as he leaned towards him. "I can't quite put my finger on it, but my instincts are usually right. Whatever happens, stay in your seat unless you hear differently from me."

"I'm afraid that in this jalopy, I can't move much anyway." The President said with a hesitant smile. "What about Kay?"

"I don't want to frighten her anymore than she already is. I need you to watch out for her if anything happens."

"Not a problem."

"It may be nothing at all, but stay on your guard." Greg said before getting out of the chair and moving to the back of the plane where his bags were stacked. He unzipped one of his bags and pulled out two Barettas, several clips of ammunition, and an Uzi. He put one Baretta in his back, stuck three clips in his pocket and placed the Uzi on the rear seat. Greg never left anything to chance. He didn't know what might happen, but he wasn't about to be unprepared.

Closing the bag, he moved back forward. When he got to the President's chair, he handed him the other Baretta and two clips of ammunition.

"I want you to hold on to this, just in case." Greg said.

"Are you serious?" The President asked with a quizzical look, like he was being handed a poisonous snake.

"I'm always serious, or hasn't Kay told you that?" Greg said with a quick smile.

Greg proceeded back towards the cockpit. He placed the bag on the floor before walking inside, and then moved back into the copilot seat.

"Everybody comfy?" Steve asked.

"Considering what they are strapped into, they're making the best of it." Greg replied. Looking out the window, he noticed that they had dropped even further since he left.

Suddenly the plane started to shudder. Greg could hear something sputter and looked out the right window to see a puff of smoke come out of the right wing engine.

"Damn!" Steve roared. "The damn engine is kicking off. Something's wrong with the fuel intake."

"Can you do anything?" Greg asked.

"Probably, but I'll need to land to check it out. Fuel line might be clogged, or the intake valve is stuck."

"Where?"

Steve pulled out the latest chart and compared the readings on the GPS.

"There's a remote airstrip outside Brownlee, Nebraska. Nothing really there but a landing strip, but I've got all the tools I'd need. According to our current location, we're only about 20 miles out." Steve said as he held onto the controls, turning off the autopilot.

"Is that close enough?"

"Easy. Would take us that long to descend anyway." Steve answered. Grabbing the intercom he made the announcement to Kay and the President. "Sorry folks, but we've run into a bit of a mechanical problem. We're going to land in about 10 minutes to check it out, so strap yourselves in, it's going to be a bumpy ride."

Listening to the intercom, Kay almost laughed inside, wondering how it could be any bumpier than it had already been.

Greg watched as Steve manhandled the plane to keep it on course. Steve had shut down the right engine and was operating on only one. They continued to decrease in altitude, skimming over the tops of trees. Greg looked out and saw nothing but rolling hills of emptiness. No homes, no cars, and barely a road in sight.

Within four minutes, Steve pointed out the airstrip that lay ahead, which was really just a flat spot, barely trimmed, between two small buildings. As they came closer, Greg scanned the entire area, trying to find some hint of danger. As they were about to touch down, he finally noticed what was out of place. Along the road that paralleled the landing strip, cut off by a row of trees, were three unmistakable sedans. As the plane touched down and slowed, Greg caught the reflection of something beyond the building at the end of the strip.

"What the hell is going on, Steve?" Greg asked, pulling the pistol out and laying it against his lap.

"Whatcha mean, partner." Steve replied. "The engine's conked out and we need to fix it."

"Damn it, Steve. Of all people, I thought I could have trusted you." Greg said as the plane continued to slow, closing in on the end of the strip. Steve was throttling down the engine, softly applying the brakes.

"Listen, my friend. You've got yourself caught with the wrong crowd. You're in the wrong place at the wrong time.

Just give yourself and them two up. I've made arrangements that you won't be hurt." Steve said with sad eyes.

"How stupid can you be?" Greg asked before he noticed Steve pull a gun from his side and point it at Greg.

"I hate to do this, but you don't give me much of a choice. This is much bigger than the both of us." Steve said as the plane was within seconds of coming to a complete stop.

Without hesitation, Greg swung up his left hand and pushed Steve's arm back, moving the gun barrel pointing behind him. The gun went of once, and shot through the side of the plane, as Greg swung around with his right hand, cracking the butt of the gun against Steve's forehead. Immediately Steve's body went limp. Greg pulled the throttles back and grabbed the wheel, turning it hard to the left. The plane creaked, as if in pain, as it turned violently to the left. As it turned and sped up, shots began to ring out from the trees and buildings.

"Hang on back there." Greg screamed through the open doorway. "Get down on the floor and hold on tight."

Once the plane had done a complete one hundred eighty-degree turn, he straightened out the wheel and sped on back down the runway. Suddenly two bodies came scrambling out of the woods, firing at the plane, sending glass shattering in the cockpit. Greg turned directly towards them, causing them both to leap out of the way to the ground. Seeing a break in the trees, Greg guided the plane to the dirt road that he had noticed earlier paralleling the runway. Bouncing along, he could hear the tips of the wings crash against the trees lining the road. It was a tight fit, and pieces of the plane started to come apart at the stress.

Fortunately the plane had a small mirror outside the window and Greg could see bodies scrambling to their cars. He knew it wouldn't be long before they'd be right behind him. Spotting another break in the trees, Greg turned the wheel violently to the right, sending the plane off the road. Almost immediately, he spun the wheel completely in the other direction. The plane almost split in two at the drastic change of direction.

"Come on baby, hold on." Greg pleaded.

The plane bounced over the road, into another field, and then back onto the road, heading directly back in the direction they came from. Directly ahead, the cars sped right towards him.

Greg smiled at the picture of their faces when they noticed the plane was now heading right back towards them. It was a simple game of chicken, and Greg knew that in this game, the biggest usually won and the cars were no match for the ungamely plane. The drivers of the cars realized the same thing and tried to veer off the road. Two of the cars bounced off the road and directly into a tree, one on either side of the road. The third found a deep ditch and rolled over.

Greg moved the throttles back forward, slowing the engine down as he pressed onto the brakes. He was amazed that the plane was still in one piece, although it would never fly again. The plane finally came to a stop near the buildings. Greg unstrapped himself from the chair and walked out of the cockpit. He found Kay and the President wrapped between the seats, a little bruised but it could have been a lot worse.

"Everybody okay?" Greg asked, trying to help them off the floor.

"What the hell is going on?" Kay exclaimed.

"Seems we've been set up." Greg replied. "There was a little welcoming committee waiting for us."

"Now what?" The President asked, brushing himself off.

"You two stay here, it's not over with yet. There are still a few members of the welcome wagon out there I have to get to know better first." Greg said as he opened up his bag and pulled out a sawed-off shotgun and holster. The holster was specially designed to allow the shotgun to be carried on the back, but had Velcro strips along the side, allowing him to pull it away quickly. He put the pistol back into his back and pulled back on the shotgun. Just to be sure, he pulled a box of shells out of his bag, dumped the shells on the seat nearby and took a handful, tossing them into his pocket.

Greg looked out the window, which allowed him to see all the way down the road. Nothing appeared to be moving. He slowly opened the door and jumped down to the road. Walking down along the tree line, he heard the faint crack of a tree limb and fell against one of the trees. Squatting down, he peered around the tree on the landing field side. There he discovered the two who he almost ran over with the plane, moving up by one of the trees. Greg stood back up against the tree, and smiled. Placing the shotgun in the holster, he stepped out from behind the tree and walked casually up along the road, whistling.

Suddenly the two jumped out from the tree, one carrying a pistol, the other an M-14 machine gun. Unknown to Greg, these were the same two that Captain Davenport had called Heckyl and Jeckyl back in Washington, D.C. Looking startled, Greg stopped in his tracks and raised his arms in the air.

"Hold it right there. Don't make any sudden moves." Heckyl hollered.

"Whatever you say sir." Greg replied. "What the hell is going on?"

"Don't give us that shit." Jeckyl responded as they came closer.

When they were within 20 feet, Greg reached down to the shotgun handle with one arm as he leaped off to one side. Both Heckyl and Jeckyl fired, but Greg was no longer where their weapons were pointing. Before they could react, Greg fired one round into each of their chests, sending them reeling backwards off their feet, and falling to the ground with a thud.

"Hell, I wouldn't give you any shit." Greg said as he stood back up. "But I will give you some lead."

Greg continued to walk towards the cars. The two that had run into the trees were smoking, while the upturned car still had its wheels spinning. Greg saw some movement in the upturned car and pointed his shotgun at it. Within a millisecond of firing off a round, the car burst into flames, the shot hitting directly into the gas tank. Greg barely heard the faint screams from within the car as he continued on to the other two cars.

"Tsk-tsk. It's against the law not to wear your seat belt." Greg said as he looked into the first car and found the passenger's head sticking through the windshield, a mixture of blood and glass. The driver's head was leaning back, the steering wheel pressed tightly against his chest. He could hear the man struggling to find air to fill his collapsed lungs. Slowly the man turned his head towards Greg, one eye opening slightly, and one arm trying to lift a pistol at Greg. Greg just shook his head, swung the shotgun around and fired. The window of the driver's side shattered, with pieces of glass, hair, blood and flesh flying out. Greg didn't show any emotion, and the once hazel eyes, were completely black again.

Greg walked over to the other car to find a tree branch had gone through the windshield, severing the driver's head. The passenger had been thrown from the vehicle and, after hitting the tree head on, was a lifeless mass of flesh at the base of the tree. In the back seat, the body was bloodied but still breathing. Greg opened the door, and the body nearly collapsed out of the car. Tugging at his jacket, Greg pulled the man free and laid him on the ground. Placing him on his back, Greg suddenly noticed the President standing there beside him.

"I thought I told you to stay inside the plane." Greg snapped.

"I thought you might need a hand. Guess I was wrong." The President replied, stepping back after seeing the emptiness for the first time in Greg's eyes.

"This is the only one I could find that was still breathing and not trying to put a bullet in me." Greg said, as he wiped some of the blood from the man's face.

"Jesus Christ!" The President exclaimed.

"What?" Greg asked.

It's the Secretary of Defense, Andrew Carmichael."

"Are you sure?"

"Positive. What the hell is going on?"

"I don't have any idea, but maybe he might be able to shed some light on things." Greg said as he slapped the man's cheek. "Wakie-wakie Andy. Time for school."

Andrew Carmichael was in a daze. His vision was blurred, mostly by the blood in his eyes from the gash in his forehead. He tried to sit up, but couldn't feel his arms moving or anything below his waist. Feeling the cloth against his face wiping away the blood, he tried to reach out, but couldn't because Greg had his arm pinned by his knee.

"Who?" Carmichael mumbled.

"Just your friendly terrorists." Greg remarked.

"Andrew. It's John Lockwood. What are you doing out here?"

"God!" Carmichael declared. "This should never have come to this."

"How about you start with why my team was sent to kill the President?" Greg said as he rested the end of the shotgun underneath Carmichael's chin.

"Is that really necessary, Greg?" The President asked as he knelt down next to Greg, putting his hand on his shoulder.

315

"What's going on Andrew?" The President said, moving the weapon away from the man's chin.

"Alexander is going to start a war against the Middle East. He's going to win the approval of Washington, Monday, and rebuild this country again."

"What the heck are you talking about? We were just about to sign an Arms Agreement. Why would he want to do that?" The President inquired.

"He and the forces behind him are sure the country is falling weak and the only way to regain its strength and prominence is through a war." Carmichael gurgled out. His mouth was starting to fill with blood, the first sign that his internal organs were starting to collapse.

"Who's behind all this?" Greg asked.

"I don't know. Alexander is the only one who deals with him."

"Who all is involved?" The President asked, trying to wipe some of the blood from the corner of Carmichael's mouth and forehead.

"I have no idea. It's beyond the imagination. It spreads across every facet of society. The rich and the poor, business tycoons, military authorities, police, anyone who believes and supports a powerful nation. More and more people are brought into the fold every year." Carmichael coughed and blood spurt out between his lips.

"I'm sorry, sir." Carmichael said as he looked up with dejected and empty eyes. The President leaned down and touched his shoulder, and noticed that his eyes went dark.

"He's gone, sir." Greg said as he stood up.

"Jesus Christ. This is a real mess." The President said, wobbling for a moment as he stood, Greg's hand holding him steady.

"But we will get it straightened out, come hell or high water." Greg replied, patting him on the back. "First let's get the hell out of here and figure out another way to get you to Washington."

"Just how the hell are we supposed to do that now?" The President asked.

"Well. There is still one good car up there by the buildings. We can drive all night and get to a safe place I know by daybreak. From there we won't be far away and we can make our final plans." Greg said, and then started to walk back towards the plane. He stopped off to check the pockets of the two bodies lying off the side of the road with holes in their chests from the shotgun blasts. Fortunately he found a set of keys, tossed them in the air, and placed them in his pocket. They both walked back to the plane to find Kay sitting in one of the seats, holding a pistol towards the door. As they walked towards the door a shot rang out, careening off the ground.

"Whoa there, Nellie. It's the cavalry. Put the gun down and don't shoot." Greg bellowed.

"Sorry." Kay replied. Greg peered around the edge of the door, to find Kay sunk down into the seat, a look of fear in her eyes.

"Its okay. It's all over. We're safe for now." Greg said as he pulled himself onto the plane. "Why don't you go down with the President and help him get the car ready." Greg tossed the keys out the door to the President. "It should look just like the other three."

Greg helped Kay out of the plane into the President's arms. He walked to the back of the plane and gathered up his bags and tossed them out the door. Remembering that Steve was still in the pilot's seat, he walked into the cockpit. Steve was still slumped over.

"Now what are we going to do about you?" Greg said as he pushed the body back into the chair. He realized that there wasn't anything to do. Somehow, when they were being riddled by bullets, one found the center of Steve's forehead.

"You got off easy, my friend." Greg said. It hurt him inside, that someone he respected had betrayed him. He wondered now if there was going to be anyone he could ever trust again. He had a long road ahead, and knew it would be a tough one. He couldn't imagine just how tough it was going to be.

Chapter 33

Greg figured it would take them at least 24 hours to figure out what happened at Brownlee, giving them enough time to drive that day and through the night before they'd have to abandon the car. The straightest course would be Highway 80, however once it turned into the turnpike just past the Indiana border, there was a chance the toll collectors might identify them, so they'd jump on Highway 65 towards Indianapolis and then take Highway 70 east.

Taking the first shift, Greg drove for 6 hours, taking stops every two hours at rest stops for bathroom breaks and getting refreshments and sodas out of the machines. They couldn't risk stopping in any restaurants. The only stops they'd make were at gas stations, but the sedan could go over 300 miles between fill-ups, limiting their risk of detection.

Kay tried to sleep in the back seat, but the day's events kept gnawing at her brain, so she tossed and turned during the 6 hours. She did manage to get some rest, while the President and Greg talked casually about sports and politics. During their conversation they discovered they both loved the Cleveland Indians and how they had endured many suffering years, until they managed to win some pennants and make it to the Big Game. Unfortunately those days had passed already, and now they were back to being mediocre.

Just past Iowa City, Kay took over the driving. The President rested in the back seat so that he'd be ready for his turn. The conversation between Kay and Greg was restrained, for lack of a better word. Greg tried to find out more about Kay's years growing up, her job, and her hobbies, but the replies were short and not very specific. Kay tried to find out more about what Greg did and how he got involved in it, but the answers were also rather general. It wasn't until the third hour of their limited conversation that they found out they enjoyed the same kind of music, the classic 70s tunes. Throughout the drive, they had attempted to find radio stations that played some form of older rock and roll, but the wide stretches of Nebraska and Iowa offered little selection other than country and western, which they also discovered it was something they weren't too crazy about either.

Once they got past the more personal aspects of the discussion, they also talked about their love of movies and reminisced about some of their favorites. Greg's favorites ranged from the remake of Robin Hood with Kevin Costner, Armaggedon with Bruce Willis and Antonio Bandera's Desperado. Kay could tell why Greg was the way he was for his selections, the adventure and unmitigated violence that came with good guys overpowering the bad. When Kay mentioned her favorites were Pretty Woman with Richard Gere and Julia Roberts along with Love Story with Ryan O'Neal and Ali McGraw, Greg just smiled and thought, just like a woman. They both laughed at how Kay had never seen Desperado and he had never seen Love Story. At least they both agreed that The Wizard of Oz was among their favorites.

As they neared Indianapolis, the sun had just set to the west. The risk of detection was almost nonexistent during the remaining part of the drive. They were clocked in darkness in their boring sedan. Traffic mainly consisted of truck drivers carrying their load across the country, paying little attention to who was in the cars below them. Greg and Kay laughed at how at one time the big fad was to have a CB radio and "handle". They both started talking in truck driver lingo with phrases as 10-4 good buddy and see you on the flip side.

Just north of Indianapolis, the President took over the driving, allowing Greg to get some rest in the back seat. Both Kay and the President could see a hint of how the past week had taken its toll on him. They were amazed at how outwardly he still looked fresh and alert after everything he'd been through, but the faint signs were still there in his eyes. Most people can put on a façade, but the eyes could never lie on what lie deep inside.

Kay was more upbeat after the last hour of discussions with Greg, and began to admire the real person inside the hard shell. Still, it was hard to get past the other hidden darkness that resided within him. She couldn't shake off the empty dark eyes when he killed Steve Puller and how quickly he changed from the fighting machine to the boy next door in the gas station in Mexico. She wondered if she could ever look at him without seeing those images flash back into her brain.

The President drove for the next 3 hours taking them around Indianapolis and into Ohio, past Dayton. The discussion was not as lively as the last hour with Greg. Kay had asked him about his climb through the political ranks and about his wife. While listening she understood how a whole country could love this man who was so honest, open and caring. As he talked about his wife, a certain glow came across his face, that even in the darkness Kay could recognize. She knew that no woman could ever replace that spot in his heart, that he loved her so much. A love that she had always dreamed of and wondered if she'd ever find it.

At the rest stop west of Columbus, Greg took over for the rest of the trip. He was now deep into familiar territory, having spent many years in this part of the country, remembering many of the sites he hadn't seen in quite a few years. While they were at the rest stop, they relaxed a bit. The evening was a clear one, with barely a cloud in the sky and the black heaven filled with stars. They sat back in one of the benches under the trees and allowed themselves a bit of peace and quiet.

"By the way, where are you taking us?" The President finally asked.

"Inquiring minds want to know do they?" Greg replied sarcastically.

"It's not one of your hidden away fortresses underground is it?" Kay asked with a smile.

"Not hardly. In fact, we're just about 4 or 5 hours away." Greg stared off into space. "I'm not sure how well we're going to be received though."

"What's that supposed to mean?" Kay asked hesitantly.

"Well." Greg paused. "These people know me as a career Naval Officer, honest and clean-cut. With the news that has been going on and my picture all over it, I'm sure they're overwhelmed to say the least."

"Who?" The President asked almost demandingly, his hands opened up as if waiting to be handed a present.

"If you must know, I'm taking you to my parent's house. They live in a remote town in western Pennsylvania." Greg replied, lowering his head. "I figure if there's someone in this world I can trust, it has to be them. I just hope they won't give me the third degree. I can face an army full of well-armed, highly trained mercenaries, but don't ever want to face my Mother's wrath."

They all laughed together. This would-be hero, the man of danger and suspense, is concerned not with the danger that lie in Washington D.C. or who might find them between here and there, but facing up to his mother now that she learns her boy isn't the All-American boy she thought he was. It was more than Kay or the President could handle.

"It's not funny." Greg declared. "She'll send all of God's wrath down on me for not telling her the complete truth. Now I'm being plastered all over the news as a terrorist plotting against the government. Is going to take a lot of explaining. That's why I'm going there with you two at my side. I need all the help I can get."

They sat and laughed for another 15 minutes until getting back in the car. Greg kept on driving while Kay rested in the back seat. They continued to chuckle at Greg's fear of seeing his Mother with all the other events that surrounded them, but little did they know, that Greg wasn't far off.

* * * * * * * * * * * * * *

The streets of Washington D.C. were almost void of activity. The nation's capital that was so alive during the day was asleep at two in the morning, except for the limousine that pulled up to the Washington Memorial. Standing at the base of the towering monument a lone figure stood. The back door of the limousine opened and Thomas Alexander II stepped out onto the pavement. The air was brisk, but warm. Lights shone on the tip of the memorial, but at the base, a dimly lit lamppost barely provided enough light to walk up the steep incline.

"Any news?" The lone figure asked.

Alexander was always amazed at how the figure always seemed to be wrapped in a shield of darkness. The face of the lone man never seemed to appear, even in the dim lights.

"Distressing news. An hour ago we learned that our friends managed to escape, taking out nine men, including Protector." Alexander said referring to their code name for the Secretary of Defense.

"Lockwood's Guardian Angel is not one to be taken lightly. He was trained by Davenport and from what I've learned was the leader of the group we sent into Acapulco. He's rather resourceful." Falcon said as he walked with Alexander around the monument, his face never meeting up with the light of the lampposts, which sent chills even through Alexander's body.

"We have people set up in the toll booths on the Ohio turnpike and checking all the train and bus stations. We have alerted the police in Virginia of the make and license plate of the car they are possibly driving. They won't take one step into D.C."

"We can't underestimate this man again. I've made some of my own arrangements with my own people. We have a few places he might try to go and we're setting up a rather exciting surprise if he should show up in any of them." Falcon said, before stopping and facing Alexander.

"How goes the vote?" Falcon asked.

"Everything is proceeding as planned. In three days, we'll have their approval and can proceed with all our plans." Alexander said.

"Good. You concentrate on the politicians. I'll take care of the thorn in our side. I don't want anything to spoil things when we are this close. It has taken a lot of sweat and blood to get here." Falcon said as he proceeded down the walkway away from the monument.

Alexander stood there next to the limousine as he watched Falcon walk off into the darkness. A dark form engulfed within another. He wondered at how someone could have amassed so much power, wealth and influence. Just being in his presence humbled even himself. The man carried about such an aura of authority and power that one felt as if his life was truly in his hands.

* * * * * * * * * * * * * * * *

An hour earlier, Greg had turned north from Pittsburgh onto Highway 79. Sunrise was still over an hour away. He reached over and placed his hand on the President's shoulder and gently shook him.

"Are we there yet?" The President said comically.

"Almost. About another 30 minutes. Once we get there, I'm going to park the car and check things out. I need you and Kay to be completely alert."

"You expect someone is watching the house?"

"I always anticipate the worst and rejoice later if it's not."

"Not a great way to go through life, my friend." The President said, placing his hands on Greg's shoulder. "When this is over, you and I need to find some time to get you reacquainted with the good things in life."

"When this thing is over, I won't have much else to go to. My team is gone and I doubt the Navy is going to be too willing to accept me back into its open arms."

"So what will you do?"

"Who knows? I've always considered going into business for myself."

"Well depending on how this ends up, I will always have a place for you."

"I appreciate that, sir. But after this, I think I'm going to stay away from the political circles."

"I don't blame you." The President said with a smile.

"But, if you ever need me, all you'll have to do is call. You're a good man, sir. I always felt that, but after these days, you have my deepest respect and admiration."

"Well, thank you. You know, Kay's right. Sometimes you can be a real nice guy."

They both laughed.

Ten minutes later they exited the highway onto Route 108. The President read the exit sign and shook his head.

"Slippery Rock?" He asked.

"Pretty remote, huh?"

"Not really. They had a pretty damn fine football team in the 70s. I used to see their scores on television all the time."

"Well, I didn't attend there. I went to another nearby college that was its rival, in almost everything. Our fraternity used to call the town, Slimy Pebble. We'd hold an annual 100 Hogs and Dogs party, inviting 100 of the schools girls over. Being a phys-ed school, you figure out which one of those they were." Greg said smiling.

Once the entered the outskirts of Slippery Rock, Greg pulled behind an abandoned building. By this time, Kay was fully awake as well, and listened to the President tell her about the town and Greg's remarks. She just shook her head in disgust when he mentioned about the fraternity party. Greg went to the trunk of the car and pulled some items from his bags and then returned to the driver side window.

"You two stay here. No following this time, sir. My parents' house is about a quarter-mile from here. If I'm not back in an hour, I suggest you get this car in motion and drive to Canada." Greg said not expecting or wanting a reply. He quickly disappeared around the building, leaving Kay and the President alone feeling somewhat uneasy.

"For the first time, I'm not too thrilled with him being gone." Kay said.

"He'll be back." The President said, attempting to reassure her as well as himself.

Greg worked his way towards his parents' house through the trees and buildings. As he neared their street, he moved with extreme caution, taking in all the surroundings and trying to find something out of place. It didn't take long. One car was sitting at the end of each block, hiding two passengers within each. A jogger went by his parents' house and rounded the bend. Greg waited five minutes and the jogger returned, following the same course. Each time he passed the car with its back to Greg, the jogger would give a glance to the occupants inside the car, not one of curiosity, but acknowledgement. Greg knew he had to handle this carefully, because if one piece of the three-ring circus was out of synch, the other two would be aware that something was happening.

Fortunately for Greg, the jogger was about his height and weight. Greg was a block away from the first car and went up two streets, one past the one that the jogger was using to fulfill his circle. Well out of view of the cars, he paralleled his parents' street and went to the one that lead to the furthest car. He moved down one block and waited behind some bushes for the sign of the jogger. He removed a small package from his pocket and inserted a small device into the clay-type surface. Within a minute, the jogger turned the corner and headed back to his parents' street. After the jogger turned the corner down his parents' street, he moved down the block and, hidden by the well-trimmed hedges along the house on the corner, maneuvered himself behind the car. Crawling to the back of the car, he turned over and attached the package to the car's gas tank. Sliding back, he went across the street and back up the road hidden by the bushes.

Returning to his original spot before the jogger went by, he waited again. Once the jogger went by, he moved on down the parallel street to the corner where he expected the jogger to turn back again. After a while, the jogger reappeared at the corner. Hidden by a tree, Greg waited until the jogger came to the tree. Without warning, Greg jumped behind him, grabbing him by the throat with one arm, and sliding a knife behind the man's ear, turning it. "One of the most effective ways to kill a man", was the words of the instructor he remembered, "to slide a knife into the brain and scramble it, causing immediate light's out." The man's body went limp instantly.

Greg hurried to remove the man's jogging outfit and sneakers, and put them on. He then raced down the street to try to catch up to the man's timing around the corner. Once he reached the corner, he slowed his pace to match that of the jogger. Rounding the corner to his parents' street, he lowered his head and made the same acknowledgement. Halfway down the street he pressed the small control in his hand and the tiny quiet town was suddenly alive when the car exploded. Turning around to keep his back on the other car, he jogged backwards. Once he reached the other car, he slowed down his pace and turned, facing the occupants and smiling. The occupants had their attention on the car that had launched upwards from the rear and then fell back down into a ball of fire. It was too late when they turned to the jogger and noticed who was there. The amazement on their faces brought a smile to Greg's face as he pointed the silencer at each and fired directly into their chests. They were caught completely off-guard.

Greg opened the driver's side door, shoving the dead driver to the side. Starting up the car he turned the car completely around and around the corner. Stopping to pick up the dead jogger and toss him and his shoes into the back seat, he drove off to where he left Kay and the President. From rounding the corner in the jogger outfit until he picked up the dead jogger took less than two minutes. The neighborhood was still wiping the sleep out of their eyes and just beginning to start peaking out their windows when he was gone.

Greg pulled up behind the abandoned building and parked the car in the wooded area. Climbing back out he went to check up on Kay and the President.

"Out for a morning jog?" The President asked, seeing Greg's new attire.

"What's that stuff on your collar?" Kay asked, and then gazed in horror when she realized it was blood. "Oh God, now what have you done?"

"We had a few onlookers waiting for us. I had to cleanse the area." Greg replied as he took off the jogging outfit.

"Cleansing?" Kay screamed at him. "Destroying would be a better word for it."

Greg ignored her remarks.

"We need to put this car with the other and walk to my parents' house from here." Greg said as sirens began to wail in the distance.

"Jesus Christ, what now?" Kay asked.

"The place is going to be a little busy for a while. It will provide us just the distraction we need." Greg said with a little grin on his face.

"You really are something." The President said shaking his head.

Greg parked the sedan in the wooded area by the other one. He kept the others away from the car so they wouldn't notice the three dead bodies inside. Grabbing his bags out of the trunk, he led the President and Kay to his parents' house through the street that was behind their house. As they went across his parents' street, both Kay and the President looked down at all the activity. A fire truck was battling a car engulfed in flames while a policeman attempted to keep the newly awakened neighborhood away.

"Part of your handiwork?" The President asked.

"They were parked illegally, facing the wrong direction." Greg replied.

Kay glanced at the President who raised his eyes and held up his hands quizzically.

At the house that backed up on his parents' house, they walked down the driveway and around the garage, to his parents' back patio. They entered onto the screened in patio, and Greg knocked on the back door. After a second round of knocking, the door opened slightly to a tall man, dressed in a pajamas and robe. The man stood there for a moment as if in shock, his mouth wide open, and a blank stare on his face.

"Nice to see you too, Dad." Greg said. "Any chance I'm still welcome here."

"Jesus Christ." The man replied. "Get in here."

They walked inside to the kitchen and after Greg placed down his bags he turned to his father and held out his hand, which was quickly met with a firm handshake.

"Dad, I'd like you to meet President Lockwood and Kay Cross. Folks, this is my Dad."

As they were exchanging greetings, a woman in a flowing robe walked into the kitchen. Kay was struck by how young the woman looked and how majestic she appeared. She just couldn't see the resemblance of either of Greg's parents in him. The man seemed so charming and hospitable, and the woman so stately.

"Honey, what's going on?" The woman asked before she noticed the others in the room. "Oh my God!" Was all she could say.

"Hello, Mom." Greg said. Once again Kay was amazed. This man who not 10 minutes ago had killed who knows how many, was standing there with an intimidated look on his face, as he confronted his mother.

"Greg Anthony Morris, what the heck is going on?" She asked, her hands on the side of her hips. Kay knew by her calling him with his middle name, that it was going to be rough on Greg. She remembered when her Mom used to refer to her with her middle name and the punishment she received afterwards.

"Mom, this is President Lockwood and Kay Cross." Greg said introducing them. "Folks, this is my Mom."

"Nice to meet you, Mrs. Morris." The President said.

"From what I hear, this is a terrorist and you're trucking around the world with him and this harlot trying to overthrow the government." She said without moving from her spot.

"I told you she was tough." Greg said as he looked at the President and received a grin in return.

"Don't you bad mouth me, young man." She said as she walked over to Greg.

Both Kay and the President were now in complete shock when Greg and his mother met face to face and then she grabbed him and hugged him close to her.

"Are you okay?" She asked.

"I'm fine, Mom. I'm sorry." Greg said.

"For what?"

"For putting you through all this."

"Honey, if you think I believed all those cock-and-bull stories you've been feeding me for the last five years, you better think again. I knew there was something going on, just sort of figured it had something to do with a woman." She said laughing.

"Excuse me." Kay interjected. "Am I missing something?"

"What's the matter, dear?" Greg's Mom asked.

"Forgive me, but the impression I got from Greg is that you were some overpowering ogre."

"Greg, you didn't pull that one again, did you?" She said as she turned to Greg. Turning back to Kay, she walked over and took her hand. "Oh, never mind his wild stories, dear. He can be a real jackass sometimes."

"Tell me about it." She replied glaring at Greg, who was standing there with a sheepish grin.

"You all look like you've been through Hell and back. Why don't you all go upstairs and freshen up while I make some breakfast."

They spent the rest of the morning getting a shower, freshening up, and eating a wonderful breakfast of eggs, muffins, donuts, fruit, sausage, and bacon. Greg started to feel like the fifth wheel with his father and the President talking with each other and his mother and Kay gabbing about Greg's shortcomings. Noticing her son's predicament, she reached over and grabbed his hand and squeezed it tightly. The rest of the day they spent talking. Much to Greg's dismay, his mother once again brought out old pictures of him when he was a kid. While his mother doted over her son's youth, Greg walked onto the back patio and sat down to put his thoughts back to the road that lay ahead. After a few minutes, his father came out to join him and they spent a good hour talking man to man.

Greg recommended that everyone get some rest during the afternoon. His father had offered up his car for the rest of their trip.   Greg didn't know what lie ahead; but he figured it was going to be rough.

Chapter 34

Six hours after the remote town had been rudely awaken by explosions and sirens; Greg suddenly awoke from his short sleep. After the President and Kay had gone upstairs to get some sleep, Greg had sat alone with his parents and talked a while before the week's events finally won over. Unable to shake the weariness, he dozed off on the couch, his mother placed a comforter over his legs. No matter how long or short he slept, Greg always woke up quickly. Today was no different, except that a new danger had crept inside his mind while he slept.

Pulling the comforter to one side, he stood up, feeling the aches and pains surge through every muscle. Shutting his mind off to the physical strains, he walked to the kitchen in search of his parents, shaking his head as if disgusted with himself. He found his mother making sandwiches on the kitchen counter, while his father was outside digging through the garage. It had been almost a year since he had been home, and for a brief moment, he just stood back and smiled, wishing he could now return to those good old days. The moment was short-lived, interrupted when his father came through the backdoor carrying two suitcases.

"I found them." His father bellowed as he came through the door.

"Took you long enough." Greg's mother replied without turning, a grin stretching across her face.

"Hi, son. We thought you'd at least sleep another hour." Greg's father said as he placed the suitcases on the floor.

"What are you up to?" Greg asked.

"Well I thought you all might need a change of clothes, so I pulled out some suitcases we had of some old clothes you could use."

"Don't you ever throw or give anything away?"

Guy Macdonald

"Oh, you know your father, dear." Greg's mother said as she finally turned, placing the wrapped sandwiches in a heap on the table. "Forever the pack rat, a trait I believe you've inherited, if I haven't forgotten."

"Well maybe not for that long." Greg said with a smile.

"Never know when things might come in handy." His father interjected.

"Well, I'm afraid we have a problem I overlooked." Greg said.

"What's that hon?" Greg's mother asked.

"Do you still have the keys to Bob and Karen's cottage up north?" Greg asked.

"Yes. They're down in Florida right now." Greg's father answered.

"Well." Greg paused briefly, trying to find a good way to put this, but realized it was just going to have to be said. "The word will eventually get out about the watch-dogs being put out of commission this morning. We need to move quickly and get you both up to the cottage before they realize what's going on and send some angrier dogs here."

"We already figured that out." Greg's father said as he walked to Greg's side. "We've already packed some things and Mom's making sandwiches for the trip."

"Where do you think you got your ability for quick thinking?" Greg's mother said with a smile, opening up some small lunch bags and putting the sandwiches inside, adding fruit, bags of chips, and small cakes. On the floor by the table, Greg noticed the cooler stuffed with sodas, water bottles and ice.

"I should have known better." Greg said shaking his head.

"We'll be ready to leave in an hour. I went out and filled up the car with gas already." Greg's father said, wrapping his arm around his son. "We'll be settled in the cottage by nightfall and you can head east."

"Sometimes you guys amaze me." Greg said laughing.

"Better let them sleep a little while longer while we finish getting ready." Greg's mother said as she folded up the lunch bags. "Is there anything else you might need?"

"No. Hopefully it will all be over in a few days."

For the next hour they made final preparations, pulled out some clothes for the President and Kay, and loaded up the car. Greg passed on any regular clothes, keeping to his military all-black outfit. Fifteen minutes prior to leaving, they woke up the President and Kay who weren't too excited about the new arrangements, but realized it was necessary.

Shortly before noon, the entire group climbed into Mr. Morris' Chevy Blazer and headed up north to Tionesta, Pennsylvania. It was a four-hour drive into the mountains of northwest Pennsylvania, at the edge of the Allegheny National Forest. The cottage was hidden away in the woods with a small lake behind it. When Kay stepped out of the Blazer, she stood there in awe, as if she was inside a post-card. Across the lake she could see the mountains begin to rise above the trees. She had imagined places like this, but never believed she would ever see one close up. The cottage was simple and made entirely of logs, cut from the trees that used to grow on the spot it now stood.

Stepping inside the cottage, the image was quite as expected. Across the hardwood floor in the main room was a massive fireplace of stone. The furniture appeared as if it had grown right up from the floor, sculpted from the same trees that had once stood there. At the back of the room was a large panel of windows that looked out onto the lake and the mountains beyond. Beyond the panel was a large wooden deck that went from one end of the cottage to the other with stairs that led down to the lake and a small pier. Antique lamps adorned the tables and walls. Mounted above the fireplace was an enormous painting of the mountains.

To one side was a staircase with wooden railings that led up to the second floor, which overlooked the main room. Upstairs were three bedrooms and a full bathroom. Behind the staircase was a passageway that led to the kitchen, dining room and a study. The kitchen was larger than most, with a central island that housed the range. Over the island hung pots and pans held up by a series of black chains. At the back of the kitchen was another large window that circled around an inset that also overlooked the lake. The dining room had a large oak table with 6 high-back chairs that sat on a large circular rug with Indian designs. The study had a large oak desk, with a leather high-back chair, and cabinets all along the walls filled with books and pictures.

After walking around the house in complete amazement, Kay realized that she never saw a phone, a computer, or a television. It was complete isolation from the outside world. This was the type of place the owners came to in order to escape, to unwind and feel at peace. While Greg and his father unpacked the car, his mother was busy straightening things up and opening the windows to let out the stale air from being closed up for almost 4 months.

"You two should go up and get some sleep. We'll leave here around 11 tonight. It's about a 6 hour drive to DC." Greg said as he walked past Kay.

"This place is amazing." The President said as he walked over to the door leading out to the back patio. "I could live here."

"My son might disagree with you." Greg's father laughed.

"Oh don't start that again." Greg said setting his parents' suitcases on the floor.

"What?" Kay asked.

"My son hated this place. He was so bored every time we brought him up here." Greg's father replied.

"Dad, I was young and restless. Time and people change." Greg retorted.

"Funny." Kay whispered.

"What is?" Greg's father asked.

"In the short time I've been with your son, I would imagine this would be his kind of place, completely isolated from the rest of the world." Kay answered.

"I doubt that. Greg likes the malls and movie theaters too much. He hates being away from the hustle and bustle."

"Not anymore Dad. I'd much rather escape into the woods on a horse, than fight with rude people in the mall anymore."

"To be honest, I could see your son living here, but it would be with a collection of high tech devices everywhere." The President said, sitting back in one of the oversized chairs with plush cushions.

"Hey, I've got hundreds of other people that want to abuse me, I don't have to stand here and listen to it from you all." Greg said as he walked back outside.

"Don't mind him. We didn't do such a good job in teaching him good manners." Greg's father said smiling. "But he is right, you should go up and get some sleep. When you wake up we'll have something for dinner before you leave. There's a bed for each of you upstairs."

Kay and the President went upstairs and fell asleep within minutes after sinking into the plush mattresses on the large beds. Greg unpacked his two duffel bags and went over all his equipment, cleaning the guns and loading the cartridges. This was his last real opportunity to get everything prepared before they got into the nation's capital and came across any unexpected confrontations. After an hour, he came inside and after talking to his parents for a while, went to the back porch and laid down on the chaise lounge, falling asleep after running through another complete set of options for what lay ahead.

* * * * * * * * * * * * * *

Shortly after eleven o'clock in the evening, the Chevy Blazer left the cabin in the hills of Tionesta with its three passengers. Greg's mother had packed an ample supply of sandwiches and drinks to get them through the trip. All three had rested well, feeling refreshed after showers and something to eat. Kay had the hardest time adjusting to sleeping during the day and being awake all night, but the tranquility of the wilderness made it easier.

Driving through the hills of Pennsylvania in the dark was not an easy task. The roads wound and curved with steep drops just off the edge of the road. The hardest part was along Route 36 until they intersected Highway 80. After three hours of driving, they turned off Highway 80 onto Route 322 towards Harrisburg. The drive across the Appalachians wasn't as treacherous as the drive from Tionesta to Highway 80, but it wasn't much easier either.

Having never been in Pennsylvania before, Kay wondered during the drive what the countryside looked like in the daytime. As they worked their way through the small towns and mountain ranges, she could only imagine the majesty and grandeur of the countryside. Greg reflected back to his Boy Scout days, when his troop had spent one summer hiking and camping along the Appalachian Trail. He remembered how he had often dreamed of coming back to this countryside and retiring in the mountains. Smiling, he remembered the discussion at the cottage and living in seclusion, and realized that his life had changed and he had come to that point where he desired the isolation and solitude instead of the congestion of city life.

Throughout the drive they came across very few cars, which wasn't unusual considering it was out of the way and dangerous to drive along in the middle of the night. They made one stop outside Harrisburg for gas; using the gas card his father had given him, to avoid contact with anyone.

At Harrisburg they took the longer route to Washington, via Highway 81 in order to avoid Baltimore. Instead they drove towards Hagerstown, and met up with Highway 70, which would take them towards the northwest side of the capital. Just outside the capital they'd turn off on Route 189 to Potomac, where they intended to remain while they carried out their plans to get the President back into office. Greg's first commanding officer used to have a houseboat in Potomac that Greg hoped would still be there. He knew the Captain was deployed, so if it was still there, it would be unoccupied, and they would 'borrow' it for a few days.

They drove through Potomac an hour before sunrise and proceeded down to the river, just south of the canals. Fortunately, the boat was still there and empty. Parking the car about ½ mile down the street, they walked along the waterfront to the houseboat. Finding the doors locked, Greg took out a small thin card, that looked like a credit card, and proceeded to jimmy the door open. The residence was nothing to brag about, with simple furniture and appliances, but for now it would be the best thing they could ask for.

"Kay, you remain here while the President and I go visit his friend. We should be back in two hours." Greg said as he pulled several weapons out of his duffel bags, placing some within the specially designed jacket and the others in a small gym bag.

"Are you sure this is going to work?" Kay asked.

"We don't have any other option. The President is positive he can trust this man and it's our only hope of getting him back to the White House." Greg replied.

"It's almost over, Kay." The President said as he placed his hands on her shoulders. "In two days it will all be over, one way or another."

Kay hugged the President with teary eyes, wondering if she'd ever see the two of them again.

"I'd much prefer to stay with you, sir." Kay said.

"Its best you stay here. We're just going to pay a little visit and head right back here." Greg said.

"Be careful." She said as they walked out the door, leaving her feeling alone and uneasy.

* * * * * * * * * * * *

Outside the large home, a black limousine was parked along the circular driveway. Hanging on one side of the entranceway was a United States Flag and on the other side, the flag of the state of Massachusetts. The first beams of sunlight were just beginning to pry their hands over the horizon. The driver of the limousine was wiping the dew off the windshield, when he felt a tap on his shoulder.

"Mind if we borrow this for a while?" The voice said. Before the chauffeur could turn around, the butt of a pistol crashed down on the back of his shoulders, just below the neck, causing him to fall limp to the ground. The voice was that of Greg Morris, who picked the chauffeur's body off the ground and moved it to the back of the car. Moving back around to the driver's door, he reached in and turned off the engine and pulled the keys out of the ignition. Opening the trunk, he loaded the chauffeur's body into it, closing the door. Moving around to the passenger door, he opened it and motioned to the bushes. The President quickly moved to the car.

"Your ride, sir." Greg said with a smile, closing the door after the President climbed inside. Greg moved back around to the driver side, put the chauffeur cap on his head he had removed from the previous owner, and sat down behind the wheel, closing the door behind him.

Within ten minutes, a well-dressed man in his mid-50s, wearing a tailor made brown suit, came out the front door and headed down the steps to the limousine. He wasn't surprised that the chauffeur wasn't there to open the door for him, a luxury he wasn't very comfortable with, having told the driver to forego unless it was raining. He opened the door and waved back at the faces of two little children in the window before climbing inside. Once the door closed, he could hear the doors lock immediately, which surprised him, but not as much as the body that was sitting across from him in the back.

"Dear God." The man said, his mouth and eyes wide open as he stared at the man across from him.

"Good morning, John." The President said.

Senator John Billows sat motionless, fear surging throughout his entire body. The only thought running through his mind was the story of a terrorist imposter, but never imagined the likeness could be so precise.

"Relax John. It is me, not a terrorist." The President said with a smile.

"What do you want from me?" The Senator said with a studder.

"John, my dear friend. Would a terrorist know about a certain Halloween frat party in which you became so inebriated from a party punch while playing a dice game, that you stumbled into every tree on the walk back to the dormitory?"

"Is it really you? They said you were killed." Billows asked.

"It's me, thanks to my good friend up front." The President said as he motioned to Greg who was looking back through the partition.

"What the hell is going on, John?" Billows asked.

"That's what I'm here to find out." The President replied as the car moved out of the driveway.

For 30 minutes they drove around the suburbs of the capital. The President told the Senator everything that had occurred and the assumptions they had made about Alexander. He told him about the villa in Mexico, how Greg had saved him and their trek across the country, including what Carmichael had told them in Nebraska. Throughout the discussion, Billows was in awe.

"I have nowhere to turn, John. You have been a good friend for many years. I have no one else I can trust. I need your help." The President finished.

"What can I do?" Billows asked.

"I need you to find a way to meet with Alexander and tell him you want to meet him tonight, alone, at midnight, by the Lincoln Memorial. Tell him you have some information on the terrorists."

"You must know, Alexander is giving a speech to the Senate today. He's making one last push to get us to vote giving him authority to take action on the terrorist countries. He's managed to push the vote up to tomorrow." Billows replied.

"Damn." The President said. "Then we have to move faster than I had hoped. Tell him it's urgent that you see him tonight. I intend on confronting Alexander face to face. If all goes well, I'll meet you at your house tomorrow morning."

"For what?" Billows asked.

"I can't tell you until then. If I'm not here tomorrow morning, then you have to do whatever you can to stop Alexander from getting the vote." The President said as the car stopped back in front of Billows' house.

"How can I contact you?"

"You can't. Just set up the meeting and stay home tonight. We'll cover the rest in the morning if all goes well."

"What if he won't meet?" Billows asked.

"Then tomorrow morning we'll have to come up with another alternative." The President replied. "I highly doubt he'll pass up the meeting if you mention something you heard from a friend in Massachusetts about the terrorists."

"What about my chauffeur?"

"He'll be fine. We're going to park the car somewhere safe and keep him as our guest until this all blows over. You'll have to drive yourself to work today. Sorry."

With that, the Senator stepped out of the limousine. He took one last glance at the President, who smiled up at him like an injured soldier, pleading for help. Closing the door he walked back up the steps to his house while the car drove off.

The car parked several blocks away from the Senator's house in a quiet park, where the Chevy Blazer was waiting. Greg pulled the chauffeur's body out of the trunk and loaded him into the back of the limousine. Within an hour and a half, they returned to the houseboat. The first phase was in motion, and now had to wait the entire day to put the next step into place.

* * * * * * * * * * * * * *

In the early afternoon, Greg turned on the television that fortunately was fed by a satellite dish, and turned to the political station covering Alexander's speech to the Senate. The President and him watched, as Alexander spoke flamboyantly about retaliation for the injustices done to the American foundation, namely the killing of the President and Vice-President. The rhetoric included references to the American Revolution and the freedom that was won for the American way of life. He reflected on the bombings in Colorado, New York and embassies abroad and how the American people will not be afraid to come out of their homes anymore. It was time action was taken, Alexander continued, to quell the barbarian acts of violence against innocent people. Finishing his speech, Alexander, reminded everyone in the Senate that the country had the technology and the will to overcome these 'animals', and if they valued their children's future, they would act quickly and vote positively tomorrow.

"Boy, he sure does put on quite a show." Greg said as he turned off the television.

"He's a born motivator." The President replied leaning back in the chair. "Alexander was well groomed for politics. Although he and I had our different views on some issues, I respected the man. During my term, he was quite instrumental in pulling the right people onto our side on many bills we tried to get enacted."

"And now?" Greg asked.

"I still respect the man, but I don't agree with him. It's true we've had terrorist acts on American soil, but we've made significant strides against the terrorist network and those that support them since the World Trade Center. Whatever cause he's after or whoever is working with him, has manipulated his thinking, but his words were powerful and will stir up a lot of old memories. He'll win the vote if we don't stop him."

"Now that sounds like a true politician. Pardon my bluntness, sir, but this guys a psycho, and the worst kind, a well funded, well educated psycho with the power to see things trough."

"You have a point." The President said with a smile.

For the next hour they watched CNN to get coverage of the impact of Alexander's speech and the military's preparations while they went over what they were going to try to attempt that night. Greg brought out the equipment they were going to be using. Kay listened intently as she wondered about all the things that could go wrong. She didn't know if she'd be up to such a challenge, and wondered how she'd react if things got out of hand. Little did she know that a hidden part of her would re-emerge tonight, when they came across their biggest challenge yet, and how much she would truly learn about herself.

Chapter 35

Clouds had rolled in during the day, and an early fog had formed, covering up the moon and stars, leaving a misty cloak around the Washington Mall. The dim lights along the narrow paths provided little to help aid anyone walking late that night. It was the type of evening that reminded the President of the story of the Boston Strangler, walking along the dark, misty streets, hunting his unwary victims. The President wondered if he was the hunter or the hunted. Greg reassured him that he was neither.

Greg and the President drove into the capital after dark, parking their car on Independence Avenue, by the Department of Agriculture, around 10:30pm. The car was parked on the north side of the road, across the street from the Agriculture building, just past the Freer Gallery of Art, to allow a clean view of the Memorial. Greg wanted the ninety minutes to walk the perimeter of the Washington Memorial to ensure that Alexander had not invited some unwelcome guests.

"Stay here until 11:30, sir, then walk towards the memorial. I'll be nearby." Greg told the President as he grabbed some equipment out of the back seat.

"And what am I supposed to do?" Kay asked from the back seat.

"You stay with the car and keep a close eye towards the monument. If you see anything unusual going on, then drive as close as possible and look for us. If you don't see us, then high-tail it out of here." Greg replied, handing her a set of binoculars and pistol. "Use this only if you have to."

"You be careful, Greg." The President said over the hood of the car as Greg disappeared into the mist.

"I hate this waiting. How the hell does he expect me to see what's going on at the memorial in this mess?" Kay asked, stepping out of the car.

"I'm sure you'll be able to see if something isn't right." The President replied, feeling the cool night air seep into his body, causing him to shiver. "Let's just get inside the car where it's at least a little warmer.

* * * * * * * * * * * * * *

Greg did a complete circle around the western end of the Mall. At this time of night in this weather, there wasn't a hint of activity to be found. Walking by the Korean War Veterans Memorial, around the Lincoln Memorial, past the Vietnam Veterans Memorial, and circling the Ellipse, he used his night vision goggles, but found no sign of danger. At eleven fifteen, he had completed his check and set his sights on the Washington Memorial. In the foggy conditions, the memorial wasn't as impressive with three-quarters of the structure hidden in the fog. Within 15 minutes, he spotted the President making his way up the path to the Memorial.

The President paced around the Memorial, wondering where Greg might be, remembering that Greg had told him to stand on the Ellipse side of the monument, to provide the least chance of being a target. Trees stood on the north side of the monument, whereas the other sides provided a long stretch of open territory.

Greg glanced down at his watch, and noticed it was two minutes past midnight. He started to worry that Senator Billows had not convinced Alexander to come out that night, until he saw two headlights driving down 15th Avenue towards the monument. Breathing a sigh of relief, he huddled behind the small ticket building that stood near the monument. The limousine pulled up near the walkway to the monument, and a lone figure walked out of the back. Greg adjusted his night vision goggles and was reassured that it was Alexander.

When Alexander walked past the ticket booth, Greg moved around the trees and came up behind the limousine. Walking up the driver's side of the car, and stopping at the driver's door, he rapped on the window, keeping his face out of view.

"Yeah?" The driver asked.

"Miserable night ain't it. Any chance you can spare some change?" Greg said softly.

"Get outta here you bum." The driver replied.

"Come on sir, spread some good fortune with a veteran." Greg mumbled as he moved his hands into the window and grabbed the man's jacket. Immediately the door swung open, but Greg was ready for that, sliding to the right.

"I'll give you some fortune buddy." The man said, but was stopped dead in his tracks, feeling a sharp pain in his neck.

"You should be more polite to veteran's." Greg said, pulling the needle out of the chauffeur's neck. Catching the body in his other hand, he dragged the chauffeur to the back of the limousine and pushed him into the back door. Removing the keys from the ignition, he hit the automatic lock and closed the driver door.

* * * * * * * * * * * *

Alexander walked up the inclined walkway to the monument, and spotted the lone figure off to his right. A chill suddenly ran along his spine as he remembered the last meeting he had at this same spot.

"What is so important you had to speak to me here?" Alexander quipped as walked up the figure standing with his back to him.

"It's a matter of National Security." The President said, suddenly turning. He smiled at the reaction he received from his would-be successor.

347

"You!" Was all Alexander could say, his eyes open wide and arms flapping at his side.

"Yes, Tom, it's me. And I'm not too happy so say the least." The President replied.

"You are a stubborn son of a bitch, I'll grant you that. I figured you'd show up sooner or later, trying to reclaim your throne."

"What the hell is going on?" The President asked.

"Haven't you heard? There's a new revolution going on."

"For what purpose?"

"To get this country back on its feet again. This country has grown soft and complacent. We rely too much on foreign power for fuel and technology that we pay way too much for. We provide relief and support to the hungry across the seas, while our own people are homeless and poor. We've allowed ourselves to become the police force of the world, rather than exerting our immense power where it should be. We were once a proud nation, emulated by the world, but after the Cold War ended, we lost our purpose. It's time to change all that, and take our place in history once again." Alexander said, sounding like the cardboard box prophets that stand on street corners.

"And for that, you'll kill the President and Vice President?" The President said, starting straight into Alexander's cold eyes.

"You epitomize the weakness this country has become. Signing arms agreements weakens this nation further. We lessen our presence around the world that demonstrated our strength and send money to nations that squander it away. A weak military leads to a weak nation in the eyes of the world and an open target."

"So you don't deny that you had something to do with the murder of the Vice President and the attempt on my life in Acapulco?" The President said closing the gap between him and Alexander.

"Hell no. It was the only way we could get somebody in the White House with the balls and intelligence to turn this nation around." Alexander said, raising his fist up into the air.

"And that someone would be you, Thomas Alexander the Second?" The President said.

"Yes. Like the great Alexander before me, who conquered Europe, I will bring this nation back to its proud status."

"You really are a piece of work." Greg said, as he moved in closer, carrying a video camera on his shoulder.

"Tom, please, you've got to put an end to this now." The President said.

"You fools. What did you hope to accomplish? Do you really think I'd come unprepared?" Alexander replied, as he showed them the transponder he had in his hand.

In a matter of seconds, two sets of headlights came barreling up 15th Avenue, heading straight towards them. With his other hand, Alexander pulled a gun out of his jacket, raising it towards the President.

"Time to finish what we failed to accomplish in Acapulco." Alexander said. Before he raised the gun, Greg had dropped the camera and rushed between the President and Alexander. He managed to push the President aside just as the gun went off. Grabbing Alexander's wrist that held the gun, he raised it, swung underneath it, and pulled it down over his shoulder, hearing the distinct crack of bone splitting. Alexander let out an agonizing scream as his hand dropped the weapon. His scream was met with the full force of Greg's left elbow, crashing against his nose, causing him to reel backwards against the monument.

Suddenly the air was filled with gunfire, emanating from the two cars only 100 feet away. The concrete around Greg's feet began to splatter as the bullets were beginning to find their range. Wheeling around, he pulled Alexander in front of him and sent him hurtling towards the cars.

Falling forwards, Alexander's body suddenly stopped and began to shake, as bullets intended for Greg were sent directly into Alexander's chest. It provided Greg the few seconds he needed to gather up the President and move to one side of the monument.

Pulling the machine gun from his side, he peered around the corner and started firing at the oncoming cars. After several rounds, one car suddenly veered to one side, the bullets piercing the windshield and hitting the driver in the face. The second car steered to the right to get a better angle on their targets, sending bullets careening off the side of the monument. Greg grabbed a hand grenade from his jacket, pulled the pin and hurled it towards the oncoming car. He guided the President around the monument, to get clear of the gunfire, when the grenade exploded, sending the car tumbling off the side of the hill in flames.

Coming around the corner, they were met with gunfire from the occupants of the first car. Greg pushed the President back around the corner and began to return fire. A bullet found Greg's leg, adding to the damage left by Alexander when he had attempted to fire on the President. Greg stumbled, hit by another bullet in his arm, but he continued to fire. As he fell to the ground, he noticed that another car had come from another direction; it's lights turning on just as it hit the sidewalk.

The occupants of the first car were unprepared for Kay's sudden arrival, as she bounced over the sidewalk, running into one of the three. She saw Greg collapse on the ground as she swerved the car between the monument and the remaining two. She reached into Greg's bag in the back seat and pulled out on of his machine guns before leaping out of the car, firing wildly towards the two would-be assassins.

"Get in the car!" Kay yelled back to the President. The President lifted Greg up from the ground and helped him towards the car, hearing a muddled groan. Kay moved around to the hood of the car and kneeling by the tire, fired directly at the two surprised killers. Screaming obscenities, she found her mark, sending both men falling backwards. Kay moved up from her squatting position and walked towards the two bodies. Upon reaching them, she swung the gun upwards, sending a swath of bullets along each body, emptying the cartridges as she screamed.

"Kay, let's go!" The President screamed as he ran towards her. He grabbed her as she continued to pull on the trigger of the empty gun. Amazed by what he saw, he pulled her around and pushed her back towards the car. Shoving her into the passenger side, he ran around the car, climbed in and sped the car off the grounds, onto Independence Avenue and west towards the Lincoln Memorial.

Gazing over, he saw Kay sitting motionless, her eyes staring emptily forward. Looking into the back seat, he verified that Greg's curled up body was still breathing.

Driving behind the Lincoln Memorial, he wound his way around on Rock Creek and Potomac Highway, out of Washington D.C. on Wisconsin Avenue, River Road and finally MacArthur Boulevard towards the houseboat.

When they arrived at the houseboat, Kay was still staring off in a daze. He reached over to find her trembling and her skin cold as ice. The moans from Greg in the back seat had stopped, but he noticed that Greg was still breathing, although barely.

"Kay, snap out of it." The President said, shaking her shoulders and staring into the empty eyes. It took several seconds, but the life seemed to reappear in her eyes. She shook her head and when she was able to see the President staring at her, she suddenly burst into tears.

"It's okay, it's over." The President said, pulling her head onto his shoulder. Her whole body was trembling, not from the cool night, but the fear that had enveloped her and sent her into a tailspin, unleashing the intense violence within her.

"Kay, I need you to get a hold of yourself. Greg's been hit. I don't know how bad, but we need to get him inside."

Kay looked up at him and shook her head in acknowledgement. She looked into the back seat and by the light of the parking area; they caught their first glimpse of the damage done. Greg lay across the back seat, which was soaked with blood. The President and Kay climbed out of the Blazer and moved to pull Greg out of the car. Greg's breathing was short and raspy. They removed the heavy jacket and equipment, lightening the already heavy form that couldn't provide any assistance. When he took off the jacket, a tape fell out of the pocket. The President breathed a brief sigh of relief and pushed it into the back of his pants.

They pulled Greg's arms around their shoulders and carried him down to the pier and into the houseboat. Kay began to push the furniture aside as the President laid him on the floor.

"He needs a hospital." Kay said.

"You know we can't take him there. The moment we're seen, it's over." The President replied, trying to undo his shirt and pants. "Get me as many towels and bandages as you can find. Also grab me some whiskey from the bar."

Within two minutes, Kay returned carrying a load of towels and first aid supplies. Dropping them on the floor by Greg's now half-naked body, she ran over to the small bar in one corner and pulled two bottles of Jack Daniels. When she returned, she almost fainted from the sight of Greg's injuries. The President was trying to wipe the blood from Greg's face that had been hit by concrete debris when the bullets bounced off the monument. Blood was oozing from Greg's left shoulder, side and right thigh, where bullets had found their target.

"Pour the whiskey over the holes to sanitize the wounds." The President said, balling up several towels.

Kay poured the alcohol over the wounds, before the President applied a towel to each. Before she placed the bottle on the floor, she took a deep gulp of the Jack Daniels for herself.

"Hold the one down on his leg and I'll get the other two." The President said as he pushed down on the towels. "Hang in there, Greg."

* * * * * * * * * * * * * *

A tall figure walked around the Washington Monument, gazing at the scene like a General observing the aftermath of a battle. He stopped by Alexander's body and knelt down beside it. After verifying that his mentor was indeed dead, Falcon stood back up and walked down towards the Reflecting Pool. When he reached the edge, he raised the video camera and tossed it into the water, unaware that the tape was no longer inside.

Falcon arrived at the scene just as the Chevy Blazer turned the corner onto Independence Avenue. He was unaware that Senator Billows had requested the meeting with Alexander. Alexander had received an anonymous letter requesting the meeting to provide information on the elusive John Lockwood and his companions. Now Falcon swore to himself for not finding out who had contacted Alexander. Leery of the information, Falcon had arranged for Alexander's reinforcements if they were needed. Now everything he had worked these long years for was lying dead at the base of the monument.

Shortly after arriving at the pool, the sirens began to wail in the background, growing louder as they neared the complex. Falcon slithered towards the trees that lined the walkway around the pool, disappearing into the foggy mist.

* * * * * * * * * * * * * *

They did everything they possibly could for Greg. After soaking up most of the blood and finally getting it to stop, they taped the bandages across his wounds, and carried him into the bedroom. They had no idea to what extent the injuries were, whether there was internal damage or not. The President was sure that the shoulder bone had been fractured.

"What are we going to do now?" Kay asked as they walked out of the bedroom.

"We're going to get a couple of hours sleep and continue on tomorrow morning, as planned." The President replied, sitting down on the chair that had been pushed along the wall.

"And what about him?"

"We'll take care of him after it's over. Hopefully he can hang on until the afternoon, when with any luck, this will all be over."

"I'll keep an eye on him." Kay said, picking up the half empty bottle of Jack Daniels and putting the cap back on.

"Let me have a swig of that before you put it away." The President said holding out his hand. Kay handed him the bottle and he tilted his head back and took one big swallow. Letting out a deep breath, he closed his eyes for a moment and let his head fall down to his chest.

"You should finish this off. After what you just went through you probably need it more than I do." The President said, handing it back to her.

"What did happen? One moment I was driving to get you, and the next minute, you are shaking me in the car. The rest is a blur." Kay said.

The President went over the entire evening's events, including Kay's killing of the two gunmen. With each detail, Kay's eyes grew wider. When he got to the part where she had walked up to the injured bodies and emptied the gun into them, she almost passed out. She almost drained the bottle of Jack Daniels when he finished his recollection.

"Easy does it there, girl." The President said, grabbing the bottle from her.

"I don't know what happened.   When I saw Greg collapse on the ground, I just lost it."

"You've been through a hell of an ordeal, Kay.   It's amazing any of us are still sane with what we've been through.   At least Greg managed to keep the tape." The President said, holding it in front of him.

They finished the bottle together, trying desperately to put the past two weeks behind them, but finding only a brief reprieve as they each fell asleep in their chairs.

Two hours later, the President awoke with someone shaking him from behind.

He quickly jumped out of the chair, almost falling as he reeled around.   The commotion caused Kay to awaken, almost sliding out of her chair.

Standing in front of them was Greg, his bandages neatly changed and dressed.   He could barely stand, but with help of the furniture was able to somewhat stand erect.

"We don't have much time left.   We need to get to Senator Billows' house." Greg mumbled.

"I'll get to John's house, you are staying here, Greg." The President replied.

"It's not over yet, sir.   I may not be one hundred percent, but I'm the only protection you have, and I'm staying by your side until it's over." Greg said, maneuvering himself around the couch until he could sit down.

"You're in no condition to go anywhere.   This afternoon, after it's over, we'll get you to a hospital.   Until then, Kay will look after you." The President responded.

"I'll make it.   I've come this far, and I will see it through.   You owe me that."

"But why do you need to go?" Kay asked.

"The President still needs to get to the Senate safely, and as long as I have one good arm and can stand on both legs, I'm going to ensure he gets there. Just because Alexander is gone, doesn't mean we aren't out of the woods. This is much bigger than Alexander, so we still need to be on our toes. Once everything is over, then the Secret Service can go back to protecting you, but right now they still believe you are a terrorist imposter, so I'm all you've got."

The President and Kay knew it was fruitless to argue with Greg. And for all that he'd been through to get them here, he deserved to see it to its conclusion. They agreed that they've come this far together, and should remain that way until it's over.

The President laughed out loud, causing Greg and Kay to stare at him in amazement.

"What's so funny?" Kay asked.

"I just felt like we were the Three Musketeers and we're about ready to say All for One and One for All." The President replied.

With that they all laughed.

Chapter 36

Senator John Billows gazed down at his sleeping wife as the first signs of sunlight slithered around the bedroom drapes. Bending down, he kissed her cheek and grabbed his watch off the nightstand. Snapping it on his wrist he noticed it read half past five in the morning, plenty of time to get a good cup of coffee and a muffin, before heading to the capital. His wife and children shouldn't be up for another 30 minutes.

Closing the door quietly behind him, he walked out of the bedroom and down the hall to the staircase. Stopping at the top of the stairs, he could smell the distinct aroma of coffee, although he hadn't set the timer on the coffee maker. Looking down the hallway, he verified that his son and daughter's doors were closed. Raising an eyebrow, he stepped slowly down the staircase, listening intently for any unusual sounds.

At the bottom of the stairs, he looked around the corner into the living room, and found it empty and undisturbed. Looking through the window on the side of the front door, he could see the new day dawning, as birds began to search for the morning worms that poked their heads out with the morning dew. There was no unusual movement as the neighborhood slowly awoke to the sunrise. Moving around the staircase, he proceeded quietly down the hallway that led to the back of the house and the kitchen. With each step the smell of coffee grew stronger, teasing his sinuses.

"Good morning, Senator. About time you got downstairs." The voice said, startling Billows. There, sitting at his breakfast table, were the President and a woman, each drinking out of a cup from his kitchen cabinet. The coffee pot was three-quarters full with a mug sitting beside it. Suddenly he felt a chill and turned to find Greg standing behind him.

357

"Let's keep it quiet and not wake up the family, Senator." Greg said with a smile.

"Good Lord, are you trying to give me a heart attack?" Billows asked, noticing the paleness in Greg's face and the way he leaned to one side.

"Calm down, John." The President said. "Excuse our impatience, but we couldn't stand around outside your front door waiting for you. We have some interesting information for you and, as we spoke about yesterday, we need your help again today."

"Did Alexander meet with you?" Billows asked, stumbling to the kitchen counter. Greg moved to the refrigerator and searched inside.

"Damn, don't you have any Diet Coke?" Greg asked.

"Sorry, this is a Pepsi family." Billows replied.

"In answer to your question, yes, Alexander showed up." The President said, taking a drink of the coffee.

"And?" Billows asked. Greg pulled out a Pepsi and closed the refrigerator door. Moving to the counter, he poured coffee into the waiting mug and handed it to Billows.

"I think you better sit this one down, Senator." Greg said, motioning him to the kitchen table.

Billows sat down across from the President. Greg moved around the table next to Kay. Billows noticed that Greg was limping on one leg and sat down rather gently. His attention then turned to the young lady sitting next to the President. Even without make-up and a visit to a hair stylist, she was still rather captivating, he thought. The strange part was the look in her eyes, distant but full of emotion. It was as though she was alone in the room, pondering on something deep, but still not completely unaware of the events going on around her. The President put his coffee mug on the table and leaned on the table with his elbows, placing his chin on his hands.

"John, Alexander is dead." The President said, shocking Billows.

"What?" Billows mumbled.

"Alexander was killed last night."

"You killed him?" Billows said, his eyes and mouth wide open in fear.

"We didn't kill him, John. We were attacked while meeting with him. I didn't want this to happen, but it did, and nothing we can do to change that." The President said with sincerity. Billows had known his old friend for a long time and knew when he was being honest.

"Dear God. What are we going to do now?" Billows said, lowering his chin to his chest.

"Do you have a VCR?" Greg asked, putting his hand on Billow's shoulder.

"Yes, in the family room." Billows replied.

"We need you to see something, John." The President said, standing up and walking over to Billows. Helping him up, the four of them moved into the family room, adjacent to the kitchen.

"By the way, this is Kay Cross, a newspaper reporter we have been with for the past two weeks." The President said as they settled into the comfortable chairs in the living room. Greg walked over to the television set and turned it and the VCR on. Pulling the tape out of his pocket, he inserted it into the slot of the VCR and pushed play.

"This is what happened last night." The President said.

Billows watched as the video relived the events at the Washington monument. It showed the statements by Alexander that outlined the charade that the country had been lied to about. The killing of the Vice President, the attempted assassination of the President, the course of action that Alexander was attempting to play out, and the attempt by him to shoot the President there at the foot of the monument. Suddenly the image was distorted, as it had dropped to the ground when Greg moved to save the

President, but it still managed to record the two oncoming cars firing at them, the killing of Alexander, and the beginning of the fight for survival that abruptly ended.

"Greg managed to save the tape before we managed to escape, thanks to Kay." The President said. Billows sat back in awe, unable to speak.

"John, we need your help to get into the Senate hearings today and get them to see and hear this tape." The President continued. "We need you to take us there and get the whole story out in the open."

"Jesus Christ. Do you know what this is going to do to the American public?" Billows asked. "They already hate politicians, and this will just break their backs."

"You let me handle that, John. You just get on the floor and submit this for everyone to see, before they stop to vote. Once they see it, I'll take care of the rest."

"And just how am I supposed to get you into the Senate? The moment you're seen, they'll arrest you or kill you." Billows asked.

"We'll get there. You just get their attention." The President replied.

"This is just too incredible." Billows said.

"I know. But we don't have a moment to lose. You're my only hope, John. Will you do this?" The President asked, standing directly in front of the Senator.

"You're a damn fine President, John, and a good friend. You know I'll be there for you." Billows replied, standing up and shaking the President's hand.

* * * * * * * * * * * * *

"It was expected that the President was going to address us all this morning before we voted, however, there has been no word from the White House. The only direction I received was that we were to continue the vote today without delay." The somewhat overweight gentleman at the podium said.

"Thank you, Senator Fairling. If there's nothing else on the floor, I move we open the ballot for voting." The Speaker said, holding the gavel up. Before he was able to strike the gavel down, he heard a distinct voice and noticed Senator Billows standing with his hand raised.

"With respect to my colleagues, sir, I request permission to address the forum." Billows said.

"The floor recognizes Senator Billows." The Speaker said, sitting back down in his high-back chair.

Senator Billows moved down to the platform and podium that faced the front of the auditorium. As he adjusted the microphone, a clerk came down the walkway, pushing a cart with a television and VCR on it, placing it to one side of the front opening, in clear view of the entire audience.

"This is rather unusual." The Speaker said leaning forward.

"If you'll allow me a slight indulgence, sir. I think you'll find this deviation from the norm to be very informative." Billows said, clearing his throat.

"Granted, but let's keep this short, Senator. We all want to get out of here today and enjoy the long weekend." The Speaker said with a round of laughter ringing through the audience.

"I'll take very little of your time, sir. What I have to say has come to me only this morning, and holds a true bearing on these proceedings. It involves the events of the last two weeks and the failure of President Alexander to appear this morning." Billows started. Immediately there was an echoing of mumbles throughout the audience.

"Order." The Speaker said, slamming his gavel down. "Proceed, Senator."

"Thank you, sir." Billows said, adjusting his stance and clearing his throat once again.

361

"My fellow Senators, we have been operating under false pretenses for the last two weeks. Our vision has been blurred by deceit, corruption and greed. The entire American public has been manipulated and lied to."

Immediately the room was filled with scores of politician's standing, shaking their fists into the air, and mumbling to one another.

"Order!" The Speaker screamed out, smashing the gavel to its base. "You're on dangerous ground, Senator. I caution you to proceed carefully."

"Mr. Speaker, you know me to hold the highest regard for this country and it's principles. The very foundation of this country has been shaken, and to demonstrate I'd like to play you a tape of some events from last night."

"Proceed." The Speaker said as Billows walked to the television set.

"Gentlemen, this tape was given to me this morning by a trusted friend, and contains a horrific story that will shock you. This event happened only last night, and will confirm what I have just said." Billows said as he pushed the play button on the VCR.

The room became deathly silent as they watched and listened to the events on the tape. In the back of the room, a lone figure stood in the shadows, and watched his dream shatter before his eyes. Disgusted, he moved to the large doors and walked out, only to bump into someone walking into the room with two other people. His eyes opened wide at the sight, and almost fell back into the door. Even though they were wearing wigs, hats, and oversized clothing, he knew exactly who they were. When the tape concluded, Billows walked across the front of the floor.

"My friends, this is not a dramatization, but actual footage. Thomas Alexander is dead, killed in the middle of this fine city, at the heart of his own deception." Billows said, standing directly in the middle of the floor.

"I announce to you that President Lockwood was not killed in Mexico, as seen by the video. I have known this man since my college years, and I am positive that there is no terrorist imposter. Only he could have known about pieces of my personal life that were so minute." Billows said, bellowing over the increased mumbling in the crowd.

"My fellow Americans, I give you President Lockwood." Billows exclaimed as he pointed up the walkway.

Three figures walked down the long hallway between the audience. When they reached the main floor, one man shook Senator Billow's hand and removed his hat, wig and jacket.

"Mr. Speaker. Request permission to address the Senate." The President said.

"The man's an imposter, arrest him." A voice screamed out from the audience.

The President walked up to the large seating area that surrounded the Speaker and held his hand around the microphone.

"Would an imposter know about your son being arrested for possession of cocaine, Dave?" The President whispered, recounting an episode in which the Speaker had asked for the President's help in quieting an embarrassing moment that was kept entirely secret between the two of them.

"Order!" The Speaker said standing up, staring at the President in awe. "I can also confirm that this man is truly John Lockwood and not an imposter. The floor recognizes the President of the United States."

"Thank you, Mr. Speaker." The President said as he made his way to the podium.

"Ladies and Gentleman of the Senate as well as the American public. I have been on a long journey for the past two weeks, since the incident at the villa outside Acapulco. I'd like to introduce two people who have been instrumental in ensuring my safe return. Lieutenant Commander Greg Morris and Kay Cross." The President said, as they removed their costumes and acknowledged the unsure applause of the audience.

"I can understand your misgivings and uncertainty right now." The President continued. "But let me assure each and everyone of you, that what you have witnessed on the video tape is only a slight taste of the deception that has been going on. I have seen first hand, how there is an element in this country that has attempted to play out a grand plan to take this country to war, in hopes that it will revitalize this country. People I, as well as these two, trusted played key roles in attempting to see to my death, the end of the peace agreement scheduled in Acapulco and taking our military to an unnecessary war."

"Granted, this country has many shortcomings. There are things that need our attention, but to go down the direction they were choosing, is not the path we need to take. The events I endured have opened my eyes to certain aspects of the country we have all forgotten, and we need to concentrate on them with complete conviction, but we cannot forget that peace is the correct way to survive. I will see to it that the signing of the Peace Agreement is rescheduled soon."

The President walked around the floor, looking into the faces of the many politicians who sat around him. He wondered how many of those in this room were a part of the secret society that was behind this. Trust on both sides of the fence was going to be a large issue over the next couple of years, especially who he could trust and who actually believed he was not a terrorist.

"I plan on meeting with each and everyone of you over the next several months. You need to be reassured of who I am, and we all need to work on finding the solutions to the difficult problems that we face in this country. The entire nation and its governing body need to refocus its efforts on our own neighborhoods and cities. Together we must find solutions to the homeless, education, crime, and family values." The President continued as he walked back to the podium.

"In some ways, these events are probably the kick in the pants this country needed to wake us up to the realities that we need to address and the politics we were sworn to uphold.

We managed to win the war against terrorism but failed to ensure the strength of our economy and its people. I don't hold all the answers, but with your support, we can find a way to make this country stronger from within. We don't need to spill the blood of our soldiers and sailors to bring this country back to its feet again, we just need to refocus our efforts and start bringing solutions within our own borders."

"Most of you who know me, know that I don't make unfulfilled promises or speak just to be heard. I promise you now though, that together, putting aside our party prejudices and outside influences, we can return to being the voices of our country and make a difference. Work with me to make this country the home we all dreamed of, and the foundation that others will admire and emulate."

"Thank you, Mr. Speaker." The President said, bowing to the table. With that, the Speaker rose from his chair and began to applaud. Within seconds the whole room was standing on its feet, echoes of applause ringing off the walls. Kay could almost hear the applause coming from every home and office that was watching the proceedings on television. The distant stare she had been under since the events at the Washington Memorial had quickly evaporated, replaced with an unflappable admiration and respect for the man standing beside her.

"You don't think I laid it on too thick do you?" The President asked with a smile.

"I think you laid it just thick enough, sir." Kay responded, smiling back as he wrapped his arms around her.

"How many times do I have to tell you? It's John. I think with all we've been through you could at least get rid of the formalities."

"Habits are hard to break.........John. But I'll do my best."

They turned their attention back to the audience that was ringing its approval. The President looked back at Greg who was leaning on the table, peering out across the room at the doors. Throughout the speech, Greg tried to make out the lone figure they had bumped into when they entered, but the shadows of the overhang kept his face out of view.

"You okay?" The President said walking over to Greg. Kay turned to look as she noticed him look at her, his eyes becoming glossy.

"I think you're back in office." Greg replied before falling to the floor in a crumbled mass. The President and Kay ran over to him, his face pale and his skin cold.

"Somebody call an ambulance." The President screamed. He looked at Kay, seeing the tears well up in her eyes.

The room became a bedlam of activity as clerks ran out the doors trying to find help.

"What happened?" The Speaker asked after having come down from his seat.

"This man has been severely injured trying to save my life on numerous occasions. We need to get him to a hospital immediately." The President said.

Greg's breathing became short and raspy. Blood was beginning to seep down his arm from the bullet wound on his shoulder. The President and the Speaker lifted him up and carried him out of the auditorium.

* * * * * * * * * * * * *

366

Secret Service agents began to crowd the waiting room that held just two occupants. Kay sat motionless while the President stood to one side of the room in deep conversation with someone from the White House she didn't know. The feelings were welling up inside her again. The helplessness she had felt during the time in their underground hideaway in Camp Pendleton, when Greg was lying on the medical bed injured from his fight with Davenport.

The conflict between the man in her dream and the one now lying in surgery continued to plague her. The warmth she felt making love to him in the Jacuzzi and the hatred afterwards bounced around inside her mind. Opposites, bombarding each other, mingled with the unknown violence from the previous evening overwhelmed her.

Noticing Kay's condition over the shoulder of the Secretary of Treasury, he shook the man's hand giving him items to look into, and moved over to her. Sitting down next to her, he put his arms around her and pulled her close. She rested her head on his shoulder, feeling the security he always provided. It was the type of security she felt from her father when she was young.

They didn't need to say anything to each other. There was no point. The President knew she was struggling within about Greg. He could tell by her discussions on the long drive from Nebraska and the way they looked at each other, that there was something going on between them. Discussions that highlighted Kay being torn with her feelings towards him, but also knowing that she truly did care for him, although she didn't quite realize it.

The quiet moment was broken when a doctor entered, causing them both to sit up.

"How is he?" The President asked.

"I won't lie to you, sir. It's not good. He's still unconscious. His injuries were very bad and he lost a lot of blood. We've done all we can do. Right now, all we can do is wait and see if he even regains consciousness." The doctor said.

"This man saved my life, doctor, so you do everything within your powers and keep me abreast of his condition." The President said, holding Kay's hand, which clenched his tightly.

"Can we see him?" Kay asked softly.

"He's in intensive care." The doctor replied, motioning for them to follow him.

They walked into the private room and saw Greg lying in the bed, his body covered with bandages, tubes and wires running from his body to the equipment that surrounded the bed. A monitor sat on the other side of the bed, echoing his heartbeat while his body was fed with nutrients. For the first time since Camp Pendleton, they saw Greg with a look of peace on his face.

"Can you leave me with him for a few minutes?" Kay asked.

"Are you sure?"

"Yes."

"I'll be right outside if you need me." The President said and walked out the door, surrounded by the Secret Service agents.

Kay sat up on the edge of the bed and took Greg's hand in hers. She reached up and ran her hand across his cheek and moved some of the hair back from his forehead. Looking at him now, the conflict slowly subsided. She was beginning to realize that no man had ever consumed her as much as he had. Never before, had someone filled her every thought and deep emotion. As she gazed at him, she wondered if he would be different now that the adventure was over. Looking at the wall, she wondered if he'd ever be able to live a normal life after everything he'd been through in his life. They were so different, but she still felt something pulling her to him. She never believed in fate, but the question daunted her on how they met and were pulled into the same vortex they had endured.

"Who are you?" She whispered, looking at Greg. "Who is the person deep inside? Are you really the man in my dream, or just some player in a nightmare that has come to an end."

"What am I supposed to do?" Kay asked, looking up at the ceiling. "We are so different. Why have you brought us together? Give me some sign."

Closing her eyes, she took a deep breath. Suddenly she felt Greg's hand slightly press against hers, squeezing her almost unrecognizably. She opened her eyes in amazement, her mouth open wide. The grip lasted only a brief moment, but it sent chills up her spine. Standing up from the bed, she moved towards the head of the bed and leaned down, placing her face near Greg's head.

"I don't know if you can hear me, but if this is really something special, you know how to find me." Kay said before kissing his forehead. She stood back up and let go of his hand.

Gazing out the window, she noticed the hectic activity on the streets below, but felt so far away from it all. Smiling, she walked towards the door, a little bit more life in her step.

Chapter 37

A robin strolled along the plush green grass, circling the stick that was sticking straight up from the ground. With each circle, it closed the gap between itself and the stick, trying to understand its purpose. Stopping, it fluttered its wings to see what kind of reaction it got, but the stick remained motionless. As it came closer, a tiny shadow began to creep along the ground, growing in size as it neared the tiny bird. Alarmed the bird flew off, just in time before the white ball landed in the spot the bird was previously standing.

"Nice shot. Hope that's not a premonition for another birdie." The gentleman said, clapping the back of the other man who was still holding the golf club.

"Hey, sometimes when you keep your eyes shut, it's amazing what can happen." The other man replied.

"Greg, give your Commander in Chief a break. You're already up five strokes. Open your eyes for a change." The voice of John Lockwood said as they both returned to the golf cart. Greg's limp was slight, but noticeable.

It was six months after their appearance on the Senate floor. Greg had remained unconscious for almost a week, but slowly regained his strength and within a month, walked out of the hospital, much to the dismay of the doctor's who wanted to keep him for another month. Greg was growing restless in a hospital bed, and needed to get back to the sunshine and fresh air.

For the next five months, Greg recuperated at the cottage in the woods in Pennsylvania. Each day, he would exercise, slowly at first, stretching out the muscles that had grown stagnant after the long hospital stay. After one month he started walking along the trails in the woods, going a little farther each day, until he could go 30 miles without stopping. As he grew stronger, Greg returned to his rigorous training routine. He had arranged to have some of his personal equipment sent up from San Diego, including a weight bench, body bag, and martial arts weapons. With each passing month, he strained and sweated, returning his form back to his previous quickness and power, with the exception of his right leg, which still suffered from the cartilage damage caused by the bullet that shattered the bone and twisted the insides of his leg.

Throughout his seclusion, he never spoke to anyone other than his parents from time to time. He never heard from Kay or the President, preferring to stay isolated while he brought himself back to health and cleared his head. There was so much he needed to think about and figure out. He managed to find opportunities to play golf occasionally, which helped him relax and clear his thoughts.

Since the episode, the entire adventure had been reported on television and in the papers. To protect Greg's personal life and avoid any retaliation from those behind the plot, his identity was not revealed and eventually was reported as having died in the hospital from his wounds, receiving a full military funeral attended by the President. Hidden away in the hills, Greg didn't watch the television or read the paper. It was now time for Greg to heal physically as well as mentally. He had to consider what he was going to do with the rest of his life now that the team was gone. With help from the President, Greg was secretly discharged from the Navy with a full pension, the least his country could do for his actions.

When he felt strong enough, Greg returned to his apartment in San Diego. When he arrived, he contemplated calling Kay, but never got farther than picking up the receiver. The next day he received a phone call from the President. Hearing that Greg was back home, he asked if they could have that golf came they had once discussed. Three days later Greg met him at the Coronado golf course.

They finished their round with Greg winning by seven strokes. Greg found it amusing that throughout the round; the Secret Service agents had infiltrated the golf course, showing up at every corner and hole. It was rather amusing to see men in suits walking around the golf course, especially in California, on an unusually warm day.

"You are still rather competitive aren't you?" The President asked as they sat down in the clubhouse.

"Sorry, sir, it's just my nature." Greg said with a smile.

"Greg, you are no longer in the military, so please, do me one favor and start calling me John."

"I'll try. Momma raised me right to respect my elders." Greg said, lifting his eyebrows in jest.

"Well you won't earn any points with remarks like that one." The President recounted and they laughed together.

"Have you heard from Kay at all?" The President asked.

"I've thought about it, but not sure she'll even want to talk to me after all this time."

"Well maybe you should read this then." The President said, handing him a newspaper. "It's quite a captivating story."

Greg opened up the paper to see it was the San Diego Union Sunday edition, dated two weeks after their entrance into the Senate. The headlines read 'Heroics, Politics and the Start of a New Nation'. Greg read down to see the story was written by Kay.

"Greg, forgive me for my bluntness, but this lady cares about you and I think you care the same for her. Quit being so damn stubborn and take a chance."

"I appreciate your concern, sir, I mean John." Greg said, catching himself once he saw the look in the President's eyes. "But we are two totally different people."

"You used to be. You don't have to be anymore. Your secret life is over and you can live a normal one if you want to." The President said leaning over to him.

"I've considered that. I'm going to reopen Steve's club after I fix it up."

"Well there you go. All you need is someone special to keep you honest." The President said with a grin.

"The memories of the missions and the team still haunt me, and I can't put that on anyone." Greg said sitting back in the chair.

"If she's the right woman, she can help you get over them. But there's something else, isn't there?"

"Yes." Greg said leaning closer. "We both know that Alexander couldn't have done this all by himself. This was way too big even for him." Greg said, looking down at the table.

"What do you mean?" The President asked.

"When we were at the Senate, we bumped into a man as we walked in. He was still standing there at the back of the auditorium while you spoke. I can't shake the feeling that he had something to do with all of this and I'm not sure it's over."

"Now that's just being paranoid."

"I've learned to trust my senses, they've kept me alive all these years. There was something about the man. I couldn't see his face in the shadows, but the whole time I watched him, chills were running up my spine. Whoever he is, I have a feeling we haven't heard the last from him."

"That was the injuries talking, Greg. For the past six months, this nation has really come alive, just like it did after the World Trade Center bombing, but instead of everyone being cautious and the Stock Market suffering, the nation and the economy grows stronger every day. The cooperation in the capital is mind-boggling. We're starting to make real progress. We're actually working on the very issues that the whole plot was meant for."

"True, but powerful men can be extremely dangerous and vengeful, and whoever was behind this is very powerful. We took from them what they had plotted and planned. It doesn't matter that we are going towards the same goal, it matters that we stole their thunder, and that will give them enough reason for revenge."

"Greg, don't you think they'd have done something already?"

"These are meticulous people, John. They went to great lengths to carry out their plans. They won't rush into anything."

"And this is why you keep to yourself?"

"Less distractions."

"That's a sad way to go through life my friend. Let me ask you something. Following along with your theory, don't you think that Kay's life is in danger too?" The President said grabbing Greg's arm. "She was just as much a part of this as you and I were. Hell, she even rubbed it in their noses with this story."

"I guess you're right. I hadn't thought of that."

"If anything, she needs you nearby to keep her out of danger."

"I see where you're going with this. Nice try, John. You're still the politician. You almost had me going there for a minute."

"Just think about it will you? Do you know that Kay spent the first four days you were unconscious in your room? I finally had to convince her to get back to San Diego and get her story written."

"They never told me that!" Greg exclaimed.

"Just do me a favor. Give her a call. It may not work out, but you'll never know if you don't try, and years from now you'll be second guessing yourself." The President said as one of the Secret Service agents came over and whispered in the President's ear.

"I'm sorry, Greg, but I have to get going. I enjoyed the round and hope we can do it again some other time, after I've had more of a chance to practice." The President said standing up, shaking Greg's hand.

"It will be my pleasure." Greg said as he followed him out of the clubhouse and to the limousine. The President stopped before climbing into the car and turned to Greg.

"Make an old man happy and give her a call." The President said before climbing into the limousine. Greg stood there at the sidewalk and watched the limousine drive off.

Greg got into his car and headed home. As he drove over the Coronado Bridge, he pondered the President's comments and the possibility that Kay's life might be in danger as well. His insides started to tighten up at the thought. Turning off the bridge and heading south towards Chula Vista, he wrestled with his feelings about Kay. He knew he was attracted to her, but also knew they were so different.

Turning into the apartment complex, he noticed a strange car parked in front of his building. Instead of turning down his alley, he continued on another block and parked his car. Reaching under the seat, he pulled the Baretta out of its hiding place. He walked around the building adjacent to his, looking for signs of irregularities. In the alcove that led into his apartment, he caught a glimpse of a lone figure standing in the shadows, holding something.

Assured that there was nobody else around, he moved along the walls of his apartment, approaching the alcove from the stranger's back. Pulling the pistol from his jacket, he raised it against the wall as he reached the entranceway. He could hear the stranger breathing on the other side of the wall.

With one quick move, he swung around the wall and placed the pistol against the stranger's head.

"Jesus Christ!" The woman's voice screamed, dropping the package she was carrying on the floor to the sound of glass breaking.

"Damn." Greg responded, pulling the gun back as he recognized Kay's voice. "What the hell are you doing here?"

"I'm fine, thank you. Great way to great visitors." Kay said; as she knelt down to pick up the package.

"I'm sorry. Lately I have a thing about unexpected visitors." Greg replied, bending down to help her.

"Well, I think you're dinner is a real bust." Kay said as she looked into the package that was now soiled from the dinner she had prepared.

"How'd you find me?" Greg said as he motioned her towards his door.

"A good friend of ours thought it would be a good idea for me to take the first step, since you haven't bothered to call or write." Kay answered as Greg opened the door to his apartment.

Greg walked inside, and took the package from Kay, laying it on the table. Before she knew what happened, he placed his hand behind her head and pulled her head closer to his, their lips meeting in a deep, intense kiss as the door to the apartment closed.

As the door closed, a camera telephoto lens slid back through the drapes of the window in the apartment across the parking lot.

About the Author

Guy Macdonald, born in New York, spent 17 years in the United States Navy reaching the rank of Lieutenant Commander. His experiences included participation in the planning and execution of amphibious forces in Desert Storm and Somalia's Restore Hope, afloat staff and NATO intelligence duties during the embargo of the former Yugoslavia, as well as Operational planning for the Pacific Fleet in San Diego, California.

During Restore Hope, he was directly involved with the Secret Service in the shipboard security arrangements for President Bush's onboard three day visit. Currently working in management for a major telecommunications company, he is married to his lovely wife Sandy while his daughter Jennifer attends The Ohio State University. He holds a Bachelors Degree from Grove City College (1978) and Masters Degree from the University of Maryland (1997) both in Business Administration. Guy is self-taught in piano and guitar and enjoys golf, movies, and music.

Printed in the United States
6564

9 780759 697362